FOSSIL
WHISPERERS

Mitch and Danica,
Congratulations on your wedding.
thank you for having our band with
vocals by your aunt Sheena for
your celebration.
    With this book enjoy a
narrative journey through the
historical Old West.
    Best wishes,
    Neil Hicks

FOSSIL WHISPERERS

HERB HICKS

FOSSIL WHISPERERS

iUniverse books may be ordered through booksellers or by contacting:

iUniverse
1663 Liberty Drive
Bloomington, IN 47403
www.iuniverse.com
1-800-Authors (1-800-288-4677)

ISBN: 978-1-5320-5333-7 (sc)
ISBN: 978-1-5320-5335-1 (hc)
ISBN: 978-1-5320-5334-4 (e)

Library of Congress Control Number: 2018908428

Print information available on the last page.

iUniverse rev. date: 07/20/2018

In memory of my brother,
Robert W. (Bob) Hicks
1941–2005
Artist, musician, teacher, art jewelry designer, and fossil hunter

ILLUSTRATIONS

(by Herb Hicks)

1. *Eohippus,* Dawn Horse
2. 1870s Fossil Hunters with Cavalry Sentinel
3. *Mosasaur Tylosaurus Proriger,* Marine Reptile
4. Frontier Fossil Hunter, Collection of Carl Grupp, South Dakota
5. *Hesperornis Regalis,* Regal Western Bird
6. *Uintatherium Dinoceras,* Beast of the Uinta Mountains (Fearful Horn)
7. *Triceratops,* Three Horn Face
8. *Brontotheres,* Thunder Beast
9. Missouri River Fossil Site, Collection of Jim and Nancy Greutman, Montana
10. *Camarasaurus,* Chambered Lizard

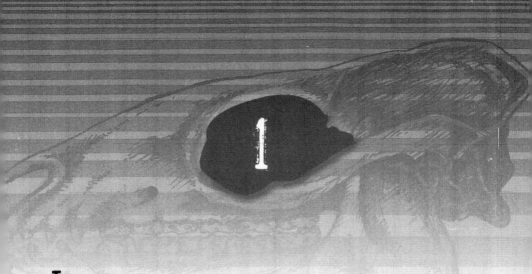

The train's steam locomotive, billowing voluminous gray puffs of smoke, rumbled across the flat, arid Western plains. Pulling a tinder car, four passenger cars, and a caboose, it raced along tracks straight as an arrow as the engine settled with ease into a motion and rhythm that gave it unprecedented speed. The gray clouds of smoke steadily followed the railcars as the repeated click-clack cadence of the wheels, crossing where the rails joined, sounded at close intervals.

The train's fireman, his face and muscular arms red hot, was perspiring profusely and cursing profoundly as he stoked the firebox and fed more water to the boiler.

"All right!" the engineer shouted. "We've got the steam now."

In a coach car, a group of young college men were trying to deal with the tedious train trip. Some played games while some were reading and others tried to sleep. In one seat, a clean-shaven, tall young man in his late twenties was sleeping and dreaming. The hot midday sun lit the top of the passenger's head of tousled brown hair as he leaned against the coach window and swayed from side to side. The book he'd been reading slid from his lap and hit the floor with a thud. His dreaming became more vehement and vocal.

"Hope against despair, hope against despair … hop—," he mumbled as he felt himself being shaken. Opening his eyes, he gazed out the window into a dazzlingly sun-drenched landscape. He was hot and clammy as he heard a familiar voice.

"Jake … Jake," the voice whispered. "Are you okay?"

Taking a moment to gather his thoughts, Jake realized the hand shaking his shoulder belongs to the voice of his friend Dan Randall, seated on the train bench across from him.

Jake Harding and Dan Randall, friends at Yale College for the last two years, were traveling from Connecticut to Nebraska. They had joined the 1870 Yale Scientific Expedition along with ten other Yale students under the leadership of Yale Professor of Paleontology Othniel Charles Marsh.

The students, all in their twenties, looking for adventure, had signed on with Professor Marsh for a fossil-hunting trip to the Frontier West. Yale College in New Haven, Connecticut, supported and financed the expedition along with donations and the help of the Union Pacific Railroad. US Army General Phil Sheridan had assured Marsh that a company of the Fifth Cavalry at Fort McPherson near North Platte, Nebraska, would be readied to escort the fossil expedition through Indian Territory. The professor had been assured that the Indian troubles caused by the Cheyenne Dog Soldiers and the Lakota-Sioux had cooled down considerably.

Jake had convinced Dan to sign on for the expedition. He had told Dan, "the most exciting part of being a paleontologist is to be able to work in the field rather than just in a lab cataloging fossils someone else has discovered. The experience of digging up a fossil that has been buried for millions of years will transform you."

Dan reached over and closed the train's window curtain, blocking out the blinding sunlight.

"You were dreaming," Dan said.

"Whew, yeah. What a nightmare," Jake said, unwinding his six-foot frame from a reclining position. "That dream seemed so real—one of my scariest."

Jake, trying to ease his stiffness, got up from of his seat; stretched his tall, lanky frame; ran his hand through his tousled hair; and started to walk down the railcar's aisle. All he accomplished was stumbling and being shuffled from side to side by the train's motion as he struggled to maintain his balance. He flopped down in his seat again. He thought, as *uncomfortable as it is riding this rail train coach car, it's much better than travelling by covered wagon.* He marveled at the thought that just a year ago, in 1869, the railroads had extended across the continent from the Atlantic to the Pacific Coasts. Before then, wagon trains would take four to six months going east to west. With the railroads, the trip could now be accomplished in a few days. *The marvels of the Industrial Age are amazing,* Jake thought as he contemplated the adventure that lay ahead.

"You were mumbling something about 'hope' again. What was that about?" Dan asked, swaying in his seat as the train picked up speed.

Jake was bounced back into a reclining pose.

"Where are we?" Jake asked, avoiding Dan's question.

"Somewhere in the middle of nowhere," Dan said. "It's hotter than hell out there. It's an endless, flat, parched, dry, brown prairie."

Dan kept ranting on about how hot and boring the train ride was and how much he already missed the cities back east, especially New Haven and his hometown of Philadelphia. Dan's father had wanted him to go into the family business; a clothing and shoe factory had made his family wealthy. But Dan chose to go to college. Dan's interest in geology and paleontology at an early age and then his hearing of Professor O. C. Marsh's work made him decide to go to Yale. Meeting and becoming friends with Jake Harding was Dan's most enjoyable reward for choosing Yale. He looked up to Jake as a replacement of the older brother he had lost to scarlet fever when Dan was ten. Jake always listened wholeheartedly to Dan's opinions, and even though he sometimes disagreed, he was not judgmental.

"Hope again?" Dan's questioning was more demanding this time.

"Oh yeah," Jake answered. "My grandpa was in my dream."

Jake began to recount his nightmare. "I dreamt I was being

chased by a huge prehistoric monster," Jake said. "It was a lizard-like beast with large fangs."

Dan was all ears. He especially liked a stirring, scary story.

"I was in a hot, steamy jungle," Jake continued. "The lizard-like creature, towering above me, charged with its mouth open, displaying rows of glistening, dagger-like teeth and arms with talons poised to slash."

"Sounds like a *Hadrosaurus,*" Dan said, "only your nightmare monster is equipped with fangs and claws."

"You're right," Jake said. "In my dream, my grandpa was trying to protect me. He was about to rescue me when you woke me."

"I remember your grandfather," Dan said. "He was a minister, right?"

"Yeah," Jake said. "I was raised by Grandpa O. Z. He was always my guardian. Whenever I'd feel depressed, his preacher instincts emerged and he'd give me a sermon on having faith, always ending it saying; 'Hope against despair.'"

Fidgeting in his seat, Jake slowly rolled his neck and pumped his shoulders up and down in an attempt to relieve his stiffness.

"Grandpa and I agreed to disagree on a number of issues," he continued. "One subject of disagreement was that of creation."

"Yeah, I'll bet," Dan said, nodding knowingly. "Your grandpa being a minster of the Church of the Brethren, and you being a student of paleontology, I can imagine your conversations were quite lively."

"My grandfather was a man of great faith and wisdom," Jake said. "His belief in Creation was founded on the Bible's book of Genesis. He explained to me his understanding of the act of Creation. The description of 'the act' in Genesis was not to be taken literally but as an allegory. He also believed that the statement that the world was six thousand years old, according to the calculations of James Ussher, Bishop of the Church of Ireland in the seventeenth century, was as false and misleading as Genesis's statement of time. Bishop Ussher calculated the date of the creation of the earth to be Sunday, October 23, 4004 BC."

"Wow. Then we should celebrate every October 23 as Earth's birthday, the way we celebrate Christmas!" Dan sarcastically exclaimed. "I love to celebrate big holidays."

"So I've noticed," Jake said. "You like the gifts and the parties."

"Yeah, darn right," Dan said. "Life should have more gifts and parties. You're always too damned serious."

"Only when I'm serious," Jake said. "Sometimes life should be taken seriously."

"Oh, I take life seriously—when *I'm* serious," Dan said with assurance and a pompous tone.

"Okay, okay," Jake said. "Let's not get into one of our ridiculous arguments just for the sake of arguing. Just be quiet for a while and don't talk so much."

"Well, sometimes there's nothing better to do than talk," Dan said. "Like right now, I'm bored with this train ride, and a good discussion might liven up this journey. How are you going to express yourself without talking?"

"There are other ways to express oneself," Jake said.

"Like how?"

"Making pictures, writing, gestures, music, dance … the arts," Jake said. "You know, sometimes what is not said is as important as what is said. Being silent gives your mind the time and space to reflect."

"Oh, what a philosopher you are," Dan said, chuckling.

"Try reading. It'll pass the time," Jake said. He picked up the book he'd been reading before sleep overcame him and handed it to Dan. Then he reached for the sketchbook lying on the seat beside him and began drawing.

"Ah, I see you are still very much taken with Darwin's theory of evolution," Dan said as he opened the book Jake had handed him. "I still can't believe Professor Marsh would give you a gift of this book.

He doesn't give gifts. To get a copy of Charles Darwin's *On the Origin of Species* is indeed special coming from old O. C."

"I believe he liked my work when I assisted him," Jake answered. "As you know, he casually knows my grandfather. He is aware of my differences with O. Z. about evolution and creation, and I think he wanted to give me fuel for my arguments with grandfather."

"I think Professor Marsh is one strange duck," Dan said. "What's your opinion of him?"

Jake crossed his arms, leaned back in his seat, and looked at the ceiling with a grimace, still trying to relieve his stiff neck. He thought for a moment before answering.

"Yeah, he is a strange one." Jake said. "He has this annoying habit of clearing his throat sometimes before he speaks. Especially if he was interrupted while deep in thought, or amazed, or embarrassed. He sounds somewhat like a horse snorting." Jake chuckled to himself. "I know he inherited a large sum of money from his rich uncle, George Peabody. As professor of vertebrate paleontology at Yale, he's a real professional. With his work he is methodical, deliberate, and possessive of his discoveries, and he can become quite quarrelsome when confronted with opposition to his findings. And he's very competitive. You know, he is so much like my grandpa, even to the extent that both men don't like to use their given names, only their initials. I must say I admire both Othniel Charles and Oliver Zeller."

"I read and hear gossip about the rivalry between Marsh and paleontologist Edward Cope of the Academy of Natural Sciences in Philadelphia," Dan said. "Do you know about that?"

"Only what I read in the newspapers," Jake said. "Seems the feud began after Marsh, who has a keen eye, pointed out that Cope had made a monumental mistake in the reconstruction of a thirty-five-foot marine saurian specimen, a plesiosaur. Cope had put the skull on the wrong end."

"Oh, no. I'll bet O. C. was gloating over finding that error," Dan said.

"No doubt," Jake said. "He delights in being right."

Jake remembered the times he had observed the professor at work in the Yale College labs preparing fossils. Marsh was painstaking in his assembling of fossil bone specimens but open to being creative in their assemblage, which could lead to some misconceptions. His attention to detail was as uncanny as were his methods. He would spend hours chipping away at the clay matrix in which the bone fossils were embedded. Muttering, he would bend down close to the fossils as though he were talking and listening to them. *It looked as though the fossils were whispering some secret to the professor. Maybe they were,* Jake thought. A mysterious phenomenon occurred while Jake himself worked with fossils that held secrets from millions of years ago. He had the profound realization that his eyes and hands were the first to come in contact with the bones after the passage of eons. This prompted his mind to conjure imagined scenarios of epochs long ago. He pushed these thoughts from his mind and continued to draw in his sketchbook.

The gentleman seated behind a huge mahogany desk in the train's plush business coach was writing intensely when he was interrupted by a loud knock on the railcar's door.

"Come in," he called, continuing to write without bothering to look up. "I'll be with you in a minute."

The conductor opened the door, admitting an amplified noise of the train's squeaking wheels and the smell of burning wood from the locomotive's smokestack. Quickly closing the door, he entered the luxurious coach car and stood in silence looking down at the stout, fortyish man behind the desk.

The bearded, balding man finished his script and then studied it for a minute before looking up.

"What is it?" he asked as he cleared his throat, making a sound like a horse snorting.

"Professor Marsh, sir," the conductor said. "We'll be pulling into Omaha in about twenty minutes."

"Good," the professor answered. Clearing his throat again, he added, "Tell the students to get their belongings together. We are going to spend a few days in Omaha getting outfitted. Have them assemble in front of the depot."

"Yes, sir, will do," the conductor said as he saluted, did a smart about-face, and went out the door to the next car.

Must have been a military man, O. C. thought, clearing his throat again he returned to reading his manuscript.

"Do you know anything about firearms?" Jake asked Dan.

"Not a thing," Dan said, shaking his head. "Why?"

"Me neither," said Charlie, one of the students overhearing the conversation.

"Why?" Jake asked, mimicking Dan. "Because O. C. told me we're going to spend a few days in Omaha doing some target practice. We'll be issued army rifles so we can bag some game for food while on our expedition."

"Yeah, I also hear," another student said abruptly, "that we'll have to fight off Injuns. I can't wait to get one of those redskin devils in my rifle sights."

Bruno Adler, a tall, husky German lad with wavy blond hair, whom everyone called Bear because of his name, size, and demeanor, was holding out his arms to imitate sighting down a rifle barrel and mouthing, *Pow.*

"Why do you say that, Bear?" Jake asked, a little perturbed by the remark.

"Because it'll be amusing to watch those wild savages hit the dust," Bear answered arrogantly.

"What?" Dan inquired, grumbling.

"It'll be amusing to kill another human being?" Jake asked sarcastically.

"Oh, come on, mister son of a preacher man," Bear bellowed, snickering. "Those animals are not human. They're vermin. Haven't you read the news about what those bastardly cowards have done to white settlers and soldiers?"

"Yeah, I've read some stories," Jake said. "You can't believe everything you read. I've also heard that the Indians were protecting their families and land from white invaders—but, you can't believe everything you hear."

"What *are* you, Harding—an Injun lover?" Bear asked, scoffing.

Jake, too reserved to push for a fight, didn't answer. But he wouldn't back away if pushed too far.

Before either one could continue their insolent banter, the coach door opened.

"Shut up and listen!" the conductor shouted as he entered the car.

Quiet befell the coach as the conductor continued with the authority of a drill sergeant.

"We'll be arriving in Omaha in about twenty minutes," he barked, stiffening his back and sticking out his chin. "Professor Marsh wants all you boys to gather your belongings and depart from the train as quickly as possible. Then you're to assemble in front of the depot and wait for him. Understood?"

"Yes, sir," the students resounded in chorus. Then a cheer went up and someone shouted, "Finally! We can get off this iron horse with its buckboard seats and stretch our aching backs!"

"That Bear," Dan whispered to Jake. "He's a strange one."

"How do you mean?" Jake asked.

Dan moved closer to Jake's left ear and continued to whisper. "I knew his family when I lived in Philly," he said. "He has a fine-looking and friendly sister, Sara, who I took a shine to. Bruno was always taunting her about one thing or another. One day that big bully got my goat, and when I tried to stand up for Sara he gave me a thrashing. I told Bruno's father about the incident, but all his dad did was laugh at me. His dad is a big investor in the Union Pacific Railroad, and his son is nothing other than a rich, spoiled SOB."

"So it would seem," Jake said, nodding in agreement.

The students carried their bags onto the Omaha depot platform and formed a small group to wait for their professor. Clean cut and naïve looking, they were oblivious to being eyeballed by some of the Nebraska frontiersmen. The students had all the appearance of being eastern greenhorns, which they were.

While the students dawdled around on the platform of Union Pacific Railroad's depot, Marsh was inside the station talking to the telegraph operator. His words were animated by his gestures as he dictated a telegram.

The professor stepped out of the depot onto the platform, cleared his throat, and began to address the students.

"Men, we're going to be in Omaha for a couple of days to get outfitted with supplies, including firearms and ammo. Tonight we'll be billeted at the army post. Tomorrow we'll take part in some target practice," he said, snorting. "Then we'll be moving on to Fort McPherson, where we'll meet up with an army escort to begin our fossil-hunting expedition."

The army had two wagons waiting at the Omaha station for the Yale party. They would be transported to Omaha Barracks, four miles from the city. There they'd receive a hot meal and a good night's sleep on army cots.

The next morning, the students reported for target practice. The army issued the Yale party Winchester '66 lever-action .44 caliber rifles, and each student was given five rounds of ammunition. The army figured they could not waste more than sixty bullets on target practice. Soldiers positioned targets in a field target range, and the students were to try to hit a bull's-eye at about 150 yards.

With the students lined in a row in prone positions, their rifles ready and steadily resting on one arm, a soldier gave the command to start firing. Most of the students just pointed their rifles at the targets and fired without really aiming. Few came close to the targets as bullets zinged and kicked up dust around the boards. One student hit just outside the bull's-eye circle. Jake placed one bullet in the bull's-eye and the other four in the next circle.

"Damn good shooting, mister," one of the soldiers said as he looked through field glasses at Jake's target.

"Thanks," Jake replied. "I've had some experience."

"Well, what about you?" the soldier asked Bear, who was just lying there sighting down his barrel but hadn't fired a shot.

"Well, sir," Bear said, "I was wondering if I could shoot standing up?"

"Suit yourself. But it's easier aiming from a prone or sitting position."

"Thanks," Bear replied. He stood and brought his rifle up against his shoulder. He took his time sighting down the barrel, took a deep breath, slowly let it out, and gently squeezed the trigger. To the soldier's surprise, a bullet hole appeared in the target about an inch from the bull's-eye—to the right and low.

"Okay," observed the soldier. "Good shot."

It shoots a little to the low right, Bear thought. Again he stood very tall and still. Everyone, including Professor Marsh, was watching Bear as he took aim and in rapid succession fired four shots, grouping them in the bull's-eye.

"Wow! I'll be goddamned," the soldier said, his field glasses trained on Bear's target. "I've never seen such marksmanship. He got four shots in the bull's-eye!"

Everyone applauded, including Marsh, himself an excellent marksman.

"It's nice to know someone in this outfit can hit something," Marsh said, "in case we ever get into a shooting match with Indians."

The train, after pulling slowly out of the Omaha station, began following the Platte River on its way to Fort McPherson, a journey of about three hundred miles.

O. C. Marsh, seated at his desk in the privacy of his coach, was rereading a letter from his nemesis, Edward Drinker Cope of the Academy of Natural Sciences in Philadelphia. Marsh scoffed at the letter as he threw it atop a pile of papers on the desk. As the train picked up speed on its way to the western outpost, Marsh began furiously writing a letter to the *American Journal of Science* criticizing Cope's professionalism.

Penning a letter criticizing his adversary was certainly not a new undertaking, for he had done it many times before. Both he and Cope had exchanged a number of letters and articles in scientific publications criticizing each other's work. Both scientists were egotistical, competitive, and Machiavellian in their attempts to discredit the other's work when vying for funds for their expeditions. But both men were making valuable contributions to the science of paleontology.

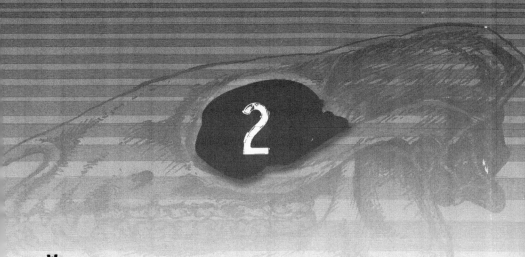

When the Yale students scrambled from the train, laden with their new gear acquired in Omaha, they got their first glimpse of the Wild West.

Fort McPherson, built mainly of cottonwood logs from trees found on the Platte River bottoms, was originally known as Fort Cottonwood; some of the veteran soldiers stationed at this outpost still called it by its original name. The fort had an array of frontiersmen, including trappers, buffalo hunters, cattlemen, settlers, and soldiers of the Fifth Cavalry.

Major General William Emory, the post commander, Pawnee scouts, and William "Buffalo Bill" Cody were at the fort to greet Marsh and his recruits. General Phil Sheridan had written Bill Cody to ask him to be of assistance to Marsh and his party.

General Emory asked Cody to address the Yale group and fill them in on the details for the trip to the Loup Fork River, the fossil bone site that Marsh was interested in.

"Today we'll assign each of you a horse and tack for tomorrow's ride," Cody said. "You'll have an escort of a company of the Fifth Cavalry—thirty outstanding horse soldiers led by Major North with Lieutenants Thomas and Reilly and two Pawnee scouts who will see to your safekeeping. There are a few small parties of renegade Sioux out there. Just be vigilant and don't go wandering off in small groups. They won't attack a group as large as you have. Your firepower would be too much for them. General Emory has asked that I continue my hunt for those hostile Sioux, so I and my men will only be going partway with your party on your geological expedition. Now, let's take a look at those horses."

The next morning at first light, Marsh and the Yale men departed the fort. They were led by Major North, Bill Cody and a dozen of his men, the Pawnee scouts, and ten of the cavalry troopers. Following the fossil hunters were half a dozen wagons creaking across the sand hills, loaded with supplies of food, tents, ammunition, picks, and shovels. The caravan included an ambulance wagon and a chuck wagon. This cavalcade of horsemen, wagons, and mules was fortified by twenty soldiers of the Fifth Cavalry bringing up the rear.

The Yale men were in high spirits as they anticipated their first fossil finds. Astride their horses, the motley crew from Yale wore long sleeved shirts of various styles and brimmed hats of different shapes. Each one carried a new Winchester rifle in a saddle scabbard. They had already begun to take on the appearance of frontiersmen. Around each man's midriff was a holstered Colt .44 revolver and a sheathed Bowie knife. A geological hammer poked its head out from their saddle packs.

Perhaps the most eager of the Yale group was O. C. Marsh himself. He had previously visited the West after attending the 1868 American Association of the Advancement of Sciences conference in Chicago. That trip, three years before, had also taken him across the Great Plains, where he became fascinated with fossils from the Pliocene Epoch (5.33 million to 2.58 million years ago). His discovery of a small fossil of a horse found in a bone bed in Nebraska was of the most interesting to Marsh. That millions-of-years-old fossil was from a prehistoric horse about the size of a fox; Marsh named it *Eohippus* (dawn horse). His discovery would become a valued, but controversial, link to Darwin's theory of evolution.

The fossil hunters, army escorts, and wagons steadily made

their way over the grassy sand hills of the Nebraska plains. The July morning sun began its climb toward a blazing noon-day glare. It would be a hot, dry, and grueling four- or five-day journey to the Loup Fork River.

The first night out, the campsite was a pleasant and welcomed break after a long ride through the rough landscape and scorching prairie heat. Tents lined up in a half dozen rows and supply wagons surrounding the perimeter with soldier sentries on guard made for a feeling of security for the tenderfoot eastern students.

After setting up camp and enjoying an evening meal, the group was entertained by Marsh's description of the plains eons ago.

"These Great Plains," Marsh explained, clearing his throat, "were at one time covered by a shallow sea that reached from the Gulf of Mexico into Canada and the far north, and west to the Rockies, covering most of central North America. This was the Cretaceous Period, from about 145 million years ago to 65 million years ago. It was the last period of great dinosaurs. This inland sea contained many wondrous creatures, some of whose fossilized bones we hope to discover on this expedition."

The students and troopers were fascinated by Marsh's story.

"After the end of this period, the seas receded and left a lush savanna that gave rise to mammals," Marsh continued, "mammals like what I've referred to as the *dawn horse*. This little two-foot-high creature had three toes on its back feet and four toes on its front, rather than hooves. It's from the Eocene Epoch fifty million years ago and is the prehistoric ancestor of our horses of today."

A huge laugh rose from the ranks of the troopers.

"I'd better check my *darn horse* to make sure all his toenails is clipped," one trooper bellowed out. "You can sure tell some tall tales, professor."

The Yale group sat in silence waiting for O. C.'s reply.

"While you're at it, trooper," Marsh said wryly, "you'd better check to see if you have a tail." This time a roar of laughter went up from the students.

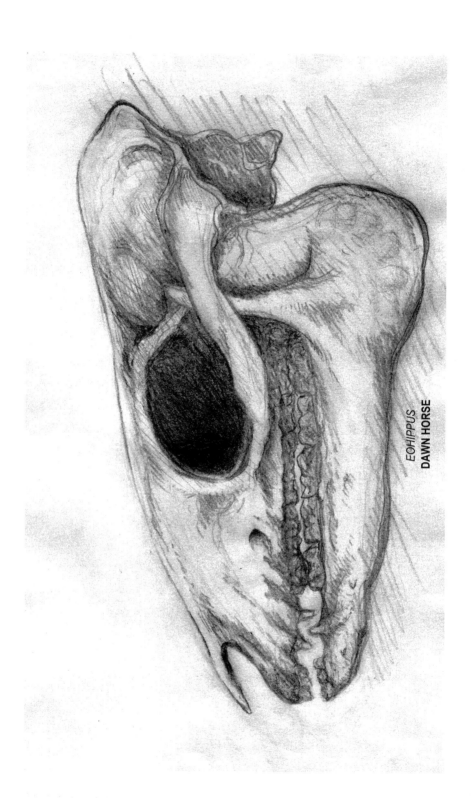

EOHIPPUS
DAWN HORSE

Northwest of the camp, huge, billowing thunderheads were rising above the darkening horizon. As the setting sun painted clouds with colors from mauve to cerise, the coming dusk brought a cooling relief from the heat of the day.

All of a sudden, members of the camp were attacked. Their attackers were not a horde of hostile Indians but another throng of formidable adversaries—mosquitoes. Mosquitoes have inhabited this planet for millions of years, longer than some of the fossils they would be collecting. The coolness of the evening brought the little bloodsucking pests out in swarms of thick black clouds that engulfed the men and horses.

Troopers begin throwing green grasses on the campfires to attack the insects with smoke.

"Better get some grease smeared on your hands and face!" one of the troopers yelled at the students as he began swatting at the insects. "Those skeeters are goin' to be nasty tonight."

As black clouds of insects invaded the camp, other distant black clouds were moving across the prairies to do the same. The wind began to pick up as the skies darkened. The heavens lit up with spiked lightning flashes, and loud rumbles of thunder echoed across the plains. A few drops of rain splattered here and there in the dusty ground, discouraging the pests' invasion. Then, with a couple of dazzling flashes and resounding booms, the skies opened up, pouring sheets of rain with such force that in a matter of minutes the campsite flooded and ended the mosquitoes' assault.

Running for cover, Jake and Dan watched the downpour and the lightning display from the fly of their tent.

"This godforsaken country is hell on earth," Dan said, shaking his soaked hat. "In one day we've rambled over a trail-less, treeless, and waterless landscape; been scorched and parched dry by a blazing sun; and been invaded by pesky bugs and drowned out by pouring rain, not to mention scared out of our wits by thunder and lightning strikes so close it made the hair on the back of my neck stand up."

Jake chuckled. "Pretty boring journey, huh?" he said.

"I'd say more like a horrendous journey."

"Darn it Dan, don't start complaining. I don't want to be arguing with you. I need to get some sleep," Jake said, yawning.

"I'm not complaining or arguing—just stating facts," Dan answered.

The next day the troopers told the students that a few Sioux were dogging their party. The students were assured that the troopers were on the guard and that the Indians wouldn't attack a group as large as theirs.

After four more days of challenging maneuvers over the waterless terrain, they arrived at the Loup Fork. Here the geologic features of the Nebraska landscape changed drastically. The rolling plains gave way to sculptured chalk cliffs and ribbed canyons leading to the river bottoms. It was a welcome site for the scientific expedition.

The party stood viewing the river from a high ridge. The river valley with its flowing sparkling waters, green patches of grass, and stands of cottonwood trees looked like the gardens of paradise to the parched men and horses. Willows framed parts of the river banks, providing cover for thirsty critters. The cool river was an oasis for elk, deer, antelope, and many other kinds of wildlife, including Indians.

"My God," Bill Cody said, "this godforsaken land is beautiful."

"What's that?" Major North asked.

"Just thinking out loud, Frank," Cody said as he turned from viewing the vista and addressed the major.

"Tomorrow my men and I will be leaving your party to track—"

"*Injuns!*" a voice hollered out.

A rifle shot rang out, and troopers jumped into action and barked orders to take cover.

"I think I got one!" Bear shouted.

"Where?" Cody demanded.

Bear, with his carbine in hand, pointed to a patch of willows in the river valley.

"Sioux!" he said.

All eyes were cast in the direction Bear was pointing just in time to see a small herd of deer high tailing it up a ravine.

"You saw Sioux Indians—with antlers?" Cody said, scoffing.

"I know there's Injuns out there," Bear said, flustered. "I think I hit one. I always have my rifle ready, and when I saw them I fired before they could get away."

A few chuckles went up from the troopers. Major North held up his hand for silence as he approached Bear.

"What's your name, boy?" the major asked in a commanding voice.

"Bruno—Bruno Adler," Bear responded. He added, "Most call me Bear."

"Well Mister Bear, Bruno Adler," the major said, "I advise that the next time you want to fire your rifle, you scout the area with some field glasses so you can see the difference between a deer, a Sioux, and a trooper—and then ask for permission. If there weren't any Indians out there now, there surely will be after hearing your rifle report echo down the valley."

The major turned to one of his cavalrymen.

"Sergeant, get me a pair of field glasses," he ordered.

The sergeant retrieved binoculars from a trooper and handed them to the major.

The major took a step closer toward Bear. Not intimated by Bear's size, the major looked up at him and held out the binoculars.

"Take these glasses. Next time you think you see Indians, use them," the major said. "Scabbard that Winchester and don't be so trigger happy."

A Pawnee scout standing near the major started chanting, "*Rahkataar uusu, Reetahkac kiriiku kuuruks.*"

"What did you say?" Major North asked.

Fossil Whisperers ~ 19

"Yellow hair shall be called *Eagle Eye, Yellow Bear!*" the scout exclaimed, holding his hands up to his eyes to imitate field glasses. The Pawnee scouts were known not only for their loyalty and bravery but also for their sense of humor.

"I know I shot an Injun," Bear mumbled to himself.

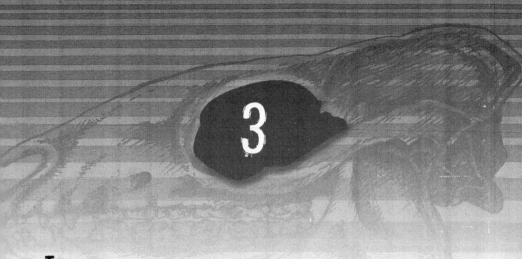

3

The serenity of the river valley was enlivened by the activity of men searching and chipping at the clay landscape with rock hammers. Fossils were to be found everywhere. Marsh instructed his students to be on the lookout particularly for horse fossils.

The group enthusiastically unearthed an assortment of mammal fossils from the Pliocene Epoch that included rhinoceroses and six species of early horses. Some of the troopers became interested in the fossil hunt and joined the students in their excavations.

The Pawnee scouts, superstitious of the fossils at first, wouldn't touch the bones until Marsh explained to them the nature of the fossils. Joining the rest of the camp in the fossil hunt, the Pawnees began bringing back fossils to the "Bone Medicine Man."

As the party searched the river bottoms and adjoining gullies, there were signs that the Sioux were not far away. Smoke from the Indians' campsites was seen often. The party knew they were in Sioux country.

They discovered Sioux burial platforms built on high stilts, as well as platforms constructed high in trees where the Plains Indians would lay to rest their dead.

At one burial site, Marsh suggested to his men they should collect the skeletons of the dead Sioux. Being in Indian Territory, the Yale men were fearful of disturbing an Indian burial site, but Marsh ignored any fear once he had an objective in mind. Not hostile Indians, the

July heat, or sudden, overwhelming, deafening thunderstorms could deter him from his single-minded quest for Pliocene fossils that he hoped to uncover on this expedition.

"Men," the professor said, clearing his throat, "we're here to collect bones. These bones are needed so we can do research on the origin of the Indian race."

The Sioux bones were added to the Yale collection.

Two days after they set up camp in the river bottom, one of the Pawnee scouts rode up to Major North's tent and asked Lieutenant Reilly to see the major.

"What is it?" the lieutenant inquired.

"I talk only with major," the scout said.

"Lieutenant, would you round up a couple of the men and see if you can scare up some deer or antelope for some fresh meat?" the major ordered.

"Yes, sir," Lieutenant Reilly replied. "How many would you like, sir?" he asked jokingly.

"Don't spend more than half a dozen bullets," Major North said, smiling.

"Now let's have our little powwow," the major said to the Pawnee scout.

"I found something you should know," the Pawnee said. "Scouting the bottoms near a gully, I found Indian tracks and blood. Look like someone was killed there, day or two ago. I track up the gully to where horses had stood and were ridden off —east across prairie. I think maybe Eagle Eye Yellow Bear shot a Sioux, like he say when we first here."

"You believe that's possible?" the major questioned.

"I believe," the Pawnee answered.

"Okay," the major said. "You and I keep this only between us. Don't tell the other men, you understand?"

"Me understand," the Pawnee scout replied.

The fossil expedition progressed along the Loup Fork to the point where the river began to be not much more than a trickle. Fossils were plentiful and easy to remove from the Nebraska clay.

Sergeant Frank Muller was fascinated by the fossils the Yale students were finding. Approaching Dan Randall, who was busy excavating a fossil bone, the veteran trooper led his horse and addressed Dan while introducing himself.

"Howdy. I'm Frank Muller," he said. "You know, a few years back I found some bones on my Pa's land. They were in stone like the ones you're digging. My younger brother has quite a collection of bones."

"Where's that?" Dan asked.

"Over in Wyoming, northwest of Laramie, near Medicine Bow," Muller answered.

"Dan Randall's the name," Dan said. "That's my partner Jake coming toward us. Looks like he found a good fossil he wants to show me."

"Look at this skull!" Jake exclaimed as he showed Dan a detailed fossil of the skull of a Pliocene horse. "What a beautiful specimen."

Two more students approached Jake to look at his find.

"Jake Harding, this is Sergeant Frank Muller," Dan said.

"What's this fossil you found?" the Sergeant asked.

"It's from a prehistoric horse," Jake said.

"That's the skull of a horse?" Muller asked, looking very puzzled at the fossil about the size of a dog's skull. "Oh, you mean like in that story Professor Marsh was telling about the first horse?"

"One and the same," Jake said, handing Muller the fossil for a closer look.

"That's fascinating," Muller remarked. "I was just telling your friend that I found some fossils similar to these on my dad's ranch in Wyoming."

"Are you a fossil hunter?" Jake asked.

"No, but my brother does collect them," Frank answered. "I'd run across these interesting-looking bones in the limestone bluffs on our ranch. I saved a number of them for my brother."

Muller turned the fossil skull over and over in his hands and then held it up to compare its shape to his horse's head.

"Well, I don't know," Muller said. "I think this is so much bull."

"No," Dan said. "It's horse."

"Horseshit, bullshit," Muller said. "Still adds up to be manure."

Jake laughed, unsure whether Dan or Frank was aware of the humor in their conversation.

"You been soldiering for a long time?" Dan asked.

"Uh-huh," Muller replied. "I joined the cavalry when I was nineteen."

"Ever been in an Indian attack?" Dan asked.

"Uh-huh, too many times," Frank answered. "One time damn near got me killed because of some deserters we had. About two years ago, near Sand Creek Colorado, we were ambushed by a party of Cheyenne. The Cheyenne are still fightin' mad over the '64 Sand Creek Massacre."

"I've heard reports about that massacre," Jake said. "Horrible reports of cold-blooded murder."

"Yeah, on both sides," Muller said.

"It must be scary being in an Indian attack," Dan said.

"Thinking about it is frightful," the sergeant said. "Being in it you don't think about being scared; you just fight to defend yourself. We lost four good men that day and a number wounded before the hostiles were driven off. That's where I earned these," he said, pointing to his sergeant stripes, "and where I got this," he added, pointing to a long scar on the left side of his neck that ran from his ear on down until it disappeared under his shirt collar.

Muller reflected for a moment. "Reckon we'd all been killed if it weren't for the Tenth Cavalry boys showing up," he said. "Those Buffalo Soldiers saved our scalps that day."

"Buffalo Soldiers?" Dan asked, fascinated with the corporal's story.

"Yeah, that's the name the Indians gave the men of the Tenth, a Negro regiment," Frank said. "The black soldiers joined up after the war and had their own regiment. They are fearless fighters against the Indians."

Frank read the worried look on Dan's face at the mention of fighting Indians.

"But don't worry, men," Frank assured them. "All the troopers on this expedition are experienced soldiers and steadfast—not like some of the deserters we've had in the past."

"We appreciate your protecting our expedition and putting up with us tenderfoots," Jake said.

"This is easy duty," Sergeant Muller said. "It's about my last assignment. When my twenty-year hitch is up in September, I'm headed back to the ranch. My curiosity about fossils has been moved. I may look for more fossils when I get back to Wyoming."

"Finding bones millions of years old is a fascinating adventure," Jake said.

"You may be right, Jake," Frank said as he looked over his shoulder toward a noise that had distracted him.

"I'll take this up with you another time," Frank said. "Right now I'd better see what all the commotion is about with that wagon and mule team yonder."

With one smooth move, he swung himself up into the saddle, turned his horse sharply, and loped off toward the wagon.

Three pistol shots rang out as Sergeant Muller rode off. Not knowing for sure what the situation was, he spurred his horse to a gallop, and on the run he drew his rifle from its scabbard and was ready for anything. He came to a quick halt and dismounted in front of a trooper who had a long, handlebar mustache and a British accent.

"Corporal Evans, what's going on?" Frank asked.

"Ay, that goddamn mule poked his bloody muzzle at a rattler and got bit," the corporal said, pointing to one of the wagon mules. "Nick shot the snake. Missed the first two shots but blew its head off on the third try."

Nick De Luca, one of the company's youngest recruits, was just lucky he had hit the snake on the third shot; he was probably the poorest shot in the company. A recent Italian immigrant, Nick had enlisted in the US Cavalry hoping to improve his English and see America.

"Luckily he didn't hit the mule," Frank said. "Where is he?"

"Nick?" the corporal asked, and then he answered his own question. "The bloke's skinning the snake over by that big cottonwood, his big trophy from the America West."

Frank tied his mount to the wagon wheel and went to talk to Nick. The sergeant harshly reprimanded the private for firing the three shots—the signal for alert.

Jake, Dan. and two other students were worried when they heard the gunshots.

"T'is no cause for concern," Corporal Evans said as he rode up to the four students. "One of our lads just killed a bloody rattlesnake that bit a dumbass mule. Sergeant Muller lambasted the private for firing those shots. Sometimes things upset the sergeant and, for no reason, he just explodes. When he gets his bloody hackles up, you don't want to cross him. I'm on my way to let the lieutenant know what's happened. Lots of rattlers around here so be careful."

"Geez," Dan said. "This godforsaken country is hell on earth."

"Must have been a damn big snake to take three bullets to kill it," Jake said.

Dan snorted and clenched his teeth. "God, I hate snakes about as bad as anything I can imagine. Why the hell does there have to be snakes anyway?" Dan said, shaking his head and hunching his shoulders.

Jake chuckled. "Dan, you're always complaining about something you can't do anything about," he said. "The snakes are here and were here long before you."

"Yeah, I know," Dan said with a little smirk on his face. "I remember the story of Adam and Eve, but no snake could get close enough to tempt me."

"And if it did you'd just talk its head off," Jake said, laughing.

"All right, you two, enough joking around," Jim, one of the students, said. "Let's head for the chuck wagon. I'm in need of some grub."

Another student, ignoring the quarrelling, was looking at a sky full of threatening thunderheads.

"It looks like another big storm is going to pound us tonight," he said. "We'd better get going and grab some chow before it hits."

4

The evening meals were usually the most pleasant time of the day for the camp—if it wasn't raining and the wind wasn't howling and the mosquitoes weren't too fierce. The food wasn't as terrible as the students had heard it would be. The men would usually enjoy fresh meat after someone had shot an antelope or a deer or an elk, which were plentiful around them.

Jake was sitting next to Corporal Evans, who was asking him about the fossils they were finding. Jake mentioned that Sergeant Muller had an interest in collecting fossils.

"The sergeant is a strange one, he is," Corporal Evans said.

"Why do you say that?" Jake asked.

"Some of the men think he's two people in one," Evans said.

"Why is that?"

"Well, most of the time he's a half-decent chap and a good squaddie," Evans said. "Then something will set him off, and he sort of becomes a madman."

"I found him very pleasant," Jake said.

"Most people do when they're on his good side," Evans said. "I think the things that set him off are a reflection of his long and horrible experiences as a soldier. He has been in some bloody battles and done things and seen things that would change any bloke's character."

"He said he was getting out of the army come September," Jake said.

"And good thing too," the corporal said. "He needs a rest from soldiering."

"Well, I like the guy," Jake said.

"And well you should," Evans said. "Just watch your P's and Q's around him."

Private Nick De Luca, who was sitting next to the corporal, listened with interest to their conversation.

"*Si e vero,*" De Luca said to Jake. "You watch it."

One of the cooks approached Private De Luca and asked what he had done with the snake he killed. Nick told him he had thrown it in the bush after he'd skinned it.

"Damn it, son, next time you get a big rattler, bring it to me," the cook said. "I make a delicious rattlesnake stew."

The thought of eating a rattlesnake struck Dan as disgusting. "I'll be damned if you'll ever catch me eating a snake," he said. "I'd have to be near dead of starvation or drunk as a skunk, or both."

"What's the difference between snake and these venison steaks?" Jake asked. "They're both meats."

"The point is, one's a crawly, slimy snake," Dan said as he took a big mouthful of coffee and spit it out as soon as it washed his tongue.

"Goddamn, that coffee's strong enough to float a horseshoe," Dan said, still spitting as he spoke.

"Ah, it's good for you. It'll put hair on your chest," Jake said.

"Yeah, Ma would say that to me when I wouldn't eat my greens," Dan said thoughtfully. "Hair on your chest. Is that supposed to make you a man?"

Jake shrugged. "Don't know. Let's see your chest."

"Don't be a wiseass, Jake," Dan fired back.

The constant sparring of words was something both Jake and Dan enjoyed. Even when their discussions got a little heated, there was no malicious intent. It was a game they played as friends.

Twilight on the prairies can linger on and on, but in this case clouds were blocking out the last fading rays of sunlight and darkness was coming fast over the plains. The colors in the bluffs were rapidly becoming muted as twilight engulfed the landscape, and large, billowing, dark clouds were building on the western horizon. Slight breezes from west to east began to increase, with gusts launching dust and sand into the sullen prairie sky. Something else was in the sky—smoke.

"Look at that!" a trooper said, pointing to the west.

Miles away, a streak of light was snaking across the prairie as far as the eye could see. A wall of thick smoke was leading the dancing light.

"I'll be damned," a trooper said. "Those damn Injuns mean to burn us out."

The flickering prairie fire, being fanned by the west wind from the oncoming storm, was advancing rapidly, sending tongues of flames licking at the prairie grasses.

"Everybody, grab picks and shovels," Corporal Evans ordered. "We'll clear a break and build a backfire to stop those bloody flames."

The men worked fanatically to make a furrow for a firebreak and then lit a backfire as the crackling prairie inferno steadily danced toward their camp. By the time the prairie blaze hit the burned-out backfire strip, there was no grass left to fuel the fire. Yet the dying flames didn't give up their attack as they hissed at the break; they fired burning ashes, propelled by the blustery wind, toward the campsite.

The men, busy stomping out cinders, were quickly relieved when the storm broke, sending a dousing rain onto the camp and extinguishing the prairie fire.

Dan, about to say something, caught an intimidating glance from Jake. He hesitated before speaking and held up his hands.

"No complaints, no arguments, and no discussion," Dan said.

The fossil operation at the Loup Fork had been successful. After almost a month of digging, the expedition had unearthed six different species of prehistoric horses and a wide variety of other extinct animals. The party now headed back to the town of North Platte and Fort McPherson.

The ride back, under the intense July sun, was scorching hot without the slightest breeze to stir the air. But there was a stirring, the whirring of millions of insects. With every step the horses took, swarms of grasshoppers were flushed from the prairie grasses. The men, covered with the little buggers with the buggy eyes, were busy brushing them from their faces, hands, and clothing. The horses were bothered by the hoppers getting in their noses, eyes, and ears and kept whinnying, shaking their heads and manes, and whipping their tails in frustration.

Dan complained about the hoppers and told Charlie that he was getting so many bugs in his mouth that one would think he was chewing tobacco.

"Stop yapping. Just spit," Charlie said.

Dan let the remark pass, unsure if Charlie meant to be helpful or critical.

As they neared the Platte River, the grasshoppers finally thinned out. They rode across an area of alkali flats where the wind came howling across the prairie, blowing alkali dust and sand that stung their faces. It seemed to Dan there was no end to the misery this godforsaken country could generate.

Jake and Sergeant Muller rode side by side as they traveled to the north fork of the Platte River. Their conversation centered on fossils, the Western frontier, and horses. Frank told Jake about his ranch that was run by his younger brother and his sister after his older brother and mother had been killed in an Indian raid a few years earlier. Frank was going home to help run the ranch. His pa was getting along in years and was being crippled by arthritis.

The party that rode into the town of North Platte looked quite different than the one that had left Fort McPherson a few weeks earlier. Tanned and dusty, many of the men supported whiskers, including Jake, who now had the beginnings of a full beard and mustache. The month's experience had turned the students of Yale College into students of the Western Frontier.

At Fort McPherson, the troopers and the Yale party were treated to a celebration dinner as General Emory welcomed the party back.

"I'm delighted to know that Major North and his troopers took good care of your expedition and brought you all back safely, except for one old mule that succumbed to the bite of a rattlesnake," the general said, addressing the party.

"Got me a nice keepsake!" Nick shouted as he stood up and unrolled a six-foot snakeskin with rattlers attached. He got a round of applause.

At dinner Jake and Sergeant Muller continued their conversation.

"Jake, I noticed that you seem to be real handy with horses," Frank said.

"My grandpa taught me all about horses," Jake said, "which included veterinary skills."

"Well, if ever you look for a job on a horse ranch, look up the Muller Ranch," Frank said. "I'll give you the address." Frank took a paper and pencil from his pocket, wrote the address down, and handed it to Jake. "Write to my brother, Chris. He handles all the affairs for the ranch, and he'll be interested in your knowledge of fossils."

Jake introduced Frank Muller to Professor Marsh, telling Marsh about Frank and his brother's interest in fossils and his ranch in Wyoming, where a number of fossils had been found.

"Wonderful," Marsh said, clearing his throat. "I'd be interested in knowing what you find. I'll give you my postal address at Yale, if you'd be as kind as to send me a description of any unusual fossil finds."

"I can get my brother to do that," Frank said. "He is the one keen on finding fossils."

"Splendid," the professor said as he handed Muller his address.

"If your brother finds any fossils of interest to me, I'll be happy to pay him for them."

"I'll be helping Professor Marsh at Yale with his research on fossils when we get back," Jake said to Frank. "But I *will* be out this way again."

"I bet you will," Frank said.

Marsh sent dispatches to New Haven detailing their recent findings. The Marsh party crated their fossils for shipment back to Yale and said good-bye to the troops at Fort McPherson.

5

In mid-August Marsh and his party boarded the train at North Platte heading for Cheyenne, Wyoming. Fort D. A. Russell at Crow Creek Crossing near Cheyenne was the expedition's next destination.

The party was outfitted at the fort with an escort of thirty troopers from the Fifth Cavalry, commanded by Captain Robert Montgomery. They travelled north of Cheyenne to explore the region between the North and South Platte Rivers.

The group explored a badlands that previously had been unknown. Here they found an abundance of fossils of giant turtles, rhinoceroses (Hyracodon), birds, and oreodonts (an ancient creature that looked like a cross between a sheep and a pig). An exciting event for the party was the excavation of the fifty-million-year-old remains of several brontotheres (related to rhino-like creatures with three toes on their hind feet and four toes on their front feet).

The expedition continued northwest toward the North Platte River. There the landscape was like a roughly carved high-relief frieze. It was a labyrinth of ravines and bluffs that changed their kaleidoscopic colors with the hour of the day.

Jake viewed the scenery before him and thought, *my god, this godforsaken country is beautiful.*

As they made their way gingerly through the maze of gulches dotted with sagebrush, one of the pack mules started braying, reared up, and fell on her side. The cavalry trooper leading the mule was almost thrown from his horse when it was spooked by the mule's distress. The trooper dismounted and tried to calm the mule, but it kept braying and thrashing about with its eyes open wide with fear and its lips curled, exposing its large teeth.

"What happened?" Jake asked the trooper.

"Got bit by a rattler," the trooper said. "I just saw its tail end slither off into the brush. Not much I can do for old Jenny here. Just wait and see how she fares."

Bruno rode up behind Jake, dismounted, and tethered his horse and his pack mule to a bush.

1870s FOSSIL HUNTERS WITH CAVALRY SENTINEL

"You guys stay on your horses and keep moving," the trooper said. "There are lots of snakes around here."

"I'll stay and keep you company, if you don't mind," Bruno said. "Maybe I can get a shot at that snake."

"He is a crack shot," Jake said.

"All right," the trooper said. "But don't go wandering off in the bush. I don't want to nurse two snake bites."

"Thanks," Bruno said as he drew his rifle from its scabbard.

As the party traveled through the badlands for another fifteen minutes, they heard a rifle shot. Bruno had bagged a ten-point whitetail. A minute later, another shot rang out. The trooper had put the snake-bitten mule out of her misery.

At the North Platte River, the party found more species of fossil horses.

Scotts Bluff stood like a gigantic clipper ship riding the plains of Nebraska. Outcroppings and bluffs rose from the level plains, creating a peculiar landscape punctuated with erect projections hundreds of feet high. The hard-rock outcroppings had been carved into surreal shapes by millions of years of erosion.

Heading southwest along Horse Creek, the men, hot and dusty, decided to take a swim and bathe in the stream before heading back to Fort D. A. Russell. They found a place where the river had a grassy bank sloping toward a gravel shore that led into a tranquil pool of cool water.

Soldiers stood guard as the students begin to strip down, their bare butts and bodies as white as the underbelly of a rainbow trout. But their hands and faces were as tanned as their leather saddles, and just as dusty. They appeared to be wearing brown gloves and face masks.

Jake and Charlie were the first to wade in. Jake was in the river up to his chest splashing cool water over his shoulders and arms.

Standing farther up the sloping bank near his tethered horse was Bear, butt naked. He was about to go to the shore and test the water when, suddenly, he reached over toward his horse, withdrew the Winchester carbine from his saddle scabbard, put the gun to his shoulder, and aimed at Charlie and then at Jake.

"Charlie, get out!" Bear yelled. "Jake, don't move!"

Midstream, Jake looked up, stopped splashing, and saw Bear with his carbine pointed at him.

"Look out, Jake!" Dan shouted. "He's going to shoot."

That son of a bitch is going to shoot me, Jake thought.

Jake froze and stared at Bear. Bear took his time carefully aiming and then fired off a round. Jake heard a splash behind him to his left and turned in time to see what he thought was a floating tree branch being knocked through the water. It wasn't a stick—it was a snake.

Bear stood tall, breathing easy. He sighted down his rifle barrel again and slowly squeezed the trigger for the second time. This time the bullet whizzed over the top of Jake and blew the head off another snake just as it was about to enter the water on the far bank.

"Snakes! Snakes!" everyone yelled.

Charlie scrambled up the bank on all fours, clawing at mud and gravel. When he realized what was happening, he stood up and ran to get his rifle. A number of others had grabbed their guns. They formed a line like a firing squad and stood naked, firing at the far steep bank.

Bear stood straight, tall, and silent in the nude and kept aiming his rifle and firing. He had a serious look on his face that was seldom seen.

The far bank was crawling with snakes slithering along the water's edge. Bullets zinged into the gravel along the cut bank as dozens of shots missed, but some found their mark.

Troopers came running thinking the party was under attack. Soon realizing the hostiles were snakes, they joined in the barrage.

Jake lay nude on the gravel bank as bullets whizzed toward the far bank.

As quickly as it had started, the volley of gunfire stopped and the snakes disappeared.

Jake got up, grabbed his pile of clothes, walked toward Bear, and held out his hand.

"Thanks, Bear," he said. "You saved my hide."

Bear shook Jake's hand with a big, bear paw grip. The two nude men stood grinning at one another on the sloping bank under a hot, summer Nebraska sun.

"You're welcome, Harding," Bear said. "I hate snakes."

"I do too," Jake said, laughing. "Next time I bathe I'll wear my gun. By the way, you really are a good shot."

"Thanks," Bear said. "That makes my score one Sioux, one deer, and about half a dozen rattlers." He bent down, picked up his shell casings, shouldered his rifle, and then turned to walk farther up the bank to where his clothes and horse were.

Jake turned and looked at Dan. Both started to chuckle as they watched Bear's bulky, bare backside go up the hill.

"You know, he does look like a bear," Jake said.

"Yeah, a rifle-totin' polar bear," Dan said.

"He's still under the illusion that he shot an Indian back on the Loup Fork," Jake said.

"Who knows? Maybe he did," Dan said.

On their way back to Fort D. A. Russell, Jake and Dan talked about the Horse Creek bathing event.

"It was lucky Bear spotted those snakes," Jake said. "He's a strange fellow, though. I don't know if I like or dislike the guy."

"Well, I wouldn't trust him any more than a rattlesnake," Dan said.

6

Back on board the Union Pacific at the end of August, the Yale expedition traveled to Fort Bridger in the southwestern part of Wyoming.

Once at the fort, Marsh met with the post commander, Major R. S. LaMotte, and Judge William A. Carter, the post trader who was also an appointed US commissioner for federal court in Salt Lake City. Carter was a special agent of the US Post Office Department who would frequently travel the wild route of the Overland Stage Company. He was a survivor of Indian attacks and stage holdups. He was one of the richest and most influential men in the territory. Marsh, Major LaMotte, Lieutenant Wann, and guide Joe Talemans met with the judge at his large home near the fort in the Black Fords Creek valley.

"Professor Marsh, I understand you're interested in exploring an area around the junction of the Green and White Rivers," Judge Carter said. "That's a mountainous region, mainly unexplored. From what I've heard from the description Indians have given about that land, it sounds like it's beautiful but a nightmare of a terrain to traverse. I wish I had the time to go with you. I do like a new adventure."

"You'd be welcome to join us," Marsh said.

"I would love to, but I have pressing duties to attend to here," the judge replied.

"The interesting Indian tales I've heard about that region describe valleys that are littered with giant fossil bones," Marsh said, clearing his throat. "I intend to see for myself."

"We have an escort from the Thirteenth Infantry for your party," Major LaMotte said. "Lieutenant Wann will be in command, accompanied by your guide, Joe Talemans. They're two of our finest men."

"Splendid," Marsh said.

"I regret that we don't have one horse we can spare, but we have plenty of mules," the major said.

Marsh looked a little concerned. He cleared his throat, but before he could speak, the major continued.

"The country you're going into is as rugged as any mountainous wilderness you can imagine," the major said. "Mules are your best bet for mounts and pack animals."

"The major is right," Talemans said. "Mules were made for that country. They're beasts of burden, they're sure-footed, and they can pack heavy loads for longer distances than any horse."

Two days later, the Yale party and their army escorts made their way through the Fort Bridger Basin along Henry's Fork into Utah following the Green River. The meandering route made travel slow going, and the rugged terrain began to take its toll on the wagons.

"Never thought I'd be riding down a canyon on the back of a jackass," Dan said.

"You're not," Jake said. "That's a mule your riding."

"I know that … you jackass," Dan said.

"Well, don't insult me or the animal by calling us donkeys."

"I don't mean to insult you or the dumb animal," Dan said. "I do thank the mule for being so sure-footed and you for being so knowledgeable."

The men were glad they were mounted on mules because the tortuous terrain tested the abilities of the animals' sure-footedness. The mules pulling the supply wagons were straining over the rugged terrain. The wooden wagons were being shaken apart, twisting and bouncing over the rocky landscape as they inched their way along the Green River.

A loud crack rang out as one of the wagon wheels broke. The wagon tipped onto its side, and supplies tumbled across the ground. The driver, unable to maintain his balance, jumped to his safety.

"What happened back there?" Lieutenant Wann yelled.

"Broke a wheel!" the wagon driver yelled back.

Joe Talemans, riding point, was trying to pick out the best route. He turned his mount and rode back to the lieutenant.

"What's going on, sir?" Joe asked.

"We broke a wheel," Lieutenant Wann said. "Joe, the wagons are not going to make it. They're falling apart."

"I know," Joe said. "I've found the best trail I could, but it's no good for wagons. At the rate we're going, we'll be here when the snows come. I think we'll have to abandon the wagons."

"You're right," Wann said. "I'll send some men back to the fort to get some packsaddles and panniers for the wagon mules. We'll load the supplies on them and leave the wagons here."

"All right," Talemans agreed. "I'll scout ahead for a place to hole up for a couple of days until we get the packsaddles."

"I'll inform Marsh of our plans," the lieutenant said.

The professor was not too happy with the lieutenant's plan. Marsh wanted to push on as he was impatient to discover those valleys strewn with giant fossil bones. The lieutenant explained that they would make better time with packsaddles loaded with their supplies than they would trying to pull wagons over the mountain passes. Marsh contained his aggravation and informed his party about the delay.

After a couple of days' delay, the party was on the move again with their supplies loaded in packsaddles on the mules. They traveled along the Green River to an unexplored area near the juncture of the Green River and White River in Utah.

Marsh, who was riding in front of Jake, turned and motioned for him to ride alongside.

"Jake, tell the boys we'll explore this section of the river," Marsh said. "I'll inform Lieutenant Wann that we'll set up camp here for a couple of days." Marsh kicked his mule and turned to go find the lieutenant.

"About time we get back to digging for fossils," Jake muttered.

"What'd you say?" Dan asked.

"Just thinking out loud about getting back to digging fossils," Jake said.

"Yeah, I hope there are fossils to be found here," Dan said. "I'll be glad to get off this seesaw mule ride so I can sit my ass on a nice soft rock that doesn't move."

Fossil hunting along the Green River produced numerous fossils. But to Marsh's dismay, and contrary to what he'd been told, there were no valleys of legendary huge fossil bones. They reached the Uinta badlands of southern Utah and then traveled through the rugged landscape to Henry's Fork and back to Fort Bridger.

At Fort Bridger, the recently found fossils were crated and sent back to New Haven. The Yale party's success in fossil collecting pleased Marsh. He decided they'd travel the new transcontinental railway to Salt Lake City and then head over to San Francisco for a few weeks of relaxation and sightseeing.

When the Yale Scientific Expedition arrived in Salt Lake City in late September, Professor Marsh was invited to meet Brigham Young, the president of the Church of Jesus Christ of Latter-Day Saints. Great Salt Lake City, founded by Mormons in 1847, flourished under the direction of Brigham Young, who started a number of ambitious building projects, including the Mormon Temple and the Salt Lake Theater.

Young invited Marsh and his party to attend a theater production at the Salt Lake Theater where some of Young's wives and daughters would be in attendance.

The fall evening air was crisp, with a large autumn moon illuminating the theater. The Yale students enjoyed flirting with Young's twenty-two daughters. After the theater production, the students chattered like adolescent schoolkids as they exited the theater.

"Did you enjoy the play, Dan?" Jake asked as he gave him a slap on the back and a chuckle.

"Gosh darn," Dan said. "I think I missed the play. But that was the best performance I've been to in a long time. Those daughters of Brigham Young are gorgeous."

"I can't argue with that," Jake said.

"It was a pleasure to flirt with them after such a long dry spell," Dan said.

"Well, I think the drought was at an end," Jake said. "It seems there was a lot of precipitation in the theater this evening."

"Well, you boys were real gentlemen this evening," Dan said, imitating Marsh and clearing his throat. "A credit to Yale, ahem."

The party traveled to San Francisco for a sightseeing tour, where Marsh again sent many dispatches to New Haven. The letters described the expedition's finds with information to be published in the *American Journal of Science and Arts*. His competition with Edward Cope was escalating. Marsh's determination to see that Yale became the leading scientific center over the University of Pennsylvania and the Smithsonian in Washington, DC was becoming obsessive. His correspondence was directed at everyone he knew who was collecting fossils. He urged them to send him their specimens so he could describe and classify them for science. He would, of course, reimburse the collectors for their efforts.

7

Frank Muller trotted easily along an all-too-familiar road toward his Wyoming ranch. The early September morning looked like it would become a sunny and mild day. Frank wondered if things at the ranch were much like he'd remembered. Was Aunt Bella still serving up the most delicious meals he'd ever eaten, and were the Wilson brothers still working the ranch along with his pa's old Pawnee friend? He spurred his horse to a lope as he got closer to his home. It wasn't just because he was anxious to see his family, but he had sensed something was wrong—terribly wrong. There were no signs of livestock that should have dotted the surrounding pasture, nor any horses in the corrals—and the scene was quiet except for a few crows cawing and scolding one another. When he approached the first corral, he saw that the gate was wide open. Beside the road laid the dead body of the Muller family's dog, a German shepherd named Schnell. His pa had named the dog Schnell because he could run so fast. Frank dismounted and examined the dead dog. A gunshot wound had claimed the dog's life. Frank's mind raced with fear as to what might have happened here. He quickly remounted.

Galloping up to the hitching post in front of the ranch house, Frank looked across the veranda and noticed that the front door stood open. He reined his horse to a quick stop, jumped down, and ran across the sunlit porch to the open door. His eyes took a second to get used to the dimness in the front room.

"Hello!" he shouted. "Hey, anybody home?"

Only the chattering crows and the snorting of his horse, bugged by flies, broke the silence.

"Pa? Jennifer? Chris? Bella? Is anyone here?"

Then he saw at the far side of the room, partway in the hallway, a figure laid sprawled on the floor, shirtless and shoeless, face down in a blotch of dried blood.

Frank quickly drew his revolver and cautiously approached the figure. He saw bullet wounds in the body—one between the shoulder blades the other in the back of the head. His worst fears were realized when he turned the body over. It was his father. Kneeling, gasping, and sighing, he reached with his left hand and closed his father's eyes. Frank shook his right hand in defiance as he gripped his revolver and waved it in the air.

"Drop your gun, mister, and put your hands high," a coarse voice behind him commanded from the front doorway. "Mister, I'll shoot you dead if you make one wrong move."

"Okay," Frank said. "Take it easy. I'm putting my gun down."

"Now slowly get to your feet," the harsh voice ordered. "Kick that gun away and turn around."

Frank was about to do as ordered when he heard another voice outside the front door.

"Chris, what's going on?" a female voice yelled out.

"Stay there, Jen," Chris said.

Frank, with his hands held above his head, did a slow turn toward the man with the rough voice and found himself staring into a rifle barrel.

"Frank?" the voice at the other end of the rifle asked. "Goddamn. Frank, is that you?"

"Yeah, Chris, it's me," Frank said sullenly. "Brother, would you mind lowering your rifle?"

"Jen, get your butt in here, pronto!" Chris hollered as he lowered his rifle.

"Damn it, Chris! What do you think I am, your pet hound?" the woman outside said as she ran up the steps and stomped across the porch. "First you tell me to stay, then to get. Oh, my God! Frank!" She stepped into the living room.

"Jennie," Frank said as he moved toward her with open arms, obscuring her view of their dead father's body.

"Oh, Frank, it sure is good to see you," Jen said as she hugged him.

"Good to see you back home again, brother," Chris said. "What's going on here? We found Schnell shot dead out by the corral."

"I know," Frank said, sighing hesitantly. "Bad news—Pa's been killed too. I just arrived shortly before you and found him dead of two bullet wounds."

"Oh no. No!" Jen cried. "I *told* him to come to town with us. Damn it!"

She ran across the room and knelt beside her father's body, sobbing. Chris followed and knelt over his father, helpless in his effort to do anything.

"Son of a bitch," Chris said. "Why didn't he come with us? I was afraid something like this would happen. This country has been crawling with outlaws and hostiles of late. Where is Aunt Bella? She was here. And the Wilson brothers—where are they?"

"Let's check around," Frank said. "Maybe they're hiding."

"God, I hope they haven't been killed or captured," Chris said.

"Looks like Pa were running for the gun rack when he was gunned down," Jen said. "The rifles are missing."

"Along with the horses we had corralled," Chris said.

"Those bastardy crooks must have taken my mare! She was in the front corral," Jen said. "Poor Lady, what's she going to do without me? What am I going to do without my horse? What am I going to do without Pa?"

She removed her hat and threw it on a chair. Her long auburn hair cascaded around her shoulders. Sobbing, she turned and stomped down the hallway toward her father's bedroom.

"I'll get a blanket to cover Pa," she said, her anger and grief mingling with the tears rolling down her cheeks as words of rage rang out. "I'm going to kill the bastards that did this."

For the first time in five years, since seeing Jennie on a short leave from the army, Frank noticed that she had grown into a beautiful, mature woman with the demeanor of a hardened frontierswoman combined with the sophistication of a lady.

"Let's take a look at the bunkhouse," Chris told Frank. "The Wilson brothers live there."

Frank and Chris crossed the yard heading for the bunkhouse. Tears welled up in Chris's eyes at the thought of his father being murdered. His thoughts echoed the words of his sister: *I'm going to kill the bastards that did this.*

Frank and Chris drew their revolvers as they approached the bunkhouse and saw the door wide open.

"Charlie? Phil?" Chris called out.

Stepping inside, they saw the Wilson brother's bodies—one shot dead lying in the middle of the room, and the other lying below the side window. Chris went to examine the body by the window, while Frank knelt to look at the dead man in the center of the room.

"They been shot twice, like Pa," Chris said. "Each a bullet wound to the body and one in the head. The sons of bitches wanted to make sure they were dead."

"Yeah, dead men tell no tales," Frank said.

"Whoever did this took the Wilsons' guns," Chris said. "Along with their horses, Pa's horse, and the herd we had. We had corralled about sixty horses we planned to sell to the army."

"Chris, Frank, where are you guys?" Jen called out as she headed toward the bunkhouse.

"We found the Wilson boys—murdered," Frank called out as he made a quick turn and went out the door to meet Jen.

Frank grabbed ahold of Jen and steered her away from the door.

"Is Bella in there too?" Jen asked.

"No, she's nowhere in sight," Chris said. "We'll keep looking."

"You don't want to see this," Frank told Jen, holding her back. She resisted his hold and started for the door.

"I want to see my friends," she said, sobbing and cursing as she entered the bunkhouse. "When I kill those murdering horse thieves, I want to remember what those goddamn bastards did to my friends and Pa."

"Let's check out the cabin," Chris said. "I know Red Arrow and his wife Sunbird were going hunting. They may still be in the mountains. Don't know where Bella could have gone."

"Jen, bring the wagon up to the house," Chris said. "We'll unload the supplies after we check the rest of the buildings."

"You know we'll get those bastards," Jen said, giving Chris an assertive look.

"Yeah, I know, sis," Chris said, nodding his head.

"I put a blanket over Pa," Jen said. "All the guns in the house are missing along with Pa's gold pocket watch. But they didn't get into the safe."

Jen ran to get the wagon and team. Frank watched her scramble over the corral fence. He was continually amazed at Jen's spunk. He remembered her as an adventurous, pleasant, sweet young girl of five years ago, when she was fifteen. She had changed from a sweet adolescent into a mature frontiers-woman.

"Let's check the cabin and the barn," Chris said. "We'll get a couple of saddle blankets to cover the Wilsons."

The cabin door was flung wide open.

"Hello Red, Sun?" Chris called out. Peering inside, Chris and Frank could see that the place had been ransacked.

"Looks like no one's here," Frank said as he holstered his revolver.

"Any sign of Red and Sun?" Jen yelled from the road.

"No," Chris called back. "Maybe they're still in the mountains. We'll check out the barn."

"Brother, Jen is a changed girl since I last saw her," Frank said.

"Yeah, she became a tough woman real fast after Ma and Johnny were killed," Chris said. "She does the work of a couple of men around the ranch. I believe she could run the place herself if need be."

"Well, she seems tough, but in a calloused way," Frank said.

Chris nodded and smiled. "Let's get some blankets," he said. "I'll tell you about our sister later."

They headed for the barn. Entering the old barn, the sights and smell brought back memories of better days on the ranch for Frank. But the stillness and empty stalls accentuated the present tragic state of affairs. Chris stepped to the side and pulled a rifle from behind a post of the door frame.

"The murderers didn't find the rifle Pa had us hide behind the barn door," Chris said. "He put this Spencer Repeater here in case we were in the barn and needed some firepower for any reason. Been some outlaws here about and a few hostile Indians."

"Good thinking," Frank said.

"Pa was extra cautious after Ma and Johnny were killed," Chris said.

They walked over to the tack room, opened the door, and found everything in order. Chris grabbed a couple of saddle blankets and shook the dust off of them.

"Well, look at that," Chris said. "There's Pa's old '60 .44 Colt revolver and holster. Those murderers missed it too."

"That's something to remember Pa by," Frank said "And there's his saddle—the first saddle I was ever seated on. Good memories."

Chris handed the saddle blankets to Frank. Lifting his dad's gun and holster off its peg, he pulled out the revolver. After examining the gun, he strapped the holster around his waist.

"I'm going to carry this gun until the day I find those murderers, and I promise I'll make them feel the sting of Pa's .44," Chris said. He shoved the revolver in the holster, and then with his fist he lashed out at a feed bag, releasing some of his pent-up rage.

Frank knew his brother's wrath could be immense and had no

doubt Chris meant to carry out his promise. He could see and feel the change in his brother and in Jennie. He felt a kinship toward them that he had never had before. He realized that he too had changed.

"Come on," Chris said. "Let's give Jen a hand unloading the wagon and then we'll give Pa and the Wilson boys a proper burial. This is one hell of a homecoming for you, Frank. But welcome home, brother. We've missed you."

A couple of hours later, the three Muller's were standing beside three freshly dug graves on Elk Hill. The blue autumn sky was waning as the fading daylight turned to somber gray. Darkening clouds in the west were backlit by the setting sun. Jen scooped up a handful of freshly dug earth and tossed it into her father's grave along with her pa's well-worn boots and hat. The three of them knelt before the setting sun, their heads bowed as Chris said a few words.

Frank and Chris began filling the graves with shovels full of Wyoming clay.

"Tomorrow we'll carve three headstones and stake them at the graves," Chris said. They climbed aboard the wagon and headed for the ranch house. "We'll keep looking for Bella. She may be hiding hereabout. I hope those bastards didn't take her."

After their evening meal, Chris poured each one a shot of whiskey, and they toasted their father, the Wilson boys, and Bella. Jennie downed her shot with one gulp, ambled over to Frank relaxing in a rocking chair, and plopped herself down in his lap. Frank began to rock wildly, snorting like a horse as Jen yelled out "Yee-ha!"

"Remember when you use to give me piggyback rides all over the place?" she asked. "And Chris would chase us saying *pa-am* while pointing at us with his wooden gun that Pa had carved."

"I recall you wanting to keep going faster and faster," Frank said. "And we did till I ran into the pig barn with you one day. You hit your head on the door frame something awful."

"I could never figure out why you always said *pa-am* for a gunshot," Jen said to Chris.

"Next time you hear a gunshot, listen close," Chris said. "I think that bang on your head made you goofy, although Pa always said it knocked some sense into you. You know I still have that wooden pistol Pa gave me? He made it look so real, even painting it gun-metal blue."

"I remember that. Pa used some of Ma's picture making paints," Frank said.

"Frank, it's sure good to have you back home again," Jennie said. "I wish Pa could have welcomed you home."

"I wish he could have too," Frank said.

"Me too," Chris echoed.

"Frank, before I hit the hay," Jen said, "we've something to show you. Follow Chris and me into Pa's study."

Jen took hold of the coal-oil lamp on the table, lifted the glass, and lit the wick. As she turned up the wick, the lamp cast a bright yellow glow around the room. She held the lamp high as she made her way down the hall to her dad's study. Frank and Chris followed her.

The door to the office was open, and the three entered. The lamp lit up the room from wall to wall, casting a warm glow over the objects inside.

"Well I'll be ...," Frank said, astounded by the display he saw before him.

Against the far wall of the room stood a five-shelf bookcase that was nine feet long and six feet tall. In it was a display of fossils.

"Chris, did you collect all those?" Frank asked.

"No," Jen said. "Pa found some, Chris found some, and I found some."

"You guys," Frank said. "Since when did you all take an interest in old bones?"

"Not long after you went gallivanting off with the cavalry," Jen said. "I even got a book about fossils."

"Is this the book?" Frank asked, picking up a book from one of the shelves.

"Yes," Jen said. "You know how I like to read."

"*Vestiges of the Natural History of Creation*, by Robert Chambers, Tenth edition, 1853," Frank read.

"I didn't understand most of the book, but Chris and I really enjoyed the illustrations," Jen said.

"Well, I'll be hog-tied!" Frank exclaimed. "You two amaze me. Interested in fossils, huh? Let me tell you about *my* fossil adventures the last couple of months in the cavalry."

Frank began his tale about Marsh, the Yale Fossil Expedition, and meeting one of the fossil hunters, Jake Harding.

"My interest in fossil bones has been stoked after meeting this feller Jake," Frank said. "He's coming out this way again next summer, and I hope you'll get a chance to meet him."

"I'd sure like to," Chris said. "He probably could tell me something about these bones."

"The interesting thing about this feller, Jake, is that he is one hell of a horse handler. He said he'd like to move west and hire out on a ranch," Frank said. "I gave him our address and told him to write to you, Chris, seeing as how you're the foreman here."

"Sounds like someone we could use around here," Chris said. "But the foreman job is your responsibility, now that you're home."

"It's been a long, tiring day," Jen said, yawning, "so good night, boys."

She headed up the stairs toward her bedroom.

"Goodnight, Jennie," they both said.

Chris stood up, grabbed a poker, stoked the fireplace and put another log on the flames.

"Another whiskey?" Chris asked as he reached for the bottle.

"Yeah," Frank said, holding out his glass. "Fill 'er up."

"It's my turn to tell a story," Chris said as he poured Frank and himself a glass of whiskey. "I aim to tell you about our little sister growing up."

"Good," Frank said. "I'm all ears."

"Here's to Jennie," Chris said, as they clank their glasses.

"To Jennie," Frank said as he took a big swallow of whiskey.

"About two years ago, right after Ma and Johnny were killed, Jen met this fella over in Laramie," Chris said contemplatively. "Claims he'd been in the army, and he and a couple of his friends were starting a stock-buying outfit over by Medicine Bow. Sweet young Jen took a shine to this guy, and he began to court her. He said his name was Harry Jackson. He came around the ranch five or six times to see Jen. Pa, Bella and I met him; he was always interested in how many livestock we were running and if we had any he could buy. Pa, Bella, and me didn't much like the guy. Neither did old Schnell. Pa was always a good judge of character, whether in horses or men. He said that this guy was slicker than hog grease. 'Don't trust that guy,' Pa told Jen, but you know sis. She has a mind of her own."

Chris took a sip of whiskey and rolled a smoke, lit it, and took a long drag.

"Jen would go with Harry on visits to his cabin over on the Medicine Bow River," Chris continued, watching the exhaled smoke curl toward the high ceiling. "He made all kinds of promises to her. Jen was smitten by this smooth-talking dandy. She didn't see Harry for long periods of time—claimed he had some cattle business in Medicine Bow or someplace. Then he'd just turn up again."

"I'm surprised Pa would let her wander off with him," Frank said.

"Well, not much he could do or say. Jen had become quite independent," Chris said. "Anyhow, 'bout a year ago last May, Jen, Pa, and I were rounding up some of our herd and feral horses over near Como Ridge. We had a campsite that was not too far from Harry's cabin." He took a breath.

"This is what happened," Chris said. He began his story.

8

The spring night was chilled by a mist that was creeping up from the river bottom. The campfire crackled and hissed, adding a small bit of warmth for the three ranchers. Walt and Chris sat on an old pine log. Walt lit his pipe as Chris dug some makings from his pocket, peeled off a paper, and rolled a smoke. They lit their smokes and gave a sigh of relief after a hard day's ride. Schnell was curled up between their feet, content to be with his human companions. Jennifer sat opposite them on a rock outcropping sipping a cup of coffee. Walt stood, picked up a dry branch, broke it, and added more kindling to the blaze. He walked over to Jen, sat down beside her, and put his large arm around his daughter to comfort her.

"Jennie, what's bothering you?" Walt asked her. "You're as fidgety as a broody hen. It's getting late, and we'll be rounding up the rest of those horses at sunup. You'd better get some sleep."

"Pa, I never did need much sleep," Jen said. "I'm worried about Harry. I haven't seen him for three weeks. I just feel something's wrong."

"Now what the hell could be wrong, Jen?" Pa asked. "Harry's a big boy. He can take care of himself."

"I know Pa," Jen said. "It's just that I think—"

"Damn it, don't go working yourself into a lather," Pa interrupted.

"I think I'll ride over to his place and see if he's there," Jen said. "It's only about an hour from here."

"Jennie, you're a damn fool to go chasing after that rascal," her father said. "I worry about you."

"And I worry about Harry," Jen said with resolve. "I'll leave early before sunup and be back in time to catch you and Chris at the corral down by Rock Creek."

Chris sat by the fire smoking and spitting as he watched and listened to his father and sister stir up a familiar argument. He said nothing; he just wished his sister would get Harry out of her system.

Later that night, Jen pulled her bedroll tighter around her neck, but that didn't relieve the sting of the cold mist that hung like a shroud among the trees and brush. Their small campfire was reduced to a few dying embers that didn't offer any heat. She'd had only a couple of hours sleep but didn't feel tired. Her thoughts were on riding over to Harry's and on her father, whom she loved dearly, but she wished he'd let her do things her own way. She was so much like him.

She glanced over at her father and her brother wrapped in their bedrolls. They were in the middle of a snoring contest. Schnell's paws were stroking as the dog kept whining, dreaming about chasing something. Jen unwound herself from her bed, rose slowly, stretched, and tossed her long auburn hair about her shoulders. She plunked her hat on her head, picked up her boots, and sat on a log to pull them on. Reaching beneath her bedroll, she pulled out her holster and revolver, strapped them around her waist, and rolled up her bedding.

A gray light in the east told Jen it was time to move out. She whispered a few assuring words to her horse. Her mare, Lady, was as tame as a pet with Jen but feisty as a wild bronco in anyone else's hands. Jen had trained that mare since it was a filly, and horse and rider were dedicated to each other. She placed the saddle blanket on Lady, swung the saddle up into place, and tightened the girth. She tied her bedroll on and reached into her saddlebag for a piece of beef jerky— her breakfast, of which she shared a piece with Schnell.

"Schnell, you stay with Pa and Chris," she whispered. The smart shepherd had to be given a command only once.

Jen quietly led her horse away from camp. Her pa, curled up in his bedroll with one eye open, watched her and the mare disappear down the trail. Walt reached over and threw a rock at Chris, waking him. Chris sat up with a jolt.

"Look out!" he shouted to no one in particular.

"Chris, it's me," Pa said. "Jennie just took off to Harry's cabin. I'm going to trail her. I don't like her going off alone in this country."

"Okay, Pa," Chris said, yawning. "You want me to go with you?"

"No," Walt said. "You break camp. You and Schnell take the horses down to the Rock Creek corral. We'll meet you there in a day or two."

"All right, Pa," Chris said.

Jen rode onto the trail leading to Harry's cabin. She hoped to find him there and get some breakfast. The first rays of a new day were just dawning as she rode up to a corral that contained about two dozen horses. The corralled horses all bore well-known brands from the area. Upon a closer look, she saw three horses with the brand "WM"—the brand that belonged to the Muller Ranch.

Jen noticed a buckboard in front of the cabin, and off to the side in a small paddock stood two horses. One belonged to Harry; the other she figured belonged with the buckboard. She dismounted, tied Lady's reins to the corral fence, drew her revolver, and walked slowly toward the cabin.

Jen thought it was strange that the corral held horses of different brands and wondered if Harry had taken up with horse thieves or if they had taken Harry hostage. She stepped around to the side of the cabin and peered in the window. It was still too dark to get a good look inside, but she could see two figures huddled together in a bed at the far end of the room.

She went around to the cabin door and tried the latch. It was open. Entering the cabin, she stood across the room from the bed, revolver in hand.

"Harry Jackson!" she shouted.

Harry rolled to the side of the bed.

"What?" he said, shaking himself awake. "Jennie! What the devil are you doing here?"

"Looking for you, you lying, cheating son of a bitch," Jen replied.

"Now wait, Jen," Harry said. "I can explain."

"Explain that blond bitch in bed with you or why our horses are in your corral?" Jen asked.

The blonde was as startled as Harry and tried to cover her nakedness with a bedsheet.

"Put down that gun and I'll tell you what happened," he said as he swung himself to a sitting position on the side of the bed. "Come on, put the gun away, darling," he pleaded. "What'd you plan to do—shoot me?"

Jen raised her revolver and leveled it at Harry. "The thought had crossed my mind," she said. "And don't *darling* me."

Harry started to stand and then suddenly reached for his gun in its holster hanging on a chair by the bed.

Pa-am! A shot rang out. Harry flopped back on the bed yowling and holding his shattered left knee. Blood gushed onto the bedding.

"Goddamn, you bitch!" he screamed. "You shot me!"

The blond girl began screaming and pulled all of the bedding up over herself like a kid hiding from a bad dream. Jen walked over to the chair, picked up Harry's shirt, and tossed it to him as he lay wriggling on the bed in pain, cursing, and holding his knee.

"Tie your shirt around that knee," she said.

Harry tried to sit up and attend to his wound, but as he tightened his shirt around his shot-up knee, he blacked out. Jen bent down to retrieve his gun from the floor.

She stood up with a revolver in each hand. Suddenly, she was startled by a voice from the door behind her.

"*Señorita,* drop those guns," the voice said with a heavy Spanish accent. "Then turn around or take a bullet in your back."

Jen dropped the guns. They bounced on the rough wooden floor as she did a slow turn. She stared into the squinty, fierce-looking, dark eyes of a very large Mexican vaquero with bushy eyebrows and a large, drooping mustache. In his hand, he held a pistol with a long barrel pointed at her.

"Oye, I know you," the Mexican said. "You're Harry's chica."

"And I know you, Carlos," Jen said. "I met you in Laramie. You're in cahoots with Harry."

"What happened to Harry?" Carlos asked. "Did you kill him?"

"Nope," Jen answered. "Just shot him in the knee. He passed out from the pain—or maybe from the shock of me shooting him. Ha!"

"Ha, ha," the Mexican laughed. "You think that's funny, but it's not goin' to be so *gracioso* when I put a hole in you."

Jen smiled, folded her arms, and laughed.

Carlos looked very perplexed as Jennie just kept laughing. The vaquero looked even more perplexed when he heard a voice from behind him. Standing just outside the doorway was Walt Muller with his Henry rifle aimed at the Mexican.

"Hombre, drop that pistol and put those hands high, or Old Henry will put a hole in you, *comprende*?" Walt said.

"*Chinga tu madre, gringo*," the Mexican answered. He spun around fast and fired his pistol at Walt—missing.

Walt fired a bullet into the vaquero's right shoulder. The impact of the shot from the Henry rifle knocked the gun out of Carlos's hand and sent him reeling backwards onto the floor.

"Pa," Jen said. "I was wondering when you'd get here. I thought you were trailing me. That's why I just poked along. I'm sure glad you followed me."

"Me too," Walt said. "I figured you may need backup. Looks like you've taken care of Harry."

"He isn't dead, if that's what you mean," Jen said. "Just shot in the knee and passed out."

Walt pointed his rifle at the Mexican's head.

"Now, amigo, roll over on your stomach," Walt said.

With great effort and moaning, Carlos did what he was told. Walt bent over him and removed a large knife from a sheath on the man's belt.

"Now, just stay on your belly or you'll get a hole in your head," Walt said. "Jennie, get your gun. If this bandito moves, shoot him."

"With pleasure," Jen said as she picked up her gun and then Harry's.

Walt went over to the bed and whipped the sheet off of it. The blonde under the cover let out a yell and started sobbing and shaking.

"Well, who are you, little miss golden locks?" Walt asked, terrifying the hell out of her. She didn't answer; she just kept bawling hysterically until Walt reached over and smacked her one. She shut up immediately and curled into a fetal position, shivering and sniveling.

Walt tore a long strip from the bedsheet, grasped it between his teeth, and bent over Carlos's prone body. He put his knee in the middle of the vaquero's back, grabbed the man's right arm, and pulled it behind the man's back. The huge man groaned and let out a string of Spanish cuss words.

"That's for the fear you put into my daughter, threatening to put a bullet in her," Walt said angrily as he pulled harder on Carlos's arm.

"Now give me your other hand," Walt said. "Or do you want a bullet in your other shoulder too?" Carlos slowly placed his left hand behind his back. Walt grabbed the two huge wrists and quickly looped the strip of the bedsheet around them, tying them like he was calf-roping.

Jen picked up Carlos's gun and stuck it in her belt. Harry was recovering from his faint and started moaning as he tried to sit up. Jen, with a revolver in each hand, had one aimed at Carlos and the other at Harry.

"Carlos, are you shot up bad?" Harry muttered.

"No," Carlos said. "The *gringo bastardo* got the drop on me—shot me in the shoulder."

"Walt, you've made a mistake here," Harry said. "Let me explain what happened."

"Oh, this should be good," Walt said, chuckling.

"Carlos and I found those stray horses around here, and we corralled them hoping to return them to you and old Tom Higgins's place," Harry said. "You must have thought we were aiming to rustle them, but that ain't so."

"*Sí*," Carlos added.

"That a fact?" Walt said. "Well, I was fixin' to hang you fellas for rustling horses, but seeing as how you got such a good story, I'll reconsider it. We'll decide by judge and jury; I'll be the judge, and Jennie will be the jury. If the jury believes you, we'll let you scoundrels go."

Jen looked at her father somewhat in surprise. She had never seen him so infuriated.

Walt gave his daughter a solemn look and a wink.

"What does the jury say?" Walt asked Jen. "Do you believe these scoundrels?"

"*No,*" Jen said. Her answer was quick and firm.

"Well, then," Walt said. "I'll get some rope. There are lots of sturdy trees here about."

"Now wait, Walt," Harry said. "You can't take—," He was interrupted by a voice shouting from outside the cabin.

"Hello, you there in the cabin, this is Sheriff Nat Boswell!" a man yelled. "Come on out with your hands held high with no guns! We've got you surrounded!"

"We've got the back covered, Sheriff," an officer said from behind the cabin.

"It's Old Boz," Walt said to Jen. "You keep these scoundrels covered while I talk to him."

"Hey Boz, it's me, Walt Muller," Walt called out. "My daughter and I are in here. I'm coming out. Don't shoot."

"Walt, I'll be damned," the sheriff said. "What in blazes are you doing here?"

"My daughter and I caught us some horse thieves," Walt said matter-of-factly. "What are you doing here?"

"Tracking a fellow who murdered a lawman down in Cheyenne," Boz said. "A Mexican hombre named Carlos Vargas. His tracks led me and my two deputies to this cabin. Have you seen him?"

"Yeah," Walt said, as he stepped into the doorway. "He's in here, tied up. I put a bullet in his shoulder." Walt motioned with his rifle toward the Mexican. "Come on in and join the festivities."

Sheriff Boswell stepped into the cabin. Suspicious by nature, he held his revolver ready.

"Hello, Miss Jennifer," he said, surprised to see her holding two guns aimed at the two wounded men. "Walt, what's going on here?"

Walt explained the situation to the sheriff, telling him how Harry and Carlos had gotten wounded.

"Don't know the blond gal's name. She doesn't say much—just bawls," Walt said. "But Harry and Carlos should be strung up for horse rustling."

"Yeah, sounds about right," the sheriff said. "But we'll let a judge take care of that."

Walt just grinned. "Yeah, I sure hope so," he said.

"Hey, Luke and Sam get in here," the sheriff called out to his two deputies. "And bring some rope."

"Okay, Boz," Deputy Luke said.

"Jackson, you and the bitch get some clothes on," the sheriff said.

"Her name's Sue," Harry said.

After Harry and Sue got dressed, Sheriff Boswell and his two deputies bound their hands. They marched Sue and Carlos out of the cabin and carried Harry to the buckboard.

"We'll put these desperadoes in the wagon," the sheriff said. "The boys and I will haul them down to Laramie where they can get patched up, put in jail and wait until they string 'em up."

"If you need a hand," Walt said, "I could go with you."

"Nah," Boz replied. "We'll hog-tie them in the wagon. They won't give us any trouble. Tell you what you can do—you and Jennie could get Harry's and Sue's horses and hitch them to the buckboard while the boys and I load their hoss- thievin' carcasses into the wagon. We'll tie Carlos's horse behind with Luke's horse. Luke can handle the wagon."

"All right," Walt said, "we'll take our horses from the corral and let the others out to range. Jen and I are going to meet my boy, Chris, over at Rock Creek."

9

"That's some story, Chris," Frank said. "What happened to the horse thieves?"

"I'll tell you what happened." Jennie's voice resounded from the top of the stairs where she stood in her nightgown with her arms folded and a stern look on her face.

"Jennie, have you been listening all the while?" Chris asked.

"Yep," Jennie answered. "And you told it exactly as it happened. But let me explain one part. When I shot Harry, my aim was off. I meant to shoot him in the balls, not the knee."

Chris and Frank laughed as Jen came down the stairs into the room and stood near the fireplace.

"Chris, pour me a shot," she said. "And I'll tell Frank what happened to those thieving skunks."

Jennie took the whiskey and began sipping it slowly. Her feminine figure was illuminated from behind by the flaming fireplace; she had all the guise of an angel of fury ascending from hell. Her face was flushed with anger, her eyes wide and piercing as a mountain lion's as she recalled her adventure.

She spoke of her humiliating relationship with Harry and of her apology to her father, brother, and Bella for being so naïve.

"Harry, Carlos, and Sue were being held in Laramie," Jen said. "Then they were being taken by train to Cheyenne for trial while a new Laramie courthouse and jail was being built. The train was held up by members of their gang, and the three escaped."

"Damn shame," Frank said.

"Yeah, Pa had it right," Jen said. "They should have been strung up when we caught 'em."

"I suspect they had something to do with murdering Pa and the Wilsons," Chris said.

"And the disappearance of Bella, rustling our horses, taking Lady, and killing Schnell," Jen said. "I have the same suspicion," she added angrily.

"Describe this Harry character to me," Frank said. "I'll keep my eyes peeled."

"Oh, he's a handsome fella," Jen said, "curly hair, black as a crow's feather, and a neatly trimmed moustache. You'll find he is quite lame in his left leg. That SOB is slicker than pig shit." Jen gave a little chuckle and a devilish smile.

Suddenly, Frank jumped to his feet, put a finger to his lips, and motioned for his siblings to be quiet. He quickly drew his gun from its holster hanging on the coat rack and motioned toward the door. Chris and Jen heard the noise—the unmistakable sound of a horse whinnying. Jen sprinted for the door.

"Don't open it!" Frank yelled, but it was too late.

Jen ran out the door and across the porch and disappeared into the dark night.

Frank followed her, revolver in his hand, and heard her yell.

"Lady! Oh, Lady!" Jen cried as she caught hold of the broken halter her horse was dragging.

The horse gave a low snort. Jen stroked the mare's head, whispering softly in its ear as she put her arms around its neck, feeling its hot lathered mane.

"You've had quite a run, old gal," Jen said. "But you got away from whoever you were running from. Let's get you cooled down and cleaned up."

"Jen," Frank said as he came running up. "Is that your horse?"

"Yeah!" she whooped. "She got away from the scum who stole her."

Chris came running out, lighting up the scene with a lantern he was holding. The mare was a little skittish toward Frank. He stuck his gun in his belt and held out his hand toward her.

"She doesn't take to strangers," Jen said. "But once she gets to know you she's the best damn friend you could have. I'll bet she gave those rustlers a bad time."

"And those rustlers gave her a bad time," Chris said. "Look here— she's been injured."

"Oh, no," Jen said. "Let me see."

Chris held the lantern up to show Jen a gashing wound across the mare's croup.

"Looks like a bullet just grazed the top of Lady's hindquarters," Chris said. "The wound bled quite a bit, which is good to keep it from getting infected. I think it looks worse than it is. I'll get her to the stables and treat that injury. Jen, you put on some warmer clothes while Frank and I get Lady cleaned up and take a close look at that wound."

Chris led the mare toward the barn while Frank held the lantern. When they entered the building, Frank held his hand up for Chris to stop.

"Someone's in here," Frank whispered.

Chris nodded. Frank drew the revolver from his belt.

"Come out of there, with your hands up!" Frank called out.

"*Mi auiti, per favore,*" muttered a voice shaken with fear.

Frank shouted his command again, louder this time. Holding the lantern high, casting a light further into the barn, Frank peered into the shadows holding his revolver at eye level.

Out of the shadows emerged a figure ever so slowly.

"Oh, Mary, Mother of Jesus, please help me ...," the voice pleaded.

"Bella, is that you?" Frank asked.

"*Si, si,*" Bella said.

"Aunt Bella, this is Frank and Chris!" Chris shouted. "You're safe."

"*Grazie, grazie*—thank you, thank you," Bella said. "Frankie, you've come home!"

Jen came running up to the barn, and as soon as she saw Bella she burst out in tears of joy.

"Oh, Aunt Bella, you're safe!" she said as she embraced Bella. "Thank God you're safe."

"Aunt Bella, tell us what happened," Chris said.

Bella told her story of how early that morning she was on her way to the chicken coop to gather eggs when she heard horses running, Schnell barking, men shouting, and gunshots. She was very afraid and ducked down, hiding in the henhouse. There were more gunshots and shouting; then it was quiet.

"Did you see any of the men?" Frank asked.

"No," Bella said. "I was hiding under the whatchamacallit—the chicken's roosting boxes. I heard men shouting again and the horses being herded out of the corrals and driven away."

"Recognize any of the voices?" Chris asked.

"None," Bella said. "But they were mean voices, yelling and cussing."

Bella described how she had waited a long time in the henhouse, frightened for her life. When she got up enough courage to move, she ran to the barn for cover. She hid in one of the stalls and covered herself with straw when she heard horses and someone coming.

"That would have been us," Frank said.

"I stay hidden in the barn, waiting a long time," Bella said. "Since I was a little girl, whenever I get scared I just curl up, close my eyes, and go to sleep. That's what I did."

"I'll take Aunt Bella up to the house," Jen said. "I'll get her cleaned up and get her something to eat. I'll tell her what's happened. You guys take good care of my horse."

"Oh, Jennie," Bella said. "I'm so happy to see you."

"And I'm happy to see you," Jen said. "At least two of my favorite ladies are safe now."

"What you mean, Jennie?" Bella asked.

"Come up to the house with me, and I'll tell you all about it," Jen replied.

10

The Yale party left San Francisco in the early part of October 1870, traveling on the Central Pacific Railway back to Fort Bridger, Wyoming. From there they headed north of the fort to explore a section of the Green River, where they found numerous fossil fishes and insects.

An army officer at the fort told Marsh about numerous bones of all sizes along the Smoky Hill River near Fort Wallace, Kansas. Marsh was anxious to explore this region as that is where a thirty=five-foot plesiosaur fossil had been found. Dr. T. Turner of Fort Wallace, the army surgeon and correspondent for Academy of Natural Sciences, Philadelphia, had sent the specimen to Professor Cope in 1868. Cope reconstructed the more than one hundred bones of the animal and called this fossil find an *Elasmosaurus platynus*. This was the plesiosaur that Marsh had pointed out to Professor Cope as having the skull on the wrong end.

For a number of years, since the establishment of Fort Wallace in 1865, it and Fort Hayes, Fort Harker, and Fort Riley had battles with the Cheyenne and Sioux. Marsh had been warned of the dangers of Indian attacks but seemingly had no fear of Indians. He led his party to Kansas and Fort Wallace to explore the Cretaceous beds at Smoky Hill River where he hoped to uncover his own *Elasmosaurus*.

At Fort Wallace, the Yale party was not as well received as they had been at other army outposts that had given them support. The post commander, Colonel H. C. Bankhead, was lukewarm to their arrival. Captain Graham, who was in charge of the escort for the Yale party, did not take kindly to civilians and greenhorns.

Kansas's big tourist attraction in the 1870s was buffalo hunting. Millions of buffalo roamed the Great Plains, but thousands were killed by passengers who shot from open train windows or hired special buffalo-hunt trains and shot buffalo for entertainment from a train platform. Others hired buffalo-hunting outfitters that led hunters to the great herds for a tame sport of shooting grazing bison. The prairies were becoming littered with buffalo bones.

General George Armstrong Custer and the Seventh Calvary were camped near Fort Hayes. He had outfitted a buffalo-hunting party for P. T. Barnum. Marsh knew the great showman from a trip he had made to Syracuse, New York, in 1869 to view the famous so-called archaeological discovery that turned out to be a fake—the Cardiff Giant. Marsh described it as being "humbug." Barnum wanted to buy the ten-foot Goliath, but his offer was refused so he had a plaster replica made. Fake or not, Barnum knew that people would pay to see it, and they did. Marsh also knew Barnum from a deal in which Marsh had purchased some valuable Mexican artifacts that belonged to Barnum but had mistakenly been put up for sale. Marsh and Barnum were not the best of friends, but both men had a respect for each other's tenacity.

Marsh heard that Barnum was in the area trying to hire James "Wild Bill" Hickok, the sheriff of Hayes City, to join his circus. But in a gambling game of cards, Wild Bill won all of the money that Barnum had intended to use to entice Hickok to join his circus. Barnum was not successful in engaging Hickok but was very successful in bagging buffalo. Marsh, hearing of Barnum's success on buffalo hunts, felt his appetite whetted to bag one of the beasts for a trophy.

"Marsh, tomorrow we're going on a buffalo hunt," Captain Graham said. "You and your boys are invited along if you care to come."

"It's *Professor* Marsh," O. C. said, clearing his throat.

"Oh, beg your pardon, Professor," the captain said in a condescending tone. "If'n you and your party want to tag along, get ready to leave at sunup."

"We'll be ready," Marsh said.

The crisp October morning was met with a brilliant red sunrise that promised it would be a great day for hunting. The Yale party was up early. With rifles and ammo, they were ready to meet with the army officers in anticipation of the buffalo hunt.

"My group is ready," Marsh said, still somewhat irritated by Captain Graham's attitude.

"Good," the captain said. "I've arranged for you and your men to travel to the high plains in wagons to watch the hunt. Marsh, you can ride in the ambulance wagon. Ricardo will be your driver."

"What do you mean *watch* the hunt?" Marsh asked, surprised.

"I can't take the risk of letting your men take part in a dangerous sport like shooting buffalo," the captain said. "I wouldn't want them or any of our horses to be injured."

Marsh was infuriated over the captain's attitude and comments. "Sir, my men are excellent horsemen," Marsh said. "And many are excellent marksmen, including myself."

"Those are my orders," the captain said. "You and your party can come along to watch or stay behind at the fort. The choice is yours—Professor."

Marsh grumbled, discontented, and some of the Yale students cursed the captain.

"It's all right, men," Marsh said. "Let's get aboard the wagons."

Marsh climbed aboard, seating himself beside the Mexican teamster. Ricardo had a smile a mile wide that showed off his crooked yellow teeth, partly hidden by a huge, bushy mustache. Marsh introduced himself. In response, Ricardo smiled, lifted the reins, smacked them across the mule's backs, and yelled. The mule team strained and rolled the ambulance wagon forward over the vast Kansas grasslands.

At the hunt site, the plains were covered with thousands of buffalo. The army officers galloped off after the main herd. The hunt was on.

Some Yale men decided to take off on foot to see if they could bag a lone buffalo straggler. Marsh offered Ricardo a cigar. They lit up and sat back to watch the hunt. The main herd was being attacked by the army officers. There were small groups of buffalo here and there and a few stragglers across the grasslands. Marsh noticed three bulls grazing about half a mile from the main herd. Marsh surveyed the three bulls with field glasses. *This is my chance for a nice trophy,* he thought.

"What'd ya see, *Señor* Marsh?" Ricardo asked.

"There's a group of three fine bulls off to the left of the main herd," Marsh said, clearing his throat. "You see them?"

"*Si,* I do," Ricardo answered.

"Well, I've a ten-dollar gold piece," Marsh said. "If you can bring this wagon within a distance where I can get a shot at them, the gold piece is yours."

"*Si,* señor, I can do that," the teamster said. "Hang on."

With that said, Ricardo cracked the whip, snapped the reins, and hollered, "Hee-yah!" As the mules and wagon bolted forward, Marsh was thrown back in his seat. The ambulance swayed and bounced over the prairie, and within minutes they were within rifle range of the three grazing buffalo. The buffalo began loping toward the main herd as the teamster steered the wagon parallel to the trio.

"Get me in line with that lead young bull," Marsh said.

"*Si, si,*" Ricardo answered. "He is a fine animal."

Marsh took the best aim he could in the bouncing wagon and fired off a shot. The next thing he knew, he was thrown back in the wagon again as the mules, spooked by the report of the rifle, went careening wildly over the prairie. He saw the young bull he'd shot stumble and then get up and continue on. Marsh almost lost his rifle in the runaway but was lucky to have lost only his hat. The teamster, with the skill of an experienced driver, brought the mules under control, and they headed back to where Marsh had last seen the wounded bull.

Ricardo brought the mules and wagon to the spot where the young bull was down. Marsh jumped from the wagon, cradled his rifle in his arm, and approached his quarry. Suddenly, the bull sprang to his feet.

"*Atencion*, Señor Marsh!" Ricardo yelled.

Marsh stood frozen for a second as the bull charged. He sidestepped the charging bull with the poise of a matador and fired a shot into the beast, downing it for good.

Marsh, who was usually quite a stoic person, was so overtaken with his triumph that he took a sweeping bow, did a little jig, and pulled a kerchief from his pocket. Wiping his sweating brow, he began tying the bandanna around his half bald head.

"*Ole*, Señor Marsh!" Ricardo whooped.

"*Ole!*" Marsh echoed.

Marsh rolled up his sleeves, reached in a pocket, and retrieved the ten-dollar gold piece. He flipped the coin to the driver.

"*Gracias*, Señor Marsh," Ricardo said, catching the coin.

Drawing his hunting knife from its sheath, Marsh set to work skinning the bull. He cut off the head to keep as a trophy of his successful hunt and then began skinning the animal to have the hide made into a heavy, warm buffalo coat.

Ricardo joined in helping Marsh with his task. By now it was late afternoon, and both men were bloodied and sweating under the hot prairie sun. As they worked at skinning the bull, Captain Graham and two of his officers rode up.

"What's going on here?" the captain asked with a commanding attitude.

"Looks like the professor got himself a buffalo," one of the officers said.

"*Si, si,*" Ricardo said.

"Ricardo, your orders were to keep the wagon and the students at the lookout point," the captain said with authority.

Marsh perturbed by the captain's surly tone, jumped to his feet and was quick to respond.

"The mules were frightened by the buffalo and started running," he said, clearing his throat. "We were careening across the prairie, and by the time Ricardo got control of the mules, we were headed for a small group of buffalo. I instructed him to bring the wagon alongside the animals so I could get a shot at one."

"*Si,*" Ricardo said. "Señor Marsh is a good shot."

The captain dismounted and addressed his two officers. "All right, let's get the professor's game loaded in the wagon and head back," he said.

While the men were busy loading Marsh's trophy onto the wagon, Ricardo smiled at Marsh, did a low bow, and mouthed the word *ole.*

As they got closer to the lookout point, Captain Graham pointed to a figure in the distance skinning a buffalo.

"Looks like one of my officers got another buffalo," he said.

To the captain's dismay and everyone's surprise, the hunter turned out to be one of the Yale students. The wagon and soldiers pulled up alongside the bloodied student to find Bruno just finishing skinning a buffalo.

"How'd you bring down this buffalo?" the captain asked. "Where's your horse, son?"

"Didn't need a horse, sir," Bruno said. "These buffalo are sure dumb. I just ran and crawled to within range of a small group and picked out this big bull. Buffalo hunting is sure a tame sport compared to other hunts I've been on."

The captain scoffed, turned, and motioned to his two officers.

"Let's get this boy's buffalo meat loaded in the wagon," he said. "We want to get back to the fort before sundown."

Marsh smiled at Bruno. "Well done, Mr. Adler."

"Thank you, Professor," Bruno said, giving Marsh a smart salute.

The captain was very quiet and solemn on the trip back to the fort. It bothered him that he had bagged only two buffalo in the all-day hunt. And to make matters worse, the two officers with him kept praising Marsh and Bruno for their kills.

"That was a good shot from a careening wagon barreling across the prairie," one of the officers said. "You bagged a fine bull, Professor Marsh."

"And, young man, to kill a buffalo on foot is as good as or better than some Indians could," another officer said to Bruno.

Back at the fort, the wagons were unloaded of their supply of buffalo trophies and meat. Buffalo tongue was a particularly succulent piece of meat and could fetch a handsome price as a delicacy when pickled and sent to consumers back east. Marsh's trophy buffalo head was sent to a taxidermist to be mounted and shipped back to New Haven.

11

It was the middle of November, and although the weather was cold, Marsh insisted that the Yale party prepare for one last exploration.

The fossil hunters, along with their guide, Ned Lane, and a military escort led by Lieutenant Blake, headed north and east of Fort Wallace traveling along the north fork of the Smoky Hill River. Here the Kansas landscape changed to rocky outcroppings, chalk bluffs, canyons, and unbelievable rock formations that were part of a Cretaceous seabed 150 to 60 million years old.

The bitter November wind chilled the men to the bone. They were issued long johns, which helped a little to stay the November cold. With gritty determination, the fossil hunters continued their fossil search.

The Yale students, who had been tenderfeet five months before, were now seasoned frontiersmen—their softness hardened by the land and their boyish looks eroded by the weather. The fossil-hunting party took on every exploring challenge with enthusiasm and courage. Even Dan realized the strength the adventure had given him. It was as Jake had said: "The experience will transform you."

The Smoky Hill River Valley looked to be a promising site for Cretaceous fossils. The fossil hunters set up camp, pitching their tents in the shelter of a high bluff. The steep cliff provided them with some protection from the elements. They placed the wagons in a semicircle at the base of the cliff to keep the horses and mules enclosed and provide a buffer against any Indian attacks. The party began the arduous task of digging fossil bones from the bluffs.

Late that afternoon, Dan let out a whoop. "Look at this!" he yelled, pointing to some fossil bones embedded in the side of the cliff.

"Hey, Professor Marsh!" another student called. "Look at this fossil Dan discovered."

Embedded in the shale and chalk cliff were the bones of a very large marine-type lizard with rows of sharp teeth. About two feet of the skeleton were protruding a half inch from the surface of the bluff, but then it disappeared into the cliff and a few inches of it surfaced again about two feet away.

"Dan, looks like you've found a large mosasaur," Marsh said. "Excellent."

Many mosasaur fossil bones were being discovered by the party, but the prize one was Dan's. This was a skeleton with almost all the parts intact, including the skull with its elongated jaws displaying rows of huge sharp teeth. Bones of three of the four flippers were also intact. Marsh was elated by this find. He and Dan were the ones doing the excavation of this specimen. It would take three days to release the fossil from its Cretaceous rock tomb. With most of the fossil bones of its skeleton still being held in place by its matrix, the parts were carefully wrapped in burlap gunnysacks and crated to be shipped back to Yale. The skull and lower jaw of the creature were meticulously cleaned at the site, and Jake set about doing a drawing of them. Marsh instructed the students to carefully wrap and crate the skull separately. The length of the mosasaur was estimated to be around eighteen feet.

The calm and cool evenings brought buffalo to the river valley to drink. Ned Lane and Jake decided to ambush some buffalo to obtain fresh meat. As the shadows elongated across the valley floor, a group of five buffalo came down a well-worn coulee trail leading to the river. Jake and Ned lay hidden in a small stand of cottonwoods and willows watching their prey amble toward the river bank. The animals were not more than a hundred yards away.

"Those two young cows in the lead," Ned whispered. "You take the first one; I'll get the second cow. Fire when I give a count of three." Jake nodded.

"One, two, three," Two shots rang out almost simultaneously. Down went two buffalo.

The camp enjoyed fresh choice cuts of bison.

The campsite was constantly troubled by coyotes howling every night. The coyotes were attracted by the smell of fresh buffalo meat but were not brave enough to break through the cordoned off and guarded circle of wagons protecting the camp. Although there was the constant alert against Indian attacks, the campers, bunched next to the base of the cliff, felt a degree of security from attacks by man or beast.

The November night was cold with a clear sky. A full moon illuminated the Kansas plains in a sapphire light, casting eerie blue shadows from the bluffs and rocks. Tonight the coyotes were especially noisy and seemed closer than usual. Jake thought *it must be the full moon that set off their howling.* The howling had disturbed his sleep. He was freezing cold and shivering as he rose from his makeshift bed on the ground to search for more blankets. His breath steamed from his mouth and nose as he rubbed his cold hands together and ran his fingers through his hair. Suddenly, a rifle shot rang out, and the camp came to life.

Damn, Jake thought, *it's an Indian attack.*

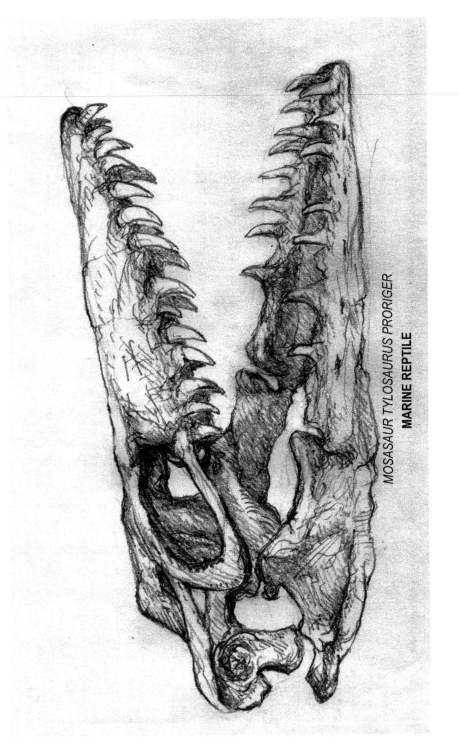

MOSASAUR *TYLOSAURUS PRORIGER*

MARINE REPTILE

Everyone began shouting and running. The mules, braying, had stampeded, and the horses were whinnying and kicking. In the bright moonlight, the men could see the stampeding mules kicking up dust as they took off across the prairie. Private Anderson, the sentry on duty, approached Ned Lane and Lieutenant Blake.

"Hell, Ned, I didn't think those mules would take off like that when I shot that varmint," the private said. "That coyote was so crazed by the smell of fresh meat that he jumped from the top of the cliff onto the chuck wagon. 'Bout scared the livin' Jesus out of me."

"Well, private, that coyote and your rifle shot scared the hell out of the mules and the rest of us," Ned said. "Looks like the mules stampeded but the horses stayed close. Guess that's horse sense. We'll take a count at sunup."

The next morning, all the horses were accounted for, but only one old mule, the one the men called Crazy Jane, was found. Nine mules were missing.

"Private, you take Crazy Jane and see if you can find those damn mules," Lieutenant Blake ordered.

"Yes, sir," the private said as he hastily prepared to depart with the old mule.

Tracking the runaway mules was fairly easy. It wasn't but a few miles out that the private discovered the wayward mules headed back to Fort Wallace. The private slowed old Crazy Jane to an easy pace as he ambled along a twenty-or-so-mile trail back to the fort.

It was late morning when a post sentry saw a group of terrified mules loping toward the fort.

"I'll be damned," the sentry said. "Looks like the mules deserted the Yale outfit."

"Looks to be more than desertion," another trooper said. "They're dragging broken halters and ropes—means they broke lose scared and ran. Get the general."

When General Bankhead viewed the runaway mules, he swore

under his breath and was thinking that he would be in deep trouble if something had happened to the Marsh party. He was under orders from General Phil Sheridan to protect the fossil hunters.

"The Marsh camp may have been attacked by the Cheyenne," the general said to Lieutenant Braden. "Get your company together to rescue Marsh and his outfit. Get going as fast as you can and have a wagon follow your company in case there is wounded to bring back. Now get."

The cavalry had just galloped off to rescue the fossil party when Private Anderson, astride the old weary mule Crazy Jane, came moseying into the fort. The worried and agitated general and some other officers ran to meet him.

After hearing Private Anderson's story, the general walked around the mule and the trooper. Eyeballing them and twirling his handlebar mustache, he gave the private an austere look of disapproval.

"Private, where in hell is your rifle?" General Bankhead barked. "That's government issue."

"It's back at camp, sir," Private Anderson answered. "But I got my revolver."

"Soldier, you never desert your weapon," the general said. "God almighty, how'd you expect to defend yourself in Indian country? And you risked not being able to protect a government mule. Maybe a few days in the guardhouse will get you to reflect on your duties."

An officer took the private by the arm while another led the mule away.

Damn, the private thought, *twice in two days my rifle brought troubles to me.*

At the Yale campsite, the evening stillness was interrupted by the outcry of soldiers and the drumming of horses' hooves. The Marsh camp was being "rescued" by the cavalry regiment led by Lieutenant Braden. The Yale men cheered and waved as the troopers rode into camp.

"Is everyone all right?" the lieutenant shouted.

"We're fine," one of the students said "The mules broke loose and stampeded."

"Yeah," Lieutenant Braden said. "They showed up back at the fort. We thought the Cheyenne had attacked you. That's why we're here."

"Well, we're all safe," Ned said. "You and your men are in time to join us for our Thanksgiving dinner, though. We have lots of grub—buffalo tongue, steaks, roasts, choice cuts of antelope meat, rabbit stew, canned vegetables, and whatnot. You can grab a cup of hot coffee and might even find a shot of whiskey for it."

"Damn, you boys sure are roughing it," Lieutenant Braden said. "Sure glad we had to come rescue you. Dismount, men. Let's join the Thanksgiving party."

The last few days at the fossil site were successful in terms of discovering more mosasaur remains. On the last day of collecting, Marsh and Jake, with a soldier as guard, explored a region farther from their camp than they had gone before. It was already late afternoon as the three of them rode along the riverbank following a buffalo trail. The professor insisted that they ride slowly so he could continue looking for fossils. Twilight was fast approaching.

"Professor, we should be heading out," Jake said. "It's a good hour's ride back to camp." The soldier nodded in agreement.

Marsh ignored them.

"Whoa," Marsh said. "There's something I want to examine."

Marsh dismounted, strode off the trail a few feet, and picked up a small fossil bone. It was almost a foot long and an inch in diameter. One end had an unusual joint. It looked somewhat like the tibia of a gigantic bird. Marsh began probing the area with his knife, searching for other bones.

"Come on," Jake pleaded. "It'll be dark before you know it."

"All right," Marsh answered, frustrated. "Let me mark this spot."

He wrapped the fossil, put it in one of his pockets, and with his knife marked the site by carving a deep *M* in the rock face.

"I'll be back," he said to the marked bluff.

They rode toward camp down the darkening trail as the blackness of night began covering the landscape. A signal gun from camp was fired repeatedly to help them find their way back.

At Fort Wallace, a large shipment of fossil specimens was packed and shipped to New Haven. Carefully packed along with them was the mysterious fossil of the bird-like tibia that puzzled Marsh.

The Yale group embarked aboard the Kansas-Pacific Railroad. Hayes City would be their first stop on the way back to New Haven. Seated in a first-class palace car, the Yale party looked out of place. They now had the appearance of old frontier explorers more than Yale students.

"Now this is the way to travel," Dan said as he pushed himself farther into the plush upholstered seat and viewed the polished wood paneling and brass fixtures.

Jake nodded. "You're right," he said. "Can you believe this is the same group that left New Haven five months ago?"

"Nope," Dan said, surveying the group of rugged-looking young men.

The Hayes City stop brought together General George Custer and Professor Marsh. The meeting of these two headstrong leaders was ostentatious. The flamboyant general, wearing a tailored buffalo coat, a muskrat fur hat with his yellow curly hair falling to his shoulders, and leather gauntlets halfway up his forearms, met Marsh on a bitterly cold and snowy December day. Custer had invited Marsh to his quarters at the fort to dine with him.

The delicious dinner of assorted game was prepared by Custer's personal chef, a woman he sometimes took along on his campaigns to cook for him. The dinner was served by two of his aides. Custer was known to have a number of pets; among them were two large greyhound dogs that attended the dinner party.

"General Sheridan and Bill Cody tell me your party was pretty damn successful at fossil hunting," Custer said. "I've run across some of those bones myself over on the Platte where I led the Seventh Cavalry on a successful campaign against the Sioux and Cheyenne."

"We did have good luck fossil hunting along the Platte," Marsh said, clearing his throat. "It was also our good fortune that we didn't have any trouble with the Indians, although there were signs we were being followed by them."

"Their days are numbered," Custer said, his blue eyes sparkling. "My command, the Seventh, is without a doubt made up of the best horse-soldiers on the plains. I predict that within a year we'll have crushed all those bastardy hostile savages and placed the rest on reservations, making the West safe for settlers and travelers."

"I am planning another expedition next year, "Marsh said. "I hope it will be safe."

"It should be by then," Custer said. "Perhaps we'll meet again next summer."

The Yale party continued their trip homebound for Connecticut aboard a first-class railway carriage.

"It's been quite an adventure," Dan said. "But I'll be glad to safely get back to New Haven."

"It'll be another adventure to sort through all the fossils we've found," Jake said. "I'm looking forward to working with the professor in the lab."

"I must admit," Dan said. "It was exciting uncovering a fossil that had been hidden for millions of years. But it'll be nice going back to the comforts of civilization after camping on the hard, cold ground; getting blasted by bizarre weather; being confronted by wild animals; and fearing being scalped, to mention a few unpleasant conditions of our adventure."

"I look forward to doing it again," Jake said with enthusiasm.

12

In mid-December 1870, Marsh and his Yale students arrived back in New Haven. Marsh now had the humongous job of sorting through the crates of fossils shipped from the West. He employed the help of half a dozen students.

That winter, Jake Harding helped Marsh sort, study, and classify some of the fossils they had discovered. Using Georges Cuvier's method of comparative anatomy, they compared the size of each fossil bone to the known anatomical structure of other animals.

The professor's examination of the bird-like Smoky Hill River fossil revealed that it apparently belonged to the wing finger of a new species of pterodactyl, the first discovered in America. According to Cuvier's correlation of parts, Marsh estimated the wingspan of the creature to be twenty feet. The largest earlier fossils of a pterodactyl, found in Europe, were only about the size of a seagull.

By spring of 1871, Marsh had published a number of articles about the Yale Western expedition. The June issue of the *American Journal of Science* carried an article on his findings of a new species of pterodactyl.

That spring, Jake's passion for fossil hunting in the Western frontier had totally captivated him. Enthusiastic about the possibility of moving west, he wrote a letter to Chris and Frank Muller in Wyoming.

But spring also brought sorrow for Jake Harding; his grandfather, O. Z., passed away in April.

"Professor Marsh," Jake said, "I'll have to take a couple of weeks off to attend Grandpa's funeral in Philadelphia and take care of my affairs there."

"Yes, yes," Marsh said. "I was sorry to hear of O. Z.'s passing. Your grandfather was an astute man and a fine gentleman."

"I'll be back as soon as possible," Jake said.

"Good," Marsh said. "I'm making plans for our summer expedition to the West again and hope you'll be able to make it."

"We'll see," Jake said. "I'll let you know as soon as I get back."

Jake hoped he would get to see his friend Dan Randall, who had moved back to Philadelphia after leaving Yale.

Jake's train trip to Philadelphia to attend his grandfather's funeral gave him the solitude and time to recall the pleasant memories he had of his grandfather. O. Z. had taught Jake many of life's skills, including horsemanship and a veterinarian's knowledge and care of horses.

Jake's thoughts were also on his plans for the future. He loved his work with fossils, and the frontier West had entranced him. He would like to go west again in the summer with Professor Marsh. The big obstacle with that plan was money. He had a small bank account, and his expenses for school had been partially funded by a trust that his grandfather had set up. Marsh had informed him that on this summer's trip to the West, the students had to pay their own way—an expense Jake could ill afford.

O. Z. Harding's funeral was a huge affair with brethren of the church attending from a number of counties. It was comforting to Jake to find Dan attending the funeral service. Jake sat grief-stricken as he listened to the eulogy to his grandfather. He had dearly loved and would miss his grandfather. Even though he was treated by O. Z.'s church congregation as a member of a larger family, he acknowledged the fact he was the last surviving member of the Harding family.

After the service, Jake and Dan talked about their plans for the future. Dan had decided to take up his father's offer to go into the family business, leaving his interest in geology to become a hobby. Jake told Dan of his desire to move west to become an independent fossil explorer and hire out as a horse wrangler.

O. Z.'s home in Germantown, the northwest section of Philadelphia, was a magnificent colonial style brownstone house. O. Z. had rented part of the house to a family of the brethren but maintained his own bedroom and a large study, taking his meals with the family of renters.

Alone and despondent, Jake reclined in a chair in his grandfather's large study. The room had a gloomy appearance about it as he felt the haunting memories of his joyful childhood overtake him. He had spent many hours with his mother and grandfather in that very room. He had never known his father. His mother had died when he was about nine, leaving his grandfather to be his sole guardian.

He sat at his grandfather's huge desk, feeling the comfort and power of the solid walnut bureau. Gazing at the German inscription carved elegantly across the center drawer, he reflected on his grandfather's guidance. Sorting through his grandfather's papers, he hoped to find some information regarding his father. He found nothing, but he did find the last will and testament that O. Z. had left. The will contained the address of a Philadelphia attorney named as the executor of his grandfather's estate. He would contact the attorney's office first thing the next day.

According to his grandfather's will, the lawyer told Jake, he was the beneficiary of a sizable bank account plus his grandfather's house in Germantown. Jake made arrangements to have the attorney act as his rental agent for his grandfather's house, with the rental fees deposited in a bank account Jake had set up. The inheritance gave Jake the financial freedom to do the one thing he desired—to be an independent fossil hunter in the Western frontier.

In late May, Jake arrived back at Yale. He informed Professor Marsh that he would go west with the 1871 summer expedition but wouldn't be returning with them. Jake's correspondence with Frank and Chris Muller in Wyoming had prompted Jake to decide to go out west and stay there, continuing his exploration for fossils. If Professor Marsh agreed, Jake would send to Yale any interesting fossils if he would be paid for them. Marsh agreed.

Frank Muller had written Jake, telling him that after mustering out of the army, he had returned to his Wyoming ranch to find that his father had been murdered and horse thieves had rustled most of their stock. Chris Muller sent a letter along with Frank's saying that he had been told of Jake's skills as a wrangler and veterinarian. Chris offered Jake room and board at the ranch in exchange for part-time work with horses, meaning that Jake would have time for fossil hunting. This would be the ideal arrangement for Jake's future endeavors.

13

Jake left Connecticut in the first part of July headed for Fort Wallace, Kansas, traveling with Professor Marsh and the 1871 Yale Scientific Expedition. He was excited about going on another fossil expedition and was eager to start his new life by making his home in the West. Jake had settled all of his affairs in New Haven and was prepared to give up his life in the East and start anew in the West. He left a modest amount of money in a bank account in New Haven but took the larger part of his inheritance in cash and bank drafts with him. He entrusted his grandfather's house in Philadelphia to a realtor whose mandate was to collect the monies from renters and deposit it in an account in Jake's name. He planned to pay his way with the inheritance monies until such time as he became gainfully employed. To protect his cash, he had sewn two deep pockets, one on each side, to the insides of his trousers legs. He had told himself that if someone tried to rob him, they would have to strip him naked. His arrangements with Chris Muller as a part-time ranch hand would allow him to be an independent fossil hunter working in the West for Professor Marsh. Marsh had also enlisted a number of other part-time fossil collectors to work the Western frontier.

Arriving at Fort Wallace, the Yale party found the July heat on the Kansas plains brutal. With five army wagons and an army escort, Marsh and his party of eleven fossil hunters were bound for the

Smoky Hill River region where he had previously found the bird-like tibia bone of a pterosaur. The party set up their tent camp not far from where the previous year's November expedition site had been.

"What a difference in this summer camp from the one last November," Marsh said to Jake.

"Yeah, from freezing to frying," Jake answered.

"Jake, you get the guys together, and we'll head out to the chalk bluffs where I found that pterosaur fossil last year," Marsh said. "Tell them to be mindful of the rattlers."

The party followed Marsh along the river bottom and down the buffalo trail Marsh had traveled the previous year. The professor's anticipation grew as he remembered the landscape from earlier. He spurred his horse ahead of his men and found the rock face where he had carved the *M*, marking the site of his pterodactyl fossil find. He reined his horse, quickly dismounted, and found the impression where he had dug out the fossil. Excited by the prospect of finding more bones of the pterosaur, Marsh took his knife and began carefully unearthing the hot Kansas clay. He uncovered a fossil bone, then another, and another. His students rode up to find the professor on his hands and knees, digging and laughing.

"This is the site, boys!" Marsh shouted with glee. "Tether your mounts to those bushes yonder. Work very carefully. Explore this site for pterosaur fossils."

The Yale men, obeying their leader's commands, were soon on their hands and knees exploring the hot Cretaceous chalk surfaces. They began finding pieces of fossils, whereas Marsh unearthed the rest of the bones that formed the whole wing of the first little fossil he had found.

The quiet concentration of the party working was interrupted when one of the men let out a yell and then a shot rang out. Marsh, some of his students, and the army guards drew their revolvers and were ready to take cover, thinking maybe it was a Sioux attack.

"It's okay!" Oscar Harger, one of the Yale students, yelled. "A rattlesnake surprised me, but I shot it."

"You make damn sure that rattler is dead before you handle it," one of the cavalrymen shouted. "The creatures' heads can still bite long after being shot."

"It's okay, sergeant," Oscar answered. "I blew its head apart."

Marsh's persistence in exploring this area in detail for fossils paid off. The fossil hunters found numerous pterosaur fossils of different species and bones that told of enormous wingspans of twenty to thirty feet.

Jake and Oscar shared a tent at the campsite. Like Jake, Oscar enjoyed the adventure of the Western frontier. They became instant friends and shared their enthusiasm for fossil hunting.

The party continued probing the hot Cretaceous chalk of the Kansas Smoky Hill River bottoms. They were successfully finding fossils, but at a price. Into the third week of exploration, with daily temperatures around 110 degrees Fahrenheit, the fossils hunters were fatigued. Under the blazing sun, a number of the party began to show signs of heat stroke. Jake was wiping the sweat from his brow as he admired a fossil he'd just uncovered when he saw Oscar collapse. Heat stroke had hit Oscar hard as he lay on the hot ground retching, moaning, and convulsing. Jake was on his feet in a second and rushed to aid Oscar. A couple of the cavalrymen came to their assistance, and someone yelled for Professor Marsh. Jake held his quivering partner. A soldier untied his kerchief and soaked it with water from his canteen.

"Let's get him in some shade," the soldier said to Jake. "Wet his brow and neck with this bandanna, and give him small sips of water."

By the time they got Oscar back to camp, his convulsions had subsided but he was beginning to have delusions. Jake placed him in the shade of some bushes and held his head up so he could take a drink of water.

"Let go of me, you red-skin devil. You're not taking my scalp,"

Oscar said, mumbling something about chasing the Indians back across the river.

"I'm not an Indian," Jake said. "I'm your friend, Jake."

Jake began to really worry about his friend's condition. Oscar was hallucinating and was hot with fever.

Marsh approached Oscar and Jake. With his slouched hat pulled down over his sweaty head, he bent down to talk to Oscar.

"Dad," Oscar asked, "did we drive off the Indians?"

"I'm not your dad. I'm Professor Marsh," Marsh said. "We weren't attacked by Indians. You've had an attack of heat exhaustion and fainted."

"My dad said it was the Sioux," Oscar said.

"Your father ain't here, son," Marsh said. "You're on a fossil expedition in Kansas, and you've been overcome by the heat. Your remarks aren't making any sense. You just rest and try to drink some water."

"I'll look after him," Jake said. "I'll make sure he drinks and rests here in the shade. It's too hot in the tent now, but I'll help him get in it this evening when it cools down."

"This evening may see a hard rain, the way those thunderheads are building," Marsh said.

As evening approached, a cool breeze brought some relief from the hot daytime temperatures. Suddenly, the wind picked up, bringing with it large black clouds discharging flashes of lightning and claps of thunder. Jake helped Oscar into their tent. Large drops of rain began to splash onto the dry clay ground. The temperature plummeted as hailstones hit the camp with the roar of a hundred cannons. Fortunately, most of the stones bounced off the tent's canvas surface, although as the hail increased in size, a few stones tore through the fabric. Jake was amazed that Oscar could sleep through such a racket but concluded that it was probably the best thing for him. The campsite, looking like it had been hit by a snowstorm in July, was covered with hailstones; some were as large as chicken's eggs.

The next morning, the sun rose to a cloudless sky as the heat began to climb again. The hailstorm had turned the chalky Kansas clay into a gummy terrain. Fortunately, none of the men had been injured, but some of the horses and mules were bruised and one horse had been killed by large hailstones whacking it on the head.

Oscar pulled on his boots and looked outside at the river of mud flowing by the front of the tent.

"What happened here?" he asked Jake, who was outside shoveling mud away from the tent's entrance.

"We got hit by a terrific hailstorm last night," Jake answered. "You slept through the whole shebang."

"Damn, I missed it," Oscar replied. "I love dramatic tempests."

"Well, we had everything," Jake said. "Thunder, lightning, wind, and rain, with lots of hail. I can't believe you slept so hard. How're you feeling this morning?"

"Not too bad, just a little tired," Oscar answered, yawning.

"Glad to hear," Jake said. "We were worried about your heat exhaustion. You were talking out of your head with a fever, saying all kinds of crazy things."

"That so," Oscar said. "I can vaguely remember being hot as hell. What was I talking about, anything embarrassing?"

"Not really," Jake said, chuckling. "Although you thought I was an Indian and Marsh was your dad."

"I apologize," Oscar said, grinning at the thought of his misunderstandings.

"It wasn't just you," Jake said. "Everyone was beginning to be fatigued by this heat." Jake took a drink from his canteen and offered it to Oscar. "We'd better get moving. We're breaking camp today and heading back to Fort Wallace."

At Fort Wallace, the party boarded the Kansas-Pacific Rail and headed for Denver for a week's rest. In the middle of August, they rode the Union Pacific to Cheyenne and then on to Fort Bridger, Wyoming, where Marsh met up with his former acquaintance, Judge

William Carter. Judge Carter told Marsh about the disorder that had befallen the garrison. The soldiers had taken a cut in pay and had inferior rations, causing many of them to desert. The number of Indian attacks had decreased in this part of the West, and the US Congress didn't see the need to support a large army. Although the Indian uprisings were diminishing, Judge Carter pointed out that there was an increase in the number of outlaws, mainly horse thieves.

Major LaMotte at Fort Bridger was again accommodating and provided the Yale party with escorts and wagons.

"Some of the recruits and officers have been lollygagging about the garrison and need some activity to keep them sound," Major LaMotte told Marsh. "I've rounded up three wagons and ten soldiers for your expedition."

"Splendid," Marsh said. "We appreciate your army's help."

"It's not *my* army, professor," the major said bitterly. "I only follow orders from Washington. Providing you with an escort is the least I can do to keep this godforsaken post active."

The party explored the Eocene rocks of the Bridger Basin and the area along Henry's Fork, a tributary of the Green River near the Wyoming–Utah border. There they set up their camp among the cottonwoods and willows. This site was a welcomed lush green and temperate location, much different than the barren hot landscape of the Smoky Hill River camp. Wild game was plentiful. The streams were teeming with cutthroat, brown, and rainbow trout. Fossils of early mammals were frequently found, and to Marsh's delight the party uncovered two more horse species of the dawn horse, *Orohippus uintanus* and *Orohippus pumilis*.

By mid-August the Yale party at Henry's Fork had concluded their fossil-finding work. They headed back to Fort Bridger to crate fossils to be sent to Yale. They would board a train to Salt Lake City and then head on to Portland, Oregon, for the last part of their expedition. Marsh received some mail at Fort Bridger and dashed off a number of telegrams about the fossil finds.

FRONTIER FOSSIL HUNTER

COLLECTION OF CARL GRUPP, SOUTH DAKOTA

As word of large fossil finds in the American West began to circulate, Marsh was not the only one who went there in the search of bones. His competitor, Edward Cope of Philadelphia, was on his way to Fort Wallace that August of 1871. Marsh received word of others exploring the area of the Western fossil sites that he considered to be his private territory.

There were a number of men at Fort Wallace who Marsh enlisted as fossil hunters. He found out that one of his men was collecting for Cope and launched into a jealous rage. Marsh's possessiveness over fossil sites and his obsession with trying to outperform Cope's fossil hunting activity escalated the competitiveness between the two paleontologists. Cope was determined to publish more papers on his findings than Marsh. This rivalry led to an all-out fossil war.

Meanwhile, Jake had decided it was time to leave the Yale expedition. As he walked toward Marsh to let him know he was leaving, his thoughts centered on the Yale professor's possessiveness.

"Professor Marsh, I'll be leaving the group tomorrow," Jake said, biting his tongue so he wouldn't mention the professor's egocentricity.

"Sorry to see you leave, son," Marsh said, clearing his throat. "You will, of course, stay in my employment for bone collecting?"

"I'll collect and send bones to the highest bidder," Jake said with assertiveness.

"I'll pay you top dollar," Marsh assured, a little taken aback at Jake's attitude.

Jake sensed the doubts of loyalty Marsh had about Jake's fossil collecting.

"If you're out west next summer, let me know," Jake said, trying to ease the tension. "I may be able to join up with your party again. You can write to me at the Muller Ranch address."

"Splendid," Marsh said, clearing his throat. "Let me know of your fossil finds."

The next morning, Jake took the eastbound Union Pacific train from Fort Bridger to Laramie.

The decelerating *click-clack* of the train's wheels and its screaming whistle meant they were coming into Laramie. The city, located on the Laramie River and high plains between the Medicine Bow Mountains and the Laramie Mountains, had a history of lawlessness due to corrupt community officials. In the late 1860s, Laramie's self-appointed marshal, "Big Steve" Long, and his two half-brothers owned the Bucket of Blood Saloon, from which they conducted their crooked dealings. Forcing settlers to sign over deeds to their property, the brothers threatened their lives or provoked them into a gunfight with the gunslinger marshal. As many as thirteen men had been killed by the fraudulent marshal. In1868, rancher Nathaniel Kimball Boswell of Laramie was elected sheriff of the county of Albany. He was a no-nonsense lawman committed to bringing law and order to the Wyoming territory. Old Boz, as he was known, organized a vigilance committee. They stormed the Bucket of Blood Saloon, arrested the three outlaw brothers, took them to an unfinished building across the street, and hanged them from a rafter. Justice was served, with the guilty being punished swiftly and efficiently.

The braking train gave a sudden jerk and then came to a stop. Jake reread the note that Chris Muller had written introducing him to Sheriff Nat Boswell. Gripping his two bags, he departed from the day-coach car, stepped onto the depot platform, and went inside the station. He asked the station agent where the nearest hotel was.

"There's a hotel just up the block on Grand Avenue to the right," the agent said. "You can't miss it. It has good rates and caters to train passengers. They also have a restaurant."

A baggage man approached Jake. "Do you have any other baggage?" he asked. "If you're planning on taking a train out tomorrow, you can check any of your baggage here and now."

"Thanks. I won't be taking a train tomorrow," Jake said. "Can you tell me where I might find Sheriff Boswell, and a bank?"

The look on the baggage man's face told Jake that his question had puzzled him.

"Why are you looking for the sheriff?" the man asked.

"Personal business," Jake said, thinking that it was none of anyone's affair.

"I didn't get your name, sir," the baggage man said.

"Didn't give it," Jake answered.

The man gave a shrug. "Sheriff's office is two blocks past the hotel. Just head north on Grand, it's on the left side of the street," he said. "You can't miss it. And the bank is across the street."

Jake hefted his bags and set off to find the hotel.

The hotel did have good rates and it did cater to rail passengers, but Jake was hoping for something a little more refined. All he needed, though, was a bed for the night, and it was still better than the tent city he'd been living in the past few months. When he signed the register, the clerk looked over his name and asked for an address. He gave the Muller Ranch as his address. He was given the key to a room on the second floor. The sparse hotel room contained a washstand, a clothes cabinet, and a small bed not much bigger than the army cots he had slept on. He poured water from a pitcher into the wash basin and splashed some unto his suntanned face and hands, combed his tousled hair and beard, and changed his shirt. He shoved the note to Boswell in his pocket, donned his hat, and went down the stairs. He decided to pass on the seedy-looking hotel's restaurant and seek someplace else to have supper. First, he would find Sheriff Boswell, and then he would deposit his money and set up a banking account.

"The stranger's coming up the boardwalk, Nat," Deputy Sheriff Luke Martins said, trying not to be too conspicuous as he looked out the window of the sheriff's office. "He kind of fits the description, all right, but he has a full beard."

Sheriff Boswell looked up from behind his cluttered desk.

"Is he armed?" Boswell asked.

"Doesn't look like it. No coat on to conceal a weapon," the deputy said.

"Is he limping?" the sheriff asked.

"Naw, he's walking straight as an arrow," Luke said. "Should I open the door?"

"Yeah, let him in," Boswell said.

As Jake approached the sheriff's office, he was surprised to see the door open and hear a voice call from within.

"Come on in," Boswell said. "We've been expecting you."

From behind the desk, the sheriff, a large middle-aged man with a full black beard, stood with his gun drawn. The deputy, a young good-looking man with a neatly trimmed mustache, held the door open with one hand; his other was on his holstered revolver. Jake was taken aback by the gun pointing at him. There was a moment of silence while Boswell studied Jake. Then, holstering his gun, he reached out his hand for a greeting.

"Howdy, I'm Sheriff Nat Boswell, and this is Deputy Luke Martins," Boswell said. "And who might you be?"

"Howdy, my name's Jake Harding," Jake said, shaking the sheriff's hand and nodding to the deputy. "I have a letter here from Chris Muller introducing me." Jake removed his hat and handed the letter to the sheriff.

Boswell took the letter and read it out loud. It explained Jake's business in the West as a fossil hunter and his part-time employment as a horse trainer, cowhand, and vet for the Muller Ranch.

"Well, by God, any friend of the Muller's is a friend of mine," Boswell said. "I know Chris. His dad, Walt, was a good friend of mine. Sorry for the distrustful welcome, but you vaguely fit the description of a wanted man. When someone at the rail station sent word of your arrival, we thought it best to be prepared, my apologies."

"None needed," Jake said. "I understand your position."

"You understand this territory is still trying to deal with a number of outlaws, some that are determined to put a notch on their guns aimed at Old Boz," the sheriff said, chuckling. "We're still trying to solve the Muller's Ranch murder case. I'd sure like to catch the bastards that killed Walt and his men."

"I'm sure you'll bring them to justice someday," Jake said.

"You're damn right I will," Boswell said. "A swift and efficient justice will be served on them."

Luke closed the office door and crossed the room to shake hands with Jake.

"Chris Muller and I grew up together. He's a good friend of mine," Luke said. "Do you know his sister, Jennie?"

"No," Jake said. "I haven't had the pleasure of meeting her."

"Well, it'll be your pleasure, I'm sure," Luke said. "When you meet Jen, she'll be surprised to meet you. I'll be going out to their ranch in a day. My cousin Lys and I are going to give the Muller's a hand with some construction work. Chris and Lys have been friends since childhood—wouldn't surprise me if they got married someday—" The deputy was about to say something else but was interrupted by the sheriff.

"You know where their ranch is located?" Boswell asked.

"Somewhere over on the Medicine Bow," Jake said. "Chris drew me a map. But I'm not familiar with Wyoming so any guidance you can give me will be appreciated."

"I'll be glad to help," Boswell said. "If you have a map Chris drew, it's probably got good directions."

"I've got to make a deposit at the bank, so I'd better get before they close," Jake said. "If you could direct me to a decent café, I need to get some supper. Tomorrow morning I need to buy a horse and tack, if you can tell me of a good livery stable."

"Claudia's Café is the best eatin' place in town. It's just across the street and two stores north, next to Iverson's Bank," the Sheriff said. "If we didn't have other commitments this evening, Luke and

I might join you. But I'll tell you what—I'll buy you breakfast in the morning and get you squared away with a horse and supplies. How's that strike you?"

"Much obliged," Jake said. "But let me buy you breakfast."

"Son, you have no idea how much I eat. Breakfast will be on me," Boswell said. "I'll meet you at, say, seven thirty tomorrow morning."

"All right, see you at breakfast then," Jake said.

As Jake walked out of the office, Sherriff Boswell thought, *I must ask Jake Harding if he owns a gun, and if so he'd better wear it in these here parts.* Another thought that crossed Boswell's mind was how much of a resemblance Jake had to Harry Jackson, with a beard. The resemblance stopped at the physical likeness, though, for Jake's demeanor was far different.

In the morning, Jake was at the café by seven. He set his two bags down by a table, seated himself, and ordered a coffee. The stranger seated at the next table glanced his way, and Jake thought he knew the person. Sure enough, he had met him before; it was the railroad baggage man. Acknowledging that Jake recognized him, the man nodded.

"Howdy. Did you find the sheriff?" the man asked, his question loaded with curiosity.

"Yes, I did," Jake said, a little snappish. "Thanks for telling the sheriff I was coming."

"Ah … you're welcome," the man said, taken aback by Jake's response.

An awkward silence followed as the two men made an effort not to look at each other.

A waitress brought Jake his coffee. Jake blew on it, took a sip, set the cup down, and extended his hand to the stranger.

"Hi, the name's Jake," he said, delighted in playing this little game of awkwardness.

Jake couldn't quite understand the strange feeling he had about his presence in Laramie. He'd felt it in the sheriff's office, the hotel, and of course with this railroad employee. Just as the man was about to shake hands and introduce himself, Boswell and Luke come into the café.

"Howdy, BB," the sheriff said. "Good morning, Jake. I see you two have met."

"Just about to," BB said.

"BB, this is Jake Harding," Boswell said. "Jake, this is Bartholomew Burgoyne. Everyone calls him BB."

The waitress approached their table.

"You look lovely today, Linda," Luke said to the waitress. "Let me introduce you to Jake Harding. He'll be working at the Muller Ranch."

"I'm pleased to meet you, Jake," Linda said. "I'm sure you'll like working at the Muller's. They're good friends of mine."

"Linda is Claudia's daughter," Luke said. "Claudia Holmes owns this café."

"You forgot to mention that Linda is your girlfriend, Luke," BB said disdainfully.

"Now don't go embarrassing my deputy and our waitress, BB," Boz said. "You behave yourself."

"Well, everyone knows that's the truth," BB said.

"That may be," Linda said. "But not everyone approves. Ma doesn't like the idea of me having a lawman for a boyfriend. Too dangerous, she says."

"You mean to say Luke's too dangerous for you or that his being a deputy sheriff is too dangerous?" BB asked, snickering.

"Too dangerous for *you*," Linda quipped, giving BB an austere look.

"Looks like I'm surrounded by dangerous people," BB said. "Thankfully I've had my breakfast, so I'll be leaving."

He pushed his chair back forcibly and flashed a sneering smile, his face flushed with exasperation. Everyone was silent as BB threw some money on the table for his meal and stomped out of the café.

"Let's order our breakfast, shall we?" Boz said, trying to ease the tension.

After a hardy breakfast and small talk about the weather and a fight that had happened the night before at one of the local saloons, Luke excused himself.

"For you, Linda," Luke said as he laid a tip on the table. "Duty calls. See you all later." He tipped his hat to Linda and made his way to the door.

"Luke is a fine deputy," Boz said, "but he sure is shy around the girls. He's been trying to get up enough courage to ask Linda to marry him. It's been festering in him for a couple of months now. But don't mistake shyness for stupidity. My deputy is a very intelligent person."

"He does seem like a fine young fella," Jake said. "But he didn't seem to like his friend ribbing him about Linda being his girlfriend."

"Oh, I wouldn't say that BB was Luke's friend," Boz said. "Those two have their differences. BB does some serious drinking from time to time, and one time after spending most of the day in the saloon, he came into the café here and started getting fresh with Linda. Luke happened by and saw what was going on, and they had one hell of a fight over it."

"Who won?" Jake asked out of curiosity.

"Neither," Boz said. "I stopped it before they killed each other. I had to lock up BB for a couple of days. When that bastard gets drunk, he's likely to kill someone. I suspended Luke for a few days till he cooled down."

"It seems like they have settled their differences," Jake said.

"Don't you believe it," Boz said. "Luke is usually cool and level-headed, but BB is a hothead and can get Luke's dander up. Then they go at it."

"Speaking of getting at it," Jake said, "if I'm going to get to Muller Ranch, I'll need a horse."

"I'll take you down to Ingersoll's Livery Stable." Boswell said.

"My friend Sylas Anderson works there. He has some fine horses for sale. I'll make sure he gives you a good deal. By the way, do you own a gun?"

"Yes, sir," Jake replied. "I've got a '60 Colt Army .44 in my bag, belt and holster included. I thought it best not to wear it around town— might give someone the wrong impression."

"A lot of people in these here parts have the wrong impression about a lot of things," Boswell said. "But I advise you to start wearing your revolver, in town and on the trail."

Sylas, a huge elderly man of Norwegian descent, had arms as large as an average man's thighs. His thick white hair and blue eyes were offset by his dark suntanned hands and his weathered face, which at the slightest provocation would burst into an enormous smile and let out a laugh as loud as a braying mule. The sheriff introduced Jake, telling Sylas that Jake was a friend of the Muller's and that he needed to buy a horse and saddle. When they shook hands, Jake was amazed at the size of the large hand that was offered him. This giant shook Jake's hand with a firm but gentle grip as if he realized the power that it contained. Sylas had a heavy Scandinavian accent and a booming voice that went with his proportions.

"Vell, I'll be dern," Sylas said. "Old Valt vas a goot friend."

Jeez, everyone in the territory must know the Muller's, Jake thought.

Sylas, with a lariat in his hand, led Jake and Boz to a small corral where a dozen or so horses were feeding. It didn't take Jake long to spot the mount he wanted.

"I'd like to take a look at that bay with the hind white socks," Jake said. "Looks like a spirited mare. I like my horses with a little spirit."

"Yah, me too—my vemmen too," Sylas said with a booming laugh.

Sylas entered the pen and lassoed the mare. Jake inspected the horse's teeth and hooves.

"Been recently shod," Jake said. "Somebody knows their business all right."

"That'd be my son, Jerome," Sylas said. "He's real goot vit horses."

Jake stood close to the horse, put his hand on its mane, and then ran it down the mare's back and croup, giving a little tug on its tail. The horse snorted and turned to look at Jake. Jake held up his hand, and the horse turned to the front and snorted again.

"How about we get her saddled," Jake said.

"I'll get Jerome to bring a saddle and bridle," Sylas said.

Jerome, a lad of about eighteen and almost as big as his father, brought the tack.

"Does she have a name?" Jake asked Jerome.

"I call her Snotra," Jerome said. "It's a Norse goddess name meaning 'smart.'"

Jake saddled and bridled the mare and rode around the outside of the corral, and then he loped about a quarter mile down the road where he stopped, dismounted, and said something to the horse. The mare was spirited with an even disposition. Jake mounted again, and the horse snorted as he turned her around and spurred the animal into a full gallop. The mare charged forward with speed and agility. Jake knew that this was the horse for him.

"By Got," Sylas said. "You got a vay vit dem horses."

"I'll take her," Jake said. "I'm going to call the horse Snort 'cause she reminds me of a professor I know, and she does have a distinct snort."

"Jake, you have a good eye for horseflesh," Boz said. "Where did you get such knowledge?"

"From an expert horseman, my granddad," Jake said.

14

Jake followed the road northwest of Laramie. The Wyoming basin sandwiched between the Medicine Bow Mountains to the west and the Laramie Mountains to the east was a spectacular vista of streams, meadows, and woods. Stands of ponderosa pines, cottonwoods, and junipers permeated the landscape. The countryside was beginning to be painted with fall colors as the aspens turned gold and orange. Jake thought he had never seen such beauty in nature and instantly fell in love with this Western landscape. He had followed the road that led to Rock River and Medicine Bow for about three hours and according to the map he had and Boswell's directions, he should soon come upon a road to the east that led to Muller Ranch.

Following the road east, he saw a ranch house sheltered in a tree-lined valley. All the way to the ranch, he kept his eyes on the terrain, looking for any sign of fossil sites. Except for a few outcroppings and bluffs, most of the land in the area had too much overburden to expose the possibility of fossil locations.

The late afternoon sun had caused both man and horse to work up a sweat. On the way to the ranch house, Jake came upon a corral with its gate open. The mare pricked up her ears and began snorting and prancing.

"Whoa, Snort. What's bothering you?" Jake asked his horse. "You don't like that corral?"

Jake reined in the mare and gave her a pat on the neck, and then it struck him what the horse wanted. Inside the corral fence was a large water trough. It had been a while since both of them had had a drink and Snort was letting Jake know. He rode into the corral, dismounted, and led the horse to the water trough. Snort shook her head and eagerly began sucking up the cool liquid. The horse's gulping water was mixed with the sound of a voice coming from behind Jake.

"Mister, get those hands high and don't turn around or I'll shoot you," the voice said, with no uncertainty.

Jake raised his hands. "Whoa, I'm a friend of the Muller's. Who are you?" Jake asked, thinking Snort's pricking up her ears had indicated more than water.

"Never mind," the voice said. "Unfasten your gun belt with your left hand."

Jake did as he was told. The holster and gun fell to the ground.

"Now turn around, keep those hands high, and walk toward me," the voice said.

Jake turned and saw the person holding a gun on him step out from around a shed.

"What's your name? And what's your business here?" the person asked.

Jake, with his hands still held high, mumbled a low "What?" as he realized that the person holding a revolver on him was a woman, a beautiful young woman. The woman was just as surprised when Jake turned around.

"Take your hat off," the woman said in her low husky voice. "Now I asked you a question—who are you?"

"My name's Jake Harding," Jake said. "I came to see Frank and Chris Muller. I have a letter here from Chris. Who are you?"

"I'm their sister, Jen," she said. "This is quite a surprise. We've been expecting you."

Jake started laughing.

"What's so funny?" Jen asked.

"Well, within two days, I've twice had a gun held on me by someone who said, 'We've been expecting you,'" Jake said.

"All right, Mr. Harding," Jen said. "You can put your hands down now."

"Thank you, ma'am," Jake said.

"Don't *ma'am* me," Jen said. "The name's Jen."

"And my name is Jake," he said.

"Okay, Jake," Jen said. "You'd better tend to your bay before she wanders off."

"Yes ma'am—uh, pardon, Jen," Jake said. "Snort and I are newly acquainted, and I don't think she realizes she's my horse."

"You're horse's name is Snort?" Jen asked, chuckling.

Jake nodded his head and turned to go catch his horse, saying under his breath, "Yes ma'am."

Jake smiled to himself, thinking; *now there's a woman with as much spirit as she has beauty. It's my lucky day to meet a horse and a woman with such great qualities.* Jake caught up with Snort at the far end of the corral, where she had found a little stack of hay to chomp on.

"Unsaddle your horse and leave her in the corral!" Jen yelled. "Bring your saddle bags and baggage. We'll go up to the house and get you settled while we wait for Frank and Chris."

Jen ushered Jake into the house as she chattered like a jaybird, telling him about Chris's interest in fossils and how she had since become fascinated with them. Jen hung her hat on a peg by the door and told Jake to do the same with his. Jake was captivated by the beautiful, spacious living room with its enormous rock fireplace, polished wood log walls, and open beam ceiling. It reminded him of his grandfather's house in Philadelphia except for the assortment of wild game on display—the deer, elk, moose, and buffalo heads mounted on the walls. But his primary attention was focused on Jen as she tossed her hair free from the confines of her hat. She ran her fingers though the long auburn waves and gave Jake a resplendent smile, inviting him to follow her. Jake's first chance to get a good look at this frontier gal told him that she was more than beautiful—she was stunning. Trying not to get caught staring at her, Jake looked around the room and commented on its spectacular design.

"Come on," Jen said, leading Jake through the front room to the hallway. "Bring your bags. We've fixed a room for you to bunk in."

Jake was gripping his bags as though they were life preservers while trying not to drown in doing or saying something stupid … but he did.

"Thanks, ma'am—ah, *Jen*," he said, embarrassed.

Jen just chuckled and opened the door to a spacious bedroom. It contained a large bed, washstand, dresser, clothes closet, desk, and chair.

"Drop your bags in here," Jen said, "and then follow me across the hall. I've got something to show you. I think you'll like this."

Jen opened the door to her dad's study where against the far wall stood display shelves that ran the length of the room. The shelves were filled with fossils. Jake was awe stricken. Never had he expected to find an exhibit like this in a rancher's home.

"Put them hands high," a voice suddenly said, loud and sharp.

A tall, husky man with a large mustache entered the room with a revolver aimed at Jake.

"Stop, Chris," Jen said. "He's not who you think. This is—"

"Jake Harding," Frank said, as he entered the room behind Chris. "Good to see you made it okay. I see you've met Jen and Chris."

"We haven't yet been introduced," Chris said as he lowered his gun.

Jen started laughing, and Chris joined in as he holstered his gun, shook his head in wonder, and held his hand out to Jake.

"Howdy, Jake," Chris said. "Sorry about mistaking you for someone else."

"Good to see you again," Frank said, walking over to shake hands.

"Good to see you too, Frank," Jake said. "I've sure had a strange welcome to Wyoming. Third time I've had a gun pulled on me—once by Sheriff Boswell, then by Jen, and now by Chris. Not holding it against any of you. Maybe it's just a Western way of greeting strangers. I don't know, but it's been unnerving."

Both Frank and Jake had perplexed looks on their faces. Jen was about to say something when Bella entered the room.

"Oh, my God! It's him!" Bella screamed and hid behind Chris.

"No, it isn't," Jen said. "Aunt Bella, this is Frank's friend, Jake Harding. We told you he would be coming to work on the ranch. Let me explain to Frank and Jake what all this kerfuffle is about."

"Please do," Frank said.

"Frank, you remember me telling you about Harry Jackson, that scoundrel?" Jen began. "Well, Jake here bears an uncanny resemblance to Harry—that is, at first glance. No offense, Jake."

"None taken, ma'am … uh, Jen," Jake said. "Now I understand why the railroad agent, the sheriff and his deputy, and you and Chris all gave me such strange welcomes."

"I've never met this Harry Jackson," Frank said. "I wouldn't know him except from your description, Jen—mainly that he has a limp caused by your shooting him."

"Only put a bullet in his leg," Jen said. "I should have put one in his black heart."

"Amen to that," Chris said.

"Anyhow, make yourself at home, Jake," Jen said. "I'm going to give Aunt Bella a hand in the kitchen. Supper will be on in about an hour. I'll bang on the triangle to let you guys know."

"All right, we'll listen for it," Frank said.

"Let's show Jake around," Chris said to Frank. "We'll go over to the cabin and introduce him to Red Long Arrow and Sunbird."

"You and Jake go on ahead," Frank said. "I've a few things to take care of. I'll catch up with you at supper."

Frank headed for the barn while Chris and Jake took off for the cabin. At the barn, Frank entered one of the empty stalls, reached up behind a rafter, and retrieved a large bottle of whiskey. He leaned against the stall railing, holding his head and shaking. After uncorking the bottle, he took a big swig and sank to the floor on his knees, mumbling. His thoughts became tangled as he began to see visions of his skirmishes with hostile Indians. He took another drink of whiskey and another as he recalled more scenes of bloody battles. Cavalry comrades alongside him were being hacked to pieces with tomahawks, pierced with spears and arrows, and then scalped and their bodies mutilated. He let out a yell and curled up in the stall, hiding from his nightmarish visions.

Jake and Chris were just approaching the cabin.

"Did you hear that?" Chris asked. "Sounded like someone yelling."

"Didn't hear a thing," Jake said, straining to listen for any sound.

Walking up the path to the cabin, Chris told Jake about his Indian friend. "Red is a Pawnee Indian who became friends with our pa and has worked for us for a number of years," Chris said. "His wife, Sakuru Rikucki, which means 'Sunbird' in Pawnee, helps Bella with chores around the ranch."

The door to the cabin opened, and Red and Sunbird appeared in the doorway.

"Sometime I hear you yell," Red said.

"Wasn't me," Chris said. "Maybe Frank yelled at one of the horses."

Chris introduced Jake to Red and Sunbird, telling them of Jake's interest in fossil bones and of his skills with horses and that he'd be staying on at the ranch.

"Red makes extra-long arrows and stains them red with wild berry juice; hence his name, Red Long Arrow," Chris said to Jake. "He and I have hunted a lot of elk and deer together. Red uses a traditional bow and arrow, although he's also an excellent shot with a rifle."

"I go to mountain hunting now, sometime," Red said. "Bring back big elk. Elk meat good like buffalo, but buffalo best. You and friend, Jake, want to go?"

"No. Not this time," Chris said. "Maybe sometime. I want to show Jake some of the horses."

"Sometime," Red said.

"Speaking of horses," Jake said, "I'd better tend to mine."

"That must be your bay in the front corral," Chris said. "That's a fine-looking mare."

"Yep," Jake said. "Her name is Snort, and she does snort—thus the name."

"Maybe I should've named my horse Fart," Chris said musingly. "Let's get a look at your horse. You can leave her in that corral for now and put your saddle in that shed next to it."

After saying good-bye to Red and Sunbird, they walked over to the corrals. Chris showed Jake some mustangs and feral horses that Red had been breaking.

"Red is one hell of a bronc tamer," Chris said. "He's a good ranch hand. He has a little quirk of asking and answering questions by saying 'Sometime' sometimes," Chris laughed. "Get your horse taken care of, and we'll go up to the house and have a 'snort' of my pa's fine Kirshwasser."

While Jake and Chris were talking, a loud clanging of metal interrupted their conversation. Frank came strolling into the corral shouting at them.

"Chow's on," Frank said. "You guys quit your jawing and git on up to the house before Jennie pounds that iron triangle into a circle."

The evening meal, comprising some of Aunt Bella's finest culinary dishes, featured a tender elk roast. The conversations centered on ranching, expanding of the western states, fossil hunting, and the problems with outlaws and renegades roaming the territory.

"I'm sure impressed with the collection of fossils you all have found," Jake said. "Were they all collected on your ranch land?"

"Most of them were," Chris said. "There's a place not far from here where Jen and I found a number of fossil bones. We'll take you there, and maybe you can help us to identify them."

"That'd be great," Jake said. "But I don't want to take you away from any work you have to do at the ranch. And you remember our agreement: I'm to help you with any of the ranch's stock for my room and board. I can always explore the area for fossils on my own."

"Oh, no you don't," Jen said. "We weren't just telling tall tales when we said the territory is being invaded by a number of hooligans passing through these parts. We always go as a team and leave a guard with the ranch house."

"Sis is right," Chris said. "Times have changed since the war. There are a number of outlaw gangs and bushwhackers that drift through. Also, some hostile Indians turn up now and then"

"Well, I'll leave the planning up to you guys," Jake said. "I'll be ready any time."

"I need a change of pace," Chris said. "Maybe I can take Jake over to the butte fossil place tomorrow. It's only about a five-hour ride."

"Hang on," Jen said. "I'll go with you. I know places where there's bones as well as you do. Frank can look after the place."

Right you are, sis. You three go on," Frank said. "I can manage just fine here. Besides, Luke and his cousin Alyssa should be here tomorrow morning.

"Great," Chris said. "Let's go tomorrow. The sooner we go, the sooner we'll be back."

"Well, you'll want to get back so you don't pass up seeing Miss Alyssa," Jen said, bantering.

"It'll be a pleasure to be around a refined young lady like Lys for a change, rather than putting up with your sassing," Chris fired back.

"Okay, you two," Frank said. "Start getting your gear together for tomorrow's ride. I'll take care of everything here."

"Let's plan on going for two days," Chris suggested.

"That'll be great by me," Jake said, "if that doesn't put you out in any way."

"All right, it's settled then," Jen said with glee. "Fossil hunting we'll go."

The rising sun was still hidden behind the eastern mountain range as Jake, Jen, and Chris finished their breakfast. They saddled their horses, loaded their gear on a pack mule, and rode toward the western range. Their destination was toward Medicine Bow over the Laramie River.

Jake thought, *now that's a graceful horse and rider,* as he watched Jennie ride down the trail ahead of them. She rode as if she were born in the saddle, which she darn near was.

"We ought to make the fossil location just in time to have lunch, set up camp, and start our dig," Chris said.

The fossil site was located between two high bluffs. Erosion had washed the clay, laden with fossils, down onto the flat plain and buried them in a shallow overburden. After setting up camp, they started searching the area for fossils.

Twenty minutes later, Jen let out a whoop as she held up a small fossil skull of a prehistoric horse.

Jake ran to her to take a closer look at her find. "That's a perfect specimen of Professor Marsh's 'dawn horse' skull," he said.

"Don't know what you're whoopin' about, gal," a stranger's voice rang out, "but I'll bet it's either gold or diamonds."

Three riders emerged from the ridge. They were scruffy looking as though they'd been on the trail for some time. The older man, who had yelled at them, had an unkempt black beard entwined with strands of gray and two dark, sinister, sunken eyes. His large, gnarled hands held a rifle across the pommel of his saddle. The two younger riders had a cockiness about them that spelled trouble. One was skinny with long red hair. He wore a patched Confederate army coat that was a size too large. The other man, sitting slouched in his saddle, was chubby. He was dressed in a tattered leather vest and a shirt that was once white but had long ago lost its luster. He wore a smirk on his stubble-bearded face as he stared through squinty eyes at Jen. Chris, who was a few yards from them, put his hand on the butt of his revolver. As he did, he was shot by the older man with the rifle. Falling backward into the clay dirt, Chris grabbed his right arm in pain.

"Now, all of you unbuckle those gun belts," the rider who shot Chris said. "Or take a bullet."

"That's my brother you shot, you son of a bitch!" Jen shouted as she started toward Chris.

"Jen, it's okay," Chris said, getting up. "It's only a flesh wound. Do as the man says. We don't want any trouble."

With his left hand, Chris unbuckled his gun belt and let it fall to the ground. Jake and Jen dropped their gun belts as well.

"Wise decision, folks," the shooter said. "Now, let's see what y'all diggin'."

"We're digging for fossil bones," Jake said. "There's nothing here of value to you."

"We'll see," the shooter said as he pointed to the red-haired rider. "Boo, hop down and take a look in those sacks. For damn sure ya'll ain't digging turnips. We hear say there's been some diamonds found in these here parts, and gold too."

"Maybe they got a sack of 'taters," Boo said as he scurried over to pick up Jen's knapsack. "I sure could use a chaw on a sweet 'tater," he snickered.

"I'm a'thinkin' we may just have a sweet 'tater for our pleasure," the smirking young rider with the leather vest said.

"You may be right, Jeb," the older man said. "I do have an eye for well-bred horses and women, seems like we have both here."

The old man reached down on his saddle, untied his lariat, and then handed it to Jeb.

"Jeb, you put this rope on that pretty miss, and then take your rope and hog-tie the two men," the old man ordered.

"Okay, Captain," Jeb said as he dismounted, undid the rope from his saddle, and started toward Jennie and Jake carrying the two ropes.

"You ain't going to put a rope on me," Jen said as she struck out at Jeb.

Jeb grabbed ahold of Jennie's arm and twisted it behind her back. Jake lunged at Jeb, landing a hard punch to his jaw that caused him to lose his grip on Jen and fall over into the dirt. A shot rang out, and Jake fell to the ground. He clutched his right leg as blood started staining his trousers. Jen let out a scream as the old man raised his rifle for another shot at Jake.

"I gave you a warning," the old man said. "Now you pay." He took aim at Jake. There was a moment of silence and then a low, barely audible *thock*. The old man sat back in his saddle for a moment. His rifle pointed into the air and fired. He made a gurgling sound as he looked at the last thing he saw—a long red arrow sticking in his chest. Then he fell forward, dead.

"Injuns!" Boo shouted as he held up Jen's knapsack and pointed toward the top of the bluff.

"Where?" Jeb asked. He jumped up, turned, and looked at the old man slumped forward in the saddle. Jeb drew his revolver. *Thock*,—again, that sound of an arrow penetrating a body. Jeb fell dead with a long red arrow embedded in his back and sticking out the front of his chest. His leather vest was stained a purplish hue from the blood.

With one flying leap, Boo was in his saddle. He spurred his black horse to a gallop, and his long red hair began flapping like a cape. He looked like a devil riding out of hell. At that moment, Jake picked up Jeb's revolver, knelt on his good leg, and fired a shot at Boo. The fleeing bandit flinched as the bullet grazed his right shoulder. The horse and rider disappeared in a whirlwind of dust.

"Damn," Jake said. "I didn't bring him down, but I gave him something to remember us by."

"Red," Jen cried out. "Where are you?"

"Up here," Red said as he appeared at the top of the bluff. "Heard the shots and came fast. Looks like some bandits found you—sometime."

"Thank God you came along when you did," Jen said.

"You all okay?" Red asked.

"I'm okay," Chris said. "Just a flesh wound to my arm." He reached for his canteen, took a big swig, and offered it to Jake.

"I'm fine," Jake said, refusing the drink. "I don't think that rifle shot to my leg hit the bone."

"Let me tend to that leg wound of yours," Jen said. She undid the bandanna from her neck and bent down to tie it around Jake's leg. "The bullet went clean through your leg."

Chris wrapped a kerchief around his wounded arm and strapped his gun belt back on his waist.

"Think you can ride?" Chris asked Jake.

"Oh, yeah," Jake said. "I'm mad enough that I could take off riding after that red-haired son of a bitch."

"You better take it easy and stay off that leg," Jen said. "We'll get you back to the ranch and patch you up." She leaned over and gave Jake a kiss on the cheek. "Thanks for coming to my rescue," she said.

"It was my pleasure, ma'am—uh, Jen," Jake said, embarrassed.

"That's all right. I take no offense to what you call me," Jen said. "I know you mean well. I'm just not used to having such a gentleman around."

Red come riding down the trail leading a pack horse loaded with an elk carcass and a large elk rack.

"Thanks for coming to our rescue, Red," Chris said. "Your timing was perfect, and so were your shots. Looks like you had a successful hunt."

"Sometime," the Pawnee said, smiling. "Got me a nice elk and two bandits."

"Who in hell were those guys?" Jake said.

"Don't know," Chris said. "Let's see if we can find out. Jen, you help Jake over to his horse. You two start heading back to the ranch and get that leg wound tended to. Red and I will take care of things here."

"Ah, I'll give you a hand," Jake said. But as he started to get up, he took a step forward and then sank to his knees, groaning.

"Oh, yeah, sure you will," Jen said sarcastically as she reached down to help Jake stand up. "Let's get you back to the ranch, if you can ride."

"Oh, I can ride," Jake said, chortling. "I just can't walk."

Jen removed her hat, gave the perspiration on her forehead a swipe, and then gave Jake a light swat on his backside with her hat.

"Good thing you can ride 'cause it's a long crawl back," she said. "Let's get back to the ranch before dark."

"Just help me up on my horse," Jake said. "I'll be fine."

"Chris," Jen said, "Jake and I can take Red's packhorse, with the elk, back to the ranch so we can take care of the meat."

"Good idea, Jen," Chris said. "Red and I will break camp, bury these scoundrels, and bring their horses with us."

Jen helped steady Jake as he stood on his wounded right leg and put his left one in the stirrup. Chris walked over to them, helped Jake swing up into the saddle, and then went over to the old man's horse, which was calmly grazing. The dead man had toppled from his saddle. He was lying on his side a few feet from his horse with the red arrow sticking in his chest. Chris turned the man over on his back and started going through his coat pockets. Red had dismounted and was checking out Jeb, who lay face down with a red arrow sticking in his back.

15

Frank, Luke, and Alyssa were building an addition to the corral when they heard three horses approaching down the road. Luke recognized Jennie riding Lady and leading a packhorse. Jake was hunched over in his saddle. Luke realized something was amiss and ran toward the horses.

"Jennie! Jake!" he called out. "What happened? Where's Chris?"

"Chris is okay," Jen said.

"Isn't that elk on Red's packhorse?" Luke asked.

"Yeah," Jake answered. "He's okay too. They'll be along later."

"We were ambushed by three bandits," Jen said. "Red came along in time. He killed two of them. The third ran off and was wounded by Jake. Both Chris and Jake were wounded. Chris got a flesh wound to his arm, and Jake's been shot in the leg. We've got to get him up to the house and take care of that wound."

Frank and Lys came running up just in time to hear Jen tell about the outlaws.

"Luke and I will take care of the packhorse and elk," Frank said.

"Alyssa, you help Jen with Jake," Luke said. "He's the feller looking for fossils I was telling you about."

"Nice to meet you, Jake," Lys said.

"Likewise, Alyssa," Jake said, tipping his hat.

"Call me Lys," she said.

Bella and Lys busied themselves in the kitchen boiling water and getting clean towels for bandages. Bella was mixing up a concoction of some kind of antiseptic and mumbling a string of Italian phrases that had something to do with *God help us*. Jen was in Jake's room trying to make him comfortable on the bed. She loosened the bandanna from his blood-stained pant leg and heaved a sigh.

"Looks like you've lost a fair amount of blood," she said. "But you'll live. Okay, let's get those boots and trousers off."

Jake bent forward and groaned as he tried to pull a boot off.

"Let me take them off," Jen said as she grabbed his ankle. "Unbuckle your belt, and I'll slip your trousers off too."

"I can take them off myself," Jake said.

"For Christ sake, Jake," she said. "I'm trying to help you here. I've nursed two brothers and a father, and you ain't made any different. Just relax. Aunt Bella has a wonderful medicine to put on your wound. She mixes up garlic, honey, and whatnot in a saltwater solution to clean the wound."

"Sounds like I should be put on a curing rack with the elk carcass," Jake said.

"You ain't no carcass yet," Jen said. "And you won't be. I aim to take good care of you," she said, pulling his boots off. "Now unbuckle your belt, raise your buttocks, and let me slip those trousers off."

"Jake," Frank said, chortling as he walked into the room. "I suspect Jen's been trying to get your britches off since you first got here."

"You shut up, Frank," Jen said. "I thought you and Luke were taking care of the elk meat."

"Luke has it all under control," Frank said. "He's better at that than me. I thought I'd see if you and Lys needed help."

"Lys and Bella are in the kitchen," Jen said. "Tell them to hurry up with the hot water and bandages—and don't lollygag about."

Jen grabbed ahold of Jake's pant legs and, with one swift yank, pulled his trousers off. Jake let out a groan as the blood-soaked trouser leg was pulled from his wound.

"Okay, hairy," Jen said. "Let's get that wound cleaned."

"The name's Jake—not Harry," Jake said, perturbed at Jen calling him Harry.

"I know your name," Jen said, scoffing. "I was referring to your *hairy* leg, not the name Harry."

"Sorry," Jake said.

"Here," Jen said as she handed him a sheet. "Cover yourself with this, except for your right leg. Leave it on top of the sheet so we can tend to that wound."

Lys entered the room carrying hot water and towels. Bella followed carrying a tray with the antiseptic solution and a glass of medicine.

"Here, swallow this," Bella said as she handed him the glass.

"Is it whiskey?" Jake asked.

"No, it's, ah, whatchamacallit …" Bella said. "Laudanum! That's it. It'll help with your pain. You can have a whiskey after you eat something. I've made a nice soup for you."

Jake downed the medicine. He winced and let out a moan as Bella began to clean his wounded leg. Jen sat on his leg to hold it still, telling him not to move. Her voice was full of compassion.

"You make a wonderful doctor, Aunt Bella," Jen said.

"I was never a doctor," Bella said. "But I was a nurse helping my father, who was a doctor during the Sicily Revolution in 1848. He was killed during that war, and the next year I came to America to escape the wars in Europe."

"I never knew that," Jen said.

"There are a lot of things you don't know about this family," Bella said. "Someday I'll tell you all about them. For now let's get this fellow bandaged up."

Jake began to drift into an ecstasy world as the opium in the laudanum began to take effect.

Later when Jake opened his eyes, the room was in semidarkness. The lamp was turned low. The first thing he noticed was a throbbing in his leg and then voices coming from the hallway. A figure got up from the chair beside him. He recoiled and brought his hands up in defense.

"It's okay. It's me," Jen said.

"Oh, God, what a nightmare," Jake said. "I dreamt I was in a shootout and got shot."

"You did get shot," Jen said. "But you're doing fine. The medicine you took knocked you out, and you were dreaming."

Jen bent over him and laid her hand on his forehead.

"Good, you don't feel like you have a fever," she said as she turned up the lamp.

"Get me my trousers," Jake said. "Please, I want to get up."

"You ain't getting up or going nowhere," Jen said.

The golden glow from the lamp filled the room. Jake couldn't help but notice the exquisiteness of the woman standing by his bedside. Voices and footsteps interrupted his thoughts as the door opened and people began flowing into the room. Chris, Luke, Lys, Bella, and Red all crowded around Jake's bed.

"Well, how's the patient?" Chris asked, first to speak.

All at once, everyone began asking about his condition.

"I'm doing fine," Jake said.

"He thinks he can get up and go gallivanting about," Jen said.

"Maybe you should hog-tie him," Chris said, chuckling.

Jen let Chris's remark slide, except for a glaring sideways glance she gave him.

"Where's Frank?" Jen asked. "I want him to get me some leg wrapping from the barn that we use on the horses. I'll wrap Jake's leg with it."

"Well, I ain't no horse. But I want to pull my load around here to earn my keep," Jake said, laughing.

"Aunt Bella, I want some of that medicine you gave Jake," Chris said with a laugh. "Plenty of time for you to pull your load, Jake, for now you rest and let that leg heals."

"Frank said he had some work in the barn that needed tending to," Luke said. "I'll go see him and get some wrapping."

"How's your arm, Chris?" Jen asked.

"Nothing but a scratch," Chris said. "Red helped me bandage it."

"Did you find out anything about those bushwhackers that shot us?" Jen asked.

"A little bit," Chris said. "I found a letter on the old man that said he was promoted in '64 to the rank of captain in the Confederate Army. His name was Jeremy Brown. The young guy, the one they called Jeb, had an envelope addressed to a Mr. C. J. Brown of Richmond, Virginia, with a postmark and address from Atlanta, Georgia, but no letter in it."

"I'll take all the information to Laramie," Luke said. "We'll see if Sheriff Boz can shed some light on those outlaws. Old Boz has a way of finding out about things."

"Meanwhile, we'll let Jake get some rest and see you all in the morning," Chris said.

Everyone filed out of the room except Jen.

"Let me take another look at that wound," Jen said.

She tenderly removed the dressing and applied some more antiseptic.

"It's looking much better," she said. "Just stay off that leg as much as possible."

"Well, I had planned on going for a moonlight stroll, if you'd care to accompany me," Jake said.

"Ah, your pain must be better," Jen chuckled. "You're able to kid around again. I'll take you up on that at a later date, when you're able to 'stroll.'"

"I'll hold you to that," Jake said.

She picked up the lamp and walked over to his bedside. Turning the lamp low, she placed it on his nightstand, bent over, and gave him a kiss.

"You get some rest. I'll see you in the morning," she said. "Good night."

Jake was almost asleep already. "Good night," he said. "And thank you for taking care of me."

For the next week, Jennie waited on Jake hand and foot, bringing him food, changing the dressing on his wounded leg, and sitting with him, either reading stories from many of her dad's books or telling him about her family and her life on the ranch. She'd even help him stand and hobble around the house to get some exercise.

It was still dark outside very early on a Saturday morning a week later, and Jake was sound asleep. But he became alert at the sound of Jen's voice and her gentle knocking on his door.

"Come on in," he called out. "I'm still here."

"Shh … quiet," Jen whispered. "Don't wake anyone. I don't want Frank to wake and follow us. It's getting so I can't go anyplace without him hound dogging me."

"He's just being caring, as a big brother should," Jake said.

"Well, I'd like a little privacy now and then," Jen said. "I don't want a chaperone."

"How about just an escort," Jake said. "I'll volunteer."

"That I would like," Jen said, giving him a charming smile and a seductive glance. "It's going to be a beautiful day, and you can escort me on a picnic."

"Every day I see you it's a beautiful day … and a picnic," Jake said.

"Oh, aren't you the sweet talker," Jen said. "I'll take that as a compliment."

"It was meant as such," Jake replied.

"We're going to get you some fresh air," she said.

"You mean I get to go into the great outdoors?" Jake asked. "Hallelujah."

"Now don't go getting all worked up 'cause you ain't gonna go running around bustin' your britches on this little outing," Jen said.

"We're going to a lovely little spot we call Cottonwood Grove. Mom and Dad used to take us there when we were kids. It's populated by beautiful butterflies and cutthroat trout in the creek that runs through it. I'll bring fishing poles. We'll have some wine and a picnic lunch with some *kartoffelkloesse* and a surprise dish. Dress warm. I'll be back shortly after I hitch Lady up to the buckboard."

"What the devil is "kar-offel-close?" Jake asked.

"Kartoffelkloesse," Jen said. "My mom taught me how to make it. It's potato dumplings. The main dish is a delicious secret—you'll love it.

"Who's all going on this picnic?" Jake asked.

"Why, just you and me," Jen said. "Are you afraid to go into the woods with just me? Don't worry; I'll protect you. I'm bringing Pa's twelve gauge. There are a lot of turkeys in that grove. Maybe I'll get me one."

"It ain't that," he said, smiling. "I just don't want any harm to come to you. I'll bring my revolver and rifle. No telling who might show up on the trail."

"There ain't a trail where we're going," Jen said. "Not likely anyone's going to show up. Hurry; get dressed. I'll be right back."

Jen was right. There was no road to the picnic grove. Jake held on tightly to the side rails of the old buckboard as it bounced and swayed with Jen guiding it over the rough terrain, seeking out the most suitable route.

"How's the leg doing?" she asked Jake.

"It's fine," Jake said. "Only thing that aches is my backside from all the bouncing."

"We're just about there," Jen said. "See that stand of trees just ahead? That's where we're going."

"I love this beautiful countryside," Jake said. "There's a nurturing beauty about this land that makes one feel free and alive. I'm sure glad I decided to move here."

"Me too," Jen said.

Jake thought, *Did Jen mean she was glad I moved here or that she felt free and alive?* Before he could question her implication, she interrupted him.

"Look at that!" she exclaimed as she pulled the wagon to a stop. "Hand me the field glasses. They're under the seat."

Jake reached under the seat, retrieved the binoculars, and handed them to her.

"Uh-huh," she said, "just as I figured."

"What'd you see?" Jake asked anxiously, "Indians?"

"Sure lots of feathers," Jen said solemnly. "Take a look with the glasses—over to your right by the poplar trees."

Jake put the glasses to his eyes and searched to the right of the poplars.

"Turkeys!" he exclaimed.

"I think they're Indians in disguise," Jen said, laughing. "I sure would like to bag a big tom for a turkey dinner."

"You're a great kidder," Jake said.

"So are you," Jen said. "We're two of a kind."

"Yep," Jake said, and then he added, "in some ways."

The place Jen selected for a picnic was beside a fast-flowing stream with huge boulders and deep cerulean blue pools. Large cottonwood trees provided a windbreak, and the ground was thick with woodland grasses dotted with juniper bushes and May flowers being inspected by a flutter of yellow-green butterflies. Jake limped around helping Jen the best he could to unload the wagon. She spread a couple of blankets on the grass and laid out the picnic basket, shotgun, two fishing poles, and an extra blanket.

"I'll unhitch Lady and hobble her," Jen said. "Can you get around enough to build a little fire pit so we can cook our picnic lunch? See if you can find some rocks to line it, but don't take any rocks from that pile of stones yonder. That's Pa's sacred pile of stones."

"Yes, ma'am," Jake said, bowing.

"I didn't mean to sound bossy," Jen said apologetically.

"Oh, you didn't," Jake said. "I would gladly do anything you wanted."

"Anything," Jen questioned. "Well, now."

"Just about," Jake said, clearing his throat.

Jake hopped around on his one good leg, and with a little effort he was able to put some weight on the other one. He rolled some rocks in a circle for a fire pit. After Jen took care of her horse, she went over and sat by Jake, who was breaking dead branches for their campfire.

"Got something here I want you to taste," she told him.

"What is it?" he asked.

"Open your mouth and close your eyes and I'll give you something to make you wise," Jen said in a sing-song voice.

Jake did as he was told. Jen unfolded a small cloth, picked up a kernel of yellow corn, and popped it in his mouth.

"Now chew slowly," she said.

Jake chewed and smacked his lips. "Yum," he said. "That was the sweetest corn I've ever tasted. Are we having some of that with our picnic lunch?"

"Nope," Jen said. "That's not for us."

"Not for us? Then who's it for?" Jake asked.

"It's for that big old cutthroat I aim to catch," Jen said. "Pa showed me a surefire way to catch trout. I cook some corn in boiling water and then add a little honey to sweeten the taste. Then I stick the soft corn on the hook with a horseshoe nail tied on the fishing line about two feet in front of the hook. The weight of the nail takes the hook to the bottom of the creek where the big trout feed. Old Mr. Trout goes crazy for that sweet yellow corn. Come on. Let's go fishing."

Standing beside the fast-flowing stream, Jen showed Jake how to rig his fishing line.

"This trout that we are going to catch is our secret delicious picnic lunch, right?" Jake said.

"Oh, I never thought," Jen said. "You don't like fish?"

"No, no, it's not that," Jake said. "I love fish. It's just that we haven't caught any yet. I've been fishing many times when I never caught a thing. You sure we'll catch our dinner?"

"My pa was never wrong about fishing," Jen said. "Now, the big trout like to lie at the bottom of a deep pool waiting for the current to bring a tasty morsel to them. *Snap*—he got it and we got him. See that deep pool beyond the big boulder about midstream? Throw your line about ten feet in front of that and let the current take the weight and hook down into that pool. Be ready to set the hook."

Jake made a cast that was short of his target, but on the second try he landed the hook midstream and the current took his bait into the pool. As soon as the bait found the depths of the pool, Jake felt a jerk on his line.

"I got a bite!" Jake yelled out.

"Set the hook and give your line a tug," Jen said. "Now reel him in gradually until some of the fight is taken out of him. Then you can land him."

And fight the trout did. He dove deep, then surfaced, and then jumped into the air shaking his head to loosen the hook but to no avail. After crisscrossing the pool, the cutthroat tired enough so that Jake could bring him to shore.

"Will you look at that," Jake said as he slid a finger under the trout's gill and hoisted the fish high to display a colorful, glistening, eighteen-inch cutthroat trout.

"Good catch!" Jen said. "I'll get another one for our dinner." She headed downstream to the next pool.

Jen and Jake were so intent on their fishing that they didn't notice a lone rider off on a distant hill. The rider, hidden partly by a tree line of pines, was observing the two anglers through a telescope.

Jen caught a fish that matched Jake's trout. After they had a meal of fresh trout, kartoffelkloesse, and a few glasses of wine, they both relaxed.

Jen was snoozing under the warmth of the noonday sun. Jake lay back on the blanket admiring the beautiful woman who peacefully reclined across from him. He pondered his next move as yearnings began to stir in his being. Moving closer to Jen, he rose to his knees, leaned over her, and gently placed a tender kiss on her forehead. She gave a low, gentle moan. Opening her eyes, she looked into his.

"Hello, handsome," she sighed, smiling.

"Hi, beautiful," he replied. "I was—"

"Shush," Jen said, interrupting him and putting her fingers to his lips.

She wrapped her arms around his neck, drawing him close. Their two lips met in a fiery, passionate kiss. Their bodies began the choreographed dance of love, well-rehearsed since the beginning of mankind.

Jake had had girlfriends before, but never had he felt the passion that overtook his mind and body as it did now. His hands, lips, and tongue began caressing Jen's body like someone's whose needs were near starvation. Jen returned his embraces with similar responses, and the two led each other into the pleasurable intricacies of lovemaking. Within minutes, they were naked and enveloped in the warmth of each other's embraces, both of them confessing their love for each other.

Huddled together under a blanket, they realized the low setting sun in the west was signaling twilight.

"We'd better get packed and head back to the ranch," Jen sighed. "Frank will be wondering about me. He is always so overprotective. Guess he still considers me his little baby sister."

"Well, you sure ain't," Jake said. "You are the most beautiful, fine woman in the world. And I love you."

"Aw, shucks," Jen said. "I bet you say that to all the girls. And you know what? I've fallen in love with you. You are a fine, true gentleman."

"Well, thank you, ma'am," Jake said. He bowed and tipped his hat, adding, "Jen, my dear."

"You darn well remember my name," Jen said, chuckling. "Let's get home before it gets dark."

Home, Jake thought. *It* is *beginning to feel like home.* He was pleased with his decision to move west.

Jen hitched Lady to the wagon while Jake started loading the picnic gear. He picked up the twelve gauge and sighted down the barrel.

"Nice shotgun," he said. "Too bad you didn't get a shot at one of those turkeys."

"Yeah, well, I got something better than a turkey on our picnic outing," Jen said, laughing.

"What a joker you are," Jake said, chuckling.

16

Jake felt a renewed purpose in life when he woke Sunday morning. He hadn't felt so alive since before he'd been shot in the leg, which he realized was almost without pain now. He had a sound and long sleep and had slept past his normal wake-up time. The sun was already coming up over the mountains as he hurriedly dressed himself, splashed some water on his face, and combed his hair. He wondered why no one had wakened him; Jen usually knocked on his door asking about his leg and if he needed anything. As he thought about Jen, he broke into a big smile. He was eager to see her that morning to tell her how much in love he was with her.

After opening and quietly closing his door, he quickly stepped into the hallway. Barely limping now, he made his way to the kitchen. He hoped that Bella could get him a cup of morning coffee. No one was around, and when he opened the front door to go to the barns, he saw Bella heading for the henhouse. He thought maybe Jen was already doing her daily livestock chores. He headed for the barn hoping to find her there.

Jake stepped into the dim light of the barn and saw a figure at the far end of the interior, cleaning a stall. He recognized Frank.

"Good morning, Frank," he said. "I'm getting around on my leg pretty good now. I was wondering if there is anything I can do to help around here."

Jake waited for Frank to answer him, but he didn't. He just turned to face Jake with a scowl and walked toward him with a strange look in his eyes. Not saying a word, Frank approached Jake face to face. The smell of whiskey filled Jake's nostrils. Suddenly, Frank doubled his fist, drew back his arm, and launched a hard right upper cut to Jake's jaw. Jake saw lights flashing and almost passed out as he fell backward onto the barn's dirt floor. Trying to clear his head and sit up, Jake was confused as to why and what had just happened.

"What is that all about?" Jake said, shaken and bleeding from his lip.

"You know damn well what that's about," Frank said in an angry tone. "I saw you and Jennie over at Cottonwood Grove yesterday. You seduced my baby ... sister!" Frank said, stumbling over his words.

"Now, wait," Jake said. "What you saw was Jen and me making love. No one seduced anyone. I love her. I'm going to ask her to marry me, Frank. She's not a little baby sister. She's a grown, mature woman capable of making her own decisions. You can ask her about yesterday. She'll tell you she's in love with me too."

"Not according to this note she left for you," Frank said. He handed Jake a folded piece of paper.

Jake struggled to get to his feet. Still groggy from the punch Frank gave him, he opened the paper and tried to focus on the blurred words. After a minute Jake's vision cleared enough to read the note.

"No, no," Jake said, shaken. "We love each other. She couldn't have written this. This ... this is not what happened. This is not what we had talked about."

Frank stood tall with his fists clinched and a defiant look on his face. Jake thought he was going to throw another punch, so he slowly backed up.

"Where is Jen?" Jake asked. "I want to talk to her."

"You won't be able to talk to her," Frank said. "She and Chris took off early this morning to Fort Laramie on business. They'll be gone for some time."

Jake just stood there leaning against a stall, still dazed by the punch. He was confused by the way Frank was acting but even more confused by what was said in the note from Jen.

"Frank, please listen," Jake said. "I want to explain—"

"You pack up your gear," Frank said, interrupting Jake. "And get off my ranch."

Jake noticed that Frank was wearing a revolver. He knew that Frank was drunk and had gone completely loco. Jake feared for his life. Not wanting to upset Frank anymore, he said he would leave.

After packing his gear, Jake wrote a letter to Jen, went to her room, and shoved it under her door. He went to the barn to get his saddle and bridle. He didn't see Frank but had the feeling of being watched. Jake carried his tack to a small, enclosed pasture where Snort was grazing. He whistled and called out to her. The mare pricked up her ears, gave a snort, and came trotting over to Jake.

"Good girl," Jake said to his horse. "Looks like you and me are hitting the trail."

Jake arrived in Laramie just as the noon eastbound Union Pacific train was pulling into the depot. It had only been two months since he had arrived in town. It crossed his mind that maybe he should take the train back to Connecticut. No, he was going to stay in Wyoming and find Jen, the girl he loved, and resolve the mystery of why Frank had turned on him. Riding down Grand Avenue, he stopped and dismounted in front of the sheriff's office. He tied his horse to the hitching rail and went inside the office. Deputy Luke was sitting at the desk. When he looked up, he was surprised to see Jake.

"Hi, Jake," Luke said. "What brings you to Laramie?"

"It's a long story," Jake said. "I want to talk to you and the sheriff."

"Well, I've got nothing but time," Luke said. "I was just going to get some lunch. Join me and I'll listen to your tale."

"I'll do that," Jake said. "I haven't had a bite today."

"I'll hang a sign on the door for Boz," Luke said. "He went to meet the train. I'll tell him we're at Claudia's."

The café was beginning to get the Sunday lunch crowd as Luke and Jake walked up to the door.

"Look at that," Jake said, pointing to a sign on the café's door. "That's just what I'm looking for—a place to rent."

The notice on the door said, "Room for Rent—Inquire in the Café."

"That's the room at the back of the café," Luke said. "Claudia rents that out. What do you need a room for? I thought you had one at the ranch."

"I'll tell you about it over lunch," Jake said. "I'll take the sign with me, before somebody beats me to the draw. Looks like Claudia's mighty busy right now, with this crowd, so I'll catch her later. `

"I noticed you're barely limping," Luke said. "That leg wound must have healed okay. Of course, with Jennie nursing it you're probably not in any pain—that is, except in your heart. I noticed you two have taken quite a shine to each other."

"I must admit you're right on that account," Jake said. "That's part of what I aim to tell you about."

They found a table, and Linda took their order for lunch. Jake started to unfold his story when Sheriff Boswell came into the café and headed for their table.

"Hang on, Jake," Luke said. "Here's Boz. He'll want to listen to what you have to say."

Jake began his story again, telling about his love for Jen and the encounter he had with Frank.

Luke and Boswell were amazed at Frank's attitude and actions.

"Maybe I should ride out that way and have a talk with Frank," the sheriff said.

"I could do that," Luke said. "I know him better than you do. Those two brothers, Frank and Chris, are sure opposites. Maybe Lys would like to go along to see Chris."

"No doubt she would," Jake said. "But wait a couple of days. Maybe Frank will cool down by then and Jen and Chris will be back from Fort Laramie."

"Okay," the sheriff agreed. "You go, Luke. Just be careful. Sounds like Frank went off the deep end."

Claudia approached their table with a pot of coffee.

"How's the coffee?" she asked. "Need a refill? Howdy, Boz, Luke, and … don't remember your friend's name, but howdy to you," she said as she began to refill their cups.

"Claudia, this is Jake Harding," Luke said. "He'd like to talk to you about renting the room."

"Is it still available?" Jake asked, showing her the "room for rent" sign.

"You bet it is," Claudia said. "It's always available to a young, good-looking feller like you."

"Watch out, Jake," Boz said. "Claudia's been known to turn a few gentlemen's heads in her day."

"Well, my day ain't over yet," Claudia said, "so you just watch it."

Old Boz laughed. "I always watch everything," he said. "That's what a sheriff does."

"You sure do," Claudia said. "Want to see the room, Jake?" She motioned to Jake to follow her.

"You go on," Luke said. "I'm buying you lunch."

"Much obliged," Jake said. "I'll get the next one."

"Put both these young colts' lunches on my bill," Boz said. "I've got to get back to the office."

"Thanks, Boz," Luke said. "Jake, we'll see you back at the sheriff's after you get that room rented."

The room that Jake rented from Claudia was just what he needed, and to his delight Claudia had a shelter and paddock in back of the café where he could keep his horse. She had an old sorrel mare of hers back there, and Snort could get along with most any other horse.

"Got me a good deal with Claudia's rental," Jake told Luke and Boz as he walked into the sheriff's office.

"Have a chair, Jake," the sheriff said. "I'd like to know more about what Frank Muller is up to and if there's anything we can do about it."

"Well, I know one thing, sheriff," Jake said. "Frank was drunk and wearing a sidearm, so I was a little worried about that. He told me if he saw me on his land, he would shoot me on sight."

"That's a serious threat," Boz said. "We'd better check on him before he does harm to someone. Luke, you'd better plan on a trip to the Muller ranch next week, maybe next Friday. That'll give Frank time to think things over, and hopefully Chris and Jen will be back."

"I'll go with you," Jake said, "but I'll keep out of sight until you find out what's happening."

"Okay by me," Luke said, "as long as Frank doesn't see you. I'll see if Lys wants to ride along."

"Be careful, you all," Boz said. "And if Lys goes with you, keep her out of sight too until you see what Frank is up to."

"Many thanks for your help, fellows," Jake said. "Right now I've got to get to the bank and then a jewelry store."

"Not planning on robbing them?" the sheriff said, laughing.

The next Thursday morning, just as the sun was breaking the horizon, Bella, following her usual routine, was on her way to the henhouse. She looked up and down the yard for Frank, wondering why he hadn't come into the kitchen for some breakfast or at least a cup of coffee. But it was no big concern as she knew he sometimes would take off early, doing whatever he did away from the ranch. Her big concern was how strange Frank had been acting the last few days. He had been drinking a lot and mumbling to himself. And when he told her that Jake had decided to leave, she couldn't believe it. When she asked him why, he just mumbled something about Jennie. Then he turned and walked away, leaving Bella wondering.

When Bella approached the henhouse, she heard Sunbird call

out to her. The Pawnee woman was in the pasture early trapping gophers. She proudly held up one of the bigger rodents she'd caught for Bella to see.

"Askuts!" Sunbird yelled in Pawnee. "Prairie dog," she added in English.

Bella nodded in recognition of Sunbird's kill. Suddenly, Bella heard a rifle shot. Her eyes caught a glimpse of a horse and rider silhouetted against the early rising sun. She shaded her eyes from the sun's rays as the rider approached the women. She recognized Frank on his mount riding in a zigzag pattern as if tracking something. When she looked closer, she saw that he was wearing his cavalry uniform and held a rifle in his right hand. He stopped suddenly and raised his rifle above his head.

"Troops halt!" he shouted. "Hostiles ahead! Prepare to fire!"

Sunbird saw Frank, and again she held up her prize dead gopher to show him, thinking that he too was hunting the varmints. She gave a little yell and spun around, doing a little dance. What Bella saw next was something she couldn't believe. Frank brought his rifle to his shoulder, sighted, and fired a shot at the Indian woman.

"Take this, you red savage!" Frank yelled.

The bullet slammed into the dirt about a yard from Sunbird, who was still dancing and did not notice the dust the bullet had kicked up. Then she heard the rifle report, and she turned and looked at Frank. Bella screamed. Frank slid from his saddle. Positioning himself on one knee, he sighted his rifle again and fired. This time, the bullet hit Sunbird in the abdomen, knocking her to the ground.

Red was just about to leave his cabin when he heard the first rifle shot. Preparing for any unknown conflict, he grabbed his bow and a quiver of arrows and ran toward the pasture. He slung the quiver of arrows over his back. He stopped by the corner of the barn, opened the barn door, and reached for the Spencer rifle—it wasn't there. A second shot rang out. He looked across the field to see Frank on horseback shooting at something. He saw Frank dismount, kneel, aim, and fire off a third round. Red realized the target was Sakuru Rikucki. He saw his wife grab her stomach as she fell backward to the ground. He rushed toward her, just reaching her as another bullet kicked up the dirt about a foot from him. Red grabbed his wife by the leg and pulled her behind a small mound of dirt and rocks that provided cover from the rifle shots. Sunbird was alive but in pain. Blood flowed from her wound as Red drew his knife and cut a couple of swathes from the shawl she was wearing. Packing the swathes over the wound, he tied the shawl tightly around his wife's midsection. The bleeding was already slowing as the blood began to coagulate, but she had lost a lot of blood.

A bullet ricocheted off a rock near Red and his wife. He peered out from around the mound and could see Frank aiming to take another shot. This time the bullet made a soft thud as it burrowed into the dirt embankment. Red shook his head in disbelief at Frank's actions. The Pawnee had only one choice—shoot Frank before he killed him and his wife. He knew Frank had the Spencer carbine that held seven rounds of ammunition. Red recalled the number of shots Frank had taken, and if he was right, he was at six. That meant he had one bullet left before he had to reload. Red strung his bow, pulled an arrow from his quiver, and tested the pull of his bow. He was ready to charge as soon as Frank spent his seventh shot. Red stood up at the other end of his dirt fort and shouted at Frank, and then he ducked down quickly as he saw a puff of dust fly up behind him and heard the rifle report—the seventh shot. Red jumped over the embankment and ran toward Frank, screaming a bloodcurdling war cry. Frank looked up from his fumbling to reload and saw the Indian rushing toward him. Frank pulled his revolver from its holster. Red suddenly stopped, nocked the arrow to his bowstring, pulled it back, and let it fly to its mark. At that same moment, Frank fired his revolver. The last thing Frank saw was the livid and questioning look in the Pawnee's eyes. Red's arrow pieced Frank's heart. At the same time, Red felt the sting of Frank's shot as the bullet hit his upper left arm. He dropped his bow, sank to his knees, and fell forward.

Bella, who had been hiding behind a tree witnessing this shocking scene, ran sobbing toward the wounded Pawnee woman. Bella was reciting a prayer when she reached Sunbird. She bent down and cradled her in her arms. Sunbird said something in Pawnee as she took her last breath. Bella yelled at Red for help, but he didn't answer. She called for Frank—no answer. Only the whispering of the sultriness of a Wyoming summer wind could be heard. The silence was broken by loud cries from Red: "Sakuru Rikucki! Sakuru Rikucki!"

About half a mile from the Muller Ranch, Chris and Jen were leisurely heading home. They'd had a long ride after herding twenty horses over to Fort Laramie on the Platte River. They had delivered horses Frank had sold to the army.

"It'll be good to get back home," Jen said. "I'm going to take me a long soak in a hot bath. But first I plan on having a talk with Frank and find out what his problem is. He's been drinking a lot of late and mumbling to himself."

"Yeah," Chris said. "He got on my butt about not wearing a hat when I was out mending a fence last week. Jeez, you'd have thought Sergeant Muller was disciplining one of his horse soldiers."

"Bella was in tears one day over something Frank had said to her," Jen said. "She wouldn't say what it was about."

"Red had a run-in with him too," Chris said.

"Our brother definitely needs our help," Jen said. "First thing we got to do is get him off the whiskey—"

"Whoa! You hear that?" Chris asked, interrupting Jen.

"Sounded like a rifle shot," Jen said. "There's another one."

"Coming from the ranch," Chris said. "Let's ride!"

Jake, Lys, and Luke left Laramie early that Friday headed for the Muller Ranch. The sun illuminated and warmed the frosty tops of buildings as Laramie began to stir with the activity of a new day. The crisp air was refreshing as the three of them rode along a dusty trail that was painted with a palette of autumn colors. Luke and Lys wanted to know more about Jake's fascination with fossils and why he had decided to move from Connecticut to Wyoming.

Jake told them of his grandfather, who had taught him about horses and passed on his love of nature. He also talked about going to Yale to study geology, meeting Professor Marsh, and becoming interested in paleontology. The study of the evolution of life forms found in fossils from when the earth began to support life, about three billion years ago, fascinated Jake to almost an obsessive level. Those fossils that traced the history of life on earth became more meaningful to him than any treasure sought by man. He explained his apprenticeship with Professor Marsh doing restoration and cataloging of fossils. But working in a lab with found fossils only satisfied part of Jake's passion. He had a need to be in the field experiencing the thrill of finding these buried treasures himself.

The three-hour ride went by quickly as their conversation shifted from Jake's love for the frontier, its natural beauty, the freedom to explore the fossil beds, and his newfound love for Jennie and the strange behavior Frank Muller had displayed.

They stopped about a hundred yards from the Muller Ranch, and Luke told Lys and Jake to wait in a small wooded area until he signaled that it was okay to approach the ranch.

Luke rode up to the veranda in front of the house and announced his presence. The front door slowly opened, and Chris appeared in the doorway.

"Luke, I'm sure glad to see you," he said. "I was about to ride into Laramie to see you."

"Well, I saved you a trip," Luke said. "Is everything all right?"

"No," Chris said, his voice cracking as he shook his head. "Frank and Sunbird are dead," he said with a sigh. "And Red's been shot."

"What?" Luke asked, surprised. "How'd it happen?"

"Come in," Chris said. "We'll tell you all about it."

"I've got Lys and Jake with me," Luke said. "I'll signal them to come ahead."

Luke gave a loud whistle and motioned for Jake and Lys to come on. They rode up to the house. The three of them dismounted, tied off their horses, and went inside.

Chris ushered the three visitors into the dining room. The long dining table was lit by a dozen candles. The large family Bible was open at the head of the table where Bella sat reading. Jen sat to her right, tears streaming down her face. The empty chair to Bella's left was where Chris had been sitting. Red, with his left arm bandaged and in a sling, was sitting in the chair next to that. Chris took his chair and motioned to Luke, Lys, and Jake to be seated at the table.

"This morning we buried Frank and Sunbird on Elk Hill, where our family and friends rest for eternity," Chris said. He then gave an account of how they had been killed. Trying to justify his brother's actions, he told what he knew of Frank's depression, partly caused by his horrifying experiences fighting as a cavalry trooper.

Bella filled in the details of what she had seen of Frank's behavior. Red, with his left arm in a sling, raised his right arm and patted his forehead, saying something in Pawnee.

"Frank *pa'ksu' kuutik yadacka*," Red said, making a circular sign above his head.

"Red says Frank's head was filled with evil spirits," Chris said.

"Frank seemed to be in some despondency when I was with him at Fort McPherson," Jake said. "He talked a little bit about the gruesome killings he'd experienced in Indian battles. I believe he may have been suffering from 'soldier's heart,' a desperate condition that a number of Civil War veterans suffered from. My granddad had counseled a number of those soldiers."

"You may be right about that," Chris said. "Frank surely was a changed man when he came home from the army."

"Bella called us together to have a memorial service for Frank and Sunbird," Jen said.

"First off, I have something to say to Jen and Jake," Bella said. "I found an envelope in Frank's room. It's addressed to Jennie from Jake. Please, Jen, if you would read it. It is personal so just read it to yourself."

Jen took the envelope and read the message. Jake took the note from his pocket that Frank had given him, supposedly written by Jen, and handed it to her. She in turn handed Jake the note she'd just read. Jake jumped up from his chair and ran to Jen. She pushed her chair back, threw her arms around him, and gave him a kiss.

Jake dropped to one knee. "Will you marry me?" he said as he pulled a ring from his pocket and held it out to her.

"Oh, yes—yes!" she exclaimed, hugging and kissing him.

Everyone congratulated them.

"Thank you, Aunt Bella, for finding that note," Jen said. "This is a bittersweet occasion. How could Frank do such a horrible thing? He was really sick."

"Now, I have a story to tell all of you," Bella said. "I had been instructed by the will of my late brother-in-law, Walter Muller, to tell the truths about this family. Walt said I would know when the time was right to speak to all of you. I believe that time is now."

Bella began telling about a hot summer day in August of 1832 when Walt, his wife Mary, and she were rounding up some strays along a fast-flowing stream by a place they called Cottonwood Grove. They saw a wisp of smoke curl upward and then spread and disappear into the clear blue sky. Thinking it may be someone camping near the grove, they rode over to take a look. When they got closer, they could see it was the smoldering remains of a burnt-out wagon. As they approached the charred wagon, they made a gruesome discovery. There they came upon two mutilated bodies with Cheyenne arrows piercing them. The bodies were so disfigured that at first it was hard to tell their gender. The body nearest the wagon was a male, and the one a little farther away toward the creek was a female. Walt poured water from his canteen on the remaining fire and refilled his canteen at the creek to finish putting out the embers. They shifted through the charred remains looking for some identification of the unfortunate travelers. There were no clues. Everything had been either consumed by the fire or taken by the attacking Indians. Walt used a broken tree branch as a shovel and began to scrape out a shallow grave while Mary and Bella gathered rocks to place on top. As Mary was gathering rocks near the creek, she heard a noise in a patch of bushes. It sounded like an animal whining. Mary always wore a revolver when riding the range, so she drew her weapon and approached the bushes. To her surprise, it was the cry of a baby. When she saw the little bundle in the thicket, she picked it up and cradled it in her arms. She removed the blue shawl it was wrapped in and found a baby boy of about three months old. Walt, Mary, and Bella concluded that the Indians had attacked the wagon the evening before and the mother had hidden the child in the bushes while she went to help her husband defend the wagon. They buried the child's parents in a shadow grave and covered it with stones. Every year on that date, they piled new stones on the grave.

They never could determine the identity of the child's parents. Mary and Walt had decided, and were delighted, to adopt the little boy. They gave him the name Frank, who grew up never knowing he was adopted. He was accepted as a Muller. Walt and Mary loved him dearly. He was somewhat of a rebellious child, but Walt always seemed to be able to handle him. One day, when Frank was about seventeen, he, Walt, and Mary got into a heated argument, and the next morning Frank had left. No one knew where he had gone. He was gone for about a year, and then one day he just showed up, apologized for his behavior, and said he wanted to come home. Walt and Mary were always the forgiving kind and were happy to have him back. Chris was only about four at this time. He looked up to Frank and followed him all over the ranch like a little colt. Frank took a liking to Chris and would tolerate his childish shenanigans.

"So, you see," Bella said, "Frank was an *adopted* Muller."

"I had no idea," Chris said. "Why didn't pa tell us?"

"I don't know, Chris," Bella said. "I know he planned to tell all you when the time was right, which is right now. He left a letter for you, Jennie, and Frank. You two can read it after I tell you the rest of the story." She took a letter from the Bible and laid it on the table in front of her.

Bella continued on with her saga, telling about the day a carriage, with a handsome young man driving and a beautiful young woman holding a baby, arrived at the ranch. Walt went out to greet them. The woman asked if this was the Muller Ranch, to which Walt replied that it was. The woman said she was here to see Frank Muller. Frank stepped out onto the veranda, looked at the woman, and addressed her in a chiding voice, asking what the hell she wanted. She told him she had a present for him. The driver jumped down from the wagon and helped the woman with the baby to the ground. She held the baby out to Frank and said that the little girl was his.

"Bullshit," Frank told her. "She ain't mine. She's yours, and probably his," he said, pointing to the young man.

The man denied the accusation and told the woman to leave the child and get back in the wagon. The woman handed the baby girl to Walt.

"Here, you take her, Grandpa," she said.

She boarded the carriage. The driver smacked the reins on the back of the horse, and they careered down the road.

Frank neither denied nor confirmed to Walt and Mary that the baby girl was his daughter, but they knew. For the second time, Walt and Mary adopted a baby. They named the beautiful baby girl Jennifer.

"Oh—oh," Jen sighed. "Is this true, Aunt Bella?"

"It most certainly is, my dear," Bella said. "You see, Jen, Frank was really your father, not your brother. Here is the letter that Walt, your adoptive father, wrote to you, Chris, and Frank. It tells the whole story."

Chris got up from his chair, turned to Bella, gave her a hug, and picked up the letter. Then he went to Jennie and put his arms around her.

"No matter what, Jennie," he whispered in her ear, "nothing can change that you are my adorable, loving sister."

17

That fall of 1871, the disposition of everyone at the Muller Ranch was as dismal as the weather. An early cold spell and snow in October made the fall roundup grueling work, and the tragic events of September had left the ranch residents with a depressing perspective. These people were of pioneer stock and no strangers to harsh conditions physically or emotionally. They made an effort to find a better life and abide their sorrow with courage and dignity.

Jake had again taken up residence at the Muller Ranch. Luke had resigned from his deputy sheriff duties and had moved to the ranch to work with Chris, Jen, and Jake. He now occupied the cabin that Red and his wife had lived in. Red had chosen to live in the bunkhouse after his wife was killed.

"There's riders' coming," Chris said as he entered the house stomping snow from his boots and slapping snowflakes off his jacket with his hat. Brushing the snow and ice from his recently grown beard, he reached for the binoculars hanging by the window.

"Whoever's coming, they're lucky to be traveling between snowstorms," Jen said as she peered through the frosty windowpane.

Chris held the glasses against the window, looking through the lightly falling snow.

"What'd you see out there?" Jake asked as he entered the room.

"Trying to make out who's riding up to the house," Chris said. "Well, I'll be. It looks like Sheriff Boz, Lys, and some another fella."

Shortly, the three riders dismounted in front of the veranda and tied off their horses. Chris opened the door to welcome them in.

"Nice day for a ride," Chris said, smiling at his little bit of sarcasm.

"Was a nice day when we left Laramie," Lys said.

"Well, you all beat the biggest part of this snow yet to come," Chris said. "Good to see all you. Come in and get warm. Don't worry about your horses. Luke and I will take care of them."

"Much appreciated," the sheriff said, brushing snow from his beard and shoulders. "I'd like you to meet my new deputy. Hal Monroe, this is Chris Muller. Hal was a lawman down Texas way."

"Howdy," Hal said.

"And who's this fine-looking little filly with you guys?" Chris asked, looking and smiling at Lys.

"I ain't so little, and I'm not a filly, you big hairy grizzly," Lys said.

Chris threw his arms around Lys, picked her up, swung her around, and dumped her in a pile of snow.

"Sure good to see you, hon," Chris said.

"Good to see you too," Lys said, laughing. "I missed you. Here, this is for you." She scooped up a handful of snow and rubbed it in his beard.

Chris laughed, grabbed Lys, and gave her cheeks a rub of his whiskers.

"Okay, children are we going to stand out here horsing around in the snow," Boz asked, "or are we going in the house to get warm?"

"You're all invited in," Jen said. She and Jake stood in the doorway motioning to everyone to come in. "All of you get in here before you let all the warm air out and the cold air in."

Boz introduced his new deputy to Jen, Jake, and Bella.

"Haven't we met someplace before?" Jen asked Hal.

"Don't think so," he answered.

"Where's Luke?" Lys asked.

"He's down at the barn," Chris said. "I'll take your horses there, and we'll tend to them. Luke will be happy to know you have come to visit."

"Tell him I brought the Laramie *Sentinel* and some mail," Lys said. "Here's three letters for you, Jake. You're a popular guy."

Jen chuckled. "Probably from old girlfriends," she said.

"Never had any 'old' girlfriends, they were all young gals," Jake said as he smiled at Jen and dodged a kick in the shin from her.

"One letter from Professor Marsh, one from my friend Dan Randall, and one from my lawyer," Jake said. "Darn, not one letter from my girlfriends." He dodged another kick from Jen. "Chris, can I give you and Luke a hand with the horses?"

"Nah, we can manage okay," Chris said. "You entertain Boz and Hal. Bet they'd like to see the fossils you and Jen have collected."

Jake was more than happy to share his knowledge of fossils with whomever would listen. He showed Boz and Hal to the room where the fossils were stored while Lys and Jen went to help Bella in the kitchen.

"Oh, jeez, look at all those old bones!" Hal exclaimed as he entered the room. Three large tables were crowded with fossils still encased in the clay and stone they had been found in, and four rows of shelving that ran the length of the far wall displayed cleaned fossils. Pinned on the walls were Jake's drawings of fossils.

"Old is right," Jake said. "They're millions of years old."

"How'd you know that?" Hal asked.

"Well, they're from a geologic period in the history of the earth called the Tertiary Period," Jake explained. "In 1830 Charles Lyell, a geologist, wrote a book about the research he did on formations of the strata of the earth. He had found that these were formed over very long periods of time and each contained traces of life from that period—fossilized remains. The long periods of time would have been millions of years, thus making the earth much older than six thousand years, as previously thought by some. The earth's exact age is only an educated guess, and the fossils we find are classified by periods from the latest to the earliest. We do know we're looking at millions of years for some of the earliest geologic periods. Maybe someday in the future, someone will find a system whereby we'll be able to accurately date the fossil record of earth's evolution of living things and its changes in environments."

Hal clicked his tongue and shook his head. "Well, that is interesting speculation," he said.

"Oh, it's more than speculation," Jake said. "The fossils are proof and a clue to the changes that took place in the formation of the earth."

"So these bones that you've found are from animals that died millions of years ago?" Sheriff Boz asked.

"Yes," Jake said. "But actually they are no longer bones. They have been turned to stone, preserved by a process of mineralization. When they were buried, if the burial site had the right conditions, a slow process of filling pores and voids began, replacing parts with different minerals. This took place over millions of years, and over time the replaced parts hardened, turning them to stone."

Hal chuckled. "I'll be danged if that isn't the most interesting tale I've ever heard," he said. "It seems like there are a whole lots of *if*s, *but*s, and *maybe*s going on in that tale."

"You know," Boz said, "it seems like doing some ingenious detective work to figure out a crime by gathering the evidence to tell the story of what happened."

"You're exactly right," Jake said. "It is detective work."

"Well, detective," Boz said, "let's look at the clues you've found."

Jake walked over to the shelving at the far wall and carefully removed a small fossil skull that was missing its lower mandible. Jake reached down to a lower shelf and retrieved a jawbone.

"This skull and this mandible are from two different animals but of the same species," Jake explained.

"Is it some kind of dog?" Hal asked.

"No," Jake said. "This animal was about the size of a dog, but it's the skull of a prehistoric horse."

"Jeez, that's a tiny foal," Hal said.

"Well, actually, no," Jake said. "It's a skull from a full-grown horse, a fossil that Professor Marsh calls *Eohippus,* a Greek word meaning 'dawn horse.'"

"Who's this Professor Marsh to say that it's the skull of an ancient horse?" Hal asked.

"He's a paleontologist from Yale," Jake said. "He's doing extensive research on the evolution of horses and a number of other species of animals by examining their fossil remains."

"If horses were as small as you say, then what did people ride?" Hal asked.

"At this time in the evolution of our planet, there were no human beings," Jake said. "We didn't appear until millions of years later."

"How can you know that?" Hal asked derisively.

"The fossil record shows us that," Jake said.

"By God, that's some kind of record—written in stone," Hal said sarcastically.

Boz, listening to this bandying of words, reached for the fossil Jake was holding. Jake handed Boz the Eohippus skull.

"Jake, I understand you studied at Yale College with Professor Marsh," Boz said matter-of-factly as he inspected the fossil skull.

"Well, I'll be damned," Hal said. "You went to Yale?"

"That's right," Jake said. "I didn't finish my course because I had a hankerin' to go hunting fossils after I went out west working with Professor Marsh on a fossil-finding expedition. I found the Western frontier fascinating and moved here. Hunting for fossils is engaging work as I find myself in touch with nature and the history of our planet."

"How'd you end up on this ranch?" Hal asked.

"Ah," Jake said. "That's a long story, but the short of it is that I know a lot about horses, taught to me by my granddad, and I was offered a job here. I work part-time at the ranch and am part-time employed by Professor Marsh to hunt fossils."

"So you're rounding up the ranch's horses *and* prehistoric horses?" Boz said with a grin.

"Yeah, you might say that," Jake replied.

"And," Boz added, "Jake has lassoed himself a pretty little filly. You see, he's engaged to Miss Jennifer Muller."

"Yep," Jake said as a big smile lit up his face.

"When's the wedding?" Boz asked.

"You'll find out later today," Jake said and left it at that.

Jen interrupted their conversation when she started banging on the dinner gong hard and fast as if it were a fire alarm.

"Well, gents," Jake said, "it's time for supper. You're in for a real treat. Bella and the girls can cook up some good chow."

While they filed out of the room, Chris and Luke came in the front door.

"We got your horses taken care of," Chris said to Boz and Hal. He introduced Luke to Hal and then showed them where to wash up before supper.

"I'll be with you guys in just a minute," Jake said. "I want to take a quick look at my mail."

The promise of a great feast was more than fulfilled. When everyone had been seated at the table, Chris and Jen filled everyone's glasses with wine.

"We have two toasts to make," Chris said. "Stand and raise your glasses."

All eight diners pushed back their chairs, stood, and raised their glasses in acknowledgment.

"The first toast goes to the beautiful lady at my right," Chris said as he turned and looked at Alyssa. "I have asked Alyssa to marry me, and she said yes, a toast to my fiancée, Lys. I love you very much—prosit!"

"Thank you all, my dear friends," Lys said. "And thank you, Chris, my dear husband-to-be. I love you dearly."

Again a cheer went up, and Chris held up his hand for silence.

"I'll ask Jake to give the next toast," Chris said.

Jake raised his glass. "President Grant has proclaimed that this year, Thanksgiving will be observed on Thursday the thirtieth of November," he said. "Chris and Alyssa and Jennifer and I have a proclamation of our own. We declare that on the day of Thanksgiving 1871, we shall have our wedding ceremonies."

Everyone gave a loud cheer and raised their glasses.

"A toast to the coming marriages of Lys and Chris and Jen and Jake," Luke said.

Everyone drank to the toast. Jake gave Jen a big hug and pulled out the chair next to him for her. Aunt Bella clinked a spoon against her glass and motioned for everyone to be seated.

"Let's eat before the food gets cold," she said. "And we'll give thanks for the good news we have just received. It's about time we let our spirits lighten with the promise of enjoyable new beginnings. Now pass the whatchamacallit." She gestured and pointed to the potatoes.

The supper had all the semblance of a festive occasion. Everyone seemed to enjoy the food and conversation, and although Jake had the appearance of being a part of the festive occasion, his thoughts were on other matters. Jen, sensing his indifference, leaned over to him, gave him a kiss on the cheek, and whispered in his ear.

"What's troubling you honey?" she asked.

"I'll tell you later," Jake replied.

After drinks were served, the conversations were filled with factual and fictional anecdotes about the weather, politics, and ranching. The latest news in the Laramie *Sentinel* was a welcome bit of information for the isolated ranchers. Boz had a long talk with Chris, Jen, and Bella about the shooting that had happened between Frank and Red. Boz said that he and Hal would be heading out early in the morning now that the snow had let up.

"Help me out in the kitchen, dear," Jen said. She motioned for Jake to follow her.

"What do you need?" Jake asked as they entered the kitchen.

"I need you to tell me what's troubling you," Jen said impatiently.

"Just hold your horses," Jake said. "I was getting around to that. I'm troubled by two things."

"About me," Jen asked.

"Oh, no," Jake said. "It's about that Deputy Hal and about the letter I received from Marsh. There's something about that guy I don't like. And Marsh's letter was a little disturbing."

"Well, I wouldn't trust that deputy any farther than I could throw him," Jen said. "There's something about him that's suspicious. But I guess I'm wary of most people I've just met."

"Yeah, I remember," Jake said, chortling.

"What about the letter?" Jen asked.

"Marsh wants me to do more than just search for fossils," Jake sighed. "He thinks I would be in a good position to do some spying on Edward Cope's fossil expeditions and then report on where and how successful those fossil sites were."

"So what do you plan on doing?" Jen ask.

"For now, I'm going to keep my eyes and ears open to both troubling matters," Jake said.

"I'm not the only one with suspicions, huh?" Jen said.

"Well, it's not all depressing news," Jake said. "My friend Dan in Philadelphia just got married to a girl named Aaliyah, and they may make a trip out west next summer."

"That's wonderful," Jen said. "When you write them, make sure you tell them we'd love to have them stay at the ranch."

The next morning, Sheriff Boswell and his new deputy, Hal Monroe, got saddled up and ready to leave. Chris and Luke were on hand to see them off. Chris asked the sheriff if he would place an announcement in the Laramie *Sentinel* regarding the upcoming marriages and handed him a paper with the particulars written on it, along with some mail to be posted. Boz thanked them for their hospitality, and he and the deputy started down the road.

The new-fallen snow crunched under the horses' hooves. Puffs of breath streamed from the men and the horses and evaporated into the cold, clear blue sky. The sun lit up the snow as though it had been sprinkled with diamonds.

Luke called out to Boz, "Have a safe trip!" Then he added, "Watch your backside."

"Always do," Boz said. He gave Luke and Chris a wave good-bye.

The two men rode side by side for about a mile, neither one saying a word. Boz slowed the pace and then stopped, pulled down the collar on his heavy bearskin fur coat, and removed his sheepskin gloves. Reaching into his coat's deep right-hand pocket, he pulled out a plug of Workman's chewing tobacco. Biting off a large chunk, he began to work it between his tongue and cheek.

"You care for a chaw, Hal?"

"Nah, don't use the stuff," the deputy said.

Boswell thrust the tobacco back in his pocket. He shoved his other hand deep in the other pocket, keeping both hands buried in the thick bearskin fur.

"These pockets keep my hands a far sight warmer than my gloves," he said. "But I guess I can't ride without using my hands, so we'll rest a spell. I got me a couple of questions to ask you, Hal."

"Yeah?" Hal said. "What would that be?"

"First off," Boz said, "what'd you think of our hosts at the Muller Ranch?"

"Oh, I don't know. Thought they were kind of highfalutin," Hal said. "I think that Jake fella is full of bullshit."

"Second off," Boz said, "I was wondering what your real name is."

"You were?" Hal said. He undid the last button on his overcoat and quickly drew his revolver from its holster. "Keep your hands well buried in those pockets, sheriff. The first move toward your gun and you're a dead man."

"Hell, I figured as much," the sheriff said, anger flashing in his eyes.

"To answer your second question," Hal said, full of cockiness, "my last name is Jackson."

"I see," Boz said. "Are you any kin to Harry Jackson, over Cheyenne way?"

"You bet," Hal said. "He's my brother."

"Kind of figured that too," Boz said. "How's old Harry doing?"

"Not bad now," Hal said. "He had a lot of pain for a while, being crippled up like he was with a shattered knee that Muller bitch put a bullet into."

"Well, that's a real shame," Boz said as he spat a big glob of tobacco into a snowdrift. "And I suppose you're the man to give retribution to that situation?"

"Well, ain't you the smart one, sheriff?" Hal said. "Harry is paying me mighty pretty to take care of the situation. You, Chris, and Jen are on my list of targets, and I'll take out that Jake guy and Luke for good measure."

"You're mighty ambitious for one gun," Boz said, fidgeting in his saddle.

"Oh, I have a plan—a good one," Hal said. "I have a record of many kills of men better than you. First, I want you to put your two hands on the pommel. Dismount while keeping your hands on the saddle, and then with your left hand unbuckle your gun belt and let it drop. You and I are going to take a little walk in the woods."

"You're the boss," Boz said as he placed his left hand on the saddle horn, turned to the right, and faced Hal. The sheriff made a move as if to dismount. Suddenly, a loud gunshot rang out as his right hand pulled the trigger of the revolver hidden in his coat pocket. The gunshot tore a hole in his coat and sent a bullet into Hal's chest.

Hal's horse reared up, sending Hal tumbling to his death in the snow. Oozing blood began to color the snow crimson.

So much for your plans, Boz thought. *I too have a plan and a record of many kills of men worse than you.*

"Hey, sheriff," Luke called out as he came galloping up the road. "You okay, Boz?"

"Yeah, just shooting a varmint," Boz said as he spat another large glob of tobacco into the blood stain on the front of Hal's coat.

Another horse and rider came galloping down the road.

"You guys okay?" Chris shouted.

"We're fine. It was like Boz suspected," Luke said. "Hal wasn't who he said he was."

"I'm glad we had that little talk last night," Boz said to Chris. "Jennie was right. There was something suspicious about Hal."

"You shot him?" Chris asked.

"Had to," Boz said. "He pulled a gun on me. Told me he was Hal Jackson, brother of Harry Jackson, and he was sent here to kill Jennie, you, and me."

"Thanks, sheriff," Chris said. "You blew a hole in his plans and him."

"What kind of cannon did you shoot him with?" Luke asked. "You sure blew a hole in him."

"Yeah, that's my new Smith and Wesson American .44," Boz said. "That revolver sure packs a wallop, especially at close range. Sure did rip a hole in my coat."

"We'll give you a hand tying his body on his horse," Luke said. "I'll ride on down to Laramie with you. I need to pick up a few supplies."

Boz laughed. "And I suppose you'll need to get a cup of coffee from Linda at Claudia's," he said.

"You know, I might just do that," Luke said, chortling.

"I'll head back to the ranch and tell everyone what happened here," Chris said. "You two take care."

"Okay, Chris," Boz said. "Come on, Luke. Let's round up Hal's horse. She bolted when I fired. By the way, there's a deputy sheriff's job open. You interested?"

"Nope," Luke said. "Had my fill of being a lawman, going to try ranching."

"Me too, one of these days," Boz said. "My brother's been after me to do that."

18

The Thanksgiving weddings were festive and beautiful events. Jen's wedding present to Jake was a Stetson hat called Boss of the Plains. Jake's present to Jen was a silver brooch in the shape of a horseshoe with a butterfly.

"I shall forever wear this beautiful brooch," Jen said, thanking Jake.

"And I shall forever wear this handsome hat," Jake said, thanking Jen.

Following Thanksgiving, everyone settled in for the winter months. Those four months slid by fast via cold and snowy scenes and planning for the spring activities. The spring of 1872 at the Muller Ranch was a welcome and busy time of the year. In late May, the skies were scattered with threating rain clouds forming in the west. A cool northwestern front was blowing the low clouds like schooners across a bay.

About a half mile from the main ranch house, Chris was building a house for Lys and himself. While Jake and Luke were busy using bucksaws and drawknives to prepare log planks for the house, Chris, Lys, and Jen were nailing in floor supports. Two young cowboys, Jim and Tom Collins, whom Chris had hired a few weeks earlier, rode up to the house construction site.

"How'd the roundup of strays go?" Chris called out.

"Real good, Mr. Muller," Tom said. "We've got seven more horses in the far corral over by the barn. That makes eighteen in all in that paddock."

"Great," Chris replied. "We're about to take a break here before that rain storm hits. You two want to join us for lunch and a coffee?"

"Yes, sir, we'd be pleased to do so, Mr. Muller," Jim said.

"Okay," Chris said. "Come on up to the house, and I'll get Bella to get some coffee and lunch for us."

After lunch Jake sat by the living room window watching the downpour turn roads, corrals, and the yard into a muddy mixture of puddles and rivulets of floating debris. He held a coffee mug in both hands as a wisp of steam floated up, warming his face and bringing a pleasant aroma to his nose. He was deep in thought. He contemplated what this deluge was doing to erode the land and expose treasures of fossils beneath the topsoil. His penchant for fossil hunting was always shadowing his thoughts. He was happy being at the ranch and being with his newfound love. But he was beginning to feel like a corralled mustang yearning for the wide-open plains. The long winter had kept him housebound except for the chores caring for livestock. The spring rains had flooded his thoughts with visions of fossil hunting. He pondered over the letter that Professor Marsh had written him about a visit this summer. His concentration was interrupted by Jen's voice.

"My, such a solemn face," Jen said as she approached Jake carrying a plate of steaming baked goods. "Aunt Bella just made a new batch of biscuits. I thought you'd like a hot one with some strawberry preserves."

"You read my thoughts, sweetheart," Jake said.

"No, not all of them," Jen said. "Particularly when you're deep in thought as you were just now. Is something wrong?"

"Wrong?" Jake asked. "Nothing is wrong. I was just daydreaming."

"Uh-huh," Jen said. "Tell me if I'm right in guessing what you were daydreaming about."

"All right," Jake said. "First, let me have a biscuit." He paused, set his coffee down, and turned in his chair. "Wait, first a kiss, and then a biscuit."

"I'll give you the biscuit," Jen said, chuckling. "Later."

"You are hilarious," Jake said.

Jen bent down, gave him a kiss, and dropped a hot biscuit in his lap.

"Wow, that's almost as hot as having you sit in my lap," Jake said.

"So, you're also hilarious," Jen said. "I do have a suspicion as to what you were thinking about."

"Yeah, what do you think?" Jake asked.

"I think you were daydreaming about exploring for fossils and wondering if this rain had exposed some for the picking," Jen said.

"You are absolutely right," Jake said. "Marsh will be here later this summer, and I would like to have some new fossils for him."

"I'm sure he would appreciate that," Jen said. "And I'd like to meet this professor who has you under his spell."

"I'm not under his spell," Jake said sharply.

"I was just joshing you," Jen said. "I know you're not. But you do have a preoccupation with fossils."

"There's no denying," Jake said. "I do have a fascination with fossils, but I wouldn't call it a preoccupation. There are a number of things I find interesting in life—the beauty of nature here in the West, the love I have for horses, and of course, not least of all, the love I have for you."

Jen went to the window. Looking out through the rain-streaked glass pane, the sheets of falling rain were almost horizontal as they were being blown by a fierce northwestern wind. Tears formed in her eyes, and the wet drops streaked their way down her cheeks. Jake stood up, walked up behind her, and hugged her while whispering in her ear.

"I love you, Jen," he said. "Tell me what's made you so sad that your eyes look like this windowpane."

She turned in his arms, giving him one of her charismatic smiles, and then she clung to his body sobbing. This was a side of Jen that Jake had never seen.

"Oh, hon," she sighed. "They're tears of sorrow and of joy. My life has been changed so much in the past year. The sudden truth about my past hit me like a mule kick. For a while it hurt too much for me to accept, but I do now. I do because I found my joy in life when I met you."

"Then let the joy in your life push out the hurt," Jake said tenderly. "I am here for you."

"I know," Jen said. "You are the kindest man I know. I didn't mean to upset you with my childish carrying on. I can blame part of my distraught outburst on this damn thunderstorm. Ever since I was a child, whenever it would rain I would feel depressed, but with you holding me I feel comforted."

"Just think of the good that the rain will bring," Jake said.

They stood in silence holding each other, transfixed by the sights and sounds of the raging storm outside their window—two lovers lost in their thoughts.

Jake assumed that rain storms like this had been going on for millions of years, molding the landscape. Earthquakes, volcanic action, freezing, thawing, and other traumatic geological events have revealed hidden secrets of the evolution of earth and life on it by exposing fossils buried for millions of eons. Jake felt he had stepped back in time whenever he uncovered a fossil and held it in his hand. In his mind's eye, he could re-create the prehistoric world as though he were eternal. He thought about the conversations he'd had with Professor Marsh regarding evolution and the study of geology and paleontology. Jake's thirst for knowledge about the changes that organisms have gone through in the history of this planet was dominant in his quest for understanding his reason for being. His experience in the physical activity of finding a fossil was transcendental, beyond his comprehension. He chuckled to himself, thinking, *Gold fever has no stronger hold over a prospector than fossil fever has over me.*

Two days later, everyone at the Muller Ranch was still cleaning up debris left from the destructive storm. A huge cottonwood tree had been blown over, and the two Collins brothers and Red were chopping and sawing the large branches into sizable logs for building and kindling. Luckily, the tree had just missed the hog pens and the chicken coop and had only brought down part of a fence. Luke, Chris, and Jake were digging trenches to divert water from the barnyard and the barn, which had been deluged with water; the yard looked like a shallow pond. While Lys and Jen were shoveling and sweeping mud from the stone pathway, Bella was mumbling a string of Italian curses as she tried to reclaim some of her newly planted garden that had been washed out.

Chris, always the optimist, approached the ladies with a smile on his face.

"I've heard mud baths are good for your skin," he said. "Anyone want one?"

"Don't you dare, Chris," Lys said. "Not unless you want to eat mud pie."

"Speaking of eating," Chris said, "isn't it about time for lunch? I'm hungry."

"You're always hungry," Lys said. "Just as soon as we wash off this mud, we're going to cook up some omelets. Bella gathered a whole batch of fresh eggs."

The ladies scrambled some eggs for omelets and sliced ham while the guys moved a couple of tables together on the veranda. Everyone enjoyed their lunch outdoors under sunny skies that had replaced the rain clouds.

"I hope this weather holds," Chris said. "I want to get the house finished before too long."

"I'll help you all I can," Luke said. "Just show me which board to nail down where, and I'll do it."

"We'll all help with the house," Jen said, "except that Jake and I will be gone for a couple of days this weekend. We'll be hunting fossils that the rains may have exposed."

"What?" Jake said. "I never said anything about going fossil hunting, let alone taking you with me."

"I know," she said. "I just know what you're thinking. You've been champing at the bit to go fossil hunting since the storm hit."

"Oh, my God," Jake sighed. "She can read my mind. I'm in trouble now. But she's right—I have a need to do some fossil exploration."

"Be careful what you think, darling," Jen said with a smirk. "You are in trouble unless you take me with you."

"Do I have a choice?" Jake asked.

"No," Jen said.

"I'd like to go with you," Chris said, "but I've got to keep at building this house."

"You're damn right," Lys interjected, "or you'll be in a lot of trouble."

"I don't want you two going fossil hunting alone," Chris said. "It's too dangerous. I think Red should go with you."

"Me love to go hunting with you," Red said as he shouted the Pawnee word for bones. "*Kiisu!* Old bones, new bones. Me hunt bones, sometime."

A day later, Jake, Jen, and Red rode their horses past the familiar fossil site where they had been ambushed by the three bandits a year earlier. Red was leading a pack mule named Mulo loaded with their camping supplies and digging tools. Jen told Jake that Bella had named the mule Mulo, the Italian word for "mule."

"This place brings back bad memories," Jen said.

"But also a new beginning for you and me," Jake said. "Red, you saved our hides that day."

"I found great joy in shooting bad men," Red said. "Sometime."

"And thank you, Jen, for nursing my wound," Jake said.

"It was my pleasure," she replied.

"How much farther is the fossil site?" Jake asked.

"We'll be there in less than an hour," Jen said. "We'll follow this ravine a little ways to where a stream meets up with it."

"I love the beauty of this landscape," Jake said. "The forest, mountains, streams, and wildlife make me feel so alive—one of the reasons I came west."

"I know the feeling," Jen said. "I haven't seen any wildlife, though. What'd you see?"

"I saw you," Jake said, grinning. Jen let out a howl and laughed.

"Me see plenty wildlife, sometime," Red said. "You want venison for camp tonight?"

"Yes, I would love a venison steak this evening," Jen said.

Less than an hour later, Jen pointed down the ravine to a stream that cascaded its fast-flowing waters down the gully. Over the ages, it had carved a deep channel into the landscape with eroding bluffs on either side.

"There it is!" she exclaimed.

"How in the hell did you ever find this place?" Jake asked.

"I didn't," Jen said. "Chris did."

The fossil site proved to be a bone bed with plenty of exposed fossils. After two days of digging, they had uncovered fossils from the Tertiary geologic period of around fifty million years ago. The fossils included fish, birds, and small mammals.

The three sat around a campfire having an evening meal of venison while recounting their discoveries.

"I believe Professor Marsh will be pleased with what we've found here," Jake said.

"We have found some interesting fossils," Jen said. "I wonder what Marsh will think of that perfect little horse skull I found."

"I'm sure he will find that most interesting," Jake said. "Don't pick at it any more than you have. Just take it as is in its stone prison. Marsh can extract it from the matrix."

"Yes, professor," Jen said, teasing. "I wouldn't dare try to extract it from its prison. It might explode into a thousand pieces, whinny, and gallop away."

"I'm not being critical," Jake said. "I'm just saying to be careful."

"Hmm," Jen said. "That's being critical."

"Hmm," Jake said. "What I'm saying is we'll have to be careful with all the specimens we've found. We're going to have a heavy, fragile load going back. I hope old Mulo is able to carry the burden."

"He can all right," Red said. "Mulo's back is very strong, sometime."

Just as Red mentioned that Mulo was strong, the mule let out a hee-hawing sound that caused Red to jump up and grab the rifle. The three horses tethered near the mule started whinnying.

"*Koo, ooks!*" Red shouted.

"What?" Jake asked, startled.

"There's a black bear over there," Jen said, pointing to the animal about a hundred yards away and wandering slowly toward their camp.

"Stand up, sometime," Red said. "Don't run. Raise your arms above your head. Stand tall. Make yourself look as large as possible."

"Okay," Jake and Jen said nervously.

"I will speak with bear," Red said, "and tell him he is not wanted in our camp. Go away … sometime."

"You can speak bear?" Jake asked apprehensively.

"Yes, sometime," Red said candidly. "When I tell you to make loud, deep growling sounds, you do so."

"What if he doesn't go away?" Jen asked.

"Then I will shoot him sometime," Red said with conviction.

Red turned and took a step toward the bear as it cautiously moved closer to their camp. Red lifted his rifle and shouted a string of Pawnee words at the bear. The bear stood up on its hind legs and made a huffing sound. Red again shouted at the bear.

"He is very old and stands up to smell and see us better," Red said.

"Jake and Jen, you now make growling sounds, and I will tell him to go sometime."

Again Red shouted at the bear as Jake and Jen growled. The old bear gave a couple of woofs, dropped to all fours, weaved back and forth, and then turned and ambled back down the way he had come, disappearing into the woods.

"Haven't had so much fun since I saw the performance of a circus bear in Cheyenne," Jen said, giving a sigh of relief.

"Me happy not have to kill old man bear, sometime," Red said.

"I'm happy old man bear didn't kill us," Jake said. "Sometime."

Mid-July at the Muller Ranch was filled with activity. Chris, Luke, and Jake had almost finished work on the new house. Red was busy breaking a number of feral horses that the Collins brothers had rounded up. Lys and Jen, with Jake's supervision, had sorted, packed, and numbered fossils found that summer. Marsh was expected to visit the ranch sometime in August.

"Lys, Luke and I are going to Laramie tomorrow for supplies," Jen told Jake and Chris. "We'll be gone three days. Do you need anything?"

"Pick up a couple of good cigars," Jake said. "I know Marsh would like a good smoke when he gets here. And you'd better get a couple of fifths of bourbon."

In the three days that the others were in Laramie, Chris and Jake had finished enough work on the house that it could now be occupied. When the women arrived home, they had merchandise piled high in their wagon. Luke, who was riding alongside with his saddlebags bulging with items, was smoking a cigar.

Jen reined the wagon to a stop. Lys jumped down and began waving and hollering at Chris.

"When will we be able to move in?" Lys asked.

"We're ready to move in now!" Chris shouted with delight. "We can start moving furniture in anytime."

"Let's start right now!" Lys said. "Come on over to the wagon and look at this."

Chris ran over to the wagon. "What is it?" he asked.

"It's a wedding present," Lys said.

"Who's getting married?" Chris asked, looking at Luke.

"Don't look at me," Luke replied.

"It's a late wedding gift for you and me," Lys said. "It's from Luke and Boz. Take a look."

"What in tarnation is it?" Chris asked as he looked at crates piled high in the wagon.

"It's a big, big, beautiful bed," Lys said.

"Wonderful!" Chris said. "Let's haul it in and try it out."

"You try out your bed," Jake said, "while Luke and I help Jen unload the wagon. We're gonna take a break and have a shot of bourbon and a cigar—that is if Luke hasn't drank and smoked all of it by now."

"No worry," Luke said. "I got you a box of fifty Y-B cigars and three fifths of Old Crow."

"And I've got a present for you, Jake," Jen said with a big smile on her face. "I'll whisper it in your ear."

Jake walked over to the wagon. Jen grabbed him by the collar, whispered something in his ear, and kissed him. Jake stood there for a moment then let out a whoop, threw his hat in the air, and kissed his wife.

"Yahoo!" he shouted. "I'm going to be a papa! We're having a baby!"

"Well, I wasn't putting on weight because I'm a glutton," Jen said sarcastically. "Or didn't you notice?"

"Oh, I noticed," Jake said. "You look great."

19

The 1872 Yale expedition spent the first part of the summer exploring bone beds in Kansas. They unearthed a number of specimens important for Marsh's research on fossil birds. Marsh's interest in birds had to do with the evolution of birds with teeth. The party discovered two fossil genera of birds. One was a pigeon-sized toothed seabird with long bones and strong wings that they named *Ichthyornis*, meaning "fish bird." The other fossil bird that most interested Marsh was a large, almost six feet in length, marine bird with teeth. It would have been flightless as it had very small wings but large webbed feet. It had sharp teeth and a long sharp beak. Marsh named it *Hesperornis*, meaning "western bird."

The Darwinian theory of evolution and the theories of the notable English biologist Thomas Henry Huxley were in accord with Marsh's own theories. The evolutionary link between birds and reptiles was a hot subject of the late 1800s. In 1862 evidence of this possibility was discovered in a limestone quarry in Bavaria: the fossil of a Jurassic creature that had several avian features (feathers plus a wishbone) and several dinosaur features (long bony tail, teeth, and claws extending from the middle of each wing). In 1863, the fossil was named *Archaeopteryx*, meaning "ancient wing," by English naturalist Richard Owen.

In early August, Professor Marsh and his party of four Yale students left Fort Wallace in Kansas after exploring the Smoky

Hill River region. Marsh was anxious to do some exploring in the Wyoming Eocene sediments and meet up with a couple of his hired fossil hunters, one of them being Jake Harding. They headed for Fort David Russell in Cheyenne, where Professor Marsh would make a side trip to the Muller Ranch to see Jake.

Jake and Chris were in the corral shoeing and trimming horses' hooves when they saw a couple of riders approaching the ranch. Jake recognized one of the riders as O.C. Marsh.

"Professor Marsh!" Jake yelled. "Good to see you found the Muller Ranch. Let me introduce you to one of the owners."

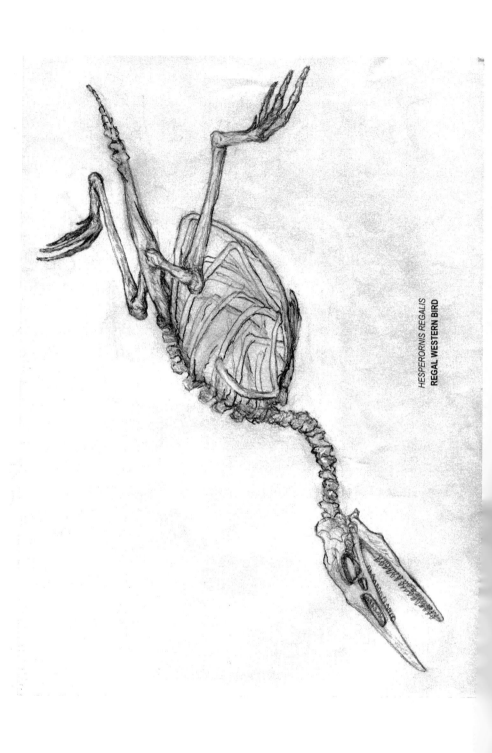

HESPERORNIS REGALIS
REGAL WESTERN BIRD

Jake introduced Marsh to Chris, and Marsh in turn introduced his guide, Ned Lane.

"Let's go up to the house," Chris said. "We can take a look at some of the fossils we've collected and meet the rest of our family."

"We have some horse fossils you may be interested in," Jake said.

"I most certainly would," Marsh said, clearing his throat. "Ever since I discovered that *Equus parvulus* horse fossil four years ago in Nebraska, I've been collecting *Equus* fossils. I have found an almost continuous link of sixty million years of evolution to the beautiful creature we know as the horse of today."

"Well, Professor Marsh, I'm sure you'll be pleased by the horse fossils my wife has discovered," Jake said.

"Your wife," Marsh questioned, clearing his throat. "Your wife is a fossil hunter?"

"Oh, yes," Jake said. "She is quite skilled and knowledgeable at that."

"How unusual," Marsh said, snorting, "a woman fossil hunter."

"You'll find that most Western women are skilled at things their Eastern counterparts wouldn't ever dream of doing," Chris said. "Did you know Wyoming women are the only females in the United States—and probably in the world—who have the right to vote?"

"Humph," Marsh said. "So I've been told."

After introductions to everyone at the ranch, Marsh and Lane were invited to lunch. Luke and Red took care of the horses. It was a crowded dinner table with Chris, Jake, Luke, Red, Jen, Lys, Aunt Bella, and their honored quests, Professor Marsh and Ned Lane.

Later after lunch, Jake, Chris, Jen, and Ned watched with interest as Marsh picked through the Muller collection of fossil bones with scrutinizing detail, mumbling to himself and making notes in a little jotter. After he'd been introduced to Jen, he had hardly said a word to her. She got the impression that Marsh was bothered by the fact that a woman could do and understand scientific endeavors like paleontology. Then she was surprised.

"Mrs. Harding," Marsh said, clearing his throat.

"Yes, Professor Marsh?" she answered. "And please call me Jen."

"All right, Jen," Marsh said. "Or maybe I should call you the Mary Anning of Wyoming."

"Who is Mary Anning?" Jen asked.

"She was a British fossil collector in the early part of this century," Marsh said. "She collected some fine specimens of ichthyosaur and ammonite fossils, which she found in the cliffs along the English Channel."

"Mary was a paleontologist then?" Jen asked.

"Well, not officially recognized as such," Marsh said, clearing his throat. "She was ineligible to become a member of the London Geological Society. Women were not allowed."

"How very quaint," Jen said sarcastically, her eyes flashing and her cheeks becoming flushed.

"Jen," Jake said, sensing a storm brewing. "Not all societies allow women to be as liberated as Wyoming women."

"It's time women were allowed the same rights and privileges as men," Jen said. "Women everywhere are beginning to realize they no longer can be cowed by possessive men, and the women of Wyoming are leading the way."

Both Jake and Marsh seemed embarrassed by Jen's comments. Neither one of them said a word, instead letting the awkward silence just hang there. Jen broke the silence.

"Of course, I meant no reflection of chauvinism regarding my loving husband and my dear brother, nor you, Professor Marsh, or you, Mr. Lane," Jen said. "I'm talking about men who are not gentlemen—scoundrels."

"We realize that, my dear," Jake said. Marsh nodded in agreement and cleared his throat.

Chris walked over to Jen and put his arms around her. "Hey, sis," he said. "I admire your spunk and couldn't agree more that there are some scoundrels in this world, but just relax and let's get on with this fossil business."

Jen was too ruffled to answer; she just nodded her head and sighed.

"Jen, Jake, and Chris," Marsh began, "you all have collected an amazing assortment of fossils. I'm particularly interested in the horse and fish fossils. I would pay you a fair price if you would sell them."

After about an hour of going through boxes of fossils and deciding which ones Marsh would purchase, they came to an agreement on price. Marsh would have the fossils shipped from Laramie back to Yale. Marsh also told Jake and Jen about the interesting bird fossils he had found in the Smoky Hill River region in the Kansas Cretaceous formation.

"These were bird fossils with teeth," Marsh said. "A most interesting discovery, as the evolutionary link between birds and reptiles may be evident here."

"That is fantastic," Jake said. "That would be in line with Darwin's theory of evolution."

"Precisely," Marsh said. "I plan to follow up on some research along that line. For now we're headed for Cheyenne and Fort Russell tomorrow to explore the Green River Basin. Jake, I'd like for you to join us."

"Normally I'd be happy to join you," Jake said. "But I have some obligations here at the ranch, and in a few days I expect my friend Dan Randall and his wife, Aaliyah, to arrive from New Haven."

"Oh, yes," Marsh said. "I remember Dan from our 1870 expedition."

Three days after Marsh left, Dan and his wife, Ali, arrived. Ali was everything Dan was not. Where Dan was reserved and reticent about everything, Ali was open to anything and delighted in new experiences and adventures. She and Jen formed an instant friendship. Jake and Dan renewed their old friendship and their interest in fossils.

"When I invited you and your wife to come to Wyoming to visit us, I wasn't sure you'd want to make a trip again to the dangers of the West," Jake said to Dan.

"Ali was delighted to get the invitation. I had second thoughts," Dan said. "But the bond of friendship is greater than the fear of danger."

After Jake and Jen showed Dan and Ali their fossil collection, they planned a fossil dig. Ali was elated at the thought of partaking in such an adventure.

Two days later, the four of them were on their way. Their horses and a wagon, driven by Jen, were loaded with camping and fossil-digging gear.

The dig site was in the vicinity of where Jake had been shot in the leg. Jen told Ali and Dan about being ambushed by robbers. Dan was worried by the story, whereas Ali was enraged. She said she would have shot them dead.

"Well, that's what Red did," Jake said. "He sent arrows into two of them, killing them. I shot one in the arm as he rode off, but he got away."

"Geez," Dan said. "Aren't you afraid he'll come back after you?"

"I doubt it," Jake said. "He was a young'un scared out of his wits. He took off like a bat out of hell, his long red hair flying in the wind as he headed for parts unknown."

The first day at the dig site was spent setting up two tents, preparing a campsite, and then relaxing in the company of friends. Early the next morning, Jake and Jen were digging for fossils while Dan showed Ali what fossil hunting was all about, such as how to dig a fossil out of its earth foundation without damaging the specimen. Ali was a serious student and quick learner. Soon, to her delight, she was unearthing fossils.

"Dan!" Ali shouted." Take a look at what I found."

"What is it?" Dan asked as he ambled around an escarpment to where Ali was digging.

Ali showed him part of a massive skull sticking out of a ledge on the side of the bluff.

"Wow! That's the oddest looking skull I've ever seen," Dan said. "Don't dig at it anymore. There may be more of the skeleton buried beneath it."

"Isn't this exciting?" Ali said. "I'm so glad I got to meet Jen and Jake and go on this trip."

"You know, honey, "Dan said, "I'm really enjoying this fossil dig. With you out here, it is a beautiful adventure, and it is good to see my old friend Jake and meet his lovely wife."

"Then you're no longer upset with me for talking you into this trip?" Ali asked.

"Of course not, dear," Dan said. "I'm glad you were so persistent. I'll go get Jake to take a look at this fossil. He may know what beast this skull belonged to."

Dan scrambled around the ridge heading to where Jake and Jen were prospecting. Just as he was about to call to Jake, he heard Ali call out and scream. *Now what?* He thought. He wasn't sure whether or not it was a cry of joy or for help. His question was answered in a minute when Ali appeared around the bluff with a stranger who was holding a revolver to his wife's head.

"Drop your belt and holster with the gun in it," the stranger demanded. "Then walk slowly toward me with your hands held high, or I'll blast this pretty lady's brains all over the side of this hill."

Dan did as he was told but not before he yelled, "Jake!"

Jake and Jen were absorbed in their search for fossils when they heard Dan yell. Just as they looked up from their digging, two men suddenly appeared out of the bush. The younger man had his revolver drawn and was carrying a coiled rope. The older fella, with a scraggly black beard, had a rifle pointed at Jake and Jen. Jake sensed something vaguely familiar about the older man, but before he could speculate any further, the man began shouting orders at Jake and his wife.

"Get them hands up high!" the older man ordered. "Billy Boy, you relieve the man of his pistol and pick up that rifle over by the woman."

As the two thugs approached, Jake thought he was seeing a ghost. The stranger looked like the robber who had been killed by one of Red's arrows the previous year, the same fella who had shot Jake in the leg.

Jen let out a string of cuss words. "Who the hell are you?" she yelled. "What do you want here, you scum? You get off our land!"

"Don't you start your bitchin', woman," the man with the beard snarled. "If'n you do, I'll blow your man's head off here and now."

"No need for any trouble, mister," Jake said. "You've got us covered; you take what goods we have and leave us in peace."

"Oh, I plan on takin' your goods, cowboy," the man said. "Then we'll leave you in peace—*pieces*."

The bearded man roared with laughter, hee-hawing like a jackass, and the boy joined in, giggling like a schoolgirl. Just then Dan and Ali came around the bluff with their hands held high, followed by a young man with long, tangled red hair that was holding a gun at their backs.

"Ah, here are your friends," the bearded man said. "The four of you squat down here in front of me so's I can keep an eye on ya'll. How ill-mannered of me not to introduce myself," he added. "My name is Josiah Brown, and this is my son, Billy Boy. I believe you've meet my nephew, Boo. You are the ones who killed my brother Jeremy and my nephew Jeb. We're here to avenge their murders."

"But we didn't kill your brother," Dan said. "I don't even know who he is."

"Well, ain't that a shame," Josiah said. "And here you are, Yankee boy, with your friends actin' all high and mighty. It's the doing of all of you that my brother and nephew is dead—killed by arrows from some damn redskin friend of yours. When we're through with you here, we'll get that red devil and everyone back at your ranch. Retribution will be forthcoming."

"We didn't murder your brother and nephew," Jake said. "It was self-defense. They were going to kill us."

"Bull crap," Josiah said. "Boo was there. Said you ambushed them and murdered Jeremy and Jeb. Boo was lucky to escape with just a bullet in his shoulder."

"He's a liar," Jake said, an uneasiness gripping his body. He began to fear the worst from these barbarous men.

"You are the damn liar, cowboy!" Josiah said. "There are certain persons upon which justice has to be served. Liars and murders head the list. And there are others that have to be held accountable for their loathsome behaviors: niggers, Injuns, Yankees, and bitchy women. I guess y'all fit in there somehow. Justice is about to be served."

"Justice, you call this justice?" Jake asked. "You set yourself up to be judge, jury, and executioner. I have two other witnesses who will testify as to the truth of what happened that day."

"And I suppose those witnesses would be an Indian and a Yankee cowboy named Chris Muller," Josiah said.

"How'd you know who they were?" Jake asked, surprised.

"I have my ways of finding out things. We've been keepin' track of y'all for some time now," Josiah said. "Billy Boy, fetch our horses. Give Boo that rifle so's he can keep these Yankee murderers covered."

Jake was more filled with rage than he was with fear. He blamed himself for the predicament that his wife and friends were in. He searched his mind for some solution. Before he could do or say anything, Dan began shouting at their bearded captor.

"Josiah!" Dan yelled. "You are nothing but a coward, holding us prisoner with no chance to defend ourselves. I purpose to offer you enormous wealth for our safe release. My family is quite wealthy, and if you let my friends go, you can hold me for ransom. My father would pay you handsomely for the exchange."

Jake couldn't believe Dan's reaction. This was a side of his friend he had never seen before. The old man squinted at Dan as he stroked his black whiskers.

"Well, now," Josiah scoffed, "I don't think y'all grasp the meaning of vengeance. It's not about money, although we'll collect our due when we loot that ranch. Our retribution will be paid by the lives who murdered our kin. Soon as my son gets our mounts, we'll play a little retribution game."

Billy Boy, spurring his mount, came crashing through the trees and bushes, yahooing as he led two other horses.

"Damn it, boy!" Josiah said. "Do you have to be so noisy as to wake the whole countryside?"

"Sorry, Pa," Billy Boy said. "I'm just excited as to what you plan on doing to these Yankee bastards."

"Just hold your horses, son," Josiah said. "I'll show you in a minute. Get our saddle strings, and you and Boo tie the fellas' hands behind their backs and tie the bitches' hands and feet. Cut a couple of strips from their clothing and gag them. I'm tired of hearing their whinin' and bitchin'."

"You want we should tie the fellas' feet too?" Billy Boy asked.

"Nah," Josiah said. "You'll see why in a bit." He waved his rifle at the four captives and then motioned for the boys to get busy.

The two young fellas did as they were told. Boo grabbed Dan's wrists, twisted his arms behind his back, and began tying his hands together. Billy Boy grabbed Jake's arm and tried to jerk it behind Jake's back. Jake would have no part of this. He quickly turned around, grabbed Billy Boy by the collar, and flipped him to the ground. He was on the lad like a calf roper, throwing him on his side while he pulled a knife from his belt and held it against the lad's throat.

"One move and I'll slit the boy's throat!" Jake yelled at Josiah. "Grab that rifle by the barrel and toss it over here, and then sit down. Now! Do as I say."

"Okay," Josiah said. "You got me at a disadvantage here. Just take it easy with that knife."

Josiah held the rifle by the barrel out in front of him. Suddenly, a loud gunshot rang out. Boo had fired his pistol close to Dan's right ear. Jake groaned, dropped the knife, and clutched his left shoulder as the bullet hit him.

"Good shot, Boo," Josiah said as he swung the rifle around and shoved his index finger into the trigger guard.

"Now, Yankee, we're going to continue with our games," Josiah said, seemingly unruffled by the turn of events. "Any more tricks from you, cowboy, and the next shot will be a bullet to your head. My trigger finger's gettin' mighty itchy."

Boo and Billy Boy got Jake to his feet and tied his hands behind his back. His wounded shoulder was obviously painful as Jake moaned and gritted his teeth. Dan was also in considerable discomfort as he kept blinking his eyes and bobbing his head, trying to subdue the ringing in his ears from the gunshot. After tying Dan's and Jake's hands, the two young attackers went to tie Jen and Ali, but not without a fight. Both women fought like wildcats, but the two boys overpowered them and, upon Josiah's instructions, bound and gagged them. Josiah had a devilish belly laugh over the entertainment that the struggling women afforded him.

"Boo, you take my rifle and guard these varmints," Josiah said. "And Billy Boy, aim your pistol at them and keep a sharp eye out while I go get my instrument of justice."

Josiah went over to his horse, untied and withdrew the pack, and then carefully unwound the leather cords that bound the package.

"This, gentlemen, is an instrument of justice," Josiah cried out as he held a large bow and a quiver of arrows over his head.

Billy Boy cheered with delight, and Boo gave out with a chilling rebel yell.

"When I was just a lad, my pappy taught me the finer points of archery," Josiah said. "Yes, sir, he could hit a possum in the eyeball with an arrow no matter how fast that varmint was runnin'. We had many a fine possum feast due to his skill with a bow, and with his coaching I became almost as good. Pa hunted all sorts of game with a bow—rabbits, turkey, deer, and even fish. But his favorite quarry was runaway slaves. They were always brought to justice by the accuracy of his barbed shaft."

"You're a madman!" cried Dan.

"You are right, son," Josiah said. "I'm mad as hell at you goddamn Yankee murderers, and I intend to do something in retribution for my brother and nephew."

Josiah strung his bow, tested the pull, slung the quiver of arrows over his back, and strode over to Dan.

"Yankee bastard, since you've got such a loud mouth, you'll be the first participant in our little game," Josiah said to Dan. "I'm givin' you much more of a chance to live than you gave my brother."

"We didn't murder your brother!" Jake yelled out. "And my friend wasn't even with us when we were bushwhacked."

"You are a damn liar, you son of a bitch!" Josiah yelled back. "Boo told me what ya'll did. One more word out of you and I'll beat you within an inch of your life so's you won't have the chance I'm givin' your friend!"

Josiah, with hate in his eyes, stepped closer to Dan, pulled an arrow from his quiver, and held the point under Dan's chin.

"This is how this is gonna work," he said. He taunted Dan with the arrow tip. "You see that big tree at the end of this clearing, the one across from the end of the bluff? Well if'n ya'll can run and make it to that tree and 'round that bluff before I can nock an arrow and get a bead on you, you're home free. When I count to three, you'd better start running. When I get to six, I'm letting an arrow fly—at you. One, two—"

Fury overtook Jake. It surpassed the pain in his shoulder as he bolted toward Josiah.

"Run, Dan! *Run!*" Jake shouted as he slammed into Josiah, knocking him down. The bow and arrow dropped from Josiah's hands as he and Jake begin to scuffle.

"Shoot that running son of a bitch, Boo!" Josiah howled as he lashed out with his boot, kicking Jake in the head so hard that it knocked him unconscious.

Boo's rifle shot brought Dan down.

"Shoot him again! Kill him!" Josiah screamed, picking up his bow and an arrow. He fixed the arrow to the string and aimed at Jake's unconscious body. Boo jacked another cartridge into the breech and sighted down his rifle at Dan lying on the ground.

Before either one of the outlaws could act, a long red arrow pierced the back of Josiah and thrust out the front of his chest, spurting blood and doubling him over. Almost instantaneously, a rifle shot rang out and Boo dropped to the ground. From the tree line, Chris and Red came running into the clearing. Billy Boy turned and pointed his pistol toward Chris.

"Don't do it, son," Chris said. "Drop the gun." The pistol in Billy Boy's hand spewed flame as a bullet whizzed by Chris's ear. Chris, running and holding his rifle at waist level fired, hitting the boy in the chest and knocking him backward to his death.

"Red, you go check on Dan," Chris said. "I'll get Jake and the girls."

Jake was coming out of his groggy unconsciousness as Chris approached him.

"Red and I took care of those bastards," Chris said. "You okay, Jake?"

"I'll be all right," Jake said. "Thanks for being here. I took a bullet to my left shoulder, but the bleeding has stopped. I'm just a little dizzy after that blow to the head. Are the girls and Dan okay?"

"Dan's been shot," Chris said. "Red is checking on him. The girls look fine. I'll get them untied. You sit a spell and clear your head."

Chris went to help Jen and Ali. He laid his rifle down as he unfastened Jen's gag and untied the rawhide cords from her feet and hands. He walked over to Ali to release her bonds as Jen wailed a string of cuss words, damning the bandits who had attacked them.

"Feel better now?" Chris asked her. She let out a sigh of relief while rubbing her sore wrists and ankles.

"Look out, Chris!" Jen screamed.

Chris turned just in time to see Jen grab his rifle and fire a shot at Boo, who was kneeling and sighting his rifle at Chris. Boo's shot kicked up dust between Chris and Ali just as Jen's bullet ripped into Boo's torso, killing him instantly.

"That's my sister!" Chris shouted.

"*Now*, I feel better!" Jen said.

Chris tipped his hat and gave Jen a big smile. "Me too," he said.

Just as soon as Chris ungagged Ali, she started screaming for Dan.

"Did they shoot Dan?" she asked Chris.

"I think he's wounded, like Jake, but they'll be all right," he said, not knowing if that was the truth or not. He tried to calm Ali as he untied her bonds.

Jen walked over to the two and handed Chris his rifle. Chris put his arm around his sister, at the same time offering a hand to help Ali up off the ground.

"Come on, you two," he said. "Let's check on your partners."

Chris, Jen, and Ali ran to the area where Dan had been shot. They saw Jake cradling Dan in his arms while Red stood nearby doing a low chant.

"I'm sorry, I'm sorry," Jake sobbed over and over.

Ali ran toward them, screaming and calling Dan's name. She grabbed Jake by the collar and yanked him back. Taking Dan's lifeless body in her arms, she began rocking and sobbing.

"No, no, no! Oh, Dan," she wailed, tears streaming down her face as she held him tightly and kissed his head repeatedly.

Jen reached out to comfort her but was pushed away. Ali withdrew further into her anguish as reality drifted away from her senses and she became consumed by her grief. She started shaking and felt sick. She turned and vomited. Chris took hold of Jen, hugged her tightly, and whispered in her ear.

"Give Ali some space and let her grieve," Chris said. "There's nothing anybody can do for Dan. Just be there for her."

Sitting on the ground, Jake was holding his shoulder and moaning. He was in extensive physical and emotional pain. Jake's grief and guilt had him blaming himself for Dan's death. He wished he could make time go backward to yesterday like he could with his flights of fantasy when he held a fossil. Jen sat down beside him and began to fashion a sling for his arm out of her coat.

"It's entirely my fault," Jake said. "If I wouldn't have insisted on his coming for a visit, Dan would be alive today."

"Jake, it's no one's fault but that damn bunch of bushwhackers," Jen said. "Now be still and let me tend to that shoulder."

"You're wrong, Jennie!" Ali screamed. "It's both our faults. It's mine and Jake's. Dan didn't want to make the trip—he hated the West. But I convinced him it would be a fun adventure, and he said I sounded just like Jake. He told me about Jake's obsession for hunting fossils and his fascination with the West. The more Dan opposed the idea, the more appeal it had for me. Jake and I are to blame for Dan's death."

"Your grief has clouded your mind," Chris said. "The tragic events here are neither one of your doing. The one responsible is that scoundrel lying over there with an arrow in his heart."

Everyone was silent for a moment. Chris took off his coat and placed it over Dan's head. The silence was broken by Jake's horse snorting.

"You're right, Snort," Chris said satirically. "It's time to pack up. Jennie, I'll hitch Lady to the wagon so you can drive them back to the ranch. Red and I will clean up here."

Chris hitched the wagon and drove it to where Dan's body was laying. He and Red wrapped the body in a blanket and loaded it into the wagon. Chris laid a couple of blankets on the wagon floor and helped Ali climb in the back where she could be beside Dan. She was sobbing again, and Jen reached out to comfort her. This time Ali accepted her offer as they hugged each other. Red helped Jake up onto the wagon's passenger seat, and Jen hopped up into the driver's seat. Chris tied Jake's horse to the back of the wagon. He brought his horse around beside the wagon and reached in his saddlebag to retrieve a bottle of whiskey.

"Here, your passengers may need a shot of this," Chris said as he handed the bottle to Jen.

"My passengers aren't the only ones needing that," she replied.

"You tend to your driving," Chris said. "Save your thirst till you get safely home."

"I'll be mighty thirsty when all this is behind us," Jen said.

Chris scoffed. "And take this. You know how to use it," he said as he handed Jen his rifle. "Hope you don't have to."

Jen gave her brother a nod, put the rifle on the floor beside her, slapped the reins on the back of the horse, and headed the wagon down the trail to the ranch. Red picked up a couple of shovels that the fossil hunters had and handed one to Chris.

It was late afternoon when Jen reined the wagon to a stop in front of the ranch house. Bella stepped out onto the veranda and asked what had happened.

"We were held up and shot," Jen said. "The bastards killed Dan and wounded Jake. We got Chris and Red to thank for rescuing us. They came along and killed the three bushwhackers—members of the same gang that held us up before. Ali is sleeping in back of the wagon. She is overcome with grief. Come help her into the house. I'll take Jake and tend to his wounded shoulder."

"Oh, my Lord," Bella sighed. She scurried down the few veranda steps to help Ali.

Just then Luke and Lys came running from the corrals. Jen told them what had happened.

"You mean Dan's dead?" Luke asked.

"Yes," Jen answered. "Those bastards killed him. He's in the back of the wagon. Would you put his body in the ice house?"

"Sure, will do," Luke said.

"I'll help you with Jake," Lys said.

"Thanks, Lys," Jen said. "For now just get some water boiling and clean towels. Then, if you would, see if you can calm Ali. I'll get Bella to work her medicine magic on Jake."

Jen helped Jake remove his shirt as he gritted his teeth and moaned.

"While Jen cleans your wound, I'll get you some laudanum," Bella said. "It'll help you forget the pain."

Bella disappeared into the kitchen to get the medication while Jen cleaned the dried blood from the wound with some water and whiskey.

"Take this drink, Jake," Bella said as she came back from the kitchen with a few drops of laudanum mixed in with some whiskey. "It'll ease the pain and help you sleep while we patch you up."

Lys brought a kettle of hot water, some clean towels, and a bottle of Bella's antiseptic that was a mixture of alcohol, honey, and thyme. After cleaning the wound, Bella looked for an exit bullet wound. Soon Jake began to feel the effects of the drug he had taken.

"I don't see an exit wound," said Bella. "The bullet must still be in his shoulder."

"He's asleep and resting comfortably now," Jen said.

"Good," Bella said." I'll probe the wound and see if I can locate the bullet. Don't worry, Jennie. He won't feel a thing. He's out cold. He should be asleep for about six hours with the medication I gave him."

"Lys," Bella called out, "put a couple of spoons, a sharp skinning knife, and a pair of scissors in that kettle of boiling water. Jenny, get me my—whatchamacallit—my sewing basket."

Bella began cutting and probing Jake's gunshot wound like a skilled surgeon. Jen helped by swabbing blood and flushing the wound with the antiseptic. After a little cutting with a knife and scissors and probing with spoons, Bella retrieved the bullet from Jake's shoulder.

"Bring that candle over here," Bella said. "I'll heat up one of my sewing needles and get this wound closed. Jake was lucky the bullet was lodged in a muscle and didn't hit a bone. He's gonna have one hell of a sore shoulder and arm for a few weeks."

"You are an amazing woman, Aunt Bella," Jen said as she gave her aunt a big hug. "I love you very much."

"And I love you, Jennie," Bella said. "Now we'll let Jake sleep. Let's go see what we can do for Ali."

It was already dark when Chris and Red rode up to the ranch. They were leading the horses loaded with gear and fossils from the camp. Jen, Luke, and Lys went out of the house to meet them.

"Thanks for bringing the horses and gear back," Jen said. "Have any problems cleaning up the campsite?"

"Nope," Chris said. "We took care of everything. Got the bodies buried and took their belongings to show to Sheriff Boswell. We packed up all your gear, including the fossils you guys found. By the way, I saw this enormous skull sticking out of the bluff that one of you had started to excavate."

"Well, don't tell Jake about it," Jen said. "The fool will want to get right back at it. Must be the fossil Ali found."

"How's his shoulder?" Chris asked.

"Bella dug the bullet out," Jen said. "She gave him something to help him sleep. He'll be out until morning."

"Good," Chris said. "How's Ali doing?"

"She's asleep right now," Jen said. "She's physically and emotionally exhausted."

"I'll go to Laramie tomorrow to see the sheriff," Chris said. "And I'll talk to Jim Vine, the coroner, to make arrangements for Dan's body. I'll talk to Ali to see if she wants to go tomorrow. No doubt she'll want Dan's body shipped back to Philly so his family can have a funeral."

"I'm going with you," Lys said. "I'm not going to sit around here while you go off looking for trouble."

"For God's sake, woman," Chris said, "I don't go looking for trouble. I just seem to stumble upon it."

"So I've noticed," she said.

Just before dawn, Luke and Red loaded Dan's body into the buckboard while Chris hitched up the horse. Jen, Lys, Bella, and Ali were having breakfast and a conversation about the tragedy when Chris entered the room with Luke and Red right behind him. All three had somber faces. Chris had his hat in one hand, and with the other he brushed back the hair from his forehead. He hesitated before speaking in a low, reverent voice.

"We're about ready to leave," Chris said to Ali. His voice broke as he continued. "I'll make all the arrangements to have your husband's body taken care of at the funeral parlor and have the casket loaded on the train for the trip to Philadelphia tomorrow."

"Thank you," Ali said. "You all better have another cup of coffee before we leave."

"That we will," Chris said. "Are you sure you're all right to make this trip today?"

"I'll be fine," Ali said. "Disaster and hardship have never been something new to my family, but the pain never gets easier. My father and two of my three brothers were killed during the war when rebels invaded our home. My mom, younger brother, and I hid in the cellar."

Jen poured coffee for everyone while Bella went to the kitchen and came back with a platter of biscuits and honey.

"I want to thank you all for your kindness," Ali said. "I don't know what I'd have done without your friendship. And I want to apologize for lashing out at Jake. I know this tragedy is not his fault and that he is a good friend. I was mad with grief over the loss of my love. But I will in time function as usual though never forgetting what I have suffered—what we all have suffered."

"When Jake wakes up, I'll tell him what you said, Ali," Jen said. "He is devastated at the loss of his friend and at the grief this has caused you."

"Before I leave, there is one other thing I'd like to share with you," Ali said, pausing to take a deep breath. "I regret I never had the chance to tell Dan. We are going to have a child."

Everyone congratulated Ali, laughing and crying as they hugged one another and celebrated the news. Chris, watching Ali, thought she looked as happy as the day he'd first met her, but he knew in his heart she was just masking her suffering. He walked over to her and touched her gently on the arm.

"Ali, we'd better be going," he said. "We've got your luggage loaded in the buckboard. Lys will drive, and you can ride up with her. I'll ride ahead and lead the way. We should be in Laramie a little after the noon hour."

By the time the morning sun was glowing low in the east, the horseman and wagon were disappearing down the road. Bella and Jen stood silently, still waving good-bye as Luke and Red headed for one of the corrals.

"Let's go check on Jake," Jen said to Bella.

Jake's shoulder was throbbing like the beating of a pow-wow drum. He was mumbling and was just opening his eyes from a drug-induced sleep that had visions of demons and monsters. He was startled by a figure leaning over him; it was his wife. Jake's muttering got louder as his eyes widened, and he grasped his left shoulder.

"Where am I?" he shouted. He began to laugh and cry hysterically. "Am I dead?"

"You're okay, dear," Jen said, distraught by Jake's hysterical state.

"What the matter?" Bella asked as she entered the room.

"He's in pain and confused," Jen said.

"He must have a fever," Bella said. "And the medication will play tricks on his mind. Talk to him calmly and give him a few minutes to get adjusted. He'll be all right. His shoulder will be sore, but I've got some ointment that will help."

"Jake," Jen said. "Look at me. Everything is all right. You've been wounded in the shoulder, but you're okay. Just be calm."

"I'm dying … dying of thirst," Jake said.

"I've got a big cup of cold water right here for you," Jen said.

"No," Jake said. "I want a whiskey. And you."

"No booze and no fooling 'round," Jen said. "You've got to get well. Just relax and let that shoulder heal."

"You and a shot of bourbon will make my shoulder heal better than ever," Jake said.

"I can tell you're already feeling much better, without me or the booze," Jen said. "Now tell me what all that screaming was about. You were mumbling something about, '*Ho pa gants des bear.*' What does that mean?"

Jake burst out laughing. "*Ho pa gants des bear?*" he said, grinning. "I was saying, 'Hope against despair.' I was having one of my nightmarish fights against fears I have in my head. But I overcome them with words my grandpa once told me: 'Hope against despair.'"

"Hope against despair," Jen repeated. "Your grandfather was a wise man. Now heed those words while I go get you some breakfast."

"Ho pa gants des bear," Jake repeated, laughing.

"Don't be a horse's ass," Jen said. "You just be hopeful and get well soon. And don't despair; I'll get you the whiskey, and me, in time."

"The time is now!" Jake shouted at Jen as she walked out of the room.

After the Yale expedition left Kansas and Marsh's visit to the Muller Ranch was concluded, the professor and his party traveled on to Fort D. A. Russell near Cheyenne, Wyoming. There they were escorted by a detachment of the Ninth Infantry led by Lieutenant Jesse Lee. Marsh's plan was to explore the Green River area and the Fort Bridger Basin, which he considered his private bone beds and was envious of anyone else digging there. But Marsh was not the only fossil collector searching the rich bone beds of Wyoming for specimens. His rival, Edward Cope, was among the fossil collectors prospecting the area.

Learning of Cope's collecting in the Green River Basin infuriated Marsh. The rivalry between the two paleontologists was escalating as both scientists tried to discredit the other by various means. This included theft, bribery, destruction of fossils and fossil sites, and attacking each other's credibility in scientific publications. A war between the two scientists on fossil collecting had been declared.

That summer and fall of 1872, both Marsh and Cope were collecting in Wyoming, each spying on the other. In the Bridger Basin, Marsh and his students were excited about a fossil they had partially uncovered.

"Professor Marsh!" one of the students yelled. "Come take a look at this huge, strange-looking skull."

Marsh saw, sticking out of a Wyoming clay ridge, a large skull of a Uintatherium, a large, hoofed, rhinoceros-type mammal of the

Eocene epoch—about forty million years ago. The skull was three feet long and had three sets of knob-like horns and long upper canine teeth.

"Excellent find," Marsh snorted. "Let's get to work extracting it from the rock."

The fossil skull was embedded in the hard rock of the cliff, and freeing it was an arduous task. After hours of carefully chipping and digging at the matrix that held the fossil prisoner, the skull was released. As they excavated the site that held the skull, they found bits and parts of the mammal's skeleton. Marsh was able to determine the size of the creature from their finds, and he figured the animal to be approximately twelve feet in length and about six feet tall, similar in shape to a large rhinoceros. Marsh made a note in his journal of the find and decided to call the fossil dinoceras, meaning "fearful horn."

As the Yale party examined the site for other fossils, Lieutenant Lee approached Marsh. The lieutenant led Marsh behind one of the wagons and handed him a spyglass.

"Take a look at the top of that hill to the south of us," the lieutenant said, "right near those pines and outcropping. Don't show yourself. Just peek around the corner of the wagon."

Marsh nodded as he lifted the spyglass to his eye. After a minute of surveying the hilltop, Marsh handed it back to Lee.

"Damn," Marsh snorted. "That's Cope and some of his men spying on us."

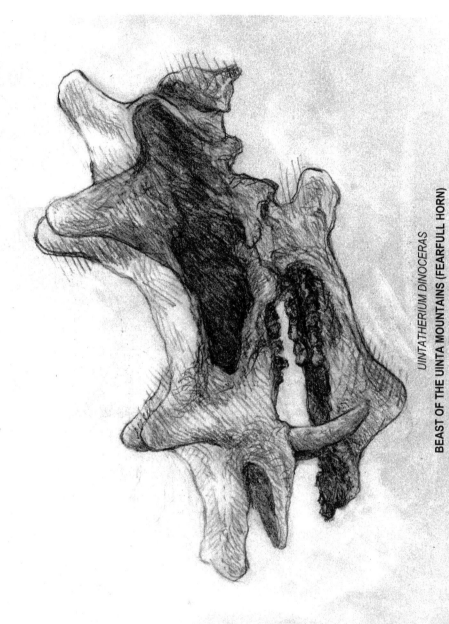

UINTATHERIUM DINOCERAS

BEAST OF THE UINTA MOUNTAINS (FEARFULL HORN)

"I thought that may be the case," Lee said. "I'm just glad it isn't a gang of robbers."

"Cope and his men *are* robbers," Marsh grumbled, clearing his throat.

Marsh quietly informed his men of the surveillance they were under and told them to go about their business as though they were unaware of being spied upon. Marsh and his party worked over the site to the last bone until they were ready to move on. The professor instructed his men to leave some pieces of broken skulls and other bones from various fossils as a plant for Cope and his men. After Marsh and his party left the site, Cope's party went down to explore the area. Finding bones the Yale party had planted from different fossil skeletons, Cope claimed them and made the mistake of thinking he had made a new find that Marsh had overlooked.

The fall of 1872 brought changes, including Jake's shoulder getting stronger every week and his wife's trim figure getting portly. Jake spent a lot of time corresponding with Marsh and cataloging fossils. Jen had an ongoing correspondence with Ali in Philadelphia, and the two were delighted that the births of their children would occur at about the same time—mid-February.

That winter at the Muller Ranch was a mixture of happiness and stress. The early, blustery winter weather was affecting everyone's behavior, but adversity would be tempered with the thoughts of the holiday season and the upcoming birth of a new family member for Jake and Jen Harding.

Jake's mind was focused on fossils, and Jen was restless with being confined to the indoors and her ever-changing metabolism. Pushing each other's tolerance, Jen and Jake were like two opposite polar forces competing for dominance.

Early one sunny, cold December morning, Jake was seated at the workbench they had installed in the room to sort and prepare fossils, intensely engrossed in fossil restoration. With a small pen knife, he was chipping and picking away the matrix from a small fossil skull when Jen pranced into the room singing. She was wearing a riding dress and jacket with a multicolored wool scarf draped over her shoulders. A thick fur hat adorned her head, and woolen mittens that matched her hat covered her hands.

"I've a wonderful idea, dear," she said, beaming and holding up her hands to display her mittens. "Let's hitch Lady to the sleigh, put some bells on her, and go for a sleigh ride. The snow is perfect after that last storm, and Lady loves to trot through the snow. It'll be good exercise for her, and the ride will buck up our winter blahs. What'd you say?"

No response. Jen was dismayed at Jake's silence.

"Hey, you old fossil," Jen said. "Did you hear what I said?"

For a moment, the silence again was deafening. Then Jake responded.

"Yeah, I heard you," he answered curtly. "Can't you see I'm busy?"

"I can see that you're *always* busy of late," Jen said disdainfully. "You've become so preoccupied with those old bones and their time that you have no sense of being alive in your own time."

"I've never felt more alive than when I'm working with fossils," Jake said. "These fossils are proof that I'm alive in my time and space as was every other creature in its own time and space. They confirm my own mortality, life, death, time past, time present, and future time. Time is the great creator of all things, for with time there is an evolution that is occurring. These old bones tell me about time and give a purpose to my life."

"Okay, *professor*," Jen said, scoffing. "Are you saying your life has no meaning without your fossil work?"

"No. No!" Jake said. "There are a lot of things that give meaning to my life—the wonders of nature, people, and most of all my love for you, my dear. But one purpose in my life is studying these fossils. It is my vocation; it's my calling. This activity is but one of life's meanings that give me a purpose. Everyone should have a purpose in life."

"You're right," Jen answered assertively, "including me. I have a few aspirations. My love and caring for you is my main purpose. How can I deal with this melancholy state of mind that I've been in so that I can achieve my purposes? I need to have a healthy body and mind to have this baby. I'm looking forward to being a mother—a good mother. I want us to be a family. How can that happen when you've been so distant of late?"

"Ha, and you," Jake said, "Not saying a word and moping around the house like you were in prison."

"I feel like I am," Jen said. "That's why I need to go for a sleigh ride. You say you love me, but do you care for me?"

"Of course I care for you," Jake answered. "Doesn't loving you mean caring for you?"

"I would hope so," Jen said. "Just show me you care."

"I will. Tomorrow we'll go for a sleigh ride to Laramie," Jake said. "We'll stay overnight at the Frontier Hotel, and I'll buy you the best dinner they have in town. Just let me finish up my work here today. How does that sound?"

"That sounds wonderful," Jen said. "Do you promise?"

"I promise," Jake said. "Your wishes are my command, your highness. Are you sure you're up for a little trip?"

"I am. I am, dear," Jen said. "It's a date."

"Good," Jake said. "I'll finish with these fossils today and pack them up with a letter to post to Professor Marsh when we get to Laramie."

"Hmm, always some plan to support your fossil obsession," Jen said as she scowled at Jake. She felt a twinge of annoyance but let go of it when she thought, *He did promise.* She knew Jake was good on his promises, and no matter his motive for going to town, she would get her sleigh ride and relief from her imprisonment.

"I *do* work for Marsh, and this trip to town will let us take care of both our wishes," Jake said.

"You sly old fox," Jen said with a little smile. "You can always make things seem like the right way. Just remember, you promised."

With that Jen threw the scarf around her neck, did a quick turn, and pranced out of the room.

The next morning, true to Jake's promise and Jen's wish, they packed the sleigh with supplies, including a large buffalo robe and a soapstone foot warmer Bella had heated. The heat from the stone should last the four-hour trip to Laramie.

Once in town, the Hardings' visit was full of joy and laughter. Both Jen and Jake were relaxed and filled with the spirit of Christmas. Jen shopped for items for the coming baby and for some Christmas presents while Jake dispatched his fossils to New Haven and picked up the mail. There were two letters from Marsh, one from Jake's attorney in Philadelphia, and a letter to Jen from Ali. Jake quickly read his attorney's letter, which was an update regarding the rental of his grandfather's house. Marsh's letters contained information on where to contact other fossil collectors who were employed by the professor. Marsh hoped Jake would get in touch with some of the other collectors and investigate some of the dig sites, as well as report on any operations that Cope may have going. Jake pocketed the letters and thought Marsh's messages sounded more like orders than requests. Leaving the post office to meet with Jen at the hotel, Jake was thinking maybe he should have been more assertive in his letter to Marsh and complained about the lateness of being paid. Marsh still owed Jake for two crates of fossils plus last month's salary. That evening, Jake escorted his wife to Ritter's Restaurant for a delightful supper. Husband and wife were completely oblivious to the rest of the world; they were absorbed in their love and affection for each other.

On February 7, 1873, Jen and Jake became the proud parents of a baby boy. The boy was named Daniel Christopher Harding after Jake's friend and Jen's brother. The healthy, robust baby boy was a joy to all at the Muller Ranch. Bella became Grandma Bella and doted on the baby night and day. In March, a letter from Ali in Philly announced the birth of her baby girl, born on February 16. The girl was named Janine Jennifer, honoring Dan's mother and Ali's friend. Even though Jen and Ali were miles from each other, their initial bond of friendship grew through their letter correspondence. To meet again someday was a solemn promise to which they held firmly.

In May, a letter from Marsh informed Jake of the 1873 Yale fossil expedition. They would be in Fort McPherson on the North Platte River in Nebraska sometime in the middle of June. Then in late July, they'd travel to Fort Bridger in the Wyoming Territory. Marsh wanted to know if Jake could join them, but Jake answered saying that he couldn't because of commitments at the ranch. Also, he didn't want to leave his wife and young son alone at that time.

21

The intense July sunrays seemed to suck up the small swirls of clay dust triggered by a hot summer wind. Jake had taken a couple of days off as a ranch hand, a husband, and a father to pursue his favorite occupation—fossil hunting. Chris and Jen had persuaded him not to go collecting alone but to take one of the Collins brothers with him. Young Jim Collins was delighted to be asked to go fossil collecting with Jake. Jim was a fine horseman and an excellent shot with a pistol and a rifle. Jim would ride one of the ranch's finer horses, a golden palomino quarter horse gelding. The horse was named Nugget because his coat had a luster like a gold nugget.

Jake and his trusty steed, Snort, followed by Jim riding Nugget were gingerly making their way up the steep side of a ravine just south of where Dan had been killed. Jake's thoughts flashed back to the horror of that ambush about a year earlier. Just as they reached the crest of the gorge, Snort whinnied and reared up as a rattlesnake struck its fangs into the horse's right leg. The snake dangled from the leg as both horse and rider flipped backward and started skidding down the chasm. Jim's reaction was quick; he reined his horse to get out of the way. Dirt, dust, and cries from both Jake and Snort filled the air as they tumbled thirty feet to the gully's floor. Jake moaned, and the horse whinnied and tried to stand but fell. Jake could see that Snort's left hind leg was broken. The bone was poking through the horse's hide. Jake lay in the dirt for a minute and then slowly rose and knelt on one leg, thankful he had no broken bones. He talked lowly and soothingly to Snort, whom he could see was in pain. Jim shouted to Jake and rode to the bottom of the ravine.

"You okay, Jake?" Jim asked as he leapt from his horse to give Jake a hand.

"Yeah, I'm just scraped up a little," Jake sighed. "But Snort broke her leg."

"I'll take care of the horse for you," Jim said as he pulled his rifle from the scabbard.

"You sheath that rifle and back off!" Jake commanded. "My horse is my responsibility," he said assertively. "I'll do what has to be done to take care of her."

Jake and his horse eyed one another with empathy. The compassion Jake felt overwhelmed him. He pulled his rifle from its scabbard and aimed it at his horse's head.

"Snort, you've given more than any horse could," he said. "I'll miss you, old friend. Rest."

The rifle shot echoed up and down the ravine, and then all was quiet, save for the cawing of some crows and a little snort from the palomino. Jake slumped down beside his dead horse. Words his friend Dan had once said came to mind: *This godforsaken country is hell on earth. Why the hell do there have to be snakes?*

"Damn snakes," Jake said.

"What'd you say?" Jim asked.

"Nothing—just that I'm sorry I yelled at you, Jim."

"That's okay, Jake," Jim said. "I know you had feelings for that horse."

"You got that right," Jake said. "Let's get this tack hidden and ride double back to the ranch."

They removed the saddlebags, saddle, and bridle from Jake's horse and carried them into a thicket of willow bushes where they hid them until they could return to retrieve the tack. It was late in the afternoon, and they anticipated it would take two days riding double to get back to the ranch. Jake took a canteen of water and some jerky, cornbread, and ammunition; stuffed them in a knapsack; and slung it over his shoulder. Picking up his rifle, he took one last look at his dead horse. Jim reached out a hand and swung Jake up onto Nugget. The palomino with its two riders set off on a long, hot ride back to the ranch.

The July heat was also felt at Fort Bridger, where Marsh and his Yale party were being outfitted to go to Henry's Fork in search of fossils. Marsh had received a telegram from Brigham Young saying that, when the expedition got to Salt Lake, Young would like to meet with the professor.

The expedition spent two weeks in the Bridger badlands collecting over a ton of fossils from the Eocene Epoch. They packed sixteen crates of fossils to be shipped to the Yale Peabody Museum and then took a train to Salt Lake City where the students could enjoy a few days relaxing. Marsh readied to meet with Brigham Young.

Marsh stepped lively up the few steps to the veranda of the beautiful, two-story residence of Brigham Young, president of the Church of Latter-Day Saints. With great eagerness, he banged the brass door knocker. Suddenly, the door opened. He was momentarily astounded by the beauty of the young woman who stood in the entrance.

"Ah, good afternoon, miss," Marsh said, clearing his throat. "I'm Professor O. C. Marsh of Yale University. I'm here to see Mr. Brigham Young."

"Why, yes, we were told you were coming," she said. "The president is in the study. I'll show you the way. Follow me."

Marsh followed the woman down a hallway, past a number of doors, and into a large study lined with shelves that were crammed with books and papers. Three gentlemen were seated in comfortable chairs. He was still feeling overwhelmed by the beauty of the woman who welcomed him, partly because of his shyness regarding women. The three men stood when Marsh entered the room.

"Professor Marsh, it is a pleasure to see you again," Brigham said as he crossed the room to shake Marsh's hand.

"The pleasure is mine," Marsh said, holding out his hand to shake. "You're doing wonderful things for this city."

"With the help of God, this city has been a good haven for us," Young said. "Let me introduce you to a couple of our brethren. Professor Marsh, this is Brother Johnston and Brother Hamilton."

After cordial greetings and handshakes, Young invited Marsh and the two brethren to be seated.

"I wanted to have a chat with you about fossil bones," Young said. "You may think it strange that a theologian would be interested in the findings of a scientist of paleontology, but let me explain."

"Please do," Marsh said.

"After reading of your research on horse fossils," Young said, "I find it very interesting that fossils of horses you've found date from pre-Columbian time. I congratulate you on your successful fossil discoveries."

"Thank you, sir," Marsh said, clearing his throat. "The West, with its variety of geological formations, is a marvelous laboratory of fossils. I've been quite successful in discovering a number of different species of horse fossils dating from about fifty million years ago. Most were found at the Loup Fork in Nebraska. We discovered a number of fossil Pliocene mammals; the most interesting were fossils of a small horse I called *Eohippus,* or as I tell my students, 'dawn horse.'"

"I'm most delighted to hear that," Young said. "I've been plagued by critics who have challenged the mention of horses on this continent in the *Book of Mormon.* They're saying there were no horses in America before the Spanish introduced them, accusing the *Book of Mormon* as being apocryphal for mentioning horses in a period that was pre-Columbian."

"Well, there were certainly ancestors of the horse we know of today," Marsh said. "Their size and anatomy, however, were a little different from the horses of the nineteenth century."

"Very well then," Young said. "I would say, according to your discoveries, horses did exist in the Americas long before the Spaniards introduced them."

"The fossil record shows that to be the case," Marsh replied, clearing his throat.

Continuing their conversation, Marsh told of his adventures collecting fossils and about the development of the Yale Peabody Museum. Young revealed plans for the development of religion, education, and culture in Salt Lake City.

As the men were ending their conversation, two women entered the room. They were dressed similarly to the young woman who had welcomed Marsh into the house. One was much older with a stern look on her face; she was so unlike the young woman he'd met earlier that he was taken aback by her appearance.

"I've brought you gentlemen some cookies and apple juice," the woman said.

"Thank you," Young said. "Professor Marsh, this is Sister Emily and Sister Mary."

"Pleased to meet you," Marsh replied, a little self-consciously.

Young rose from his comfortable chair and walked over to a large desk at the far end of the room, where he retrieved a book.

"I've a little gift for you, Professor," Young said as he handed Marsh a Bible, "A memento of our visit."

The summer twilight was slowly fading. Buildings were silhouetted against a deep blue sky as dusk enveloped the ranch. Jake and Jim, riding double on Nugget, came trotting up the road. The door of the ranch house opened, and Jen came running out.

"Jake! Jim! You all right?" she shouted as she jumped off the veranda and ran toward them.

Jake dismounted and ran to meet her.

"We're okay," Jake said. "Just had an accident with Snort, but Jim and I are all right."

Jake was telling Jen about what had happened to his horse when Chris came running up.

"What's going on?" he asked. "I heard Jennie shouting."

Jake continued with his story about his horse and the rattler.

"That's a damn shame," Chris said. "Snort was a fine mare. Thankfully you guys are all right. You've got a nasty bruise on your cheek, Jake. You'd better take care of that."

"Come on, hon," Jen said to Jake. "Let's go in the house and get you cleaned up and fed, you too, Jim. Bella will cook up something tasty for you guys. Bet you're both starving."

"Yes, ma'am, uh, Mrs. Harding, thank you," Jim said. "I'll just take care of Nugget first."

"Don't worry about the palomino, Jim," Chris said. "I'll look after him."

"The name's Jen," Jen said, smiling at Jim.

Jake and Jim had washed up and were eating when Chris and Lys came up to the house.

"You guys look almost human all cleaned up," Chris said.

"Sorry to hear about Snort," Lys said. "She was a fine mare."

"Yeah," Jake said. "It was a hard loss, and then having to leave her for scavengers to dispose of was tough."

"Well, we'll get you a good horse," Chris said. "You take a pick from any of the stock. We'll make it a gift from the ranch."

"No, you won't," Jake said. "I'll pay for the horse."

"You should pick the palomino," Jim said.

"Don't you like that horse?" Jake asked.

"Yeah, I do," Jim said. "But I can ride any horse on the ranch, and my horse didn't get killed."

"What'd ya think, Jake?" Chris asked.

"Nugget's a fine horse," Jake said. "It'd be an honor to ride him. Let me buy him."

"No, sir. He's a gift," Chris said. "Nugget is yours. Starting tomorrow, he's your charge. I'll make up ownership papers."

"Much appreciated. Thank you, Chris," Jake said. "I still think I should pay."

"Let's have a toast to that," Jen said. "I'll get some glasses. Jake, you can't argue with my brother. He's a horse trader from way back."

Jen went off to the kitchen for glasses and a bottle of whiskey.

"We had to leave my saddle and some supplies we hid in the ravine," Jake said. "I'd like to get that cache as soon as possible."

"Was that near Bushwhackers Butte?" Chris asked.

"Bushwhackers Butte," Jake asked. "Where's that?"

"That's the name Jennie and I gave to those bluffs where you were twice attacked," Chris said. "Where Dan was shot."

"Yeah, we were about a mile down the ravine south of there," Jake said. "Let's call that place Rattlesnake Ravine." Jen came over to Jake with the whiskey and cringed at the thought of rattlesnakes.

"Well, you ain't going riding off again to get into more trouble," Jen said hotly as she poured her husband a drink and gave him a stern look. "I need you around here."

There was a pause. Embarrassed by the conversation, Jim kept shoveling food in his mouth. Chris gave his sister a look of condemnation, walked over to her, and put his arms around her.

"Sis, we all know your concern for Jake's safety, but a man's got to take care of his business. Jake's got to recover his belongings," Chris said. "I'll get Red to go with him and a pack mule to bring back the saddle and equipment."

"All right," Jen said. "But Danny and I need him around here for the next few days. Jake, you promised you'd help me with that rock walkway."

"And so I shall, my dear," Jake said.

Four days later, Jake and Red were getting ready to ride off to get the cache Jake had left by the ravine. Before they left, Chris and

Jake were having their second mug of morning coffee on the veranda while Jen was getting Danny his breakfast.

"Got to tell you something," Chris whispered to Jake. "I saw a strange-looking skull that Ali had uncovered that time you guys were at Bushwhackers Butte. Wasn't supposed to tell you about it when Dan was killed and you were shot up. Jen said you might go right back out there at the time if you knew. When you're out that way, you might want to check it out. It was sticking out of that bluff across from where Dan was shot."

"Thanks. I'll take a look," Jake said. "It sounds interesting."

The door opened and out stepped Jen with Danny in her arms.

"Let's go see Daddy," she said. "He's riding off today. You never know when we'll see him again."

Jen walked over to Jake and put Danny into the arms of his father. The little boy made a gurgling sound and flung his arms up and down.

"Hey, big fella," Jake said as he lifted up the boy. "Tell your mom you'll see me in five days."

Jake, riding his newly acquired palomino, Nugget, and Red, riding beside him on a pinto gelding called Buck, led a pack mule on their way to Bushwhackers Butte and Rattlesnake Ravine. After spending a night camping, they arrived at the ravine at midmorning the next day.

"The mare's body is just beyond that patch of bushes," Jake said. They rode down the ravine toward the ridge where Jake's horse had the encounter with the rattlesnake.

Dismounting, they walked a few yards to where Jake had left his dead mare.

"What the hell?" Jake said. "She should be right here. Maybe a bear dragged her off."

The Pawnee was down on his hands and knees examining the ground and sniffing.

"No bear," Red said. "Cheyenne."

"The Cheyenne took my dead horse?" Jake asked. "Why would they take a dead horse?"

"Eat," Red said.

"Eat my horse?' Jake questioned, surprised.

"Sometime," Red said, pointing to the ground. He continued. "Cut horse here. Drag off."

"Why would they want to eat my horse?" Jake asked.

"Buffalo going," the Pawnee said. "Hungry. Sometime."

"They must have found her soon after she died," Jake said. "I thought scavengers would pick her bones. Never thought the scavengers would be Cheyenne. Let's get my saddle."

Searching where Jake had hidden his saddle, they found nothing. The Cheyenne had taken that also.

At Bushwhackers Butte, Jake found the fossil skull Chris had told him about. Digging it out of the cliff's clay side, he found a very large skull and jawbone. It looked like the skull of a rhino with three horns. One horn protruded from its beak-like pincher snout, and two others grew out of either side of the top of its skull. The skull had a bony frill extending back and up from the two horns on its head. They loaded the large, heavy skull on the mule.

After they returned to the ranch, Jake showed Chris the fossil skull. They had never seen one like this. Two days later, after Jake had cleaned the fossil, he did a drawing of it that he sent to Marsh for identification. Marsh knew of this skull and was very interested in finding more like it. He had named it *Triceratops*, "three-horn face."

22

The Harding's and Luke were getting ready for a trip to Laramie, where they would check the mail, pick up supplies, and meet with Linda. Luke had asked Linda to marry him, and a wedding was planned at the ranch in September. Jake drove the buggy with Jen and little Danny as passengers. This was Danny's first trip away from the ranch, and the seven-month-old was thrilled to be riding in the wagon and taking in all the new sights and sounds. They traveled at a leisurely pace. Luke, riding his bay mare, would make the horse do some bucking and rearing for Danny's entertainment.

When they rode into Laramie, the August sun was high in the sky, sending sweltering rays onto the dusty town site. Beyond the distant horizon, thunderheads were building and summer evening thunderstorms were a real possibility. Jennie and little Danny were dozing in the seats of the buggy. The parched travelers were anticipating some food, drink, and shade.

"Let's head for the Frontier Hotel," Luke said to Jake. "We'll get you, Jen, and the boy checked in there and a give you a chance to wash off some of that trail dust. I'll take the buggy and horses over to Claudia's Café. We can get the horses watered and stabled behind the café. Claudia's old sorrel died last year, so there's only Linda's horse, Pepper, there now, plenty of room for our horses. After you get settled at the hotel, I'll meet you at Claudia's for a cold drink and some food."

TRICERATOPS
THREE HORN FACE

"Sounds good to me," Jake said. "I'll bet Linda will be glad to see you."

"Well, I sure hope so," Luke said with a grin.

After helping the Harding's unload their baggage at the hotel, Luke tied his horse behind the buggy and drove it to Claudia's Café.

The café had only a few customers left over from the noon meal. Linda was clearing some dishes off of one of the tables when Luke walked in.

"Well, look what the cat drug in," Linda said. "Hi, honey."

Luke crossed the floor to her, grabbed her by the waist, pulled her to him, and planted a big kiss on her lips, causing her to spill a glass of water.

"Hey," she said, teasing him. "Slow down, cowboy, I ain't no heifer you can rope, tie, and brand."

"Oh, you're much prettier and feistier than any heifer, my dear," Luke said. "And on September 5, I plan on putting my brand on you." He did a quick turn to address the few customers at the far end of the café. "We're getting married on the fifth of September at the Muller Ranch. You're all invited."

"Yahoo!" shouted one of the patrons, who obviously knew Luke. "We'll be there."

"What's all the yelling about?" Claudia asked as she entered the room.

"I was just telling the folks here about our wedding date," Luke said as he gave Linda another hug.

"Well, hello there, Luke Martins," Claudia said. "Do I get a hug too?"

"You bet," Luke said, and he gave her a hug. "Good to see you, Mrs. Holmes. How've you been?"

"I'm fair to middlin'," Claudia said. "But my daughter's been flustered ever since you proposed to her."

"Well, me too, Mrs. Holmes," Luke said. "Jake, Jen, and their little boy, Danny, came to town with me. They're over at the Frontier Hotel and should be here shortly. Could we board two horses and a buggy in your back paddock?"

"Of course you can, but only if you call me Claudia," she said. "If'n you need a place to bunk, you can use the spare room. It's available until mid-next week."

"Thanks, Claudia. I appreciate that," Luke said. "I'll take care of the horses and put my gear in the room."

"I believe there's a little hay left in the corral," Claudia said. "Sylas comes into the café early for eggs and coffee; he eats half a dozen eggs at a time. I'll tell him to bring some fresh feed for the horses."

"Oh, I can't wait to see that little boy," Linda said. "Last time I saw him he was just a couple of months old and cute as a button."

Luke was about to go tend to the horses when Jake and Jen, carrying Danny, walked into the café.

"Oh, my goodness," Linda exclaimed, holding out her arms. "Look who's here!"

"Danny, let's give Auntie Linda a big hug," Jen said, walking toward Linda.

Danny had always taken to Linda, and Linda had adored the child from the first time she saw him. She took Danny in her arms and started kissing and hugging him.

"Oh, I want one of these, "she said as the child wiggled and giggled.

"Soon enough, my daughter," Claudia said with a sigh, rolling her eyes.

After greetings were exchanged, Jake and Luke took the wagon and horses to the corral in the back of the café. They unharnessed the horses and pumped fresh water in the trough for the thirsty animals.

"Claudia said I can use the spare room for a couple of days," Luke told Jake. "So I'm going over there to wash up. I'll meet you in the café."

"Okay," Jake said. "I'm starving and could whet my whistle."

A table in the café was set for six people. Jake, Jenny, Luke, and little Danny were seated at the table enjoying cold drinks. Claudia and Linda were busy setting other tables, getting ready for the supper diners. Claudia came over to the table and plopped herself down in a chair.

"I've been doing this restaurant business for too many years," she said. "It's about my time to be put out to pasture."

"Ah, you're too young for that," Luke said.

"My son-in-law-to-be is a great kidder and a *smooth* talker," Claudia said, chuckling. "But I love him, especially since he gave up being a lawman."

Linda approached the table in time to hear the conversation. "Me too," she said.

"Well, what if I went back to law enforcement?" Luke said. "Which reminds me, I've got to go see Sheriff Boswell tomorrow. I have to make sure he's invited to the wedding."

"You won't find a Sheriff Boswell 'cause he is now *Marshal* Boswell," Claudia said. "He's the warden of our new territorial prison. I should bring all of you up to date on Laramie's latest news. We have a new sheriff; his name is John Brophy. Old Boz became a marshal last month and is now the warden of our new prison. The prison is just outside of town to the west and was opened in the spring. Boz has been a busy fella with his marshal duties, plus he is buying a part interest in a ranch east of the Medicine Bow Mountains. Also, he and his brother George are investing in a soda ash works near here. I'll get you the latest copies of the *Sentinel,* and you can read all about our city's activities."

"Your meals are ready," Linda said. "Mom and I will serve you, and then we'll join you. We're sure you'll find that our new cook, Evelyn, prepares some great food."

It was a long and joyous meal, and by the time everyone was through eating, visiting, and enjoying a last cup of coffee, supper time patrons were already beginning to fill up the café. Little Danny was fast asleep in his mother's lap. Claudia was back in the kitchen, and Linda was taking food orders along with Joanne, another waitress who had just come to work. Late afternoon advanced, and a breeze stirred up wisps of dust, bringing with it the scent of rain.

"We'd better be getting back to the hotel before the rain hits," Jake said, reaching for his wallet. "I'm buying dinner."

"No, you're not," Linda said. "The treat is on Mom and me."

"Oh, no," Jen protested. "You can't do that."

"Yes, we can," Claudia said as she appeared from the kitchen. "When we come out to the ranch for the wedding, you can treat us."

"That's a promise," Jen said. She handed Danny to Jake and gave Claudia and Linda a hug.

Jake held Danny in one arm, opened the door, and followed Jen out of the café onto the boardwalk and into a windy, dust-blown street.

When they arrived at the hotel, they found their room on the second floor to be hot and stuffy. Jake laid Danny on the bed and opened the window to a cooling breeze and a splattering of large raindrops.

"Oh, that feels good," Jen said. "I'm going to sleep sound tonight after that long, hot ride."

"I'll be sawing logs the minute my head hits that pillow," Jake said, yawning.

Jen undressed Danny, washed him with a wet cloth, and got him ready for bed. Jake laid a blanket on the floor next to the bed to make a place for the boy to sleep. The room was darkening as evening approached, and echoing sounds of thunder could be heard in the distance. A flash of lightning lit up the room; after a few seconds, a loud bang of thunder announced the beginning of a heavy downpour. Jake lit a lantern, and he and his wife got ready for bed just as the rainstorm hit with full force. Yet even with the window open to the cooling rainstorm, the hotel room stayed hot and stuffy. They both removed all of their clothing and climbed into bed, pulling just a sheet over their naked bodies. Jake blew out the lantern. Eerie shadows were cast across the walls of the room as lightning flashes lit up the heavens.

Jake was hot and drenched in sweat as he lay on the bed watching intense flashes of blue light coming through the window. He struggled to get out of bed to close the window. Scuffling, he made it to the window and peered out into the dark streets of Laramie. Bursts of light and animated shadows caught his eye. Then he saw it. Appearing out of the darkness was a gigantic beast, illuminated by the blue flashes, lumbering toward the hotel. Its huge head, with three large horns and jaws showing rows of dagger-sharp teeth, sat atop a neck and body that easily could reach the second-story window of the hotel. A flash of lightning lit up the street, and he saw his friend Dan Randall standing below in front of the hotel. Dan motioned for him to come. Jake was dazed by a blinding light and a sharp bang. He yelled and jumped as he felt himself being pulled back.

"Jake! Jake, darling," Jen said as she pulled him back into the pillow. "Wake up. You're having a bad dream."

He groaned, blinked his eyes, and sat up in bed. "Oh, I was dreaming," he said.

"You sure were," Jen said. "You were moaning and groaning. And you're soaked with sweat. Were you having another nightmare about monsters?"

"Yeah," Jake said. He threw the sheet off of him, rolled out of bed, and ran naked across the room to close the window. It was stuck. Struggling to close it, he was showered by the driving rain. There was a blinding flash of lightning and a loud crack of thunder. He jumped back a step as the window sash slammed down.

"Wow," he said. "That was close."

Jen chuckled. "Ain't you a sight for sore eyes," she said, "standing there buck naked, soaking wet, and being lit up by flashes of lightning."

Danny woke up and started crying.

"Come on, my two boys," Jen said. "Climb into bed with Mommy, and she'll protect you from the storm."

"All right," Jake said. "Let's get some sleep. We'll want to get an early start in the morning. We'll meet Luke and Linda for breakfast, get to the post office and the bank, and be on the road home before noon."

"What?" Jen said, perturbed at Jake's plans. "I thought we were going to stay another day. I have plans to shop for a few things. What's your hurry? You think the erosion that the storm caused will expose fossils that somebody else might find?"

Jake didn't answer. Jen picked up little Danny, who was sniffling. She carried him over to the window and pointed down at the street.

"Look out there at that river of mud—and horseshit," she said. "We don't want to be traveling in that just so you can get to your fossil hunting. It's going to be muddy as hell for a few days at least."

"Okay, you've made your point," Jake said. "We'll stay another day."

"Thank you, dear," Jen said snappishly. She laid Danny back down in the middle of the bed and crawled in beside him.

Jake lay down beside Danny, pulled the sheet up over himself and Danny, and rubbed the boy's back.

"Let's get some sleep," he said.

But sleep wouldn't come. Jake's thoughts were troubling his mind as he lay in the dark watching the fading lightning strikes cast shadows around the room. He wondered if his dreams were a premonition of things to come. He'd had this daunting feeling about Dan beckoning him to come with him in several dreams. He also thought about hunting fossils and told himself that is what he wanted to do; *he must do what he must do,* although he agreed with Jen that it'd be too muddy for a few days to do any digging. He resolved that to be patient would be best for now, even though he found himself being less and less patient these days.

After two days of sunny skies, hot weather, and winds, the mud-caked landscape was beginning to dry out. Luke and Linda were on horseback; and Jake, Jennie, and little Danny were riding in the carriage and just pulling into the ranch yard. Chris and Lys came out of the house carrying a wooden box and sat it beside some others that were stacked on the veranda.

"How was Laramie?" Chris asked. "I see Linda came back with you guys."

"We captured her," Luke said.

"I bet you did," Lys said as she jumped off the veranda and went to give Linda a hug.

"Didn't take much capturing," Jen said. "We're delighted to have her along."

"What're you doing with all the boxes?" Jake asked.

"We had one hell of a hailstorm the other night," Chris said. "Knocked out the windows in the back spare room where we had stored some of Pa's old stuff. Everything got soaked, and we thought it was time to sort through the boxes and see what we should chuck and what we want to save."

"Well, don't chuck anything until I take a look," Jen said.

"We won't, sis," Chris said. "That's why we're stacking the stuff out here on the porch, so we can all take a look."

"Hey!" Jake shouted. "Is that a violin on top of those boxes?"

"Sure is," Jen said. "That was Pa's old fiddle. He tried to teach me how to play it, but I could never get the hang of it."

"You never told me you had a violin," Jake said.

"You never asked me," Jen replied.

"Mind if I take a look at it?" Jake asked.

"Go ahead," Jen said.

Jake hopped down from the wagon and stepped up onto the veranda. He snapped open the violin case and took out the instrument, plucking the strings and twisting the tuning knobs.

"Out of tune," he said. He picked up the bow and twisted the end to tighten the hair. Drawing the bow across the strings, he kept turning the tuning knobs.

"Nice tone," he said. Then to everyone's amazement, he started to play a tune.

"Hon, I didn't know you could play the violin," Jen said, surprised. She clapped her hands with joy.

"You never asked me," Jake said as he kept playing.

"Oh, I know that song," Lys said. "It's 'Home Sweet Home.' My daddy taught me to sing it while he played the piano. He was forever playing that song after he came home from the war."

She jumped onto the veranda, stood next to Jake as he played the violin, and started humming the tune. Then as the words came to her and Jake repeated the refrain, she started singing.

> Mid pleasures and palaces
> though we may roam,
> be it ever so humble
> there's no place like home.

Everyone applauded, yelled, and whistled.

"I have a request!" Linda yelled.

"We don't play requests," Jake said, and then he turned to Lys. "Do we?"

"You have to take this one," Linda said. "I want you two to play that song at my wedding."

"That's a request we can do," Jake and Lys said in unison.

Jen was absolutely delighted that Jake could play the violin. She could hear her father's musical voice speak once again, and her first thought was that Jake could teach their son to play.

"How in the devil did you ever learn to play the violin?" Jen asked.

"Thanks to my grandfather," Jake said, "who was the most patient man I know. He spent hours tutoring me on the fine art of fiddling, which has stuck with me all my life."

"By God, ain't that the truth?" Jen said, laughing.

It was a large wedding celebration for Linda and Luke on September fifth at the Muller Ranch. A multitude of guests came from near and far. Linda's brother, Jon Holmes, who lived in Chicago, came to join in. Linda's father had been killed in the Civil War, so Jon gave away the bride. Claudia, Evelyn, Joanne, and Aunt Bella organized the kitchen help for the preparation of a side of beef cooked on a spit. The enormous feast included all the trimmings plus kegs of beer. The fall weather was beautiful with sunny blue skies above a kaleidoscopic landscape. Guests were delighted to hear Jake and Lys perform some musical numbers, as they had promised. A number of games and activities for all ages gave the party a carnival feel. Sylas Anderson was cheered on by guests for his ability to make ringer after ringer in the horseshoe-throwing contest. Kids and adults played bat-the-ball games, tag, and hide and seek.

The new Mr. and Mrs. Luke and Linda Martins were astounded when they read the wedding card given them signed by Chris and Lys Muller, Jake and Jennie Harding, and Bella Muller. The card was a deed to a large amount of acreage on the Muller Ranch. In addition to wishing them a happy life together, the card stated that they were the sole owners of the described land, which was close to the Muller's ranch home, where the Martins could do what they pleased with the property. The Muller's hoped they would build a home on it and become neighbors to the Muller Ranch.

23

That October, back at his residence in New Haven, Professor Marsh was catching up on his correspondence. He was somewhat dismayed to read the news about the financial crises caused in part by the Franco-Prussian War and the redeeming of American bonds bought by European investors. The Panic of 1873 had little effect on Marsh personally as his financial position was secure because of his Uncle Peabody's trust fund. But he was concerned about government funds for support of geological surveys and building western railroad routes, both of which had employees who would keep an eye out for fossils that were unearthed and sent to Marsh at Yale. Marsh's adversary, Edward Cope, was also using the geological surveys to his advantage to obtain fossil specimens. The feud between the two rival paleontologists was ongoing, expanding, and at times resorted to underhanded methods to try and disgrace each other. Both scientists had spies reporting on finds and activities at fossil sites. Their classification and nomenclature of fossils was often hurried and inaccurate, and sometimes specimens that had been found by others were declared to be their new discoveries. The two scientists were prolific in their collecting and publishing results of their knowledge of prehistoric life.

Marsh had spent the winter and spring sorting through the huge collection of fossils that Yale had obtained. He wrote articles for the

Journal of Science describing, classifying, and illustrating his discoveries and was elected to the National Academy of Sciences.

In the summer of 1874, Marsh received a letter from General George Custer inviting him on an expedition to the Black Hills of the Dakota Territory. As tempting as the offer was, Marsh declined, as he was pressed by business with the Peabody Museum and cataloging the Yale fossil collection. Then, in the fall of 1874, a letter from General Edward Ord, Commander of the Department of the Platte (a military district that included Nebraska and the Dakota territories), told Marsh he should take a look at a vast deposit of fossils near the Red Cloud Agency, where the army had an outpost called Camp Robinson. Arrangements would be made to obtain wagons and supplies and to enlist some soldiers and officers who were interested in fossil collecting. The letter kindled Marsh's desire even more to obtain fossils from that region. He had one of his fossil collectors in the area. Hank Clifford from Sidney, Nebraska, could be his guide. He decided to make a trip, once again, to the western bone beds. He sent a letter to Jake Harding asking if he would join him.

Jennie was shaking her head and chuckling to herself as Jake read her the letter.

"That's crazy," Jen said. "Marsh wants you to meet him in Cheyenne at the end of October for a fossil-hunting trip to the Dakota Badlands? What about winter weather and hostile Indians?"

"It won't be any more difficult than other expeditions I've been on," Jake said. "Marsh has made arrangements for a secure and safe trip."

"This fossil expedition is not a good idea," Jen said, shaking her head.

"Let me finish the letter," Jake said. He read Jen the part about having wagons and army soldiers on the expedition. "We'll have tents, warm clothing, and plenty of food supplies. I'll be gone for just a few weeks."

"You really think you should go?" Jen questioned.

"Yes," Jake said. "According to Marsh, this is a large bone bed waiting to be explored. It could be a major find."

"Okay, you just better be back here by Thanksgiving."

"Now how could I miss our anniversary?" Jake asked.

"By freezing your ass off and losing your scalp," Jen said sarcastically.

On October 29, Jake rode into Laramie to catch the train to Cheyenne, where he would meet Marsh. In Laramie, he took his horse to be boarded at the livery stable, where he told Sylas he'd be back in about a month.

It was a short train ride to Cheyenne and a short walk from the station to the hotel where Jake met Marsh. Two soldiers were with Marsh when Jake walked into the hotel lobby.

"Good to see you again, Jake," Marsh said. "I wasn't sure if you'd make it. Let me introduce you to Lieutenant Glen Hopkins and Sergeant Paul Weber. The army has provided us with some supplies and horses and sent the lieutenant and the sergeant to escort us to Fort Laramie tomorrow."

After introductions, Marsh invited the three men to dine in the hotel restaurant. When they were all seated, Marsh bought each a whiskey before they ordered their meals.

"Lieutenant Hopkins has been telling me about some of the troubles with the Indians at the Red Cloud Agency on the White River," Marsh said. "Seems the treaty, the government and the Sioux signed in '68 at Fort Laramie, has been violated by the US Government."

"That's right," Hopkins said. "It was that treaty that guaranteed the Lakota Sioux a large reservation that includes much of the western Dakota Territory, the ownership of the Black Hills. It also says that the Powder River Country was closed to travel by all whites. That isn't the only problem. The Indian agencies have been cheating the Sioux on their annual disbursement of rations. Some of the food supplies are spoiled and not fit for human consumption. With the buffalo scarce, the Indians are starving."

"Skirmishes that the Army had with the Lakota Sioux during the Indian wars, before the Laramie Treaty, were bloody battles," Sergeant Weber added. "Those battles were fought over expansion of railroads and the encroachment of white settlers, hunters, and gold-seeking miners. The Sioux are fierce warriors, and led by Chief Red Cloud. They defeated the army at Powder River in '66."

Jake took a swallow of his whiskey and looked at Marsh, who seemed a little taken aback by the soldiers' story.

"What's the situation today at the Red Cloud Agency?" Jake asked.

"Well, Chief Red Cloud, desiring peace for his suffering people, somewhat reluctantly signed the treaty. Surprisingly, Red Cloud has tried to keep the peace between Lakota leaders and the Bureau of Indian Affairs agents," Hopkins said. "The agency, in the fall of 1873, was moved from its location on the North Platte River in Wyoming Territory to a site overlooking the White River in the northwest corner of Nebraska. At present the agent at the Red Cloud Agency is Dr. John Saville. Red Cloud and Saville have had their differences, but the greatest menace is two other young Sioux leaders, Sitting Bull and Crazy Horse. Red Cloud does try to keep them in check."

"Red Cloud seems to be an Indian that one could reason with," Marsh said snorting. "I would like to meet with him to get the Sioux's permission to go into the badlands."

"Saville assuredly can set up a meeting between you and Red Cloud," the lieutenant said.

"Going into Indian land may be a bit difficult," the sergeant said.

Jake was silent. He slowly took another sip of whiskey and thought maybe Jen was right; *this doesn't seem like a good idea.* He had no desire to get into a skirmish with Indians. But then Marsh could probably get the Lakota Sioux to give them permission to hunt fossils in the badlands. The professor with his dogged determination had the gift of convincing people to give in to his way of thinking.

After Marsh and Jake were outfitted at Fort Laramie with horses, four wagons, and a small detachment of army escorts, they arrived at the Red Cloud Agency on November 4. There they met Hank Clifford, their guide, who filled them in on the Indian situation. The agency was surrounded by thousands of tepees and reservation Indian tribes of the Sioux confederation who had gathered for the annual distribution of rations. The Indians were distrustful of Marsh's men, thinking they were gold hunters who had brought wagons, equipment, and soldiers into the area. When the news spread about General Custer finding gold in the Dakota Black Hills in August of 1874, many unwelcomed gold prospectors came to the Black Hills, which were sacred land to the Sioux; they called them *Mako Sica*. Custer violated the Sioux treaty of 1868 by taking his troops into the Black Hills in the fall of 1874. Due to the Panic of 1873, the US Government was hungry for gold.

The angry Oglala Lakota Sioux told the Indian agent, Saville, to tell Marsh to take his wagons and leave. Saville knew the trouble the Sioux could cause. The past February, the agency had had trouble with them over the lack of rations, and their demonstrations had turned violent. They had killed Saville's brother-in-law, Frank Appleton, who was an agency clerk. In response, Saville sent for the army at Fort Laramie. After settling things down with the rebellious Lakota, the army established a post not far from the agency. It was named Fort Robinson in honor of a cavalry officer killed by hostile Sioux.

"We've had some serious problems with the Sioux, and they are upset with your presence here," Saville told Marsh. "I think it would be best if your party left the area and forgot about going into the White River Badlands."

"If I could talk with Red Cloud and explain the purpose of our expedition, I'm sure we could work things out," Marsh said in his assertive manner. "The area is an enormously rich fossil field for

Eocene mammalian specimens. We have traveled a long way for this opportunity to explore it for fossil bones."

Jake agreed with Marsh. "All we want to do is look for fossils," he said.

Saville agreed to arrange a meeting between the Sioux and Professor Marsh.

In a large tent the army had erected, a feast was held to honor the Sioux leaders and ease tensions between the Marsh party and the Indians. Marsh and Chief Red Cloud were introduced, as well as other Sioux, including Sitting Bull and Sword. Marsh and Red Cloud were two men of the same persuasion. Both men were resolute and outspoken in their beliefs. They were in awe of each other, although neither would openly show it. They both gave long and candid speeches on the matter at hand—fossil hunting in the White River Badlands.

The Sioux argued bitterly because they were suspicious that the white men would go into the nearby Black Hills to look for gold after they were allowed into the White River Badlands. Marsh assured the Sioux that his intentions were only to collect fossils in the White River Badlands. He also assured them that he would take their complaints about the agency's misappropriation of food and supplies allocated to reservation Indians back to the US president. After much bickering, Marsh obtained Red Cloud's permission to go into Sioux land. The conditions were that the party was there to look for fossils only. An escort of half a dozen or so Sioux Braves, led by Red Cloud's brother-in-law, Hunts the Enemy, would accompany Marsh's party to monitor their activity. Marsh would pay each Indian escort $1.50 a day. Red Cloud advised Marsh to stay south of the White River to avoid any contact with Lakota Sioux tribes that were not reservation tribes and were very hostile toward whites. The Lakota tribe the Miniconjou was to be especially feared.

The next morning the ground was covered with snow from a storm that passed during the night. A northwesterly wind whipped the recent snowfall into billowy drifts, and the temperature dropped below freezing. It was in these frigid surroundings that Professor Marsh's fossil hunters readied to cross the desolate prairie headed for the badlands.

"I hope this isn't the kind of weather we can expect every day," Jake said as he mounted his horse and eased himself into a cold saddle. "This expedition to the badlands looks like it'll be one of our coldest digs."

"It'll be brutal," Marsh said. "But once we start collecting, you'll love it."

The professor's obstinate obsession with collecting fossils couldn't be stopped by harsh weather, hostile Indians, or wild animals.

You'll love it—Marsh's words echoed in Jake's mind. *You know he's right,* Jake admitted. *I'm addicted to fossil collecting as much as Marsh—and I love it.*

The fossil hunters' November trek over the bleak, frozen prairie was disheartening. Men and horses were exhausted and chilled to the bone by the ever-present bitter wind and freezing temperature. The guise of the landscape was monotonous. The wind rippled the highlands turf of snow-glazed grasses like waves on a restless ocean, taking one's eye to the distant low horizon. There seemed to be endless miles to this two-dimensional terrestrial landscape. And then, gradually, islands of outcroppings began to appear among the undulating grasses. Appearing in the distance like a prairie mirage, a Gothic city of graven cliff castles and palaces carved by eons of erosion met their eyes. Steep ravines like the canyon streets of some metropolis appeared. An immense cityscape of sculptured rock pinnacles displayed varied sizes and shapes of multicolored earth— the White River Badlands. Jake sighed with relief to have conquered the frozen prairie trek, but he still felt one fear: confronting the hostile Miniconjou Indians.

Hank Clifford guided the wagons and horsemen slowly down a

deep gully to find some shelter. There they would set up their camp in this massive, surreal maze of earthworks.

Arriving at the narrow ravine's flat bottom, Jake quickly dismounted. As soon as he hit the ground, he started stomping his feet and rubbing his hands to get some warmth to his extremities. A soldier next to him did the same thing.

Marsh and Hank loped over to where Jake and the soldier were talking. After dismounting, they too did some stomping to take the chill off from the long ride.

"We've still got a couple of hours of sunlight," Marsh said to Jake. "We'll let some of the troopers set up camp, and you, Hank, and I will do a quick scout around for bone sites."

"Sounds good to me," Jake said. "I'm anxious to get started, might warm me up." The young soldier standing beside Jake looked dejected and was just about to say something.

"What's your name, trooper?" Marsh asked the soldier before anything else was said.

"Charlie," the soldier said. "Charlie Adair, sir."

"Well, Charlie, check your rifle, mount up, and come along with us," Marsh said, clearing his throat. "I'll tell the lieutenant to set the camp here. The four of us will return at sundown. We'll eat then."

The young trooper was delighted to join the fossil hunters. He quickly withdrew his rifle from the scabbard on his horse and then jacked the lever to make sure it was loaded.

"Hope we don't have any trouble with hostiles," Charlie said. "But if we do, I'll be ready."

"I think we'll be okay," Hank said to the soldier. "Look yonder along the top of those cliffs. What do you see?"

"Indians!" the trooper exclaimed as he started to bring his rifle to bear.

"Yep," Hank said nonchalantly. "Don't worry; those are Red Cloud's sentinels keeping an eye on us so we don't slip over into the Black Hills looking for gold."

The four mounted their horses and started off down the ravine to inspect the badlands for bones.

"According to reports I have, we should find many bone beds," Marsh said. "A few years back, Joseph Leidy and F. V. Hayden found an abundance of mammal bones from the Eocene era in these badlands."

"I hope we find them before we get snowed in," Jake said.

"We will," Marsh said. "Look there!"

Poking out of the ground was part of a large fossil bone.

"Wow," Charlie said. "This is exciting—only gone about a hundred yards and already found some old bones."

"Old is right, son," Marsh said. "Probably thirty million years old. Looks like the femur of a large ungulate mammal. Let's get it excavated."

Even before Marsh was through speculating on what the fossil was, Hank and Jake had dismounted, gotten their hammers, and were on their way to the bone. Marsh followed with a small shovel while Charlie looked on in awe. Jake was always meticulous with his excavation of fossils, even more so than Marsh and certainly much more so than Clifford. Hank had excavated and shipped to Marsh, in New Haven, fossils that had been hurriedly unearthed and damaged.

"Take your time," Jake warned Hank. "This looks like a good specimen. We don't want to damage it."

Hank just laughed. "I've been digging fossils for a long time and know how it should be done," he replied arrogantly.

"We got problems here, men?" Marsh asked, clearing his throat and addressing Jake and Hank in a tone that indicated he was a little annoyed.

"No, no problem," both men answered.

"Okay, then," Marsh said. "Let's get to work on this bone. For now just dig enough from around the bone so I can measure its size and inspect it. We don't have to dig it all the way out of the ground. We can do that tomorrow. We don't have much time now, and I'd like to explore some other areas before supper."

Jake and Hank chipped away the clay earth, and Marsh shoveled a trench around the large bone.

"It is just as I thought," Marsh said with pleasure. "Looks like a femur of a Megacerops. It's a little over three feet. We'll leave it as it is and finish collecting it tomorrow. Let's move on and look for other bones."

No sooner had he said that than they found a bone bed strewn with exposed fossils. They immediately began to do some digging. The sun was setting, and long shadows were cast along the gorge as the temperature began dropping.

"This is brutal," Jake said. "I'm freezing my ass off—and everything else."

"We'd best be getting back to camp to get some warmth and food," Marsh said. "We'll get at this site early tomorrow."

There was plenty of food at camp; their cook had great culinary skills and was able to prepare hot, nourishing meals, seemingly a miracle in the middle of a frigid no-man's-land. The men were appreciative of the food, but finding warmth amid the November weather was another matter. In their tents they crawled into beds piled high with blankets and buffalo robes trying to keep warm. The mornings were frosty, with ice in their water barrels and frozen boots, clothing, and horses' tack. Most of the men had beards that were frosted with icicles. The men who didn't have whiskers didn't bother to shave in the frigid temperatures. After having a hot breakfast, the men were eager to start working to keep warm.

On the first morning of collecting, some of the men finished excavating the large Megacerops femur bone, while others found a diversity of bones at the bone bed site discovered the evening before. They had their work cut out for them, as miles and miles of badlands were scattered with fossil bones. Work went on for a week as the weather got increasingly colder and threating snowstorms were inevitable. Marsh knew they had pushed the time limit for their collecting and figured only a couple more days of exploring would be available before the grasp of winter would be inescapable.

Marsh was very pleased with the fossils they were finding. Among their discoveries were a number of fossils of ammonites (coiled, chambered mollusks), pterosaurs (large flying reptiles), Archelon (large sea turtles ten feet in length), and a number of Eocene Mammalia, of which two were of the most interest to Marsh. Mesohippus, a descendant of the "dawn horse," was about the size of a deer and had three toes on each foot. Other fossils were from large, rhino-like beasts, such as the Megacerops, which was the size of a small elephant. Marsh had been studying and writing papers on these and was delighted to have additional specimens to research. The Sioux patrolling the Marsh expedition were satisfied to see that the white men were collecting only bones. They concluded that Marsh should be known as Chief Old Bones.

"Professor Marsh!" Charlie Adair yelled as he rode up to a group of collectors.

"What is it?" Marsh asked as he looked up from his digging.

"Lieutenant White wants to see you at camp right away," Charlie said.

Marsh loped his horse the short ride back to camp. As he neared Lieutenant White's tent, he saw two Sioux, two troopers, and the lieutenant standing out front talking. Marsh dismounted and tethered his horse to a rope line in front of the tent.

"Afternoon, Lieutenant," Marsh said. "What's this about?"

"Professor Marsh, my interrupter tells me the Sioux say we're in danger of being attacked by the Miniconjou," Lieutenant White said.

"We always knew that," Marsh said, clearing his throat. "That's why the army is escorting us."

"I'm well aware of our duties, Professor," Lieutenant White said, a little peeved. "The Sioux say the Miniconjou are preparing a war party. They could attack us any day now. I think we should pack up and hightail it out of here, right now."

"Damn it, Lieutenant," Marsh said. "I'm not going to just throw all our fossils in the wagons to be broken to smithereens bouncing over the prairies. We have to have at least a day to pack them properly."

"Well, damn it, Marsh," the Lieutenant said, "I say we go *now*. I'm not willing to risk my scalp for your damn bones."

"We'll go when I say so," Marsh said angrily, clearing his throat. "Do not forget that I'm in charge of this expedition. You and your men are here to escort and protect this crew. If you yourself choose to desert now, please do. We'll start packing this evening and finish up by tomorrow. We will leave then."

"I'll be reporting this incident when we get back to the agency—*if*, God willing, we get back," Lieutenant White said.

"Fine," Marsh said. "When you do, say hello to General Ord for me."

The two Sioux, who were observing this altercation between two strong-headed white men, were finding the argument quite amusing. One of the Sioux, who understood enough English to get the drift of the conversation, turned to one of the troopers and pointed to Marsh.

"Chief Old Bones—Chief," the Sioux said.

"It appears that way," the soldier said.

Marsh told Jake and Hank about the possibility of an attack on their camp by the Miniconjou. He instructed them to get the men busy packing and loading the piles of fossils they had excavated into the wagons.

"We want to be ready to move out of here by noon tomorrow," Marsh said. "Too bad we have to cut our exploring short."

"Just as well," Jake said. "It's getting colder, and the men are starting to complain."

"Well, I'm not paying them to complain," Marsh said. "I'm paying them to dig."

It was a little past noon the next day when the party of fossil hunters had the wagons ready to go. They had four wagons loaded to the top with bones.

Marsh approached Lieutenant White, who was shouting orders to some soldiers but became very quiet when he saw the professor.

"You seem a little anxious today," Marsh said, grinning.

"Professor, are you ready to leave?" Lieutenant White asked coldly. "I'd like to leave before we have to fight our way out of here."

"My men and I are ready," Marsh said. "Lead the way."

Later that evening they arrived back at the Red Cloud Agency. After unhitching the wagons, the soldiers and fossil hunters looked forward to bunking in the barracks at Camp Robinson, an army outpost just two miles from the agency. There they could sleep in some warmth. Marsh informed them that he would meet with Red Cloud and the Sioux so they could examine the wagons and make sure they were not bringing back loads of gold. After that, the fossils would be crated and taken to the Northern Pacific railhead, just a few miles from the agency, for shipment to New Haven.

The next morning Marsh and Jake met with Chief Red Cloud and a party of Oglala Sioux. After examining the wagons the Indians were satisfied that the white men were not collecting anything but bones and rocks. Red Cloud was impressed with the white man's honesty.

"I am surprised and honored by your promised word," Red Cloud said. "Most white men do not honor their promise."

"I have no reason to lie to you," Marsh said. "It is as I said: we only want to collect these bones—to study them, to learn from them."

"These bones speak to you?" Red Cloud asked.

"Yes, they do," Marsh answered. "They murmur great secrets to us."

"What do they tell you?" Red Cloud asked.

"They tell us of the time they lived in their world—many, many years before you and me," Marsh said. "That world's mysteries are whispered to us by these old bones. One must listen very closely."

"My people know of some of these bones and their stories," Red Cloud said. He pointed to a large skull almost three feet in length. "We know the story of this bone."

"What do you know of this large skull?" Marsh asked.

"That is skull of Thunder Horse," the chief said. "Thunder Horse would come down to earth in thunderstorms to chase and kill buffalo across the plains. One time, during a loud thunderstorm, Thunder Horse drove a herd of buffalo into a Sioux camp where the people were starving. The people were able to kill many buffalo. The Great Spirit had sent Thunder Horse to help our people get food."

"Chief," Marsh said, "I shall call this creature's fossil *Brontothere*, meaning 'Thunder Beast.'"

"Professor Marsh," Red Cloud said, "you and your man, Jake, shall come as guests to my camp. You are first white men I trust."

Jake began to do a drawing of the *Brontothere* skull.

Later at Red Cloud's encampment the two white men were honored guests. This indeed was a special occasion. The Sioux were mistrustful of any white men.

"I know men of honor," Chief Red Cloud told his people, "and I know men of lies. I have found trustfulness in these two white men and hope in their promises to see the Great White Chief in Washington and tell of the bad food and lack of supplies by the Bureau of Indian Affairs."

The two white men were impressed by Red Cloud's intelligence and his skills as a leader of his people. The Sioux chief told Marsh and Jake about the misconduct involving the bureau's distribution of rations. The US Government had promised to help the Sioux if they signed the 1868 Fort Laramie treaty. The US would give those signers rations of food and supplies and protect their hunting grounds and sacred land (the Black Hills) from white intruders. Red Cloud gave up his war against the white man, as his people were suffering from hunger and disease; he finally agreed to the treaty. But not all Sioux tribes signed, and Red Cloud tried to make peace between all the leaders of the various Sioux tribes. Two chiefs who opposed Red Cloud were Crazy Horse and Sitting Bull, members of the Sioux Hunkpapa tribe. Red Cloud did his best to calm the tension between his band (the Oglala Sioux) and the other Lakota bands.

Jake and Marsh viewed some of the rations that the Sioux had received from the Bureau of Indian Affairs. They were outraged by what they saw and by what they heard about the corruption of US agents at the Indian agencies. The quality and quantity of goods for the Indians were dreadful—rotten foodstuff, damaged goods, and insufficient supplies.

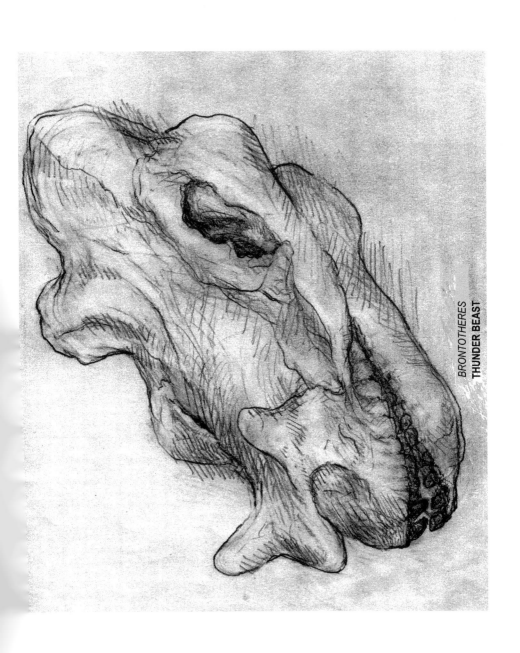

BRONTOTHERES
THUNDER BEAST

"We kept our word," Red Cloud said. "I have ended my war and have agreed to the Great Sioux Reservation of the Fort Laramie Treaty. Yet the US white chiefs would lie and cheat our people."

"Yes, yes," Marsh said. "I can see that and agree that something must be done."

"We were promised food and blankets and cattle if we agreed to the reservation borders," Red Cloud said. "The white men would bring cattle to the agency intended for us and then stampede them so that most ran back to where they came from. They would round up a few strays and return them to the agency saying they had delivered all the cattle we were promised. There was never enough beef to feed our people."

"And those dishonest cattlemen and agents would charge the US Government for a full shipment of cattle," Marsh said, infuriated. "Those and other corrupt suppliers, who were to provide goods to the Indian agencies, will be exposed and disciplined for their fraudulent dealings. I will see the Great White Chief, President Grant, and demand a full investigation of these misdeeds. This I promise you, Chief Red Cloud."

"If Professor Marsh makes a promise," Jake said, "you can bet he'll keep it."

"I believe that is so," Red Cloud said.

24

Jake was fortunate in getting back to the ranch two days before the first big snowstorm of the season came blowing in. Thanksgiving was just days away. After the arduous White River Badlands trip, he was happy to be home.

Once Thanksgiving Day arrived, Jennie and Aunt Bella put the last of the traditional Thanksgiving dishes on the huge dining table. Waiting to be seated, everyone at the ranch was standing at the table oohing and aahing in anticipation of eating the Thanksgiving feast offered before them.

"All right, everyone. Take a seat," Jen said. "I will give the blessing."

Jake, Jennie, Danny, Chris, Alyssa, Luke, Linda, Aunt Bella, and Red were all seated at the big dining room table as Jennie began to say the blessing.

"Today is the wedding anniversary of the Muller's and the Harding's. This Thanksgiving 1874 is an occasion to reflect on all that we have to be thankful for," Jen began. "Jake and I are thankful for the youngest member of this family. Our son, Danny, is our most precious gift and delight. The oldest member of our family is one who has been steadfast in serving this family with her love and guidance and with her culinary and nursing skills for more than five decades. We love and thank you, Aunt Bella. Another elderly member of our family of friends is Red Long Arrow. My father, Walt, and Red were like blood brothers, and Red has worked hard keeping our ranch secure and productive. And Red, thank you for saving our lives at Bushwhackers Butte, not just once but twice."

Jen cleared her throat, coughed, reached for her glass, poured herself some wine, and took a sip.

"Excuse me," she said. "My throat is parched. I know you're all waiting to eat so I'll hurry, but I've got to say my thanks."

"Take your time, sis," Chris said. "We're not starving, and we thank you for your comments."

"Welcome to the newest members of our family, our dear friends Luke and Linda. We love that you've decided to make your home here—about time you two joined up. I'm so thankful for my loving brother Chris and my dear sister-in-law Lys. My brother is the main reason the Muller Ranch has continued to be the legacy our father had hoped it would be. Lys, I thank you for having such loving care for my brother."

Jen paused, took another sip from her glass, and continued.

"To my loving husband and best friend, Jake, thank you for your love. It has made my life complete. I'm so happy we found each other. And I'm happy you made it back from your last fossil expedition in time for this celebration. From the stories you've told us about the troubles with some Sioux tribes, you're lucky they didn't take your scalp. And if you hadn't made it back in time for our anniversary and Thanksgiving, *I* would have had your scalp. Just kidding, my love. You have a lovely head of hair, and I like it right where it is."

Jen raised her glass of wine.

"To all, a happy Thanksgiving and happy anniversaries."

"To Jen," Chris said, raising his glass. "My dear sister is one of a kind. We all love and admire your abilities and loveliness. And speaking of loveliness, my wife would like to say a word."

"Thank you, Chris," Lys said. "Thanks to Jen for the blessing—I should say, thanks to soon-to-be *Aunt* Jen. Chris and I are going to have a baby in the spring."

Everyone congratulated Chris and Lys. Danny was beginning to fuss, so Jake picked him up and Jen brought a bottle of milk for the little boy.

"He's hungry," Jen said, "like all of us. Let's eat."

Winter was fairly mild that year, and Jake found pleasure in caring for the horses and spending some time cleaning and doing drawings of his collection of fossils. Christmas came and went like a chinook wind, but the memories of pleasant holidays lingered throughout the winter. Jen loved to curl up in front of the huge fireplace reading *The Scarlet Letter: A Romance* and *Pride and Prejudice,* the two books Jake gave her for Christmas. Jake's present from Jen was a new Smith and Wesson revolver, the same model that Marshal Boswell used, an American .44. Luke had picked it out for Jen after she had told him Jake needed a good revolver for protection when he went off fossil hunting. Jen had Jake's initials engraved on the grip of the revolver. Uncle Chris gave Danny a wooden horse he had carved, which Danny carried with him wherever he went.

On May 27, 1875, Lys and Chris became parents of a baby girl they named Harper. Everyone adored the new baby girl. Young Danny was in awe of his newborn cousin.

Jake had packed a crate of fossils to ship to Marsh along with some drawings. He took the crate to Laramie to be shipped to New Haven and to pick up the mail and some supplies for the ranch.

When he arrived back at the ranch, he went through the stack of mail. There were several letters to Chris and Lys, a letter to Jen from Ali, and a letter and packet to himself from Marsh. Opening the letter, Jake found a long overdue payment from Marsh.

"About time he paid up," Jake said to Jen. "I hesitated to send him that last crate of fossils, but I'm glad I did as now we're squared up."

"What's the package about?" Jen asked.

Leafing through the papers, Jake found a number of clippings from the New York *Tribune* that Marsh had sent plus a letter asking him to check out some fossil sites.

"The professor sent some interesting articles about his meetings with President Grant and the Bureau of Indian Affairs," Jake said. "Remember me telling you about Marsh promising Chief Red Cloud that he would take the Sioux Indians' concerns about mistreatment to the US Government?"

Jake held up the newspaper clipping to show Jen.

"Oh, yes," Jen said. "When that professor gets a burr under his saddle, he doesn't give up until he's got it out. Let me read that article while you're reading his letter."

"There are a number of *Tribune* articles about him and Cope," Jake said. "There are also two issues of the *American Naturalist.* One has his article about birds with teeth. Remember? He was telling us about that when he was here."

Jake found two letters from the professor. One was full of news about new fossil sites in the West that had been discovered by Marsh's fossil hunters and about his ongoing rivalry with Edward Cope.

In a separate letter, Marsh asked Jake if he would lead a party of fossil hunters on an exploration into the Dakota Territory along the Missouri River and into the Judith River area before Cope explored that region. Marsh said he'd like to go to that Missouri River region himself but was far too busy at this time attending to business at the Peabody Museum. He was also conducting investigations against the Bureau of Indian Affairs regarding mistreatment of Indians and their treaties.

Jake thought that leading an expedition up the Missouri River would be an opportunity to establish himself as a professional fossil collector and not just a hired student fossil hunter.

"Jen, Professor Marsh has made me a promising offer," Jake said.

"Oh, yeah?" she said sarcastically. "Is his highness going to make you a knight of his court?"

"Come on now. Don't be so negative," Jake said. "Marsh has given me the opportunity to fulfill my aspirations."

"Mm-hmm. You're at his beck and call," Jen said.

"He's asked me to head my own fossil expedition, which he will support financially," Jake said.

"And—where and when is this journey?" Jen asked.

"It'll be along the Missouri River through the Dakota Territories and into Montana, sometime this summer," Jake said.

"I thought you'd told me there were hostile Indians in that region," Jen said.

"There may be," Jake said. "But I'm sure through Marsh's friendship with Chief Red Cloud; arrangements can be made for a safe trip."

"But no guarantee of that," Jen said. "You would be taking a huge risk."

"My dear," Jake said, "there are no guarantees in life. Everything is a risk, especially if it is exploring the unknown in the search for knowledge. Besides, I have my new revolver to protect me."

"Maybe I shouldn't have given you that present," Jen said, "if it gives you a false sense of security."

Jake didn't want to get into an argument with Jen over fossil exploring and taking chances in the wilderness. He just wanted to assure her he'd be careful and that no harm would come to him.

"Jen, I'll have Marsh get us army escorts and Indian scouts," Jake said. "We'll be well protected, or I won't go."

"You get that guarantee from Marsh," Jen said, "and I'll feel much better about this deal."

"I'll send a letter to Marsh stating my—*our*—demands for a safe journey," Jake said. "And I'll get details about the time and route. Next time Chris goes to town, I'll have him post it."

A week later, Chris and Luke had hitched horses to the wagon and were ready to leave for Laramie on business. Loaded with mail to be posted and a list of items to be purchased, they waved good-bye to Jen and Bella, who were hanging laundry out to dry.

"We'll be back in three days!" Chris yelled. Jen and Bella waved back.

Jim Collins came riding up to the house and rode over to Jen, tipping his hat to her.

"Morning, ma'am," he said. "Is Jake about?"

"He went down to the east corral to talk with the horses," Jen said.

"Talk with the horses …," Jim said. "That's funny, ma'am."

"Not funny," Jen said. "He does talk to horses, as he talks to his collection of bones, to himself, and everything else—'cept me. And the name is Jen, remember?"

"Yes ma'am—uh, er, Jen," Jim said. "I'll go find him. Have to have him look at an injured filly."

Jim found Jake at the corral just as Jen had said, seemingly talking to a blue roan gelding named Dusty.

"Jen said I'd find you here, talking to the horses," Jim said.

"Well, I'm here," Jake said, "but I ain't exactly talking to the horses. I'm communicating with them best I can."

"How's that?" Jim asked.

"They respond to touch, visual signals, and sounds in a very subtle way," Jake said. "The language of the horse is gestures. They're intelligent and sociable animals that want to interact with us. But they are also suspicious of our intentions and are on guard against our mistreatment of them. The way to get their trust, to train a horse, is to think like one."

"My ma always told me to use some horse sense," Jim said. "Guess she meant to be on guard."

"You're probably right," Jake said.

"How'd you learn so much about breaking horses?" Jim asked.

"My grandfather taught me to train horses, not to break them," Jake answered.

"Train a horse, break a horse—they both mean the same," Jim said.

"They don't necessarily mean the same," Jake said. "Some bronco busters break horses by treating them so harshly that they break the animal's spirit. The horse becomes stressed to the point of resigning its fate to human commands because of fear. To beat a horse into submission does not make a well-trained horse. To train a horse you have to gain its trust. You do that by attentive visual and tactile signals, and the most important thing is patience."

"I can see the difference," Jim said. "I know wranglers who use one or the other methods—break or train."

"I've met both kinds too," Jake said. "I've seen and rode horses that for no apparent reason will try to throw you when least you expect it—unreliable animals. Once you teach a horse to trust you, you'll have a reliable working animal."

"I think old Stretch that I've been riding for the last few years had the right training," Jim said. "He'll obey any command I give him."

"Well, he's not just obeying your command," Jake said. "He trusts your command. He may not understand the purpose or results the signals may lead to; he just trusts you."

Jake gave Dusty a few scratches on the withers, removed his halter, whispered in his ear, and gave the horse a pat on the rump. The horse walked off and then began to lope to the far end of the corral where other horses were feeding.

"Now, what is it you wanted to see me about?" Jake asked.

"I found a filly in the upper east range cut up from what looks like a mountain lion attack," Jim said. "She's got scratches on her hindquarters and hind left leg. She probably kicked the lion and ran away. I brought her in for you to look at. I got her in a stall in the barn. She's a pretty little filly, black as coal."

"Okay, let's go take a look at the little gal," Jake said.

After Jake got the filly quieted down, he cleaned her wounds with a saline solution. Luckily, the slashes were not very deep. Making sure the wounds were cleaned, Jake applied a mixture of sugar and honey to help with the healing.

"You stable her and keep an eye on her for a few days," Jake said to Jim. "Let me know how those wounds are healing."

"Will do," Jim said. "You're a fine horse doctor, Jake. I like that little filly. I believe I'll call her Midnight. See ya' later, doc."

Over two weeks had passed since Jake sent his letter to Marsh. Anxious for a reply to his requests, Jake headed to Laramie to check the mail and tend to some supply business.

When he arrived at the Laramie post office, he was greeted by Gus, the postmaster, and a box overflowing with mail.

"Seems you people at the Muller Ranch are quite popular," Gus said. "You got a stack of mail from far and wide."

Jake hurriedly sorted through the mail looking for a letter from Yale. Finding two he quickly tore them open and read their messages. One contained a check for his last shipment of fossils to Yale Peabody Museum. The other was a letter from Marsh agreeing to Jake's terms for the fossil exploration into the Montana/Dakota Territories. It also instructed Jake to send a telegraph as soon as possible and let him know if he was available for the trip. Marsh would then make the necessary arrangements and set the date. Jake was thrilled to get this news and immediately sent a telegraph message. He told Marsh he would accept the position and to send a telegram back as soon as all the arrangements had been made.

"How long before Professor Marsh will get this telegraph?" Jake asked the station operator.

"It'll arrive in New Haven as soon as I complete coding it," the operator said. "But it's late back east so it may not be delivered until morning."

"Amazing," Jake said. "We live in an amazing age."

"That we do, mister," the operator replied. "Do want me to request a reply?"

"Yes, please," Jake said. "Can you deliver it to the Muller Ranch?"

"Sure can," the operator said. "It'll cost a little more, and Joey, my son who usually makes the deliveries, looks for a gratuity."

"I'll make sure he gets one," Jake said.

Jake rode out of town and pushed his horse to a gallop as he headed back to the ranch to tell Jen the good news—or what he hoped would be good news to her.

After Jake told Jen of the letter from Marsh, she had countless questions about when, where, how long, how many participants, and what kind of protection he would have for the expedition.

"Marsh is taking care of all the arrangements," Jake said. "He is getting an army escort, wagons, and supplies and will send me a telegram when all is arranged."

A couple of weeks later, two teenage boys rode up to the ranch with a telegram. They jumped from their horses, tethered them to the hitch rail, ran across the veranda, and pounded drumming beats loudly on the front door. Bella came to the door.

"What's the commotion all about?" Bella said as she opened the door.

"Is Mr. Jake Harding here?" the older boy asked.

"He's around somewhere," she said. "I'll ask his wife to get him. Who are you, and what do you need him for?'

"We're delivering a telegram to him," the older boy said. "I'm Joey and this is my little baby brother Bobby."

"I'm not your little baby brother. I'm your younger brother, you nut," Bobby said as he punched Joey on the arm.

"Okay, boys," Bella said. "You guys take a load off your feet. Sit here on the porch in the shade. I'll get Jake and you two some cookies and a cold drink."

"Thank you, ma'am," the boys said in unison.

A few minutes later, Jen returned with Jake.

Jake read the telegram and gave it to Jen to read.

"I'll get a pencil and paper to write a reply," Jake told Joey.

"Okay, Mr. Harding," Joey said with his mouth full of cookie. "My pa said to wait for a reply—and delivery payment and a tip for me and Bobby."

After the boys had their fill of cookies and lemonade and their pockets were lined with a generous tip, they headed back to Laramie with a reply to Marsh's message.

"So, you plan to go to the Dakota Territories—in August?" Jen asked, letting the words roll slowly off her tongue.

"Yeah," Jake answered with a questioning tone. "Marsh has everything arranged—the transportation, army escort, a scout, and three other fossil hunters. It'll be an easy, successful dig."

"And safe, I hope," Jen said. "It'll be the months of August and September that you'll be gone?"

"Two months," Jake confirmed. "But I'll be back to you and Danny before you know it. Between now and August, I'll be putting in a lot of hours getting some things done around the ranch. Let me know what you need done before I go."

In mid-July Jake received a packet from Marsh stating all the details for the Montana/Dakota fossil expedition. He was to meet three other fossil hunters who Marsh had hired in Cheyenne on August 4. From there they would take the train to Franklin in Idaho Territory. Then a long, tedious, and uncomfortable four- or five-day stagecoach ride would get them to Fort Benton in Montana Territory, where they would meet Captain Williams, the fort commander, and receive the arrangements that had been made for their fossil expedition.

On August 4 in Cheyenne, Jake met with the three other fossil hunters at the Union Pacific Hotel. Jake knew one of them, Sam Williston, from earlier. He had collected for Marsh before. Sam was from Kansas and had studied with B. F. Mudge, professor of geology at the Kansas Agricultural College. Considering Sam's knowledge and experience with fossils, Jake didn't know why Marsh hadn't appointed him as leader of this expedition. Jake wondered if Sam found any discomfiture in being second in command; after all, he was better schooled in geology and paleontology. Perhaps it was because Sam had at one time prospected for Cope. Whatever it was, Jake was pleased that Marsh trusted his competence to lead the expedition.

Jake had not met the other two fossil hunters before. Russel Kenny and Allan Hendricks were two young adventurers eager to learn more about fossils. Both men had been Marsh's students but grew up in the West, where they acquired skills as hunters and horsemen.

It was an easy train ride from Wyoming to Ogden, Utah. There they gave up their relatively comfortable, upholstered, second-class day-coach seats and boarded a narrow-gaged-rail train to Franklin, Idaho. The rail platform at Franklin was the end of the line for northbound rail travel and connected passengers with the Holladay Overland Mail Stagecoach Line going to Helena, Montana. They climbed aboard a Concord Stagecoach, where they would be jostled and swung back and forth in a thirteen-by-eight-foot wooden carriage suspended on a leather strap bracing for four days on their way to Helena.

Finally, after three and a half days of being tumbled about in the carriage, breathing dust and gnats, and eating food at way stations that seemed to be made of the same ingredients they were inhaling, they rolled into Helena. The town had started as a mining town first known as Last Chance Gulch. Since the 1864 gold strike, the city had grown fast, with wealthy residents contributing to the booming businesses and architectural designs. The fossil hunters decided to stay the night at the Cosmopolitan Hotel, one of the finest brick-and-stone structures in town.

"Hang the expense," Jake said. "After that stage ride, we deserve a good night's rest, along with a bath and a decent meal. We'll bill Marsh for the hotel costs."

"I'm all for that," Al said. "But after a bath and some grub, Russ and I are going to have a look-see at the Montana nightlife."

"You young guys get the dust out of your throats—and britches," Jake said. "Me, I'm going to hit the hay."

"Me too," Sam said. "Tomorrow's journey to Fort Benton will be another bucking 150-mile coach ride. You guys be ready for it."

Early the next morning, Jake was waiting for the First Nation Bank of Helena to open its doors so he could obtain the money from an account Marsh had set up for the fossil expedition. Taking the largest amount of the deposit in cash—but leaving some for the return trip—Jake stuffed the cash in the two pockets Jen had sewn on the inside of his trousers for security against robbers. This was known as banking to stage passengers. He then went to Al's room at the hotel and banged on the door.

"Al, you up?" Jake shouted. "The stage leaves in two hours for Fort Benton. Time we grab a hefty breakfast for the trip."

"Yeah, yeah," Al mumbled through the door.

Jake stepped next door to Russ's room and pounded on the door.

The door opened quickly. "Mornin'! I'm just about ready," Russ said briskly.

Al opened his door and poked his head out.

"What in the hell happened to you?" Jake asked when he saw the blackened eye and bruised left cheek of Al's face. "Have a run-in with one of those tough Montana cowboys?"

"Almost," Russ said, chuckling. "It was a Montana *cowgirl*. She clobbered Al with a beer mug. She threw it at some guy who ducked, but Al didn't."

"She didn't mean to hit me," Al said. "She apologized."

"Yeah, and she bought us a couple whiskeys," Russ said. "She and Al got to be *real* friendly."

From within Al's room, a female voice called out. "Honey, come back to bed," she said. "It's too early to get up."

"I think I'll pass on breakfast," Al said to Jake.

"Don't miss the stage," Jake said. "Two hours."

"I'll be there," Al replied.

An hour later Al came into the restaurant, a little unsteady on his feet, and plopped himself into a chair. Sam, Jake, and Russ were just finishing their second cup of coffee after having a huge breakfast.

"Coffee, strong coffee," Al said to nobody in particular.

"Hear you had a rough night," Sam said to Al as Jake and Russ chuckled. "You had better have more than just coffee before the trip."

After drinking a couple of cups of strong coffee, Al and his three companions were ready, once again, to board a Concord Stagecoach. This time it would be a thirty-hour rough ride. Al reached in his pocket for his wallet to offer to help pay for the coffee.

"Damn!" he exclaimed. "My cash is gone."

"Looks like your Helena cowgirl friend collected her earnings," Jake said, laughing.

"I guess she wasn't the refined, honest little lady I thought she was," Al said. "Good thing I banked some of my cash in my boots."

25

When the stage arrived in Fort Benton, Al was still sleeping.

"Guess I should have drank more whiskey and stayed up later," Russ said. "It seems like Al is the only one who had a pleasant coach ride."

Fort Benton was the end of the line of civilized settlements. The fort had originally been a fur-trading post established in 1846. It sat on the banks of the upper Missouri River and served as a port for steamboats during the high water season, from spring until mid-summer.

Departing from the coach, Jake grabbed Al's leg and shook him.

Al sat up, rubbed his eyes, and moaned. "My eye's sore," he said, "and I've a terrific headache."

"And well you should have, thanks to your Helena lady friend," Jake said. "Come on, sleepy head. We're here."

"She was no lady," Al said. Then he asked, "We're where?"

"Fort Benton," Jake replied. "I'll go find Captain Williams and see about the arrangements Marsh made for our expedition."

Captain Williams was a spit-and-polish military man who held a tight rein on the men under his command at the garrison. When Jake asked about the supplies and escort Marsh had arranged for the fossil hunters, the captain shook his head.

"Not a good idea to go into the Missouri River valley at this time," the captain said. "There's been a lot of trouble with the Blackfeet,

Crows, and Assiniboine Indians. And the Sioux to the south and east of us have attacked a number of white settlements. They're upset over whites colonizing their land and gold miners going into the Black Hills. Now on top of that we've had trouble with whiskey and gunrunners. There is a lucrative trade in the illegal selling of whiskey and guns to the Indians. There's a trade route through here into Canada called the Whoop-Up Trail. It's traveled by traders using ox-drawn wagons loaded with illegal goods, mainly whiskey."

"Whoop-Up Trail," Jake repeated. "That's a great name for a whiskey route."

"Yep, but that's not why it was called Whoop-Up Trail," Captain Williams said. "The ox-drawn bull trains usually had three wagons pulled by as many as sixteen oxen. The teamster, a bull whacker, walked alongside the oxen cracking his long bull whip to keep the animals moving. That was called 'whooping them up'; thus the name of the trail. The bull trains use that trail from here into Canada to a location by the confluence of the Oldman and St. Mary's Rivers. There at Fort Hamilton, also known as Fort Whoop-up, illegal trades are negotiated. The army has its hands full trying to deal with the Indians and the illegal traders."

"We don't plan on going north toward Canada," Jake said. "We want to go east and south to the Judith River."

"Be that as it may," Captain Williams said, "I'm limited for soldiers for an escort. My orders are to deal with the local dangers at hand. And we don't have a horse or wagon to spare."

"I've noticed the town is full of wagons and teams," Jake said. "Perhaps we can hire a teamster and wagon and other supplies."

"There's no doubt that's a possibility, "the captain said. "But do you have any idea of the costs here in Fort Benton?"

"No," Jake replied. "But Professor Marsh was rather generous in funds for this expedition."

"Well, if you want to wrangle some equipment and supplies from the locals, okay," the captain said. "I'll see if I can get a half a dozen soldiers, but no more than that, to volunteer for an escort, providing you're willing to pay for them."

"Fine," Jake said. "We can come to some agreement."

The captain was right. The prices of everything in Fort Benton were extravagantly high. Jake didn't know if Marsh knew of the expenses in the Montana Territory but was thankful he had budgeted for a large expenditure.

MISSOURI RIVER FOSSIL SITE

COLLECTION OF JIM & NANCY GREUTMAN, MONTANA

After three days of searching and haggling, the fossil team finally obtained the necessary items for their expedition. They had, at great expense, hired a large, well-built Conestoga freight wagon with a four-mule team and a teamster. Henrik Bachmeirer was a burly giant of a man who spoke English with a heavy German accent. They also hired a tough-looking frontiersman as a cook. Andy Lacombe, whose tanned and weather-beaten face was etched with lines, told of the many miles he had traveled along the Missouri River valley and Judith River fur trading and serving with the army as a scout and cook. He drove a two-horse team pulling a well-equipped chuck wagon, in which sat an alert, large dog—a cross between a shepherd and a wolf. Six soldiers, mostly young recruits looking for adventures outside of garrison duty, volunteered to accompany the group. They were under the watchful eye of an older cavalry man, who was also a scout, Corporal Stevens. For some reason, he had been busted down from a sergeant; it was obvious where sergeant stripes had once adorned his coat.

Jake purchased four horses that were sound but would require some horsemanship to ride. Supplies of food, ammunition, rifles, picks, shovels, and tents rounded out the necessities this outfit of four fossil hunters, two wagon drivers, and six soldiers needed.

In the last week of August, the fossil expedition, with twelve men, twelve horses, four mules, one dog, and two wagons left Fort Benton headed across the rolling prairie to the mouth of the Judith River, a tributary of the Missouri River.

Traveling across the vastness of the windswept prairie was a mind-numbing trek. To entertain themselves, the men devised a number of activities. The German teamster, Henrik, and the cook, Andy, would have knife-throwing contests. Andy's dog, Smokey, could do a number of tricks. The most amazing feat the dog would do is attack a selected person. Andy would point at someone and say, "Get." The dog would run to the person, grab him by the sleeve or trousers, and pull him over to Andy. But if Andy told the dog to "go," the dog would viciously attack the person with the intent of wounding or killing. Andy let the dog demonstrate his "get" behavior but never issued the "go" command; everyone took Andy's word that the dog could perform that feat with no problem. Andy named the dog Smokey because when he found the dog as a pup, he was laying between two smoldering, burnt-out wagons that settlers had probably lost to an Indian raid.

A couple of days later, the group descended into the Missouri River Valley and made their way to the abandoned military outpost of Fort Claggett. The lush green flora of the Missouri River Valley was a welcome relief from the monotony of the dry prairies. Jake could imagine Lewis and Clark enjoying the beauty of the river, its shores lined with willows and large cottonwoods, as they made their way up this part of the Missouri River toward the Rocky Mountains in the early part of the 1800s.

The Missouri River was known as the Big Muddy. Its dexterity to twist and turn its course as it looped through the landscape, constantly dissolving land in its path and shifting sandbars in the wake of its strong currents and whirlpools, made it one of the muddiest rivers in the world. It was a treacherous river to navigate as areas of its banks containing large cottonwood trees would be carved away, sending the trees into the swirling waters and their heavy roots sinking to the bottom. These fallen submerged trees would collect debris flowing down the river to form enormous snags that could lie just below the surface, unseen in the muddy waters. If a part of this snag was seen above water, it was called a sawyer. River boatmen were constantly on the lookout for sawyers.

The fossil hunters set up camp near the banks of the river, taking time to rest a day and get organized before journeying on to the Judith River badlands. Al had volunteered to help Andy do some cooking. Both were excellent chefs, guaranteeing the fossil party some delicious-tasting meals.

"Al, do you like fish?" Andy asked.

"Love it," Al said.

"Good," Andy said. "You and I are going fishing for a catfish."

"A catfish?" Al asked. "Just one?"

"The Missouri is known for some monstrous cats," Andy said. "If we get a good-sized one we can feed the whole camp. Come on. I'll show you how to rig up a throw line."

Andy uncoiled two lengths of lariat, each about forty feet long. He tied two lengths of four-foot twine at five-foot intervals from the ends of each rope. Rummaging around in his chuck wagon, he came up with four large fishing hooks. He tied a hook to each end of the four lengths of twine. After wrapping and tying a heavy rock to each one of the rope ends, he carefully coiled the ropes to avoid tangling the hooks and handed one to Al.

"We got our lines, hooks, and weights," Andy said. "All we need now is our bait."

Andy called Smokey and told Al to follow. Instead of heading toward the river, Andy and his dog headed toward the prairie.

"Where are we going?" Al asked, puzzled that they weren't headed for the river.

"Right over this little knoll there's some gopher holes," Andy said. "We'll get Smokey to get us our fish bait."

Andy stopped and motioned for Al to wait and Smokey to sit. About twenty yards across the flat landscape were little mounds of dirt with yellow rodents scampering about. Andy whistled a loud, shrill pitch, and the little mammals sat up to look around, as if commanded by the signal. Pointing at them, Andy told Smokey to "go." The dog took off like a shot, and just as soon as the little rodents saw him coming they all disappeared into the burrows. The dog slowed to almost a stop when he saw the disappearing act and approached the burrows with a cautious gait. He sat beside one of the burrows with his head cocked and tail twitching. Andy whistled another loud, shrill note, and a gopher poked his head up from the burrow in curiosity. Smokey's jaws were swift and sure as the dog snatched up the gopher.

Andy yelled, "Get!" and the dog came running with the dead rodent clutched in his jaws.

"Here's our fish bait," Andy said, holding up the dead gopher. "We'll skin it, slice it up, and tempt old Mr. Catfish with a meal he's fond of—raw meat."

They each baited their hooks with bloody gopher flesh and entrails. Then they whirled the rock-weighted end of the throw line over their heads and flung the line out into the Missouri. Al tied his line to a log, while Andy wrapped his around a large rock on the shore.

"All right," Andy said. "Now we'll leave the lines overnight and check them in the morning. Hopefully we'll have fish for dinner tomorrow."

Early the next morning, Al and Andy were at the riverbank retrieving their throw lines. Andy pulled his line toward shore, but Al's seemed to be caught on a snag.

"I've got a fish on my line!" Andy shouted. "Looks like about a ten-pound cat."

He pulled the fish up on the shore, whacked it on the head with a rock, and went to help Al free his line from the snag.

Both of them tugged on Al's line. Then it tugged back.

"That's no snag," Andy said. "I think you've hooked a big cat."

Both men pulled on the line, and slowly it came toward the shore. The first hook emerged with the bait gone. They struggled with the line to pull in the second hook, and a huge fish thrashed in the waters. They saw the enormous head of a gigantic catfish. It took a great effort to pull the fish up onto the shore, and when they did, they both started whooping and hollering. On the beach lay a massive catfish about four and a half feet in length and weighing around a hundred pounds.

"What a pig! You were right, Andy," Al said. "All we need is one good-sized fish for the whole camp."

"I'd say that's a good-sized fish," Andy said. "Let's gut this pig and get him cooked."

The next day's trip reached the Judith River badlands. The sculptured shapes of the canyons and the palette of colors there were familiar to Jake, much like other badlands he had explored. But the gorges were deeper and the walls were steeper than what he had seen before. This would mean arduous excavating for fossils.

As soon as they established a camp, the four fossil hunters were off to explore the sandstone formations. They found a multitude of bones that had been exposed by erosion but also had been so badly weathered that in many cases only the teeth of species had survived as fossils. Some of the bones just crumbled as soon as the explorers touched them. These were bones from the Cretaceous period, eighty to seventy-five million years ago.

Jake and his crew ventured farther into the Judith River badlands, finding numerous large pelvic and femur fossil bones and teeth of various sizes. After a month and a half of digging in the badlands, they traveled farther northeast toward the White Cliffs area. In mid-September, they were very successful in finding a number of fossils but no complete skeletons.

"I think I've made an unusual find," Jake told Sam one afternoon. "At first I thought this fossil was the horn of an animal, but after I'd removed it from its matrix and cleaned it, I realized it was a large tooth with serrated edges."

Jake handed the fossil to Sam. It was about eight and a half inches in length and two and a half inches at the widest diameter.

"By God, you're right!" Sam exclaimed, turning the fossil over in his hands and running his fingers along the serrated edge. "This is the largest damn tooth I've ever seen!"

"What animal would possess such enormous teeth?" Jake asked. "Can you picture the size of this carnivorous creature?"

"I can only imagine how gigantic the beast would be," Sam said. "It's terrifying."

For a moment Jake visualized a dinosaur with huge teeth. He took the tooth from Sam, and in his mind flashed a scene from his nightmares of monstrous dinosaurs. He blinked, groaned, and dropped the tooth.

"Easy," Sam said. "Don't break that valuable specimen."

While Jake and Sam were examining the unique fossil tooth, they were interrupted by a trooper who come riding up to them.

"Horses and men are coming," the trooper said. "Best you grab a gun and take cover. Be ready for anything. They could be Indians or outlaws."

The fossil expedition took cover behind the chuckwagon and the freight wagon. Within minutes the riders appeared over a ridge, and to the fossil party's relief it was a patrol of cavalry troopers.

"It's Captain Williams and Sergeant Graham!" one of the escort troopers shouted.

"I'm glad we met up with your group," Captain Williams said. "Looks like you're all doing fine. We've been on the trail of some gunrunners. Have you seen anyone?"

"Neither a hide nor hair of anybody," Jake said. "But we have seen a lot of wild game, which gives us a supply of fresh meat. You and your men are welcome to share some with us this evening."

"Thanks for the offer, but we need to get after those outlaws before their trail gets cold," the captain said. "They've been selling guns to the Sioux, who seemed to be amassing weapons for some kind of confrontation."

"We'll be finished here in a few days," Jake said, "and then head up to Cow Island landing to ship the fossils to Omaha."

"Well, you may not be able to do that," the captain said. "Due to the dry year and a low snow pack in the mountains, the Missouri is running low. The last steamboat, a week ago, trying to get to Fort Benton couldn't make it past Claggett Landing. I doubt if a stern-wheeler can get to Cow Island."

"How in the hell are we going to get these fossils down the Missouri?" Jake asked.

"You probably won't," the captain said, "at least not this year."

Andy was listening to this conversation and didn't agree with the captain.

"There may be a way," the cook said. "It would be a week's hard travel, but I believe we could do it if we left tomorrow for Fort Buford in the Dakota Territory."

"Yeah, Fort Buford may have boats coming up that far for another couple of weeks," the captain said. "But how are you going to get to Fort Buford without boating down the Missouri?"

"We'll ride our horses and drive our wagons there," Andy said.

"Oh, sure you will," the captain said sarcastically. "And you'll just fly over the Missouri Breaks, some of the steepest and tallest of any badland formations."

"Let's take a look at your map, Jake," Andy said. "I'll show you how we could do it."

Jake got the map out of his saddlebags and spread it on the ground. Then he, Andy, Sam, and the captain huddled around the unfolded chart on which Marsh had marked routes to possible fossil sites and mailed to Jake.

"I know we can do this because I have done it before. It's no easy trail, but if we can get food and supplies at Cow Island for a week's trip, we can make it," Andy said. "We would need our cavalry escort with us."

"We'll have Marsh pay for them if they're willing to make the trip," Jake said.

Andy pointed to a spot on the map and outlined his plan. "We head for Cow Island where there are some places to ford the Missouri near Cow Creek," he said. "We need to get to the north side of the Missouri. The natives and buffalo herds have used these crossings for years. We go up Cow Creek Canyon, which is a constant grade but can be navigated if it's dry. The canyon has high walls, but the floor is relatively flat and wide, except for a couple of steep grades. But if it rains, we'll get bogged down in the gumbo of mud from the silt of the canyon floor." Andy laughed, "Don't do any rain dances."

"Yep, I know the freighting route you're referring to," Captain Williams said. "It's been used to get to Fort Benton in low river season. But how's that going to get you to Fort Buford three hundred miles away at the confluence of the Missouri and Yellowstone Rivers?"

"Instead of turning northwest to Fort Benton, we'll go north toward the Bears Paw Mountains up onto the high plains and turn east," Andy said. "Then we'll travel the high grass prairies to Dakota."

"It'll be a long, hard trip," the captain said.

"Didn't say it would be either short or easy," Andy said. "If this weather stays as hot and dry as it's been, we'll be in good shape. But we should pack up and leave tomorrow."

Jake and Sam agreed with Andy, and early the next day, they broke camp and loaded all of their fossils into the freight wagon. By midmorning they were headed northwest on a trail to Cow Island.

"Henrik and his mule team seem to be able to handle that big wagonload of fossils okay," Sam said.

"Yeah," Jake said, "slow but steady. Good thing we're on gentle, rolling land for now, but it'll be rougher going not too far ahead."

Corporal Stevens had ridden up a slope to the west of the party to scout the lay of the land from a higher point. Jake's thoughts of getting the fossils down the Missouri were interrupted by someone shouting. He saw the corporal riding at full gallop down the slope waving and yelling something. As he got closer, Jake heard what he had feared.

"Indians! Indians!" the corporal was yelling. "Head for the canyon ahead!"

About half a mile from the party was a gorge that was dotted with outcroppings. They could use the canyon as a fortress.

Jake and his party spurred their horses to a gallop. Andy smacked the backs of his chuck wagon horses with the reins, as did Henrik with his wagon team of four mules. The chuck wagon took off with great speed. But the mule team, straining with their heavy load, was slow at picking up speed and bounced across the rolling land, falling further behind. Corporal Stevens was gaining on the freight wagon and motioning for Henrik to make a jump onto his horse. About thirty Indians appeared, charging down the slope whooping and yelling. They were gaining on the mule team, and a fusillade of bullets and arrows rocketed toward the lumbering wagon. An arrow impaled Henrik's neck and one penetrated his back. He slumped forward and bounced off his seat to his death. The corporal let out a yell, turned in his saddle, and fired his pistol at the advancing party of Indians. It was a hopeless effort in trying to avenge the teamster's death, but it gave the corporal a little satisfaction that he did something. He was thankful that his horse was sure-footed and fast. He outran the Indians and in no time caught up with the chuck wagon. He holstered his handgun and pulled his rifle from its scabbard. Jumping onto the wagon he whacked his horse's backside, and the horse, now without a rider, sped off to catch up with the fleeing fossil party.

"Welcome aboard, Sergeant Stevens," Andy said, and then he asked matter-of-factly, "Who are your guests?"

"Oh, just some old Sioux friends," the corporal replied nonchalantly as he petted Smokey, who was sitting close by Andy. "I'm going to climb to the back of your wagon and extend my invitation to them. By the way, it's *corporal*, not *sergeant*."

"Not to me, it ain't," Andy said. "As far as I'm concerned you should be a general. Your friends don't seem to be too friendly."

The hard-riding fossil party had just entered the entrance to the ravine. Two of the troopers had seen Corporal Stevens leap onto the chuckwagon. When the corporal's horse came galloping toward them, they decided to ride out toward the wagon to give some firepower support. The two inexperienced and brave (but foolish) soldiers, Privates Wally Whitney and Nat Jacobs, rode toward the advancing Indian war party. Firing their revolvers they added firepower to the corporal's rifle shots coming from the back of the wagon. Even though the chuck wagon was bouncing and swerving, Corporal Stevens was able to bring down an Indian with every shot by aiming at the larger target, the horse. Stevens was shooting the standard army-issued rifle, a Springfield carbine .45 caliber single shot. Even though it was a single shot, Stevens was quick at reloading and the Springfield had a long range, helping to keep the Indians at bay. A few of the Indians had repeating rifles they had obtained from gunrunners. The corporal was reloading when Nat rode up along the left side of the wagon yelling like an Indian warrior and firing his Colt .45. Some of the Sioux were closing in on the wagon. A bullet from the young trooper's revolver slammed into the face of an Indian brave. His painted features exploded into a grotesque mask as he fell backward. The other trooper, Wally, approached on the right side whooping, hollering, and firing his revolver. He didn't have to aim; the warriors were charging all around him in a thick and close group.

Arrows whipped through the air, and repeated gunshots whizzed bullets by the troopers and the wagon. Young trooper Nat gave out with a gasping groan as an arrow penetrated his chest and blood began to spurt across the withers of his horse. He fell to the ground; his body was trampled by an Indian's horse. Its rider, wielding a tomahawk, rode to the front of the wagon. Andy ducked as he jumped on board.

"Go, Smokey! Go! Go!" Andy yelled. The dog leapt at the Indian's throat and sunk his teeth in, ripping and tearing flesh. The warrior collapsed into a bloody, gurgling, quivering heap, and Andy pushed the Sioux's body off the wagon.

"Good boy," Andy said, petting his faithful dog. He continued racing his wagon into the canyon's entrance with the charging Indians kicking up a cloud of dust not far behind.

Trooper Wally Whitney yowled loudly as an arrow embedded itself in his thigh and his horse reared. Controlling his horse, he followed the wagon into the mouth of the canyon. A barrage of gunfire erupted from Jake and his fossil party, who had fortified themselves beside the canyon's entrance. The Indians scattered and retreated, staying just beyond rifle range.

Andy pulled his wagon to a stop beside the outcroppings that Jake, Sam, Al, Russ, and a trooper were using for cover. Corporal Stevens jumped from the wagon and helped Wally off his skittish horse, being careful not to brush against the arrow sticking in the trooper's thigh. Andy and the corporal helped the wounded soldier to a safe place behind the rocks where Jake and the others were barricaded.

"I'll get my medicine kit out of the wagon," Andy said. "Then we'll get this young trooper patched up good as new."

"Where's Nat?" Wally asked Corporal Stevens.

"I'm sorry," the corporal said. "Private Jacobs didn't make it."

"Am I going to die out here too?" Wally asked. "I'm sure in a lot of pain."

"No way are you going to die," Stevens said. "I promise you that. We're going to get that arrow out of your leg, and you'll be fine."

"I got everything we need," Andy said as he come running back from the wagon. "I've done this a few times before, so don't worry. The Indians have their medicine bundle, but I have my medicine bag. But first, some medicine for the surgeon."

Andy opened his bag and withdrew a large bottle of whiskey. Uncorking it, he took a big swig, gave a long sigh, and then handed it to Wally.

"Patient's turn," he said, "for courage." Wally hesitantly took a sip and started coughing. "Good medicine, huh? One more shot for the doc and we'll get that thorn out of your leg. You'll have a couple of nice souvenirs from this campaign—a Sioux arrow and a beautiful scar."

While Andy was preparing to remove the arrow from Wally's thigh, two of the soldiers, who had shielded themselves behind another embankment, were taking potshots at the retreated Indians. The Indians were mingling about, tempting the white men to shoot.

"Stop wasting ammunition!" the corporal yelled. "They're out of range!"

Andy, displaying the skill of a surgeon, removed the arrow from Private Whitney's leg. The private moaned and passed out from the pain. Andy finished bandaging the wounded leg and took another big swallow from his medicine bottle. Then he offered the bottle to Corporal Stevens and Jake.

"A little tonic for the soul," Andy said. "It'll be good for what ails you."

"Speaking of what ails you," Jake said, taking a swig from the bottle, "what ails *me* is that I feel responsible for the loss of two lives."

"You weren't the cause of those deaths," Corporal Stevens said. "Don't put that guilt on you. It was those savages that killed our two men."

"I was slow to respond to the attack and couldn't seem to focus in on a target," Jake said. "I was terrified."

"All of us were frightened," Andy said. "Fear is a good reaction."

"I was told once," Jake said, "that in the heat of battle you don't think about being afraid; you just fight."

"Who told you that?" Andy asked.

"A soldier," Jake said.

"Well, that's a bunch of bullshit," Andy said. "If you hide your fears and deny them, they'll be submerged only to surface later to haunt you. It's best to deal with fear now on the surface and have … hope against despair."

"What?" Jake said. "Where did you hear that—hope against despair?"

"Al told me in one of our conversations while doing food preparations," Andy said. "We'd cover a number of topics besides cooking. He told me about what you'd said about your grandpa. By the way, who was this soldier who told you not to recognize your fear?"

"He was a cavalry sergeant," Jake said. "He's dead now—went crazy."

"Hmm," Andy said.

"Well, I'd rather remember my grandfather's words than the sergeant's," Jake said.

"Good idea," Andy said.

"We'll have more than just hope," Corporal Stevens said. "We'll have a plan to defeat the attacking Sioux."

26

Corporal Stevens instructed Andy to get his wagon moved to the middle of the canyon's opening.

"Turn it so the water barrel is facing away from the attacking Sioux," the corporal said. "Too dry here to lose our water supply. When Andy gets the wagon in place, all of you meet here and I'll explain our strategy."

Andy turned his horses around and after getting the wagon in position, he unhitched the team, led them farther into the canyon to let them graze and have some water. Everyone gathered around Corporal Stevens.

"I figure the Sioux will try to get us by attacking our main defense and then flanking us, making us fight three major forces," the corporal said. "I've seen them do this before, so we are going to put up a decoy and catch them in crossfire. Time is short, so we'll have to set up our defenses in a hurry."

"You and Andy have the experience. Tell us what we need to do," one of the troopers said.

"We'll set up the wagon as a decoy for our defense," Corporal Stevens said. "We'll fortify the attack side of the wagon with sacks of flour and beans. A volunteer and I will be shooting from inside the wagon. The rest of you will be on battlement positions to the north and south sides of the ravine. We'll get the Sioux in a crossfire as they swoop in on what they think is our main defense—the wagon. The south side has a natural fortification with the outcropping there; all it needs is a few more rocks to make it quite secure. We'll need to pile up more rocks on the north side defense."

Private Whitney had regained consciousness in time to hear Corporal Stevens outline his defense plan. The young private admired the older corporal's abilities and experience and thought of him as a father figure.

"I'll volunteer to be in the wagon with Corpora. Stevens," the private said.

"No, you won't," the corporal said. "You've been wounded and need to stay out of the line of fire."

"I'm wounded in the leg," Wally said, emphatically, "not in the eye or trigger finger. You know I'm a good shot. You can use me, and I need to do it for Nat."

"All right," Corporal Stevens said. "Just keep your head down and don't do anything foolish."

"Foolish?" the private asked. "Like what?"

"Like trying to be a hero when you and Nat, outnumbered a dozen to one, rode headlong into a pack of bloodthirsty savages," the corporal said.

"Yeah, that was dumb," Wally said.

"All right, men, let's get to work," Corporal Stevens said. "First we'll get those rock piles fortified. Then get your rifles and revolvers and a lot of ammunition within easy reach of where you'll be stationed. We've lost two men; let's not lose anyone else. Wally and I will be in the center in the wagon and four men in each of the two side defenses. Ten of us should be able to have enough fire power to defend our positions."

"I sure in hell hope you're right," said one of the soldiers with a nervousness in his voice.

"He is right!" Andy said. "The sergeant has gotten us out of worse predicaments than this, that's for sure."

"You've served with the sergeant— um, corporal before?" Jake asked.

"Yah damn right," Andy said. "And those sons of bitches that busted his rank should have promoted him instead. They were a bunch of pompous brass desk-jockey soldiers that were jealous of his soldiering abilities and military—"

"All right, Andy, enough," the corporal said. "Let's get on about our business with the Sioux."

"Pardon," Andy said. "I didn't mean to rattle on about old irritates. I just wanted to affirm that your charge will get us out of this situation."

"I believe we'll be just fine if we all pay attention to details of my plan," the corporal said. "I figure the Indians will be waiting for the late afternoon sun to be lower so we'll have to shoot into its glare. We may have up to an hour before they're finishing with their pow-wow and come at us again. When they began their attack they'll most likely come straight at us using rifles. That's when Private Whitney and I will start firing."

"We have a couple of Winchester '66 repeating rifles you and Private Whitney can use," Jake said. "They hold fifteen rounds each."

"That's great," the corporal said. "That will keep a barrage of bullets firing so the Sioux will think all our fire power is from one position; the wagon. Hopefully they'll fall for our decoy. You on the side fortresses, stay out of sight, have your revolvers fully loaded, but don't fire until they're within range. When they're closer they'll probably split into three groups, using arrows, lances. and tomahawks, attacking the wagon from straight on and the left and right sides. That's when they'll be within revolver range. Make your shots count as they pass in front of your fortress."

"What if they don't divide into three groups?" a trooper asked.

"Then aim at the main group's horses. Warriors thrown from their horses will be an easier handgun target. But remember, they'll be brandishing knives and 'hawks. Your revolvers should serve you well, but have your knives handy if it comes to hand-to-hand fighting."

"It seems to me there are a lot of ifs in your plan," another soldier said.

"You're right," Corporal Stevens said, "As there are many *ifs* in any thing you do. If your plan doesn't pan out, then you reinvent. Your success is dependent on how creative you are with your job. Your job, trooper, is soldiering."

"I understand," the trooper said. "Thanks,—sergeant."

"Yeah, sergeant!" everyone shouted.

"First thing, let's get the horses tethered farther back in the canyon," Corporal Stevens said. "The Indians will try get at them to keep us from any escape."

The corporal handed Wally a spyglass.

"You rest that wounded leg," he said. "But put your eyes to work. Watch those Sioux, and when they start to move toward us, you let me know. Now get your guns and ammo and take up a position in the wagon."

Wally was elated at being assigned a responsibility and a position in the wagon alongside the corporal.

"I'll give you a hand with your saddle and get your horse taken care," Private Bob Gordon said to Wally.

Jake and Al, carrying rifles, came walking over to Corporal Stevens. Each had a Winchester 1866 rifle and a carton of shells.

"These Winchesters will help you out," Jake said.

He and Al placed the rifles and ammo in the wagon.

"Much obliged," Corporal Stevens said. He climbed into the wagon, pushing the rifles and ammo ahead of him. "You boys ready for this?"

"More than ready," Jake said.

"Looking forward to it," Al said.

Both of 'em liars, the corporal thought.

It was getting on to late afternoon; hot, dry, and still with a blazing low sun in the cloudless western sky. On the ridge of the hill west of the fossil party, a line of Sioux warriors were poised. Wally, with the spyglass glued to his eye, did a quick count. He counted twenty-one.

"Here they come!" he shouted.

A plume of dust, backlit by the late afternoon's low sun, was being kicked up behind the Sioux as they charged down the hill whooping and yipping. The loud, frightening shrieks were part of their war strategy as much as their painted bodies were meant to intimidate their enemies.

The corporal and private waited patiently until the Indians were within rifle range. Then the corporal's rifle roared and the private's rifle followed suit. The two soldiers jacked rounds into their rifle's chambers and fired as fast as possible. A few warriors fell from their mounts. Then the Indians did what Corporal Stevens had predicted and hoped for. They split into three positions; front center, north right flank and left south flank. A shower of arrows fell upon the wagon. Many were bounced from the canvas's resilient surface, a few ripped through the fabric, while some were stuck in the wagon's wooden sides and into the sacks of flour and beans. Only a couple had shot through the small opening that the two soldiers used as a gun port.

An arrow grazed the corporal's left side, causing a slash that bled profusely. He dropped his rifle and grabbed at the slash. Seeing all the blood gushing from the wound, Private Wally's first thought was that the corporal had been mortally wounded. The corporal saw the horrified look in the private's eyes.

"I'm okay," Corporal Stevens said. "You mind your post—keep firing." The corporal quickly used his kerchief as a bandage, took off his belt, and tightened it around himself, holding the kerchief over the cut. He picked up his rifle and turned his attention back to the advancing Indians.

The north Indian flank was fast approaching the fortress that was manned by Russ, Andy, Private Carson, and Private Morris. The attacking Indians, some firing arrows while others wielded lances and tomahawks, were screaming battle cries as they reached within handgun range of the north defense. A cascade of arrows fell on the rock pile. An arrow hit Private Morris in the shoulder, knocking him backward and causing him to drop his revolver.

Russ, Andy, and Private Carson frantically fired their revolvers into the howling pack of oncoming warriors. Several Indians fell from their horses. Two warriors jumped their ponies onto the fortress's pile of rocks. Russ shot one in the head just as the warrior was about to throw his lance. The other brave, tomahawk in hand, jumped from his horse and landed on top of Private Carson. The private pointed his gun at the Indian's chest and pulled the trigger, but the firing pin fell on an empty chamber. Private Carson ducked and held up his arms in defense. The warrior flinched, thinking the gun would fire. He swung his hatchet, missing the soldier's head by inches. The Indian quickly brought his tomahawk up again, this time for a death blow. A grey streak of fur flew through the air, and canine teeth chomped down on the warrior's arm. The Indian dropped his hatchet and screamed as bones crunched.

"Go, Smokey! Go!" Andy's voice rang out. The Indian grabbed the dog's throat in his left hand with a stranglehold. Andy took careful aim with his revolver and fired a bullet into the warrior's left cheek, blowing out the right side of the Indian's face as the bullet passed through his head. The warrior fell dead on top of Private Carson, who was now being covered with the Sioux's blood. The private was so traumatized he couldn't speak. He looked at Andy and just mouthed the words *thank you*. Smokey sat beside Andy, looking at him with bright eyes, his tongue dangling from the side of his mouth and his tail wagging. Suddenly there was a swishing sound. The dog gave a yelp and fell on his side with an arrow quivering in his chest. Andy turned to see an Indian standing behind a dead pony and nocking another arrow. Andy fired his revolver at the warrior before he could string the arrow. The Indian yelled and fell across the dead pony.

As the Indians began retreating, Andy kept firing, as did Russ, until their revolvers' hammers fell on empty cartridges. They reloaded and kept firing rounds—and a string of cuss words.

Jake, Sam, Al, and Private Bob Gordon were able to hold off the war party that was attacking the south side fortress. Fortunately the white men had the element of surprise on their side. The Indians, intent on swooping down to take the wagon stronghold, were surprised by the barrage of bullets that came from the outcropping before they got to the wagon. They pulled up short of attacking the wagon and directed their charge toward the white men's south defense. Indians and their mounts were being shot and held back by heavy gunfire.

One brave, riding a large palomino, had made it between the defense line and the wagon and had come up behind the fossil party. Jake saw the brave behind him and turned to confront him. The Indian brave, astride his horse, sat tall with his lance poised to strike. His appearance was terrifying. His face and half-naked body were painted with black, yellow, and red zigzag designs. The warrior, posed like some famous hero's statue, glowered at Jake for a moment, and then yelled a chilling war cry, kicking his horse into a charge. Fear mounted in Jake as he faced a charging monster of his nightmares. He took aim with his powerful revolver. He had put faith in his weapon to overcome the threat. He fired his gun, putting a bullet in the horse's chest. The palomino faltered as the Indian jumped to the side, throwing his lance at Jake. Jake ducked the thrown spear as the stumbling horse crashed into Jake's left side with a glancing blow. Knocked to the ground, Jake lost grip of his revolver. The horse fell on its side as blood gushed from its chest. The stallion began to kick up clouds of dust as it flailed in the throes of death. The warrior rolled in the dirt, withdrawing a knife as he did. He sprang to his feet, leapt on top of Jake, and slammed an elbow into Jake's eye. The Sioux's knife sliced across Jake's left cheek, leaving a cut from the side of his nose to his ear. Jake managed to grasp the Indian's right forearm and push the knife just inches away. Jake could taste his own blood flowing from the cut. He turned his left shoulder and cheek into the ground; spitting dirt, he pushed up with his right arm with all the strength he could muster, keeping the knife from slitting his throat. Looking to his left, he saw his .44 lying in the dirt. Stretching out his left arm, he searched for the gun and found its handle. Quickly bringing the gun up under the Indian's chin, he pulled the trigger. The Smith and Wesson roared, and blood and flesh flew into Jake's face as the Indian's head exploded. A loud ringing filled Jake's ears, and then all was quiet. To his left, the dead palomino lay motionless; to his right the brave, now painted with blood, was still. No gunshots came from the fortress; no yelling could be heard from invading Indians—nothing. There was only silence. He couldn't move. His vision was clouded, and then sounds began to slowly emerge as he felt pain. Suddenly a distant voice called his name.

"Jake! Jake!" an anxious voice called out. "Oh, my God, you're hurt." A blurred face appeared.

"Who's that?" Jake asked, moaning.

"It's me," Al said. "Are you all right? You look a mess. Give me your hand, and I'll help you up. The Sioux are retreating."

Jake reached his right hand out for help, still holding his revolver in his left hand. Al started to pull him to his knees. A stabbing pain ran down the left side of Jake's head, and he realized he couldn't hear from his left ear or see from his left eye. He let out a yell as Al pulled him to his feet.

Another yell broke the silence. A piecing Indian war cry came from the north fortification. Everyone turned to see Andy leap over the rock pile, yelling and running toward a dead Indian lying across his dead pony. The dead Sioux was the Indian Andy had shot the one who had sent an arrow into his dog's chest. Andy pulled his knife from its sheath, rolled the lifeless Indian off the dead horse, seized the warrior by the hair, and ran the knife around the Indian's hairline from front to back. Then he turned the Indian's body face down on the ground and grabbed the back of his hair. Putting his foot between the dead Sioux's shoulders he gave a powerful tug, ripping the scalp from back to front of the Indian's head. Andy stood over the body holding the scalp high and yelled a loud, chilling war cry.

"By God," Wally said to Corporal Stevens, "he sounds just like an Indian."

"Yep," the corporal said, chuckling as he watched Andy doing his little war chant.

Russ and Private Carson helped Private Morris, who still had an arrow embedded in his shoulder. Russ cut off the end of the arrow and pulled it from Morris's shoulder. Morris didn't make a sound; he just gritted his teeth as sweat and tears streamed down his face. Russ patched the arrow wound as best he could with a couple of bandannas.

Andy tied the Indian's scalp to his belt and went to pick up his dead dog. The four of them walked back to the wagon, exhausted from their encounter.

Sam and Al helped Jake over to the wagon while Private Gordon went to check on the horses.

"Oh, no," Al said when he saw Andy carrying his dead dog. "I'm sorry."

"Yeah," Andy said. "He was a good trooper."

"I'm sorry too," Jake and Sam said, echoing each other.

"Jeez, Jake," Andy said. "I damn near didn't recognize you. What happened? Your face looks like a fresh buffalo chip that the buffalo stepped in. You okay?"

"Yeah, I will be," Jake said, "soon as I get this filth cleaned off my face and get you to look at my cut cheek."

"I'll get my kit and tend to you and Private Morris," Andy said. "Meanwhile, you get that shit washed off your face. Use plenty of soap and water and clean that cut with some whiskey, inside and out. Here's a bottle. I'll get another."

Andy treated the wound to Private Morris's shoulder and then sat down beside Jake, uncorked the bottle of booze, and swallowed a big mouthful.

"Looks like you'll need some stitches to close that cut," Andy said. "Another inch or so to the right and your nose would be gone, and another few inches lower and your throat would've been slashed. How'd that all happen?"

"My gun was knocked from my hand by an Indian's charging horse," Jake said. "The brave launched at me with his knife and slashed my cheek while I was struggling to avoid having my throat cut. I turned my cheek to the side and saw my gun lying in the dirt. I was able to reach it and blew his head apart, splattering myself with his blood."

"You were fortunate," Andy said. "You turned your cheek—Matthew something."

"Matthew something," Jake repeated. "Oh yeah, the Bible, the Sermon on the Mount in Matthew 5, 'turn the other cheek.' You know the *Bible?*"

"Some," Andy said. "My father was a French-Canadian missionary. My mother was Cheyenne."

"Uh-huh," Jake said with a knowing grin.

"I never did subscribe to either one's way of thinking, at leastways not fully," Andy said. "I suppose your grandpa taught you the verses."

"He did," Jake said, "but with his own interpretations. To turn the other cheek meant to be able to take a personal, nonviolent insult with grace and nonviolence. But you have to be able to defend yourself from the harm of an unjust aggression."

Both men felt an affiliation to each other with the knowledge of their similarities and differences. Andy got his needle and thread and stitched the cut on Jake's cheek. Neither one said a word during the procedure. Jake just gritted his teeth and hummed a familiar tune while Andy whistled soft and low.

"There ya go," Andy said. "Good as new. That scar will add character to your handsome face."

"I thank you, 'doctor' Lacombe," Jake said. "You are a man of many talents."

"*Merci beaucoup*," Andy said. "Well, as the saying goes, 'I have seen the elephant.' Getting late, I better get a shovel and give Smokey a proper burial before the sun goes down. Then I'll rustle up some grub. I'll get Al started on that."

After talking with Al, Andy found an old blanket in the wagon to wrap Smokey's body in. Carrying the wrapped body of his dog and a shovel, he started down the gulch to bury his furry friend. Someone called out his name, and Andy turned to see Private Carson running toward him.

"What is it?" Andy asked, a little irate.

"I wanted to tell you how sorry I am for the loss of your dog," Carson said, out of breath from running. "Smokey saved my life, you know."

"Yeah, I know," Andy replied.

"If'n I'd kept track of my shots, I wouldn't had an empty gun and I'd have kilt that Injun," Carson said. "As it was, Smokey and you saved me."

"Yeah, I know," Andy said again. "Well, I reckon it's a matter of paying attention to detail. Now, as far as your detail, you are now on burial detail. Here's the shovel. This is as good as any spot. You dig, I'll swig."

Andy let the shovel fall toward the private. He laid the shrouded body of Smokey down and reached for the bottle in his pocket.

The sun had set, but enough light remained to see the silhouettes of sentinels the Sioux had posted on the ridge. Jake and Corporal Stevens sat beside the wagon to finish eating and have a much-needed cup of coffee.

"Do you think they'll try an attack tonight?" Jake asked the corporal.

"I doubt it," Stevens said, "At least not a full-scale attack. There'll probably be some night snipers trying to get our horses, so we'll take turns at guard duty."

"By the bye," Stevens began, "how's the cheek?"

"It'll be okay, "Jake said. "Only hurts when I smile. How's your side?"

"It'll be okay," Stevens said. "Only hurts when I laugh."

The night seemed darker than usual. A breeze was stirring, and a few clouds had invaded the sky, obscuring the brightness of a fall moon. No sneak attacks from Sioux night marauders were coming; in fact, there were no night sounds at all. This worried the corporal as complete quietness was as much a disturbing sign that something was wrong as was utter commotion.

At first morning light the sounds of nature were heard: birds chirped, insects buzzed, a hawk screamed, and the distant bugling of an elk in rut was heard. Corporal Stevens's thoughts were positive. He loved the sights, sounds, and smells of nature. He and Private Whitney were having coffee from a big pot that Andy had hung over a fire. They watched a beautiful orange sunrise. Wally scanned the western hill with the telescope as the east rising sun lit up the geographies of the hillside.

"They're coming! The Indians are coming!" the private yelled.

"Where?" The corporal asked. Then he saw a cloud of dust rising from beyond the west hill. The morning light caught the swirling dust column, turning it from purple to blue as a wind from north to south bent its ribbon sideways.

Everyone grabbed their guns and ran to their positions. The shapes of men on horseback began to emerge, lining the crest of the hill.

"Looks like they got reinforcements," Wally said.

"Let me see the telescope," Corporal Stevens said.

Before he even looked through the scope, he knew what he saw. He couldn't believe his eyes.

"I'll be damned," Stevens said when he saw a column of blue coats. "It's the army."

Cheers and whoops erupted from the fossil party as the army regiment advanced down the hill toward the camp. The company stopped for a minute by the cargo wagon. A small detail of troopers stayed behind the main column to investigate the overturned Conestoga freight wagon and the body of the teamster. Not a single Sioux body was present. Sometime during the night the Indians had removed all of their fallen warriors. No bodies were left on the battlefield except for Henrik's, the trampled remains of Private Nat Jacobs, and half a dozen carcasses of horses. Even the bodies of the two dead warriors that were in the camp had been taken—one at the southern fortress and the other at the northern side near the horses. Jake was amazed that the Sioux had carried away their dead during the night without being detected. He began to believe myths he'd heard about them.

Captain Williams, leading his company of cavalry troopers, rode up to the chuck wagon where Corporal Stevens and Private Whitney were waiting. After saluting the captain, the corporal filled him in on the details of the encounter with the Sioux.

"We were sure glad to see you coming over the hill, captain," Corporal Stevens said. "Another day of fighting is about all we had left in us. Our ammo supply was running low."

"Well, fortunately we came along when we did," Captain Williams said. "I believe those Sioux had just gotten guns and ammo from the runners we were after. Say, you got any hot coffee left in that pot?"

"Plenty," the corporal said. "You're welcome to help yourself."

Jake, Sam, Al, Russ, and Andy joined the captain and corporal, each pouring themselves coffee as Sergeant Graham rode up.

"Cap'n," he said, "I got a burial detail to take care of the teamster's body. The Indians mutilated him something awful—cut off his hands, feet, and genitals; poked out his eyes, and—"

"Spare me the details, sergeant," the captain interrupted. "There's a trooper's body out there. See if you and some of the boys can find him. Identify him and give him a proper military burial."

The sergeant saluted, turned his mount, and rode off to do his duty.

"Well, mister bone hunter," the captain said to Jake. "Did you find what you came for? Looks like you got scratched digging for bones. It seems to me this expedition cost a lot of dollars, plus two lives."

"I'm truly sorry for the lives lost," Jake said, "but I didn't take them. The Sioux did."

Andy said something under his breath.

"Jake put up a courageous fight against the Indians," the corporal said.

"Excuse me, gentlemen," Jake said, giving the captain somewhat of a half a salute. "I've gotta get my horse and ride out to Henrik's grave to pay my respects and check out the wagonload of fossils. There's one I want to take back. The rest can stay."

Al, Sam, and Russ got up, all of them saying they'd ride out with Jake.

"I'll get a bridle and ride one of my horses along with y'all," Andy said.

The burial detail had just finished the grave for Henrik when the five men from camp rode up. The wind had picked up, and dust was swirling over the freshly dug grave and around the overturned wagon. The wagon was lying on its side; a broken front wheel was hanging off the end of an axle. A dead mule, full of arrows, was still harnessed to the tongue tree of the Conestoga. Fossil bones and smashed crates were strewn about.

"What'd you guys want to do with this busted wagon?" one of the troopers asked.

"We're going to leave it," Jake said. "We just want to pick through the fossils for one particular one to take with us."

"The Sioux must have taken the other three mules," Andy said.

"They'll probably eat them. We'd better get at it, looks like there's a storm brewing."

After a quick search of the scattered bones, Jake found the fossil tooth he'd been looking for. It was still intact in the small, unbroken crate he had packed it in. *The Indians must have been disappointed at not finding guns in the wagon,* he thought. Sam, Al, and Russ found some small skulls to be saved. Andy found a small vertebra. He liked its shape and asked Jake if it was okay for him to keep it. He intended to use it as a talisman.

Dark clouds moved in, and lighting began to light up the western sky. The smell of rain was in the air as the fossil hunters and troopers rode back to the chuck wagon. The wind blew a dotted splattering of large raindrops, and the fossil hunters sought shelter in and under the chuck wagon. The troopers donned slickers, and the horses turned their backsides to the storm. The rain began to fall hard and heavy. In no time the site became saturated with rivulets of water pouring across the once-parched land, turning it into a quagmire.

"We'd have never made it up Cow Creek Canyon after this rain," Andy said as he fingered his fossil talisman.

"All we have to show for all our efforts is three small fossil skulls and one very large fossil tooth," Jake said, trying not to be despondent.

"And a couple of black eyes, a slashed cheek, and a few scrapes and bruises, not to mention insect bites, sunburns, and saddle blisters," Sam said, chuckling. "Professor Marsh should be impressed."

"A successful expedition, I'd say," Russ said. "We found some fossils, kept a few, and had an interesting visit with the Sioux Nation."

"Right," Al said. "And we got to keep our scalps."

In the second week of October, after a week of retracing their steps from Fort Benton by stage and rail, the four fossil hunters were aboard the Pacific Union train and pulled into the Cheyenne station. Jake planned on going on to Laramie, but the other three men departed there for their homes in Kansas.

"This has been one hell of an adventure," Sam said.

"Well, I ain't gonna miss the Judith Badlands, or the Sioux," Russ said.

"I'm going to miss you guys," Jake said. "It was my pleasure to know you. I hope we'll meet again."

"Only next time let's go to California," Al said. "I've always wanted to see the ocean. We can roam the beaches looking for seashells."

They all shook hands and departed their separate ways. A couple of hours later Jake was in Laramie. Tired of traveling, he decided to check into a hotel room, eat a good meal, and get a good night's sleep before heading out to the ranch the next day.

Early the next morning Jake headed for the livery stable to see Sylas Anderson about renting a horse and saddle. Sylas was pitching hay in the corral next to the stables when Jake walked up.

"Vell, goot day to you, Mr. Harding," Sylas said, leaning his pitchfork against the corral's fence. "Goot to see ya back. Chris told me you'd be gone awhile lookin' for bones."

"Good to see you too," Jake said. "I need to rent a horse and saddle."

"Ya, you betcha," Sylas said, walking up to Jake. "My God, vhat happened to the side of your face?"

"Oh, I had a little disagreement with an Indian," Jake said. "I had to have some stitching done."

"Yeah, vell whoever did the needle and thread work did a fine job," Sylas said, taking a close look at Jake's wound. "Looks like it's time for dem stiches to come out. I can do that if you'd like."

"Suits me fine," Jake said.

Jake was amazed at the dexterity that Sylas's gigantic hands displayed in removing the stiches. Sylas gently applied some ointment to the scar, stuff he said helped heal cuts on horses. He patted Jake on the cheek, telling him to pick out a horse and saddle and get on home to his family.

Jake headed for the post office, where he picked up the mail for the ranch. He purchased an envelope and some writing paper and wrote a letter to Professor Marsh detailing the fossil party's exploits and explaining their failure to bring back fossils. Next he went to the telegraph office. He wanted to soften the blow of the detailed letter by sending a wire to Marsh saying that he had found a fossil tooth and should be expecting a letter about the failure of the expedition.

The road to the ranch seemed longer than usual as Jake was haunted by thoughts of what he considered his failure to lead a successful fossil expedition. He couldn't come to grips with the idea that the failure to ship fossils to New Haven was caused by circumstances beyond his control, specifically hostile Indians and weather. Virtually all of his life, Jake had a feeling of confidence in his own abilities, but now, with his big chance to obtain some recognition in a profession most dear to him, he judged himself a failure. The supposedly scientific expedition turned out to be a military exploit that had cost human lives. How would Professor Marsh view Jake's abilities now? Foremost in his mind was the embarrassment he felt at being a failure in his wife's and son's eyes. His aspirations and passions for fossil exploration were still intact, yet he felt depressed over what he considered his failure.

He rode his horse at an easy trot along the winding road to the ranch until he could see the buildings in the distance. He stopped and swung down from his saddle. Stretching his aching back and legs, he took a drink from his canteen while thinking about how good it would be to get home—home to a familiar and safe place with Jen and Danny. His gloomy mood disappeared while he thought about being home again. He quickly checked and tightened the cinch on his horse and was just about to mount when he saw a horse and rider galloping toward him. A voice called out his name. It was Chris Muller.

"Howdy, Chris, good to see ya," Jake said. "You're in a mighty big hurry today."

"Glad you made it back safe and sound," Chris said. "I was at the post office in Laramie and heard you were back. I'm glad I caught up with you. You don't seem to be in a hurry to get home."

"I been just poking along," Jake said. "I had a lot of thoughts going through my mind … slowed me down."

"My God," Chris said as he got closer. "What happened to your cheek?"

"Oh, that," Jake said, chortling. "I started to shave off my beard and cut myself."

"Damned good thing you didn't finish shaving," Chris said, chuckling.

"I'll tell you all about it later," Jake said. He swung up into his saddle. "Let's head on home."

The dining table at the ranch house was filled with people welcoming Jake back home. Chris, Lys, and Harper; Jake, Jen, and Danny; Luke and Linda; Jim and Tom Collins; Red; and Bella were enjoying a much-appreciated feast prepared by Bella, Lys, Linda, and Jen. Everyone toasted a welcome home to Jake. Jen was distraught over Jake's wounded cheek, but Jake kept telling her that it wasn't painful and that he was lucky to still have his scalp intact. It upset Jen that Danny wanted to continue tracing his daddy's scar, but Jake deemed it a badge of honor.

"Jake is going to tell us all about his fossil hunting in Montana," Chris announced after enjoying the evening meal. "Isn't that right, Jake?"

"Right you are," Jake said. "You've been champing at the bit to hear the story, Chris, so I might as well start now before it gets too late. It's a long tale, so everyone get a drink and get comfortable."

Jake spent almost an hour describing the adventures of the Montana fossil expedition. He detailed a number of events, like finding the enormous fossil tooth and meeting the enigmatic Monsieur Andy Lacombe. He left out some bloody details of the Indian skirmishes other than to say they were frightening and brutal. His audience was in awe of the recounting of the expedition. Describing the fight he had with the Indian warrior, when his cheek was slashed, he assured Jen that the Smith and Wesson revolver she had given him saved his life. Jen let out a sigh as she squeezed her husband's hand. Danny and little Harper were asleep, curled up next to each other on a big bear rug Jen had laid on the floor. Jake took another sip of his whiskey and stood up.

"You all enjoy another drink," Jake said. "I'm going to get something from my bags to show you. I'll be right back."

When Jake came back, he was carrying a package about a foot long and half a foot wide. It was thickly wrapped with sacking and bound with leather saddle strings. He laid the bundle on the table, carefully untied the strings, and unwound the fabric. The wrappings revealed a fossil almost nine inches long and three inches thick. Inside the wrapping were sheets of sketch paper with a number of drawings and calculations scribbled on them.

"This is a tooth," Jake said, holding up the fossil. "It's from a dinosaur of about 165 million years ago, probably from a Megalosaurus, which means 'great lizard.' When we found it, Sam Williston and I did some calculations using Georges Cuvier's comparative anatomy. A tooth this size would have come from an animal that was of enormous proportions. Its skull would have been a little over four feet in length, its body length around thirty-eight feet, and it would have stood about twelve feet high."

"Holy cow," Chris said. "That's one hellova big side of beef."

"That's right," Jake said, holding up the fossil tooth and running his fingers up and down its edge. "This serrated edge says this creature was a carnivorous animal. That is, it ate meat. It was not an herbivore, a plant-eating creature like a horse, cow, or a buffalo."

"Whew. That's a terrifying monster," Luke said. "I'd hate to be on its menu."

"Yeah, you wouldn't be much more than a mouthful for that dinosaur," Jake said. "I have a feeling that the Judith River area of Montana, where we were, contains fossil bones of this dinosaur yet to be discovered. Perhaps a future discovery of a whole skeleton of this creature is possible."

"Well, you're not the one to make that possible," Jen said. "You're not roamin' around that Indian country again."

"I hadn't really planned on it," Jake said. "There are plenty of other fossil sites waiting to be explored."

"They're just going to have to wait," Jen said. "I'd like to have you around here for a while."

"I guess that answers the question I was about to ask," Chris said.

"What's that?" Jake asked.

"Day after tomorrow, the Collins boys, Red, and I are going to drive a herd of horses over to Fort Laramie," Chris said. "I wanted to know if you'd come along."

"He can't," Jen said.

"I can't?" Jake asked.

"You, Danny, and I are going fishing," Jen said. "Down by Cottonwood Grove."

"Sounds good to me," Jake said.

28

A silvery November dawn illuminated the large snowflakes as they drifted by the ranch house's window. Jake gazed at the scene, feeling a moment of peace. He placed the steaming cup of coffee he was holding on the table, opened a flask of whiskey, and poured a shot in the cup. He was finding more and more that a morning shot of whiskey helped him get started for the day. It seemed to ease his mind of the weighty thoughts that he still had about the Montana fossil expedition.

This past month Jake had been happy to be home again with Jen and Danny and to attend to his horse wrangler duties with animals he most admired. Jake let his thoughts wander for a minute, downed the rest of his coffee, and then slipped on his mackinaw and hat. The mackinaw was a gift from his wife. It had belonged to her father, who had traded some beaver pelts to a fur trader for it. Jake quietly opened the front door. He could hear Bella moving about in the kitchen. It was early, and Jen and Danny were still asleep. Jake stepped out into the fluttering snowfall and headed for the stables.

When he was a few yards from the barn, he called out to his horse, Nugget. A loud whinny came from the stables, which brought a smile to Jake's face. *That horse admires me as much as I do him,* he thought. He called to Nugget again.

"I'm in here," a voice answered.

"Quit horsing around," Jake said, laughing as he stepped inside the barn to see Red mucking out a stall. "Good morning, Red. I suppose you speak horse too."

"Sometime," Red answered.

"How was the trip to Fort Laramie?" Jake asked. "I haven't seen you since you got back."

"Trip okay," Red said. "Horses not. Thieves stole ten and one killed." Red held up ten fingers and then one.

"Chris didn't say anything to me or Jen about horse thieves," Jake said.

"No tell Jennie," Red said. "Chris is very angry at horse thief."

"I'll bet he is," Jake said. "I'll have to ask him about that. I'm going to ride Nugget over to the east paddock to take a look at the stock there. See you later."

It was still snowing, and with no wind the flakes just drifted down gently, covering the contours of the landscape like a satin sheet. Jake let Nugget move along at his own pace, enjoying the ride on a well-trained horse.

Jake thought it strange that Chris hadn't mentioned a thing about the horse thieves. No sooner had he thought that when he saw Chris riding along the fence line of the pasture.

"Yo, Chris!" Jake shouted, waving his hat.

Chris waved and motioned for Jake to ride over. Chris dismounted and began inspecting a broken part of the paddock fence.

"Howdy, Jake," Chris said as Jake rode up.

"You're out and about early," Jake said. "Is everything okay?"

"Right as rain," Chris replied. "Thought I'd get a head start on things before the snow got too heavy, but it looks like it won't amount to much."

"No, I don't think so," Jake said. "I wanted to check on a couple of horses."

"Before you ride off, give me a hand with this fence," Chris said.

"Sure thing," Jake said as he dismounted. "I just spoke with Red, and he tells me you had some trouble with horse thieves on the way to Fort Laramie."

"Yeah, we did," Chris said. "I was meaning to tell you about that. But you can't breathe a word of it to Jennie."

"Why not?" Jake asked.

"I don't want her to be worrying about it," Chris said. "You see, I know who the horse thieves are. They're a gang that's headed up by Harry Jackson, the fella whose leg Jennie put a bullet in and the brother of that phony deputy who Sheriff Boswell shot."

"I remember," Jake said.

"If Jennie knew Harry was back around this territory, it would worry her sick," Chris said. "I've told all the boys to keep a sharp eye out for him and his gangs—shoot them on sight for horse thieving. We had a shoot-out with them when they killed one of our horses and got away with ten. I think Jim wounded one of their men. I got a good look at Harry."

"I won't say a word to Jen," Jake said. "And I'll keep my eyes open for any strangers around here."

The first snowfalls of winter were light, fluffy, and beautiful, but what followed in the coming months were winter's ravages. Howling winds with blinding snow and subzero temperatures were trying conditions for man and beast. Midwinter melancholy beset the inhabitants of the Muller Ranch, but they were able to cope with this adversity through their communal understanding, companionship, and love.

Jen and Jake were at opposite poles with their winter attitudes. Jen's disposition was full of optimistic views; winter painted a beautiful, white, sparkling countryside; Thanksgiving and Christmas were celebrations of family joyfulness; and reflections of past seasons were positive in anticipation of another spring.

Jake was struggling with depressing thoughts that lingered in his mind and seemed to be more pronounced with the falling temperatures and longer periods of darkness. He was having recurring nightmares of his battles with frightening monsters. He loved his work as a horse wrangler and fossil collector, and his love for his wife and his son were a comfort to him. But his mind was plagued with doubts of his competence after what he considered failure with the Montana fossil expedition. His correspondence with Marsh was disappointing, as the professor didn't seem very interested in Jake's discovery of the huge fossil tooth, nor did he indicate any interest in Jake's doing further fossil explorations for Yale. All Marsh said in his letters was that the Peabody Museum had tons of bones that were being separated from rock by a staff of excellent paleontological apprentices. Jake assumed that Marsh meant that Yale had more than enough fossils at present. Jake's collection of fossils, needing preparation, had also grown—not by tons but at least by pounds. He found solace in his work and spent long hours preparing, cleaning, cataloguing, and illustrating his collection of bones.

Winter finally gave way to beautiful spring days, making working outdoors a pleasure that Jake always looked forward to. He had just finished repairing a railing on a corral fence. He picked up another rail and started toward the next repair when Jen come riding up.

"Morning, hon," she said. "What a beautiful spring day. I hope all of May is this nice. Join me for a little ride and lunch. Bella is taking care of Danny."

"I'd love to join you," Jake said. "Just let me finish this one repair."

"Okay, but hurry," Jen said. "It's much too lovely a day to waste on working. I made us some ham sandwiches and boiled some eggs."

Jake hurried his repair job to the railing and went to fetch his horse. He had let the gelding pasture in the nearby paddock.

"Where are we going on this ride?" Jake asked. "I told Chris I'd get that corral repaired by today."

"Don't you worry about that," Jen said. "I told my brother you could take the day off."

"Oh, you can't just go and do that," Jake remarked, shaking his head.

"Oh, but I can," Jen said. "You forget us Wyoming women have the right to a vote."

"Uh-huh," Jake said calmly. "So, where are we going on this ride?"

"Mainly following our noses," Jen said. They rode at a leisurely trot across the pasture to the far side. Once the noonday sun warmed the land, the scents of spring became more apparent.

"I've always loved spring," Jen said. "It's so invigorating. The fragrances, the colors, the sounds, the weather it's neither too hot nor too cold. Spring is so full of wonderful promises. All my senses hunger to embrace it. Look, there's a perfect place for our luncheon."

Jen pointed toward the end of the pasture where a huge haystack sat on a gentle slope, giving it good drainage. It was surrounded by a stacked log fence that kept livestock away from it. The sun's rays glistened and illuminated the stacked hay. In the distance a few horses could be seen grazing contentedly on spring's new growth.

"Come on. I'll race you there," Jen said as she kicked Lady in the flanks. The horse responded and took off at a gallop with Jen yahooing.

Jake just shook his head. He knew that Nugget could probably outrun Lady, but he let Jen's horse get a lead before he spurred his horse into action. Jake didn't want to win the race as he knew his wife's determination for trying to be the best at everything. He admired his wife's competitive spirit. He loved her for that, and if she loved him more if she won, he loved that too.

The haystack was a lovely spot with a beautiful view of the foothills and the Medicine Bow Mountains. Jen and Jake climbed through the fence, covered a patch of ground with some hay, and spread out a blanket that Jen had in her bedroll. Jen took a canteen and her saddlebags with their lunch and laid out sandwiches, tin cups, biscuits, and jam. While she did this, Jake took the horses down the far end of the slope to a small spring creek. He rigged a rope between two trees to tether the horses and then slackened the horse's cinches. He reached up behind his saddle and lifted off his saddle bags. As he did, he noticed two riders off in the distance near the tree line. His gaze followed them as they disappeared into the pines. He grabbed his rifle and headed back to the haystack.

"Got the horses tethered near that little stream yonder," Jake said, sitting himself down on the comfortable blanket.

"You always care for the animals, don't you, hon," Jen said.

"You bet," Jake said. "I can read those horses' thoughts. I know when they're thirsty and hungry, tired, or in pain."

"Guess that's one reason we hired you," Jen said. "What's your rifle for? Are you still worried about Indian attacks?"

"Nah," Jake said. "Just being prepared. You never know when there might be a grouchy spring grizzly about."

"Well, I've got just the thing to take the grouchiness out of any animal," Jen said. She filled a cup from the canteen and handed it to Jake. "Prost."

Jake took the cup, and even before he had a sip he detected its scent.

"Whiskey, Rye whiskey?" he asked. "A whole cup of whiskey, are you aiming to get me drunk?"

"No, dear, just relaxed," Jen said. "You've been so wound up all winter. You need to unwind, and if getting drunk is a way for you to relax—then yes."

"Prosit," Jake said as he took big mouthful. "Whew, that's some potent stuff. Where'd you get that?"

"Bella gave me that," Jen said. "Some bottles she said Walt had."

"Well, here's to Bella and Walt," Jake said. "Let's have something to eat."

"Ah, let's have another drink," Jen said. "We can eat after we work up an appetite. You need some relaxing exercise."

"Jen, honey, I know what you're getting at," Jake said, "but this is neither the time nor the place."

"This is the right time and a beautiful place," Jen said, her eyes flashing and giving Jake a coy look.

"I promise you the right time will be tonight, at home," Jake said, sighing apologetically. "When you asked why I had my rifle with me, my answer wasn't completely truthful. I didn't want to worry you, but I saw some horsemen up on the ridge. They weren't any of our boys. I just wanted to be on the lookout for any strangers."

"Honey, I understand your skittishness," Jen said. "With all the bad things you've had happen, I know you want to be vigilant. And I appreciate your concern for our safety. But don't let your worries become obsessive."

Jake had made a promise to Chris not to mention to Jen that Harry Jackson's gang had rustled some of their cattle and to be on the lookout for them. He intended to keep that promise. He couldn't identify the riders he saw, and that's all he told Jen.

"Well, I wouldn't say I'm obsessed with my concerns," Jake said. "I just want to be alert to any possible danger so we don't repeat any past tragedies."

"Amen to that," Jen said. "Now let's have a drink and something to eat and enjoy our afternoon. Here's to your promise of a thrilling evening." Jen leaned over and planted a kiss on Jake's lips. He in turn pulled her to him and kissed her passionately.

"Here's to our rendezvous this evening," Jake said as he picked up his cup.

The rest of the afternoon they ate and drank, and Jen read to Jake from the book she had in her saddlebags, *Two Years before the Mast*.

The long, sunny afternoon was relaxing. Jen was so absorbed in her recitation of her book that she became startled when Jake began snoring loudly. She closed the book and pinched Jake's nose shut. He snorted, coughed, and started fumbling for his rifle by his side.

"What—what the hell?" he said. He sat straight up with his rifle in his lap and focused his eyes on something moving across the pasture.

Realizing it was a large whitetail buck, he brought the rifle up to his shoulder.

"Stop! Stop!" Jen yelled. The deer bounded and ran down the other side of the draw. "We don't need the meat," she said. "Besides, he's such a beautiful animal. Let's not harm him."

"You're right," Jake said. "How long have I been asleep?"

"What's the last thing you remember me reading to you?" Jen asked.

"Hmm …," he mused. "There was something about the ship spotting an iceberg."

"You slept a long time," she said.

Two hours later, Jake and Jen were riding into the ranch yard.

"I'll take Lady to the stables and take care of her and Nugget," Jake said.

"Okay, I'll check on Danny and help Bella with supper," Jen said.

Jake led the two horses to the stables, where Chris and Luke were working on repairing a stable door.

"How was your afternoon?" Chris asked. "Jen said she was giving you the afternoon off. Or did she put you to work?"

"Nah, it was a relaxing day," Jake said. "I'm glad you two are here. I've something to tell you."

"Good news or bad news?" Luke asked. "I hope it's good. I've had all the bad news I can take for one day."

"Yeah, I guess so," Chris said. "Linda broke her foot this morning," he explained to Jake. "She was riding that damn roan, and when she got off to open a gate, the horse stepped on her foot—shifted his weight and wouldn't get off. She about damn near bit that horse's ear off trying to get him to move."

"I'm sorry to hear that," Jake said. "Not about the ear but the foot,—well, maybe both. Anyway, what I've got to tell you guys is that while we were riding over in the south pasture, I saw a couple of riders on the ridge. They weren't any of our boys."

"Did Jennie see them?' Chris asked.

"Nope, but I told her I saw them," Jake said. "But I never let on it could be Jackson's gang. She knows nothing of the horse rustling."

"Good," Chris said. "I don't want her to worry about the whereabouts of Jackson."

Two months later, in a middle of a hot July day, Luke came galloping into the ranch yard yelling and waving newspapers. Jen and Danny were by the steps of the veranda tending some flowers.

"What ya yelling about?" Jen asked as Luke reined his mount to a stop in front of the veranda and dismounted.

"Strike the triangle loud as you can," Luke said. "Get everyone over here."

"Are we being attacked?" Jen asked.

"No," Luke said. "But the army was. I have some newspaper accounts of a tragic attack."

Within minutes of the triangle reverberations, people began running to the ranch house. Bella invited everyone into the dining room. Luke and Jen were standing at the large table studying newspapers laid out before them. Everyone from the ranch was there except for Red and Tom Collins, who were out on the range.

"What's going on?" Chris asked as he and Jake walked through the door, their spurs jingling. They had just come in from riding the fence line in the north pasture.

"I just got back from town with the mail and a number of newspapers with some dreadful news," Luke said. "I'll let Jenny read it to you. She's a much better reader than me."

"Before I read this article, I just want to say that some of you know some of the people involved in this tragedy," Jen said. "The Laramie *Sentinel* of July 7 and 8 carried this news, but the most complete details of the event are from the Bismarck *Tribune*, so I'll read from that paper." She laid the papers out in front of her and started reading.

First Account of the Custer Massacre
Tribune Extra
Bismarck, D. T., July 6 1876
Massacred
Gen. Custer and 261 Men the Victims
No Officer or Man of 5 Companies Left to Tell the Tale
3 Days Desperate Fighting by Maj. Reno and the Remainder
of the Seventh
Full Details of the Battle
List of Killed and Wounded
Bismarck Tribune's Special Correspondent Slain
Squaws Mutilate and Rob Dead
Victims Captured Alive. Tortured in Fiendish Manner
What Will Congress Do About It?

Here Jen stopped reading, put down the paper, and asked for a glass of water.

"Let's all take a break," Bella said. "I'll get some water and put on some coffee."

"I believe this calls for a whiskey," Chris said.

"I'll bring a bottle and some glasses," Bella said.

"I believe my husband had once met General Custer," Jen said. "What was he like, Jake?"

"I only met him from a distance, through Professor Marsh," Jake said. "Arrogant."

"Who," Jen asked, "The professor or the general?"

"Both," Jake replied.

There was silence; no one said a word. They just nodded with austere expressions. Jen continued reading from the newspaper.

She read of the accounts of Custer being instructed to find the Indians and report their position to General Terry, who would join forces with Custer and wipe them out. General Terry had urged Custer to take additional troops, but Custer declined any assistance.

He had full confidence in his men to defeat any Indian force he met. On June 24 Custer pushed on toward the Little Horn, one of the branches of the Big Horn River. There he found and attacked the large Sioux village from the north. Indians were riding in all directions, seemingly retreating. Meanwhile, on June 25, Major Reno, under orders from Custer, had attacked the village at its head from the south with three companies. A bloody hand-to-hand conflict occurred in which many were killed and wounded. Fortunately they were reinforced by four companies of cavalry led by Colonel Benteen. They made their way back across the Little Horn River, and at the ford the fiercest fighting occurred. The Sioux came at them from all sides. No word came from Custer. Colonel Benteen with a company of his charged a large party of the Sioux, scattering them with their brave assault. The fighting continued until the afternoon of the twenty-seventh. The Indians suddenly began to leave. That afternoon General Terry and his command arrived, but there was still no word from Custer. Their victory celebration was short lived when Lieutenant Bradley reported that he had found Custer dead, along with one hundred and ninety cavalry men.

Jen stopped reading.

"I need a drink," she said. Then she reached for a glass, poured a shot of whiskey, and took a big swallow. "I'll read a little more and then leave the papers for anyone who wants to read the rest."

She continued reading.

Gen. Terry sought the spot and found it to be too true. Of those brave men who followed Custer, all perished; no one lives to tell the story of the battle.

All the dead were stripped of clothing and many of them with bodies terribly mutilated. The heads of some were severed from the body. The privates of some were cut off; while others bore traces of torture.

"There's more," Jen said. "And a list of those killed and wounded, quite long. I'll leave the paper on the table."

She took her half a glass of whiskey, walked around the table, and sat herself down on Jake's lap.

"Hell of a thing," Jake said. "Hell of a centennial celebration for our country."

"It could have been you in Montana," Jen said, sighing.

Two months later folks were still getting news reports and talking about the June twenty-fifth Custer massacre at the Little Bighorn River. The Sioux knew the area as the Greasy Grass River. Later it was found that Crazy Horse led the Sioux attack on the Seventh Cavalry, killing Custer and his men. Sitting Bull was involved only as a medicine man but was not in the raiding Indian war party. Chief Red Cloud's whereabouts were unknown. Some thought he was behind the plot, whereas others claimed he had nothing to do with it. It was Jake's opinion that Red Cloud did not initiate this attack, as Jake had met Red Cloud and knew of his desire for peace.

29

One afternoon in the middle of September, Luke brought a stack of mail back from Laramie. Jake had a letter from Professor Marsh and one from Sam Williston. Chris had a letter from Captain Ken Egan of Fort Laramie and one from Sheriff Brophy, the new sheriff of Laramie. Jen had a letter from Ali in Philadelphia, and the Collins brothers had a letter from their uncle in Denver.

Marsh's letter told Jake that his informers said Cope was on a fossil expedition in Montana traveling to the Judith River Badlands. Jake remembered his journey there. *What a hell of a time to be going into that country,* he thought. *The Sioux are probably roaming that area like a swarm of irate hornets.* Marsh wanted to know if Jake would be available for a fossil expedition next summer to parts of Wyoming and Colorado. Jake would have to think about that. Sam's letter said that Marsh had also asked Sam about a fossil hunt next July, and Sam wanted to know if Jake was interested because it had been a pleasure working with him before and hoped to do it again.

Chris's letter from Captain Ken Egan of Fort Laramie was a request for any horses the Muller Ranch had for sale. This was to replace horses lost in the battles last June at Little Bighorn and to furnish mounts for the army's retaliation against the Sioux. Chris would accommodate his friend's request. The letter from Sheriff Brophy told of a meeting he'd had with Marshal Nat Boswell, now warden of the new Wyoming Territorial Prison. Boswell had informed the sheriff that members of a gang headed by Harry Jackson were in the territory and to be on the watch for them. Chris let everyone at the ranch know of this, except for Jennie.

Two weeks later the ranch hands had rounded up a herd of about one hundred horses for the army. Chris, Red, and Jim and Tom Collins would drive them to Fort Laramie while Jake and Luke stayed at the ranch and took care of business there.

Detailed news of the Battle of Little Bighorn battle was still circulating. There were reports of the Indians crossing the border into Canada. A letter to Jake from Sam Williston told of how Marsh's adversary, Edward Cope, had just gotten out of Montana before some Indians, being chased by the army, made their way to Canada at the Cow Island ford.

In 1876 the US Government passed a bill that was known as the "sell or starve" rider to the Indian Appropriations Act. This stated that all reservations allocations would be cut off unless the Indians terminated hostilities, let the government change some boundaries of reservations, and ceded the Black Hills to the US Government. This, of course, was in direct violation to the 1868 Fort Laramie Treaty. Only full-blooded Indians residing on the reservations would receive benefits from this act. The US Government also ordered the slaughter of all buffalo herds, thus depriving the Indians of their basic living needs.

Most white Americans viewed the Custer defeat as a "massacre of the innocents," while some saw the American government as the aggressors who had illegally declared war on the Sioux under US president Ulysses S. Grant.

Jake was contemplating these opposing sentiments while cleaning and restoring fossils in his collection. He thought *why have human beings, throughout history, waged war on one another? Maybe some men were by nature violent, evil to the core, devoid of compassion. Some may feel a need to find purpose in life by having power over others and being in control. Greed was surely an instigator of violence.* Jake detested violence. He saw no reason for it other than in protecting oneself, as his grandfather had taught him. A loud knock on the door brought Jake out of his deliberations and for a moment startled him.

"Door's open," Jake said. "Come on in."

"Hey, you old fossil," Chris said as he entered the room. "How are the bones?"

"If you're asking about mine, they're fine," Jake said. "If you're asking about the fossils, they're as interesting and puzzling as ever."

While Chris was visiting with Jake, Lys was in the front room talking with Jen. Little Harper and Danny were playing on the floor.

"We've all been invited to a wedding in Laramie on November 9," Lys said. "Linda's friend Joanne Walker is getting married. Chris and I are going. Come with us. We could have Bella look after the kids. The Collins brothers and Red will be staying here. There will be a big shindig at Claudia's Café."

"Sounds like fun," Jen said. "Who is Joanne marrying?"

"You won't believe it," Lys said. "Jerome Anderson."

"Sylas's boy," Jen asked.

"Yep," Lys answered. "It should be a humdinger of a party. Luke and Linda are going into Laramie in the first part of November to help Claudia set up the café."

"I want to go," Jen said. "I need a break. I'll talk to the boss about it."

"I thought you *were* the boss," Lys said, laughing.

"I am," Jen said, "only he doesn't know it."

Meanwhile, Chris's and Jake's conversation was similar.

"What you think, Jake?" Chris asked. "Let's take a couple of days off and kick up our heels in Laramie."

"Sounds good to me," Jake said. "I'll ask the boss."

"I thought you *were* the boss," Chris said.

"I am," Jake said. "It's just that Jen doesn't know it."

Claudia's Café was packed with wedding guests. Claudia had the help of friends in setting up extra serving tables and a couple of guys at the door telling anyone with firearms to leave them on a table near the entrance. With all the drinking that would go on, Claudia didn't want any gunplay. She had hired Shana and Helen, friends of Joanne's as extra waitresses and kitchen help. The food was excellent, and there was plenty of it. The guests washed down the food with a lot of beer and whiskey. Some of the entertainment was provided by Jake playing the violin and Lys singing. A small group of musicians played for the dance after everyone had their fill of food. The bride and groom were honored with the first dance, and people were amazed at the dancing ability of the couple, especially considering their differences in size. Joanne was a petite, gorgeous young gal with dark hair and a pair of flashing dark eyes to match. She was demonstrative and quick on the draw (as her mother, Carolynn, said of her). Joanne was the opposite of her new husband. Jerome, with his blond hair, blue eyes, and muscular build stood six feet six, towering above his bride. Cautious and pensive, he was the antithesis of his wife. But somehow they seemed to fit as they whirled around the dance floor.

"They say opposites attract," Jen said to Jake. "Just look at those two kids. Come on take me for a spin around the dance floor."

Jake did just that as the dance area quickly began to be crowded. Linda and Luke also joined in the dancers. The café was noisy with laugher, and the more people drank, the louder the volume of laughter and talking became. Sylas danced with his new daughter-in-law while Joanne's mother danced with her new son-in-law.

It was a festive occasion with everyone enjoying themselves, except for a few who were experiencing the viciousness of alcohol intoxication. Sitting at a corner table drinking heavily were three men, two of whom were unknown to local people; but one was a well-known local. His name was Bartholomew Burgoyne, better known as BB.

Jake and Jen were kicking up their heels on the dance floor when Luke and Linda came over.

"I've had enough of this," Luke said. "My two left feet and I are going to sit this one out. Come on, Linda."

"Thank God," Linda said. "My feet are getting bruised from being stepped on."

Luke escorted Linda back to the table where all their friends were sitting. He noticed that across the room Jerome was talking with his father, Sylas, while Joanne visited with her mother and some friends.

"Come on, Chris," Luke said. "Let's have a word with Jerome and his dad."

They strolled across the room while Linda, Lys, and a couple of their gal friends chatted and laughed at something in their conversation. Shana was serving them drinks when suddenly Linda was grabbed by the wrist and forced up and out of her chair. The tray of drinks Shana was holding went flying.

"Come dance with me, you sweet thing," a rough voice said.

Linda was so surprised for a moment that she didn't know if she should scream or haul off and sock the intruder. Instead she just coldly looked into his eyes.

"You let go of me, BB," she said. "You're drunk." She stomped on his foot and got loose of his hold.

"Why you little bitch," BB said. "That'll cost you a little kiss." He grabbed her arm, twisted it, and bent down, trying to kiss her mouth, but she turned her head.

"Ow!" she yelled. "Bartholomew, you're hurting my arm."

"You bastard," Shana yelled. "Let her go and get the hell out of here!" She grabbed a glass of whiskey from the table and threw it in his face.

"Shit," BB said. "You're another wild bitch that needs taming. You want a little kiss too—or maybe more?"

Luke and Chris had just started talking with the Andersons when they heard Linda yell. When Luke saw what was going on, he ran across the room followed by Chris. BB's two drinking companions also saw the commotion.

"I hate to just sit around and watch while BB has all the fun," the first stranger said.

"Yeah, me too. Let's join 'em," the second stranger said.

Luke ran over to BB, grabbed a hold of his vest, and landed a solid punch to his gut. Linda had scooted under the table to the other side next to Lys.

"You son of a bitch," Luke said. "Get away from my wife!"

BB grabbed his gut, let out a moan, scowled, and swore at Luke.

"Ha, when I get through with you, Deputy Luke," BB said, "I'm going to show that bitch wife of yours what it's like to be with a real man, not one who hides behind a badge."

"I don't have a badge anymore and I never hid behind the one I did have," Luke said. "This time around I'm not letting you off as easy as I did before."

Luke took a step to lunge at BB when suddenly a pair of strong arms came from behind his back, enclosed him, and held him fast. Then BB landed a swift punch to his jaw, and Luke went down on the floor moaning as the room spun around with flashing lights.

"Good shot!" the man with the strong arms exclaimed. "That'll take care of him."

No sooner had the stranger with the strong arms said that when he was whirled around and a fist slammed into his nose busting it and spurting blood down his chin and shirt. The man dropped to the floor dazed.

"That's for my friend Luke," Chris said. "Now it's your turn, BB."

Luke was recovering from nearly being knocked out. He rolled over and sat on top of the bloody-nosed stranger holding him down. Chris threw a punch at BB but missed as BB stepped to one side. Readying himself to deliver another punch, Chris suddenly felt arms holding him back, and BB advanced for a hit.

"Yahoo! Hit him, B!" the voice behind Chris said, and then the person moaned and dropped his arms. Jake had come up behind the second stranger and landed a hard punch to his kidney. As the stranger bent over in pain, Jake threw an upper cut that knocked him out. BB came at Chris swinging his fists. Chris ducked and tackled BB, sending him reeling backward knocking over a table as they crashed to the floor. Sylas and Jerome broke through the crowd of spectators, and each grabbing a downed fighter. Sylas picked up BB, pinning his arms and holding him up off the floor. BB kicked his legs like a child being held off the ground against his will by a parent. Jerome held stranger number one's arms tightly behind his back. Stranger number two was no problem; he was still out cold from Jake's punch.

"Gus!" Sylas yelled. "Get some rope. Ve need to hog-tie some mavericks."

A minute later Gus showed up with a couple of lariats. The three party crashers were bound and tied while someone went to get Sheriff Brophy.

Within a short while, Sheriff Brophy arrived with one of his deputies.

"We'll get these two fellas and BB locked up," the sheriff said. "I recognize one of these hooligans. His name is Durant. He's wanted for bank robbery, belongs to a gang headed up by Harry Jackson.

"Now that is interesting," Chris said. "I'd sure like to get Jackson and all his gang. They rustled some of my horses, among other things I suspect them of."

Jen gave Chris a bewildered look but didn't say a word.

The next morning at breakfast Shana served everyone plenty of strong coffee. The guys were nursing hangovers and bruises from the party. They apologized to Claudia for busting up some of her furniture.

"No, never mind," Claudia said. "You guys did good in getting rid of some trash."

"Told you it would be a humdinger of a party," Lys said. Jen and Linda laughed.

"Do you think the boys had fun?" Linda asks.

"I'm sure they did," Jen said. "We all did."

The spring of 1877 was a busy time at the Muller Ranch. With a new herd of horses to attend to, Jake had decided no matter what Marsh had in store for him, he'd take a year off from fossil hunting. He would, however, get caught up on cataloging fossils he had collected. Spending time working at the ranch and being with his wife and son were his priorities for the moment.

Meanwhile, that spring, O. C. Marsh received a telegram from Arthur Lakes, an amateur geologist and fossil hunter, who stated that he and a friend had found gigantic fossil bones near Morrison, Colorado. Would the professor be interested? he asked. If so, the telegram asked him to send instructions regarding shipping the bones to him. Marsh did not reply. His interest lay mainly in prehistoric bones of mammals and birds of the Cretaceous period. The discoveries of such enormous bones from the Jurassic Period were few and far between, and the speculation of some paleontologists was that these fossil bones were from some aquatic creature, more like a whale than a land dinosaur. Some dinosaur bones being discovered at this time were from large dinosaurs, but the bones that Lakes was beginning to excavate were gigantic compared to former discoveries. Excited about his find and not discouraged by Marsh's apathy, Lakes sent the professor a crate of the huge bones along with a letter and sketches of bones and of the geological cross-section of hills. Lakes also sent a crate of bones to Edward Cope in Philadelphia. Lakes offered to collect and sell fossil bones to whoever was interested and paid the most.

The starting shot was fired for the largest race for dinosaur bones in history. That summer Marsh and Cope were leading the pack in the Great Dinosaur Rush, also known as the Bone Wars. Marsh sent

Benjamin Mudge, one of his leading fossil collectors in Kansas, to Morrison, Colorado. Sam Williston was now in charge of Marsh's fossil collecting in Kansas. Mudge met with Lakes and hired him to collect for Marsh. Marsh had beat Cope to the Morrison site, but Cope had received information on a fossil find near Canon City, a hundred miles from Morrison. Cope hired Oramel Lucas, a school teacher and botanist from Canon City who had discovered this fossil site, which had easier digging conditions because the soil was softer than the hard sandstone on the steep hillsides of the Morrison site. Cope was being sent huge vertebrae fossils, larger than the fossils found at Morrison. Based on those vertebrae, Cope calculated that the animal could have reached up to 130 feet in the air. Marsh and Cope were challenging each other with one discovery after another.

Marsh sent Sam to Canon City. Sam's first attempts at locating bones were not too successful, but then he found the pelvis and tail of a large dinosaur. The bones, embedded in hard sandstone, were broken but arranged in the correct anatomical order. The vertebrae in the tail had unusually large dorsal plates and spikes. Further investigation later at the Morrison quarry uncovered more bones of that species of animal with its backbone plates and tail spikes. Later that year, Marsh pieced together the unusual bones of this dinosaur and decided to call it *Stegosaurus,* meaning "armed roof reptile." Marsh and Cope spent the fall and winter in their studios. Both paleontologists were dealing with the preparation of the huge bones that had been excavated in Colorado. Marsh had a large staff at the Peabody Museum to help with the reconstruction of six of these Jurassic giants. Cope was not as fortunate in having a large staff, but with an able assistant he still managed to piece together five different dinosaurs.

30

In the later part April 1878, Jake received a letter from Marsh saying that Sam had gone to Como, Wyoming, to a bone bed that promised to be a valuable fossil quarry. In the fall of 1877, Marsh had received word from the Union Pacific station agent and the section foreman at Como Station that these two railroad men, who had been out antelope hunting, had discovered a vast deposit of giant fossil bones. Marsh immediately sent Sam to Como Bluff to investigate. In the letter, Marsh asked if Jake could meet with Sam at Como Bluff to check out the discovery. Jake agreed to go there in the middle of May. He was already aware of the Como Bluff fossil find as he had read two newspaper articles about the discovery that had been leaked to the Laramie *Daily Sentinel*. One article published on March 29, 1878, and another on March 30—titled "The Como Crocodile"—reported the find and that the search for fossils through the Bighorn country would be under the direction of authorities at Yale College. The railroad station agent at Como was suspected of leaking information about the fossil find. The news article reported an inflated value paid for fossils. The finders had hoped to receive considerable amounts of money for their discovery.

On May 10, Jake was headed for Como Bluff, about forty miles from the ranch. He rode Nugget across the dry rolling plains dotted with sagebrush and low bluffs. Late that afternoon Jake arrived at Como Rail Watering Station, which consisted of two buildings and a water tower. There he found Sam Williston and the two railroad men packing crates of bones for shipment to New Haven.

"Hey, Jake," Sam said. "Good to see you. You surprised me. I expected to see you on the northwest-bound train this evening, but here you are on horseback."

"Hello, Sam," Jake said. "My horse needed the exercise. Meet Nugget." Jake dismounted and let the reins drop as he had trained his horse to wait until given a command.

"Meet the two guys who stumbled onto this outstanding fossil find," Sam said. "Ed Carlin and Harlow Reed, meet Jake Harding, one of Marsh's employees, and Jake's horse, Nugget."

"Another one of Marsh's flunkies," Ed said as he turned his back on Jake and walked toward Nugget.

"Pleased to meet ya," Harlow said, extending his hand. "Don't pay no never mind to Ed. He's been working in the sun too long."

Ed, the Como station agent, was an outspoken, haughty, shifty individual whom Jake didn't trust from the beginning. On the other hand, Harlow Reed was the strong, mild-mannered type of frontier man who had been a guide, game hunter, and Indian fighter. Jake thought of him as being quite dependable.

While Jake was being introduced to Harlow, Ed picked up Nugget's loose reins, grabbed a hold of the saddle horn, put his foot in the stirrup, and swung himself up into the saddle.

"Your horse looks like he could be fast," Ed said. "Mind if I take him for a run?"

"I'd prefer you didn't. He's had a long ride," Jake said. "I'll ask you to get down off my horse. I don't think he likes you astride him. I warn you he may start bucking."

"Well, he ain't gonna buck me off," Ed said. "I've tamed many a bronc."

Suddenly Ed kicked the horse hard in the flanks and galloped off across the plain. Ed was right; the horse was fast. Then as fast as he had taken off, Nugget came to a halt, arched his back, and shot straight up in the air like a geyser. Ed went flying, landing in the sagebrush. The horse turned and trotted back to Jake, dragging his reins and leaving Ed to walk back.

"Good boy," Jake said as he rubbed his horse's head. *I warned him.*

Sam and Harlow were laughing but not so loud that Ed could hear.

"Marsh told me a little about the find and about some of the huge bones that have been shipped to him from here," Jake said.

"Jake, you won't believe the size, the quantity, and the quality of the bones we're extracting from four pits we've started," Sam said. "But it seems like we're not the only one's interested in this site. We've seen others snooping about. I suspect they are Cope's men."

"I'm anxious to take a look at the quarry sites," Jake said. "I hope we can head out to Como Bluff first thing in the morning."

Como Bluff, about two miles from Como Station, is a seven-mile-long ridge that is an anticline: an arch of rock strata that folds downward in opposite directions from the crest. The ridge lies near the towns of Rock River and Medicine Bow.

Early the next morning Jake filled a washtub with water from the tower for his horse. He had Nugget hobble trained so the horse could roam to find grass but wouldn't stray. Jake followed Sam and the two other collectors to the fossil site.

"This is, without a doubt, the best bone bed I've ever seen," Jake said to Sam.

"This is quarry number one, the best of the four so far," Sam said. "We're going to spend some more time digging here before we open a fifth site."

The four fossil hunters soon found bones to unearth and were busy digging until their noon break.

"We should bring that damn horse of yours to the pits to help us lug back some of these bones," Ed said to Jake. "We could make a rock-sled and sling a pannier over its back."

"Not a good idea," Jake said. "Nugget is a horse, not a mule, and I wonder if Marsh would be willing to pay Nugget a wage."

"Hell, no," Ed said. "He ain't even paid us what he owes."

"Yeah, I know about Marsh and his late payments," Jake said.

"That palomino of yours should be put to work," Ed said, getting worked up over what Jake's horse had put him through the day before.

"That ain't goin' to happen," Jake said.

"Well, maybe we should put a pannier on *your* back," Ed said. "If you don't want that nag of yours to help us, you could be our mule."

"Mister, I've had about enough of your insults," Jake said. "First you called me Professor Marsh's flunky, and then you call my horse a nag. Just keep your big mouth shut, or I'll shut it for you."

"You know, Mr. Harding, both you and your horse are full of horseshit," Ed said, snickering and jabbing his finger at Jake.

Sam and Harlow sat in silence watching this little exchange. Sam, shaking his head, knew of Jake's temperament and his admiration for horses. Sam was about to say something to calm the brewing storm, but before he could, all hell broke loose, starting with a string of insults, shoving, and then punches. Jake grabbed Ed's right arm and landed a solid punch to his gut, knocking the wind out of him. Ed bent over and then came up swiftly with a left upper cut that hit Jake on the right jaw, sending him reeling against the side of the bluff. Scuffling and throwing punches at each other, they managed to bloody each other's noses but not much more than that. Harlow and Sam stepped in and stopped the fight.

"All right, now, you fellas had your little fun," Sam said. "I hope you've got enough fight in ya to dig up some fossils. What I'm going to do is have Ed and I work quarry number four and Harlow and Jake work number one. So let's get at it."

"Shit, Sam, you know number four is so damn far away it takes half a day to haul the bones to the station," Ed grumbled. "That's hard work."

"I know," Sam said, "but you seemed to have a lot of energy. Harlow and Jake will be working just as hard. No need to be begrudging."

Without much further grumbling, everyone attended to their jobs and found the arrangement manageable, though not completely agreeable. Nugget was content to graze the prairie, finding what grasses he could among the sagebrush.

That summer the weather was comfortable at Como Bluff, and the fossil sites were very productive. By late July, many well-preserved new species of Jurassic dinosaurs were being discovered. Tension had grown between Ed and Harlow, partly due to their relationship with Marsh. Harlow felt a loyalty to his employer, but Ed did not. Harlow also thought that Ed was slacking off at his job. The tensions were at a point where they were just simmering, but at least not boiling—not yet. Jake would find relief from this antagonistic behavior by taking his horse for evening rides across the rolling countryside.

"I'll be going to New Haven next week," Sam announced. "Marsh said he'd like my assistance in the museum until next spring."

"Well, good luck with that," Jake said. "I'll be going back to the ranch in the first week in September to help with roundup."

Harlow and Ed were left to work at the fossil site for the fall and coming winter and to work out their differences. Sam went to New Haven, while Jake returned to the ranch.

As much as Jake enjoyed digging for fossils, he was glad to be back at the ranch. When he rode up to the ranch house, Jen, who was sweeping off the front walkway, dropped her broom and ran to greet him. Jake swung down from his saddle and scooped her up in his arms.

"Oh, I'm so glad your home, you wandering vagabond!" Jen exclaimed. "I've missed you more than ever."

"But not as much as I've missed you," Jake said. "Where's Danny?"

"He's with Uncle Chris," Jen said. "Those two adore one another.

They're down behind the barn doing some target practice. Danny said he's going to learn to shoot a gun."

"I'll take Nugget to the barn and see them," Jake said.

"Don't be long," Jen said. "And tell Chris to come to the house to see me."

About a half hour later, Jake, Chris, and Danny came walking up to the house. Danny was riding on Jake's shoulders yelling, "Giddyup!" while Chris and Jake were yelling, "Yahoo!"

"What'd you want to see me about?" Chris asked Jen.

"I need you to endorse a check from the Fort Laramie horse sale," she said.

"Okay, where is it?" Chris asked.

"In the salamander," Jen said.

"Uncle Chris, what's a salamander?" Danny asked all ears to this conversation.

"You see that big box over in the corner of the room?' Chris said to Danny, pointing to a large iron safe. "In that strongbox is where we keep money and important papers. They are safe in there as nobody but us has the key to open it. Even if there was a fire, that box would not burn up. There is another kind of salamander, a lizard that supposedly can go through fire without being hurt. That's why that vault is called a salamander."

"I saw a picture of a lizard in a book Mama showed me," Danny said. "It looked scary."

"I'll bet it did," Chris said. "It was probably a dinosaur."

Danny loved books, and that February 1879, on his sixth birthday, he was given a sketchbook journal. He took after his dad in that he loved to draw. His big birthday surprise was a pony. He named the horse Happy because it was a gentle, happy horse and made him happy. Uncle Chris gave him the toy pistol that Walt Muller had carved that looked like a real gun. Chris promised his nephew that he would take him target practicing with a real gun.

Winter digging for fossils at Como Bluff was miserable. Not only was the weather cold, but the relationship between Ed and Harlow was frosty. Each man had enlisted help from other railroad track workers and the two antagonists went about their work at different ends of the ridge without much communication between them. Harlow became suspicious of Ed's work and found out that he had been working another part of the bluff with some men and shipping fossils to Cope. Harlow was working quarry number four but without much success. Harlow informed Marsh of the situation brewing at Como and asked for reinforcements. In April, Marsh asks Arthur Lakes to go to Como. In the meantime, Marsh informed Harlow that he should abandon quarry four but to first destroy all the bones he saw in that site. Marsh did not want any fossils to fall into the hands of his competitor. Harlow complied with the request, smashing bones and caving in part of the quarry.

Lakes arrived at Como station in mid-May, and with Harlow they began to work quarry number three. At the end of May, Jake rode his horse to Como station to join in the excavation of bones in that quarry. About a half a mile from that site, they discovered some fossils and opened a new pit. This was quarry number six, and it was producing a number of mammals and aquatic reptiles. At quarry number six, the fossil hunters made an astounding discovery. A giant sauropod was uncovered that measured seventy-five feet in length and stood fifteen feet tall at its hip.

Marsh journeyed to Como Bluff in June to check on Wyoming's most notorious dinosaur bone beds himself. He was delighted to view the new discovery. Cope had already named this sauropod *Camarasaurus*, meaning "chambered lizard," from a discovery of its bones sent him from a collector in Colorado. Marsh decided that because of the size and location of this find that this sauropod was different from Cope's and named it *Morosaurus grandia*.

"This is truly an amazing geological formation," Marsh said, excited to survey the new bone beds. "I hear reports of other parties collecting at this site. We must establish, lay claim to, and protect our quarries at this ridge."

"We'll need more help," Jake said. "Recently we were in a rock-throwing battle with some other collectors who thought they could chase us from our site. But we stood our ground. It was fortunate it was not bullets being fired back and forth. But things have quieted down since Ed left and there's a new agent at Como station."

"I've seen a quarry of Cope's. It's about played out, and his men are looking for a new site," Arthur Lakes said. "We do need more help in excavating and to protect our quarries."

"I will see that you get some help," Marsh said. "Arthur, with your draftsman skills, can you make some maps of the positions of the bone beds in this area and send them to me?"

"That I will do," Lakes said.

A week later Marsh returned to New Haven. Arthur was doing more drawings and landscape watercolors of the area along with the mapping Marsh had requested. Harlow felt that Arthur was slacking off in his excavating duties.

By the beginning of August Marsh's crew had grown to six men who helped keep guard at the quarries. They had opened quarries seven, eight, and nine. Quarry number nine became a major yielder of Jurassic mammal specimens. Into September, even more quarries were opened. At quarry number thirteen, excavations turned up a huge *Brontosaurus,* along with almost a dozen different dinosaur species. The fossil discoveries were wonderful, but relationships were not. Harlow was becoming increasingly irritated with Arthur. Arthur's slacking off from digging peeved Harlow, but most of all it was Arthur's condescending English manners that annoyed Harlow.

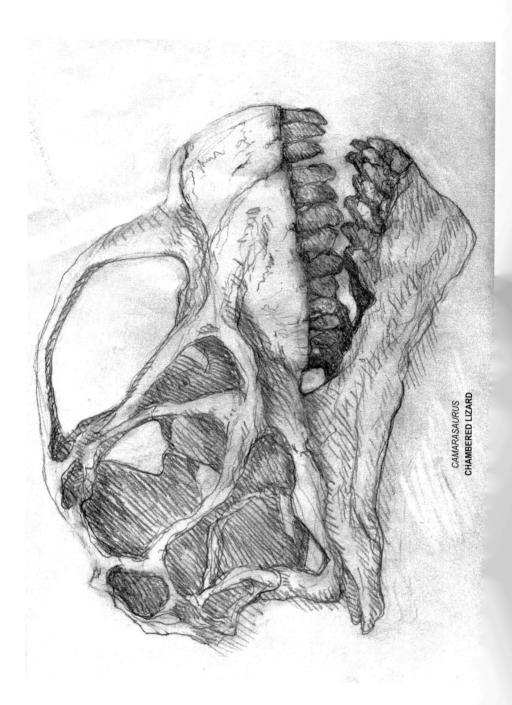

CAMARASAURUS
CHAMBERED LIZARD

"Jake, I'm going to send a letter to Marsh telling him I'm quitting this bone business," Harlow said. "I can't take working with Lakes and his high horse ways. You know, it seems everyone in this business is at one another's throats, excepting you and me."

"Well, I guess you and I are not in competition with each other," Jake said. "I've decided this is the last season I'm working for Marsh. I do love fossil hunting, but I'm going to do it on my own time and terms."

"Maybe I'll go back to working on the railroad or collect for somebody else," Harlow said. "You need a collector?"

"Well, you never know," Jake said. "We'll keep in touch. I'll be leaving for home at the end of the month. It'll be nice to get back to the ranch and my family."

31

Jake rode at an easy trot on his way back to the ranch. He enjoyed the warmth of the late September sun. The temperature was just as he liked, neither too hot nor too cold. He thought over his conversation with Harlow. The competition between fossil hunters was becoming like the gold miners' rivalry. Would there be the possibility of shooting confrontations at fossil sites? He was glad he had made the decision to quit prospecting for Yale. He'd build his own collection. In the last few years he had gained an enormous amount of knowledge about the history of life on Earth recorded in the fossil record. Pushing all his anxieties aside, he was feeling better about himself than he had since his Montana/Dakota experience.

He took a break for himself and Nugget. He was feeling a little stiff and thought he had noticed his horse favoring his back left leg. Jake dismounted, took a hoof pick from his saddlebag, and grabbed a hold of the horse's back leg. He lifted the hoof and began examining it. He cleaned some gravel from the hoof, lowered it to the ground, and gave his horse a gentle pat on the rump. Nugget snorted, and Jake laughed. He viewed the distant Laramie Mountain Range as the low afternoon sun lit its pronounced profile in indigo and mauve, contrasted by the ocher earth tones of the high plains.

"By God, this is the most beautiful country I've ever seen," Jake said, addressing his words to Nugget.

Suddenly, Jake felt a searing pain on the right side of his head.

He pitched forward, landing face down in the prairie soil. Throbbing pain and a red darkness overcame him. He couldn't move, he couldn't see, and his face pressed into the dirt. For a moment or so, there was silence, and then he faintly heard the sound of voices.

"Good shot. You got him," a voice said. "I'll get his horse."

"I'll check his pockets," another voice said. "He's got a fine-looking revolver there. I'll get that."

The voices were slowly disappearing, distorted, and then suddenly he was falling, a thud and silence, nothing but black—silence, nothingness.

The warm fall evening was filled with squeals of delight at the Muller Ranch. Danny and his cousin, Harper, were riding on the pony, Happy, supervised by Jen and Lys.

"Okay, you guys one last ride on Happy," Jen said. "It's time to get ready for bed."

"Ah, Mom, I want to stay up and wait for Dad to come home," Danny said.

"Well, he may not be home until early morning," Jen said. "We can see him then."

"I thought Jake would be home by this evening," Lys said.

"Well, that was the plan," Jen said. "He said he'd be home on the twenty-seventh, but you know Jake—he probably found another fossil he just had to dig out."

"Yeah, just like Chris," Lys said. "Sorry I'm late, hon. I had just one more horse to look after," she said, imitating Chris. "Harper and I are going home. We'll see you tomorrow."

"Come on, Danny," Jen said. "Let's take care of Happy."

The cool September nights were illuminated by a large harvest moon. Jen tried to sleep, but it was useless. She lay in bed with the coal-oil lamp turned just high enough that she could see to read. She would read a passage and then read it again. Her mind was not focused on the book she was reading but was troubled by her concern as to why Jake wasn't home yet. She listened to the pair of owls who had nested in the big cottonwood tree by the barn, hooting at each other. Then she heard the familiar creak from the hallway floor boards. She reached over to the night table, turned the lamp up a notch, and swung her legs out of the bed. She pulled on a housecoat and went to the bedroom door.

"Jake?" she asked, opening the door. "Danny?" There was no answer.

The hallway was dark. She turned and went back to the nightstand to get the lamp. Just as she reached for the lamp, a hand clasped over her mouth, and the barrel of a revolver was thrust in her face.

"Shh," a voice commanded. "Quiet, or you and your boy are dead. Put your hands together behind your back."

Jen did as ordered and felt a cord wrapping her hands together. Her assailant holstered his revolver and then tied a kerchief across her mouth to gag her.

"Okay, turn around," the voice said.

She turned and looked into the face of a man with a black beard and blue eyes as cold as ice. A revolver—that she recognized—was withdrawn from his holster and poked hard against her left breast.

"I want the key to that safe in the front room," he said, "after which you and I will have some fun for old times' sake. Now where's the key?"

Jen's eyes widened as she shook her head and tried to laugh, but her gag held fast and all that came out was a little yelp.

"Well, darling, finally you recognized me," he said as he holstered his gun. "I was beginning to think you'd forgotten me. But I didn't think you could. I'm the same old Harry, except for the stiff leg you gave me. But I always had a stiff for you—"

"Mommy," Danny said as he came into the bedroom. He was carrying the toy gun Chris had given him. He pointed the toy at the stranger. "Stick 'em up," he said.

Harry turned toward the boy and placed his hand on his revolver. "What's your name?"

"Danny," the boy said. "And that's my mom, and I might shoot you. My uncle Chris said guns are for shooting bad guys. You are bad for tying up my mom."

"Now wait a minute, Danny," Harry said. "You wouldn't want to shoot me. I'm an old friend of your mom's."

Jen was sitting on the edge of the bed trying to undo her tied hands and shaking her head. Harry drew his revolver, and at that moment, in the dim light of the lamp, he realized the boy was holding a toy gun.

"Okay, Danny," Harry said. "You come over here and sit beside your mom. You know you can't shoot me with that toy."

"You're right, but I can," a voice from the doorway said.

A shot rang out. Harry was pushed backward to the floor by a rifle bullet to his right shoulder. His gun went flying from his hand and landed on the bed.

"Grandma Bella!" Danny cried out. Bella stood in the doorway holding a smoking rifle.

"Are you okay, Danny?" Bella asked. Danny nodded. "Let's help your Mom."

Bella untied the gag around Jen's mouth while Danny picked up the revolver Harry had dropped on the bed.

"Dad's gun," Danny said as he held the revolver and saw the initials on the handle.

"Yes, I know, son," Jen said. "Be careful. It's loaded. Thank you, Bella."

Bella struggled trying to untie Jen's hands. The knots were tight but finally gave way.

"Look out! He's got a gun!" Bella shouted.

Bella pushed Jen out of the way as Harry fired at her with a derringer he'd had hidden in his boot. Another shot rang out as the

American .44 revolver that Danny was holding roared. Harry fell back to the floor, a gaping hole in his chest.

"Oh, my God!" Jen wailed. "Bella! Danny!"

Blood was seeping through Bella's nightgown where she'd been shot in the upper arm.

"It's okay," Bella said. "I'll be okay, Jennie. Take my neckerchief and tighten it around my arm."

"Hola, Harry!" a voice yelled from the hallway. "*Donde estas?*"

Jen grabbed the .44 pistol and leveled it, pointing half way up the bedroom doorway. A large figure carrying a rifle appeared in the doorway. It didn't take Jen but a second to recognize him.

"Hello, Carlos," Jen said as she pulled the trigger, sending the Mexican to his death.

"Jen! Jennie!" voices shouted from down the hallway, and then came the sounds of running footsteps. "It's Chris! Are you all right?"

Chris came running into the room, almost tripping over the dead Mexican. Then Lys, who was a few steps behind Chris, appeared. More voices and footsteps came from the hallway, and Luke and Linda came rushing into the room.

"We heard gunshots," Luke said. "Is everyone okay?"

"We'll be okay, we were waiting for Jake to come home." Jen said. "Bella's been shot in the arm. Now it's our turn to patch her up. Aunt Bella, you just lay back on my bed, and we'll take care of your arm."

"There are some clean cloths and antiseptics in the kitchen, in the upper right-hand whatchamacallit ... cabinet," Bella said, grimacing. "Also, there's the bottle of medication ... and a bottle of whiskey."

"Linda and I will get the stuff from the kitchen," Lys said. "Chris, you and Luke get some lamps. We need more light in here."

"Look what I found," Chris said as he pulled the Mexican's body away from the doorway. He reached into Carlos's vest pocket, pulled out a pocket watch, and held it up.

"Pa's gold watch," he said. "Our suspicions were right, sis. They were the bastards that killed Pa."

Jen was so upset that she couldn't speak. She just wept and nodded her head as she held Danny tightly in her arms while Lys and Linda attended to Bella's wounded arm.

After gaining her composure, Jen told everyone about Harry's attack and how Bella and Danny shot Harry.

"I shot the bad man," Danny said, "like the way you showed me, Uncle Chris."

"Danny, that took a lot of courage," Chris said. "We're all proud of you for rescuing your mom and Grandma Bella."

"You were very brave, son," Jen said. "I'm glad your uncle showed you how to shoot. I know Daddy will be proud to know how you used his gun to save us."

"First thing in the morning we'll follow up on any leads as to Jake's whereabouts," Chris said. "In the meantime you help take care of Bella while Luke and I clean up this mess. Looks like you got your revenge, sis."

"I wouldn't really call it revenge as much as it was justice," Jen said, sighing. "I'm worried as to what has happened to Jake. Harry had his gun, and my worst fear is that there's only one way he could've gotten it. Please find Jake and bring him home."

"I promise you I will, sis," Chris said.

32

In the first week of April 1881, young Danny, his mother Jen, Uncle Chris, Aunt Lys, and cousin Harper were standing on the Laramie railroad station platform waiting for the eastbound Union Pacific.

"When you get to Philadelphia, make sure you tell Ali and her daughter, Janine, to come visit us," Chris said to his sister. "We'd sure love to have them. Unless you think Ali would be too upset over the memories the West has for her."

"I'll see what she says," Jen said. "Darn, the station agent said that train would be here in ten minutes. How long have we been waiting?"

"Don't worry, Mom," Danny said. "We'll be on that train soon enough. Then you'll be wondering when we'll get off."

"You got all the papers you need for the property?" Chris asks. "The lawyer's address in Philadelphia and the real-estate papers, and—"

"Stop it, Chris," Jen said. "I'm not a child. I've got everything taken care of."

"I know you're not a child," Chris said. "You're just my little sister, my little, strong-headed sister."

"Hooray!" Danny said. "Here comes the train."

Three days later, Jen and Danny arrived in New Haven. The next day they would tour the Peabody Museum, and the day after that they would meet with Professor Marsh. The Peabody Museum had been completed in 1876, and two years later Marsh built a mansion on Prospect Street hilltop, part of the Yale property he had purchased.

The large brass Victorian door knocker resounded against the huge oak door.

"Okay, Danny," his mother said. "I think you've banged it enough. I'm sure the professor heard it."

"Wow, what a palace," Danny said as he took in the view of the front of the three-story brownstone mansion. "Marsh must be a rich man."

"That he is, son," Jen answered.

Abruptly the door opened, and Marsh appeared.

"Ah, good day, Mrs. Harding," Marsh said. "And who might this young man be?" Marsh extended his hand to the boy.

"Professor Marsh, this is my son, Danny," Jen said. "And please call me Jen."

"Ah, yes, I remember, Jen," Marsh said. "I'm pleased to meet you, Danny. You are the spitting image of your father. Jen, I was sorry to hear of the misfortune that befell your husband. Please do come in."

They entered a large octagonal room that was filled with artifacts and trophies from the American West and other parts of the world. Most notable was a large buffalo head mounted on one wall, the one that Marsh had shot in Kansas.

"What a magnificent home you have," Jen said.

"That it is," Marsh said. "This room is where Chief Red Cloud and I had a pleasant visit. I call it my wigwam; I believe the chief was impressed."

"Well, I'm sure impressed," Danny said, "as I was with our visit to the Peabody Museum."

"I'm sure your father would have admired the accomplishments of the museum's laboratories," Marsh said.

One of Marsh's house staff entered the room, and Marsh gave him orders to serve some refreshments. As he brought them in, Marsh told Jen and Danny about some of his fossil-hunting adventures in the West.

"I love fossil hunting," Danny said. "My mom, dad, and uncle taught me a lot about fossils, and I've found quite a few on my own."

"That is wonderful, my boy," Marsh said.

"Someday I hope to become a scientist of paleontology, like you, professor," Danny said.

"The science of paleontology is still in its infancy, but within the last ten years I have pushed the boundaries forward. I have learned much about the prehistoric world through the study of fossil remains," Marsh said. "Fossil bones have been known to man for thousands of years, but only within the last couple of centuries are we finding their true meaning. At one time fossils were thought of by some as bones of ancient, giant dragons. Others thought they were bones of giant humans that existed before the great flood, as mentioned in the Bible. The ancient Greeks and Romans believed they were bones of creatures described in their mythology. Indians believe they are bones of mythical beasts of their legends. Today we know fossils give us many clues to the nature of prehistoric life. The future study of fossils hold even more revealing facts about the history of life on Earth. You, Danny, could be a part of that paleontological study."

"My dad has a big collection of fossil bones that I'm studying," Danny said.

"Jake had written to me about the fossil collection he had amassed," Marsh said to Jen. "What are you planning to do with that collection?"

"My son and I are looking to donate part of the collection to the University of Wyoming in Laramie," Jen said. "Danny and I have an interest in fossils and want to keep part of the collection. We want to keep those Western bones in the West."

"My dear Mrs. Harper," Marsh said, "you do know that Jake was contracted by me to collect for Yale. Our museum should have first choice of the specimens in that collection."

"Professor Marsh, I know Jake collected for you," Jen said. "And I know that he duly shipped the fossils collected for Yale to you. Our fossil collection was collected by me and my husband on our ranch land."

"Can you substantiate that?" Marsh asked, snorting.

"Yes, I have witnesses to prove that," Jen said, her aggravation beginning to escalate, "probably to a greater degree than you can prove that you don't owe Jake for back payments."

"Well, if you think you should give that collection to another university, go ahead," Marsh said, irked at Jen's insinuation. "It's of no importance, for no museum will have the quantity and quality of new fossil discoveries that Yale shall have."

Two days later, after taking a train from New Haven, Jen and Danny departed the train at the Philadelphia Broad Street Station. There they met Ali and her daughter, Janine. The long overdue reunion between Jen and Ali was filled with hugs, kisses, tears, and laughter. Danny and Janine immediately became friends.

"What a beautiful daughter you have," Jen said. "She takes after her mother and father."

"And your handsome son takes after you and Jake," Ali said.

Both women cherished memories of their pasts; the good times were vividly recalled and the bad segments softened by time. Ali had inherited her mother in law and father-in-law's large house and property in Philadelphia. She and her daughter invited Jen and Danny to stay there. Ali had a carriage waiting for them, and they traveled through the city to the Randall's home.

After two days of reunion and reminiscing, the four boarded a carriage bound for Germantown in the northwest section of Philly. There they would meet with the Harding's lawyer. Jen Harding was now the legal owner of the property, and she was to meet with the lawyer at the house Jake's grandfather had built. The decision of what to do with the property was yet to be made.

Jen was in awe of the house her husband had known as a child. The lawyer turned the key and opened the door to the large colonial-style brownstone.

"Wow," Danny said. "Dad must have loved this house."

"He surely did," Jen said. "Quite often he talked about spending his boyhood in his grandfather's house."

"Mrs. Harding, folks," the lawyer said, "let me show you around, and then you can explore this wonderful home at your leisure. There are no renters at present, but we have had an inquiry, just last week, as to its availability. I thought it best to wait until you've made a decision as to what you wanted to do with the property, Mrs. Harding."

"My son and I haven't come to any decision as of yet, but we'll let you know," Jen said.

While Jen, Ali, and Janine toured the many rooms of the house, Danny plopped himself down in a large chair in the room that once had been his great-grandfather's study. He closed his eyes for a second and imagined his father as a boy playing in this enormous room. It was an experience so real that he quickly opened his eyes to see if he could catch a glimpse of that little boy. He admired the huge walnut desk: O. Z. Harding's favorite sanctum. Danny ran his hand over the polished walnut wood, pulled the chair from it, and sat down behind the bureau. Feeling like he was the captain behind the helm at the bow of a great ship, he scanned all the drawers, compartments, and pigeonholes. His gaze fell on the center drawer, which had a beautiful engraving carved in it. Suddenly his thoughts were interrupted by voices and laughter.

"Ah, there you are," his mother said. "Catching a little snooze?"

Jen, Ali, and Janine entered the room followed by the lawyer.

"It's all so big and beautiful," Danny said. "Knowing that Dad grew up here in this house, this room, and this desk—wow!"

"I know, son. It's overwhelming," she said. "Ali, Janine, and I had a spectacular tour of the house. What do you think we should do with it?"

"I don't know," Danny said. "Take it back to Wyoming?"

"If only we could," Jen said.

"Well, maybe we could take Great-Grandfather's desk back home," Danny said.

"That's a possibility," his mom said, giving the lawyer a questioning look.

"I could arrange to have the desk shipped to Wyoming," the lawyer said, "if you so desire."

"Oh, could we, Mom?" Danny asked.

"Okay," Jen said to the lawyer. "Make the arrangements as soon as possible. I'll pay whatever charges there are."

"Thanks, Mom. That's the best thing I could have to remember Dad," Danny said. "The desk has some interesting lettering carved on the middle drawer, but I can't read it. It's written in another language."

"That's German," the lawyer said as he walked over to the desk. "I can translate the inscription for you."

"Yes, please do," Jen said.

"*Hoffnung gegen Verzweiflung*," the lawyer said, reading the German writing. "It means, 'Hope against despair.'"

Fifteen hundred miles west of Philadelphia in Laramie, Wyoming, Chris, Lys, and Harper had just sat down to lunch at Claudia's Café. After ordering their meal, Chris laid the stack of mail on the table that they had just retrieved from the post office.

"Help me sort through this mail," Chris said to Lys as he handed her half the bundle. "Looks like everyone we know decided to write us at the same time."

"Here's one from someone we don't know," Lys said. "It's from the Denver Health Medical Center."

"Read it to me," Chris said.

Lys opened the letter and started reading.

14 April 1881

Dear Proprietor of the Muller Ranch,

Permit me to introduce myself; I am Dr. Joseph Hagen of the Denver Medical Center, Colorado.

I have a patient whom is listed only as John Doe. He was in a state of semi-consciousness (comatose) due to a gunshot wound to the right side of his head and a blow to the back of his head when first found in Sept. of 1880. He was discovered at the bottom of a ravine by two hunters near Rock Creek rail station. He was loaded on the train at that station, and as happens I was a passenger on that train. I took him under my care and brought him to Denver with me. Unable to tell us his identity and with no identification on his person we have yet to know his name. The last couple of months John Doe made a remarkable recovery from his comatose state, but he is now impaired with amnesia. He has lost the memories to his past.

Recently we have been given a clue as to his identity. A man from Laramie City recently moved to Denver and became a patient of mine. He told us he thought Mr. J. Doe had been employed by the Muller Ranch of Albany County, Wyoming. If this be the case would you be willing to come to Denver to make identification?

This of course, raises the question; is there any of your employees missing?

Please reply to this letter or send a telegram to me at the address listed above.

Yours in good health,
Dr. J. H. Hagen, MD, PhD.

"Oh, my God," Lys said, loudly enough for everyone in the café to hear.

"That's unbelievable," Chris said as he snatched the letter from Lys's hand and started reading it.

"Everything okay here?" Claudia asked as she passed by the Muller's table.

"Oh, yes," Lys said. "We think we have received wonderful news."

"You and Harper wait here," Chris said. "I'm going to telegraph Denver right away. Don't tell a soul about this till we find out what it's all about."

After Chris had sent a telegram to Denver and returned to the café, Lys had read the stack of mail and was talking with Claudia.

"Lys just read me a letter she got from Jen," Claudia said. "She sounds like she's having a great time in Philadelphia."

"Jen said she was shipping a desk to the ranch that belonged to Jake's grandfather and to expect it soon," Lys said. "She and Danny will be coming back in the middle of July.

"Good," Chris said. "We will be going to Denver by train on business soon. And we'll be looking forward to seeing them in July."

Four days later, Chris and Lys were on a train headed for Denver.

"Harper is thrilled to be spending some time with Linda and Luke," Lys said. "They'll have her spoiled to no end by the time we get back. I already miss her."

"I'll bet she won't even miss us," Chris said. "She has become so independent in the last year. Before you know it she'll be grown up and on her own."

"Oh, I hope that doesn't happen too soon," Lys said.

"Time changes things, my dear," Chris said. "Speaking of which, it has been eight months since Jake disappeared. Do you really think it's possible that this Mr. John Doe in Denver could be Jake Harding?"

"I guess we'll soon find out," Lys said.

The office of Dr. Joseph Hagen in the Denver General Hospital Trauma Center was cluttered with books, papers, medical journals, and charts. Chris and Lys, with a leather valise, sat patiently in front of a large desk waiting to see the doctor.

The door opened, and a stout, sixty-year-old man with a neatly trimmed, graying goatee entered.

"Ah, Mr. and Mrs. Muller," he said. "I hope I haven't kept you waiting too long. I'm Dr. Hagen. I hope you had a pleasant trip from Laramie."

"The train ride was very pleasant," Chris said. "I'm Chris Muller, and this is my wife, Alyssa."

After the formalities of introductions, Dr. Hagen seated himself behind his desk, drew a deep breath, dropped his hands palms down on a stack of papers, and then exhaled.

"Well, Chris and Alyssa," the doctor said, beaming, "I do believe we may have solved the mystery of who our Mr. John Doe is. The information you sent me regarding the scars on his body—the scar on his left cheek, one on his right leg, and one on his left shoulder—match up with Mr. John Doe's. But our final evidence will be your meeting with the man. Did you bring the articles that I had asked of you?"

"Yes, we did," Chris answered. "We have them in this valise."

"Good," Dr. Hagen said. "I must tell you that over the last couple of weeks, our patient's health and memory have improved. Considering the trauma this man has suffered, he is doing remarkably well. I have hope for his full recovery, someday."

"That's good news," Chris said.

"We have neither medicines nor medical treatment that can cure amnesia," Dr. Hagen said with the solemn voice of a preacher delivering a sermon. "We know so little about the workings of the brain, but we do know that time may be the great healer in this case. John's memories are buried deep inside his mind under layers of time. They must be dug out, and we hope his brain can peel back those layers to reveal the memories. This could happen today, tomorrow, next week, next year, or possibly, *God forbid*, never. If this man is Jake Harding, as we suspect he is, the best treatment would be to place him in the environment he once knew to familiarize him with people, objects, and experiences of the past that may help trigger his memories. My suggestion is that you take him back to your ranch in Wyoming for his treatment. Now let's go see our patient."

The Muller's followed the doctor to a large, open area where a number of patients were enjoying recreational activities.

"We have employed Mr. John Doe in doing some housekeeping chores. He seems to enjoy keeping busy," Dr. Hagen said. "You see that fellow across the room cleaning those windows? That's our Mr. John Doe."

"Oh, no," Chris said, disappointed. "That's not Jake Harding."

Alyssa started crying, and Chris put his arm around her.

"Well, let's meet the man," the doctor said. "I'll introduce you."

As they approached John Doe, Chris and Lys saw a clean-shaven, tall, thin, gangly man with a severe scar on the right side of his head with no hair on that side. The hair he did have was highlighted with streaks of gray. The man was moving slowly, meticulously cleaning a window.

"John," Dr. Hagen said, "I have some people I'd like you to meet."

When John turned around, Chris looked into his eyes.

"My God," Chris said, "you *are* Jake Harding."

For a moment, no one said a word—except for Lys, who, feeling faint, sighed.

"Let's sit at the table over there," the doctor said, "and we can talk."

"Okay," John said, staring at Chris with a puzzled look on his face.

Dr. Hagen introduced everyone and told John that Chris and Lys were from the Muller Ranch in Wyoming.

"Do you remember them?" the doctor asked John.

John looked at Chris, then at Lys, and shrugged his shoulders.

He paused for a moment. "I don't know—I can't remember," he sighed.

"You take your time," Dr. Hagen said. "They—we believe you are Jake Harding, and we're going to help you remember your past. To help you remember, we'll keep calling you Jake. Lys and Chris would like to ask you some questions."

"Jake," Chris said, his voice straining, "I want to help you remember who you are. Your name is Jake Harding, and you have a wife named Jennifer and a son named Danny. Do you remember them?"

"No," Jake answered without hesitation.

Chris had trouble composing himself as he sat before the shell of a man he once knew. Chris moved closer to his friend, looked into his eyes, and held his gaze there.

"Jake! Jake Harding!" Chris shouted. "I'm your friend and brother-in-law, Chris Muller. You *must* remember me. I promised your wife, Jennie, I'd bring you home."

Jake sat back in his seat, alarmed at the outburst from Chris.

"Okay, Chris, calm down," Dr. Hagen said. "Everyone just relax, and let's show Jake some articles that may jog his memory."

Chris sat despondent as Lys opened their valise and took a photograph from it.

"Do you recognize these people?" she asked Jake, showing him a photo of Jen and Danny. "Take a good look at it."

Jake looked long and hard at the photo and then laid it on the table, rubbing his fingers over it.

"There's something about those faces," he said. "They look ... happy."

"They were," Chris said. "But now they are sad because they miss you. Please come back, Jake."

Chris reached into the valise and brought out a package that was carefully warped in broadcloth. He laid the bundle on the table, and unwrapped it exposing a small fossil skull and a drawing of that skull.

"Do you recognize this?" Chris asked Jake. "You are a fossil hunter. You found this skull and did this drawing."

Jake took the skull gingerly in his hands, slowly turned it over and over, and then laid it back down. He picked up the drawing, tracing its lines with his fingers. Suddenly, past events flashed through his mind like galloping wild horses.

Everyone sat in silence for what seemed like an eternity.

"I remember ...," Jake finally said with tears welling in his eyes, "a fossil skull of a prehistoric horse. *Eohippus,* 'dawn horse.'"

33

Chris sent a letter to the ranch telling everyone about finding Jake, what had happened to him, and that he had amnesia. They were bringing him back home.

A week later, Chris, Lys, and Jake were on a train returning from Denver to Laramie.

Jake stroked his new growth of beard as he watched a spring shower splatter the moving train's window. Patterns of wet designs swirled against the glass pane. The wet streaks triggered a memory. A recollection from his past formed in his mind as he thought about his wife and son. Although he couldn't remember their faces, for a moment he recalled his wife looking out a rain-streaked window. Her back was turned toward him as she said, "Whenever it would rain I would feel depressed, but with you holding me I feel comforted." He was unable to capture more of that memory.

Jake looked at the two passengers, contorted into sleeping poses, on the train's bench across the aisle from him. As he studied their features, glimpses of past memories flashed through his mind. Chris and Alyssa were becoming more familiar recollections of his past. He was feeling refreshed as though he had awoken from a deep sleep.

"Laramie, Laramie City, Wyoming, next stop, fifteen minutes," a conductor shouted walking down the aisle.

Chris unwound his tall frame and shook Lys.

"Wake up, darling," he said. "We're coming into Laramie."

Lys yawned and stretched. "Laramie," she said. "We're here already?"

"How you doing, Jake? Get any sleep?" Chris asked.

"A little," he said. "I had interesting dreams that gave me reason to believe I had something to do with horses."

"That's great," Chris said. "You had a lot to do with horses. Your recollections are beginning to come back. I reckon when you get to the ranch you'll see a lot of things that will jog your memory."

Lys and Jake went from the train station to the post office, which was located in a mercantile store a few doors from the depot. Chris went to get the horse and buggy that Lys and he had left at the livery stable. After getting the mail, Jake and Lys browsed through merchandise in the store while waiting for Chris. Jake's eye was drawn to a light-colored, broad-brimmed, high-crown hat. The merchant, sensing a sale, approached Jake.

"Here, sir, try it on," he said as he picked up the hat and handed it to Jake.

"I'm just looking," Jake said.

"That's okay," the salesman said. "Just set it on your head and look at yourself in this looking glass. That is one of the finest hats made—Boss of the Plains, by J. B. Stetson, a genuine fur-felt hat."

Lys came walking up to Jake.

"I see you found your hat," she said. "Put it on."

"No," Jake said. "It's not my hat."

"Ah, but it is," Lys said. "You had one just like that. Your wife gave it to you. And I'm buying you that one. Now put it on."

Jake felt cornered by the salesperson and Lys. He hemmed and hawed and then plopped the hat on his head.

Just then Chris walked into the store and whistled.

"Now *that's* the old Jake," he said. "You gotcha old hat back."

No argument could persuade Lys and Chris not to buy Jake that hat.

The ride back to the ranch was filled with conversation around the many questions Jake kept asking about his past. Feeling more relaxed and receptive to questions, he began to remember a few remnants from his past. He kept adjusting his new hat as he was telling Chris and Lys about his recollection of a spacious room filled with large pieces of furniture and books.

"O. Z.! Grandpa O. Z.!" Jake suddenly shouted. "I remember my grandpa!"

"Wonderful!" Lys said. "Dr. Hagen was right—your memory is slowly coming back."

When Luke saw the carriage coming up the ranch road, he ran to meet it. He was a little taken back at seeing Jake's condition but concealed his disbelief as he approached the buggy.

"Good to see you all made it safe and sound," Luke said. "I'm sure happy to see you, Jake."

"Jake, do you remember Luke Martins?" Chris asked.

"Um, can't say I do," Jake replied. "Maybe it'll come to me."

"We've got a big surprise for you, Jake," Luke said. "Day before yesterday we got a delivery that Jennie sent from Philadelphia. It's a big desk. It was your grandfather's, according to Jennie's letter with the delivery."

"My grandpa's desk is here?" Jake asked, his eyes widening with surprise.

"Let's get up to the house," Lys said. "Have Jake look at that desk and everyone get some food and drink."

Jake sat behind the desk in the ranch's large living room. He ran his hands over the polished walnut bureau. Grinning, he traced the carved letters on the middle drawer.

"My grandfather's desk," he said, chuckling. "I can't believe it. I remember."

The next morning, Chris came up to the house to see Jake.

"Jake, I'm sending a letter to Jen and Danny, informing them of your return," Chris said. "Take a look at what I wrote. You want to add something?"

Jake read the letter describing in candid detail his return to the ranch and his recent mental and physical condition.

"That's a fine letter," Jake said. "I won't add anything. Seeing as how I can't remember much about my wife and son, I wouldn't know what to say."

"All right," Chris said. "Luke's about to go to town. I'll have him post it."

It had been almost a month since Jake's return to the ranch. He spent his time drawing fossils in his room and talking to horses in the corrals. Progress in his remembrances and physical appearance was being made due to the companionship of his friends at the ranch and the nourishing food Bella kept stuffing him with.

By the last week of May spring was in full bloom in Wyoming. Jake was in a corral checking on the health of a pair of two-week-old foals.

Chris ran up to the corral, waving a paper.

"Hey, Jake!" he shouted. "A telegram from Jennie was just delivered. She and Danny will be coming home on the fifth of June. They'll be on the morning Laramie train. I'll pick them up in the buggy. You want to go with me?"

"No," Jake said. "I'd rather wait here at the ranch."

A couple of days later, Jake decided he would get his thoughts together by taking a long ride. He ended up in a cottonwood grove with a fast-flowing stream running through it. Dismounting beside a pile of rocks, he loosened the cinch on his saddle and led his horse to the stream. He splashed the cool, clear water on his face while his horse noisily sucked and gulped a drink. Jake's gaze was fixed as he watched the water swirl and eddy around a large boulder. The flowing water carried a yellow-green butterfly to a deep pool behind the boulder. Suddenly the surface of the pool erupted as a large trout surfaced and snatched the insect. Jake's thoughts swirled in his mind as remembered images flowed fast and clear as the spring creek before him. He caught the reins of his horse, tightened the cinch, and swung up into his saddle. Spurring his steed to a gallop they headed back to the ranch.

That night more images of his past flashed through his mind as he tossed and turned in his sleep. The next day he sat at his grandpa's desk reading until late afternoon. Looking out the window he saw a buggy coming up the road. As it passed the corral Jake donned his hat and ran out the door. The buggy slowed to almost a stop, and a beautiful woman and handsome boy jumped down and ran toward the house.

Jake yelled, and they yelled.

Their shouts resonated across the ranch's yard.

"Jennie! Danny! Danny! Jennie!"

"Jake! Dad! Dad! Jake!"

WORKS CITED

Bakker, Robert T. *The Dinosaur Heresies.* New York: Kensington Publishing Corp, 1986.

Capps, Benjamin. *The Indians.* New York: Time-Life Books Publishing, 1973.

Edgar, Blake and John Gattuso. *Discovery Travel Adventure: Dinosaur Digs.* New York: Langenscheidt Publishers, Maspeth, 1999.

Forbis, W. H. *The Cowboys.* New York: Time-Life Books Publishing, 1973.

Gardom, Tim with Angela Milner. *The Natural History Museum Book of Dinosaurs.* London: Carlton Books Ltd., 1997.

Gould, Stephen Jay. *Dinosaur in a Haystack: Reflections in Natural History.* New York: Harmony Books. 1995.

Jaffe, Mark. *The Gilded Dinosaur: The Fossil War between E. D. Cope and O. C. Marsh and the Rise of American Science.* New York: Crown Publishers, 2000.

Lawson, R. W. *Lakota Leaders and Government Agents: A Story of Changing Relationships.* :Lincoln. Nebraska State Historical Society, 2001.

Nevin, David. *The Soldiers.* New York: Time-Life Books Publishing, 1973.

"O. C. Marsh Papers," accessed 29/Aug / 2017. http://marsh. dinodb.com.

O'Neil, Paul. *The Frontiersmen*. New York: Time-Life Books Publishing, 1977.

Ostrom, J. H. and J. McIntosh. *Marsh's Dinosaurs: The Collection from Como Bluff*. New Haven: Yale University Press, 1966.

Ottaviani, Jim. 2005. *Bone Sharps, Cowboys, and Thunder Lizards: The Gilded Age of Paleontology*. New York. Diamond Book Distributors, 2005.

Russell, Jesse and Ronald Cohn. *Bone Wars*. Edinburgh: Lennex Corp., 2012.

Wheeled, Keith. *The Railroaders*. New York: Time-Life Books Publishing, 1973.